Ali McNamara attributes her over-active and very vivid imagination to one thing – being an only child. Time spent dreaming up adventures when she was young has left her with a head bursting with stories waiting to be old.

When stories she wrote for fun on Ronan Keating's website became so popular they were sold as a fundraising project for his cancer awareness charity, Ali alised that not only was writing something she enjoyed ing, but something others enjoyed reading too.

Ali lives in Cambridgeshire with her family and two Labradors. When she isn't writing, she likes to vel, read, and people-watch, more often than not mpanied by a good cup of coffee. Her dogs and a ve of exercise keep her sane!

To find out more about Ali visit her website at w.alimcnamara.co.uk or follow her on Twitter: liMcNamara

Step Back in Time

Ali McNamara

SPHERE

First published in Great Britain as a paperback original in 2013 by Sphere

A CIP catalogue record for this book
is available from the British Library.

ISBN 978-0-7515-5023-8

Typeset in Caslon by M Rules
Printed and bound in Great Britain by
Clays Ltd, St Ives plc

Papers used by Sphere are from well-managed forests
and other responsible sources.

MIX
Paper from
responsible sources
FSC® C104740

Sphere
An imprint of
Little, Brown Book Group
100 Victoria Embankment
London EC4Y 0DY

An Hachette UK Company
www.hachette.co.uk

www.littlebrown.co.uk

For 'All the Lonely People'

Acknowledgements

As always, I must start by thanking those without whom books like this just wouldn't happen.

Everyone at my fantastic publishers Little, Brown, who work so hard with me on producing and promoting my books. Huge thanks to you all, especially Rebecca, my editor.

My agent, Hannah, and everyone at the Marsh Agency who help sell my stories around the world. Hannah, I'm running out of nice things to say about you with each book! You are one of the nicest, most genuine people I've ever met, and if you weren't my agent I'd be very jealous of the authors whose books you looked after!

My family, Jim, Rosie and Tom – I just wouldn't be able to do this without your never-ending love and support. I know it's not easy living with this writer sometimes, but having you all around me makes it very easy for me to do this thing I call work!

Lovely, wonderful readers! Thank you for embracing the

madness that spills forth from my imagination onto the page by continuing to buy my books! I love hearing from you too. The emails, Twitter and Facebook messages I get mean so much to me. Thank you for letting my make-believe worlds become a part of yours.

A special thank you to Lisa Devlin who was my font of all things Take That for the nineties part of the story. Thank you, Lisa!

During the writing of this book, I could happily have Stepped Back in Time quite a few times to try to change a number of things that happened to me. But as a character from one of my other books says, and Jo-Jo discovers during this story: good or bad, 'everything happens for a reason'.

It really does, I promise you!

Ali x

Hello, Goodbye

One

'Watch it, love!' the London taxi driver calls from his black cab as I dash across the busy road, weaving in and out of the congested lunchtime traffic, and into the nearest coffee shop to order my much-needed caffeine fix.

I should have waited and crossed at the pedestrian crossing, I know, but I'm in a hurry, and I haven't got time to wait for some silly green man to start flashing. You encounter enough fully grown ones doing that when you've lived in London as long as I have.

London. Full of noise and people and traffic – lots and lots of traffic – but I adore it and wouldn't want to live anywhere else. Of all the cities I've visited across the world it's still my favourite, and I've been to a few. We travelled a lot when I was growing up. My father had a good job with an international banking firm, and my mother, the quintessential business-man's wife, made it her duty to travel with him. My two sisters and I got used to travelling across the globe with them, so moving home and country every few years became second nature to us. But London, our original home, has always remained my favourite city to this day.

'Skinny caramel latte for Jo-Jo!' the barista calls, as I'm jolted from my trip down memory lane.

'Yes, that's me!' I shout. Thanking him, I grab my coffee from the counter and dash out on to the King's Road.

I love my coffee. Actually, I'd be lying if I said it's only that; it's probably more of an addiction. But when you live the kind of life I do, you need to be firing on all cylinders at all times of the day and night, and caffeine gives me that ability.

That's another thing I love about London these days – you're never more than a few steps away from a Starbucks, a Costa, a Nero's, or many of the other fine coffee houses opening up every day. I sigh with pleasure at the thought of all that variety, and take another sip from my latte.

Striding briskly along the King's Road I slip on my sunglasses while I continue to drink my coffee. I'm good at multi-tasking, always have been and I wouldn't have got where I am today if I wasn't. I smile proudly to myself as I think about exactly where that is: my own accountancy firm, with a small set of offices out in Ealing. It had taken long hours and many years of work – and occasionally kowtowing to the type of people you wouldn't want to wipe your feet on, let alone make a cup of tea for. But I'd got there in the end and earned what I'd always wanted.

I've adored numbers since I was a child and have a very mathematical, logical brain. I take after my father in that. I much preferred science and maths lessons to English and history at school – I never had enough imagination to think up stories, and I could never see the point in dragging up the past. I much preferred to concentrate on the present, on what was going on in my life at that very moment. Black and white and clear-cut, that's how I liked my subjects, and it's just how I like my life to be today. No complications.

I don't have time for those.

I turn my face up towards the bright afternoon sun and feel the rays immediately begin to warm my skin. I should really try and get out of the office more often. I'd noticed this morning when I was getting ready for work how pale I was starting to look, even for me. But it isn't surprising considering how many hours I spend at my desk every day. Long work hours and a healthy outdoor glow aren't usually the best of friends. So even though, as usual, I'm pushed for time today, it is a joy to walk through London on this gorgeous summer's afternoon.

I'm on my way to return some yearly accounting books to a second-hand record shop. I make it a rule that we personally deliver accounts back to our clients if we can; it adds an individual touch to the business and makes us accountants seem more human and friendly to our clients. This was something I'd done regularly when I was a junior, but as I moved further up the hierarchy of the firm, eventually becoming a partner, and then sole owner of the business when my partner sadly passed away, my outings during the day have become rare. I'm lucky if I stop for lunch these days, let alone leave the office during work hours.

Even though I shouldn't, I stop to browse in one or two shop windows as I walk along the road. They're all trying to tempt customers in with goods guaranteed to make their summer that little bit better, and an outfit in the window of the Peter Jones' department store in particular catches my eye. The mannequin is wearing a dark navy French Connection leather jacket, white T-shirt, red Ted Baker jeans and matching bright red Miu Miu pumps. I really like the whole outfit, but it's not at all what I'd normally wear. It's completely impractical for work, and that's what most of my wardrobe consists of these days – work-based clothes, mainly suits in practical, neutral shades suitable for an accountant. When would I wear bright red trousers? I rarely have time to go out and socialise. When I get home at night I'm either too tired, or still too busy with paperwork to go out dressed like that.

So I use the glass of the window to straighten my charcoal grey jacket, and smooth some stray pieces of hair back into the low ponytail at the back of my head. Then I leave the window and the outfit for someone much more deserving, with a much more exciting life than me.

My iPhone rings in my bag. It's Ellie, my PA.

'Hello, Ellie, problems?'

'Yo, Jo-Jo.' Then she giggles at me. 'Ha! Yo Jo-Jo, funny, that is.'

I roll my eyes. Ellie has only been with us since the beginning of the year – this is her first job since she moved to London from Liverpool. But she came with excellent references and what she lacks in etiquette she certainly makes up for in efficiency and, I have to admit, bags of personality.

'Ellie, is there a problem at the office?'

'Err, no. I was just ringing to tell you your mam phoned again and could you call her back. She was pretty insistent I pass the message on immediately, this being the fourth time she's called, 'n all.'

I sigh. My mother is very old-fashioned and still won't call me on my mobile number. 'I don't trust the things, Jo-Jo,' she says. 'It just isn't right carrying a phone around in your hand-bag.'

'It'll be about their party again,' I tell Ellie. 'She's still harassing me about it. I almost missed a family party once because of work and now my mother doesn't trust that I'll show up for anything.'

I'd been really late to my father's sixtieth birthday celebra-tion because a meeting with a new client had run on much longer than expected. But what nobody knew was that that par-ticular meeting was fundamental to me becoming a partner in the firm at such a young age. It was incredibly important. But no one other than me seemed to appreciate that. Certainly not my mother – she hadn't spoken to me for a fortnight afterwards. But even now, I still felt bad about spoiling their night . . .

'Just agree to go, then,' Ellie suggests. 'A fancy dress party – that sounds awesome. My folks would never do something like that for *their* anniversary.'

'It may sound like great fun to you, but it's hell on earth to me, Ellie. I hate dressing up. Why can't my parents just hold a civilised drinks party for their fortieth wedding anniversary like normal people of their age?'

'Aw, Jo-Jo, I think it's fab that your parents are still partying. I bet they were right goers in their time, eh?'

I cringe at the thought of my parents being called 'goers'. But Ellie's right; from the stories I've heard they were quite, er . . . free-spirited when they first met.

7

'I'm not sure I'd describe them as *goers*, Ellie, but they were very passionate about their music.'

And I should know. My sisters and I have had to live with their Beatles obsession all our lives. My older sisters were christened Paula and Georgina after Paul McCartney and George Harrison, and I was expected to be a boy (because of the way my mother was carrying me, apparently) and was going to be called John, after John Lennon, of course. But within minutes of my birth that swiftly had to be adjusted to Jo-Jo, for obvious reasons. But I'm still stuck with Lennon as my middle name. Something I never reveal to anyone! I'm just glad they stopped at three children – I didn't fancy having another sibling called Starr, or heaven forbid, Ringo.

'Is that why the party has a music theme?' Ellie asks. 'Your mam was telling me all about it on the phone. Oh, wow, think of all the costumes you could wear for that!'

I screw up my face. The thought of dressing up as some has-been pop star makes me feel physically ill; it's just not my thing at all. But Ellie, unaware of my torment, continues.

'If it was me, I'd go as Rihanna, or Lady Gaga, or even Madonna.'

'Madonna?' I ask in amusement. 'Isn't she a bit before your time, Ellie?' In theory, she was a bit before my time too, but Ellie, at twenty, makes me feel much older than my twenty-nine years.

'No, Madge is retro these days. Retro is cool, Jo-Jo, don't you know?'

I lost touch with what was cool many years ago. In fact, I'm not sure I was ever *in* touch with it.

'If you say so, Ellie. Look, much as I'd like to stay and chat with you about how to be cool, I have to get these accounts back to George at the record shop.'

'Oh yeah, sorry. Say hi to George for me, won't you, and be sure to call your mam as soon as you're done!'

Really, Ellie was far too informal for an employee. I'd have to speak with her when I got back.

'There'll be plenty of time for that later.'

'No time like the present!' Ellie sings cheerily down the phone. 'Ta-ta for now!'

'Goodbye, Ellie,' I say seriously, but I have to smile as I end the call. You just can't be in a bad mood when Ellie's around.

I continue down the road, past all the modern high street shops, until I come to an area of the King's Road commonly known as World's End. George, the owner of the shop I'm about to visit, once told me it was named after the pub I'm standing opposite now – the World's End Distillery – while I wait to cross on a zebra crossing.

The pub is an odd-looking building, completely detached from the other shops and houses that line that side of the King's Road. While they are all scrunched together in long terraces, it stands proudly isolated from the rest, like a king watching over his subjects. Even the shape of the building is regal, with its pointy apexes reminiscent of the spikes of a crown. I bet that building has seen some changes over the years, I think, as at last the traffic pulls to a stop so I can be allowed over the crossing.

I never get this type of pedestrian crossing. I can handle the pelican type with its red and green man. That's easy, it's self-explanatory what you do and when. But this zebra type with its flashing orange beacons always confuses me; when do you step out and what are the orange lights supposed to be doing before you're allowed to cross?

But I have no time right now to worry about the rules of zebra crossings or I'll be late. And I hate being late. I admonish myself for pausing to browse the shop windows as I did, but it was so enjoyable for once being out in the sunshine. Hurrying past Vivienne Westwood's famous boutique, I see the huge clock on the front of her shop that runs backwards. What is the point of a clock going backwards? I wonder, stopping to look at it for a moment; life is about moving forward, not back. Then, a few more steps down the road and I've reached my destination – Groovy Records. I smile every time I read that name; George has owned this shop since the sixties, and back then that might have been a cool name for a record store, but now it just sounds dated and wrong. But, surprisingly, George is still keeping the shop running all these years later, and with a small profit again this year, as I'm about to tell him.

I open the door to the shop and, as always, a small bell rings over my head.

'Hi, George,' I say as I see him bending over behind his counter sorting through a box of old records.

He straightens himself up slowly and with care. 'Jo-Jo,' he says, looking surprised. 'Golly, is it that time already?' He looks at an old wooden mantle clock behind the desk. 'Well, so it is, 2 p.m. on the dot. How are you, my girl?'

'I'm good, thanks, George. I have your accounts.' I hold up his battered old account book. 'All present and correct, and I'm pleased to say you still turned over a profit again last year.'

George nods knowingly as if that was never in doubt.

'Good, good,' he says distractedly. 'Now, have you time for a cup of tea, child?'

'Of course I do,' I say, smiling and quickly hiding my Starbucks cup behind my back. 'You make the best cup of tea in London.'

George nods again in agreement. 'That I do. Take a seat, I'll be right back.'

I sit down on a wooden chair that stands in the corner of the shop and wait. Even though I've just downed a large cup of coffee, I wouldn't want to disappoint George and so I'll always take a cup of tea from him. I may barely have time to set foot outside the office these days, but this is one lot of accounts I always take the time to return myself. George loves nothing more than for someone to sit and take a cup of tea with him, so he can recall one or two of his many stories about the past.

As I look around the shop, the familiar rhythmical ticking of the clock behind the desk immediately begins to calm any panic I felt about being late. The shop never changes that much. It has always had the same décor for as long as I can remember. George always arranges his stock in exactly the same way, and he always keeps a vase of bright, cheery sunflowers on the counter next to his till. I glance up at the posters on the wall showing pop stars and rock bands through the ages. Classics icons such as the Rolling Stones, Michael Jackson and David Bowie take their place on the wall next to more modern artists like Take That, Madonna and Coldplay. George even has a One Direction poster up now, although I very much doubt he has much call for their music in here amongst the records, cassettes and the few CDs that he keeps in stock.

Most kids these days download their music to their iPods and smartphones, don't they?

Some music starts to play in the shop. Ah, what is it George is playing for me today? I wonder. He always likes to try and educate me about some old band or other when I'm here. But today I happen to know this tune. How could I not? It's a Beatles track, 'Hello Goodbye'.

George appears from the back carrying two mugs of tea; he passes me one with *Choose Life* emblazoned across it. 'I'll give you the modern one,' he explains. 'I'll just take my good old Abbey Road mug.'

'Modern?' I ask, examining the motto. 'What's choose life?'

George shakes his head. 'Jo-Jo, you must know Wham – George Michael's old band? Everyone was wearing T-shirts with this slogan on when they were around.'

'George, Wham were about in the eighties, I'm hardly going to remember what people were wearing then, am I? I wasn't born until 1983.'

'Ah, yes, of course,' George nods. 'The eighties seem like only yesterday to me.'

And just as he says that, the music changes to another Beatles classic, 'Yesterday'.

'Hey, how did you do that, George?' I laugh. 'You timed it perfectly.'

George lifts his head and listens to the track. 'Another great,' he says. 'You know who this is playing, of course?'

'Yes, I can never mistake the Beatles – I had their songs played constantly to me from the time I was born until the time I left home.'

'Of course. You've mentioned before that your parents were

Beatles fans.' George pulls another chair up beside mine. 'Great band – I miss them.'

'You knew the Beatles?' I exclaim, astonished. 'I'm no great fan of theirs, but that's really cool.'

'Not exactly *knew*. They were customers from time to time – in their early days, when they first moved to London.'

'Wow!'

'This shop has seen a lot of customers over the years.' George looks fondly around the four walls of posters. 'I'm not sure what will happen to it when I'm gone.'

'Don't be silly, George, you've got years in you yet,' I say lightly. 'Don't you have anyone to leave this place to?' I ask as an afterthought. 'No family?'

George shakes his head. 'There's family, but they're not interested in music the way I am. I'm sure they'll just sell it.'

I know George must be well into his seventies. I can't bear the thought of this shop closing down when he's gone. It's his life's work.

'We'll need to find someone to run it for you then, won't we? Someone who shares your love of music.'

'I can't tempt *you*, then?' George asks, smiling.

'Definitely not! I know nothing about music. Never have done, never want to.'

'But why? That's quite unusual for someone of your age, surely?'

'Blame my parents – I guess I just got put off having it drummed into me when I was young, no pun intended,' I grin. 'You always hate what your parents like, don't you? It's one of life's unwritten rules.'

George thinks about this. 'But music is one of the few

things that can bring people together, Jo-Jo, whether it's through their love of it, or their taste in a particular band. Music unites the world.'

I hadn't expected George to be quite so poetic. 'I guess you could be right.'

'I know I'm right,' George says without hesitation. 'Think about all the couples that have a special song, one tune that they regard as theirs. You always remember the music you walk down the aisle to, or you break up with a boyfriend or girlfriend to, and the first time you ... well, you know,' George says, raising his white eyebrows at me.

'George!' I tease, smiling now. 'I'm shocked.'

'Ah, don't be,' George says with a wave of his hand. 'I was young once, you know? People say it's love that makes the world go round, but it's not, it's music.'

'Maybe it's a bit of both,' I say. 'Not that I need to worry about that right now.'

'Still no Mr Right?' George asks sympathetically. 'There wasn't the last time you were in either, if I remember rightly?'

'Definitely no Mr Right. Not that I'm looking, mind. I'm far too busy for all that sort of nonsense.'

George looks at me disapprovingly. 'A pretty girl like you with no beau on her arm, criminal that is.'

'I hardly think so. And now you sound like my mother; she's always telling me I need to find someone before it's too late. How can it be too late, George? I turn thirty this year, not sixty, for goodness' sake. I've still got plenty of time.'

'But don't you get lonely?' George asks. 'Every time I see you you're rushing here and there for your work, but you don't seem to do anything else as far as I can tell. Sometimes it's nice to have someone to share things with at the end of a hard day.'

I think about this. 'No, I don't think I'm lonely; I quite like my own company. When you've grown up with two older sisters to bicker and fight with, it's wonderful to have a peaceful house to yourself to chill out in.'

George's bright blue eyes regard me knowingly from behind his silver-rimmed spectacles. 'Sometimes we think we know what we want, but we don't actually know what we need until we find it.'

'What do you mean?'

'You just never know what fate will throw at you, Jo-Jo,' he says mysteriously. 'It has a funny way of showing us what we sometimes didn't know for ourselves. For instance you never know when or where you might meet someone ... ' George looks towards the shop door. And, as if by magic, it opens.

'Hey, George!' A young man wearing a sharp charcoal grey suit and a crisp white shirt strides confidently through the door. 'Long time no see, buddy! Oh, I'm so sorry,' he says apologetically when he sees me. 'I didn't know you had company.'

'This is Jo-Jo McKenzie,' George says, introducing me. 'Jo-Jo, this is Harry – he's one of my best customers.'

'I sometimes think I'm your *only* customer,' Harry says, a wide, relaxed smile spreading across his face. 'I was quite concerned when I had to go away and work overseas for a few months. But I see I needn't have worried, because you have two of us to keep you afloat!'

'Oh, I'm not a customer,' I explain. 'I'm George's accountant.'

15

'Accountant?' Harry puzzles. 'Not possible. Accountants are boring middle-aged men. Not ...' he struggles.

'Not what, Harry?' George asks, a smile spreading across his own lips now. His eyes dart between us.

'Well ...' Harry struggles. 'Not people that ... look like you, that's all.' He waves his hand in my general direction and pretends to look with great interest at a poster on the wall. Unfortunately it's the One Direction poster, so he hastily turns his head back towards us. He smiles nervously.

'It's OK,' I reply. 'Sadly it happens a lot, even in this day and age – stereotyping.'

'Oh, I wasn't stereotyping you,' he says hastily. 'I'm a fairly modern chap when it comes to women and jobs, and you're hardly masquerading as a brickie or a bare-knuckle wrestler, are you? Not that there would be anything wrong in that if you were,' he adds hurriedly when he sees the look on my face. 'I was just wondering if I knew you, that's all? Have we met before?'

I wasn't expecting this. 'Erm, I don't think so?'

'It's just ... you look awfully familiar to me.' Harry inspects me more closely. 'Are you absolutely sure?'

I consider Harry with more care now too. Not that I need to, really. He's quite a good-looking chap with his chestnut brown hair and deep blue eyes, which are still looking down at me intently. 'I don't think so, I'm sure I'd have remembered if we had.' To my horror, I suddenly realise that I've said this out loud, when I very definitely meant to keep it to myself.

Harry grins. 'That sounds like a chat-up line.'

'I can assure you it isn't,' I reply, furious with myself for blushing.

16

But Harry appears to be deep in thought. 'You said you were an accountant . . . that rings a bell somewhere . . . let me think.' The shop goes silent for a moment and we watch while Harry prowls around. I glance over at George, but he just shrugs.

'I've got it!' Harry suddenly exclaims, swivelling around to face us again. 'Of course, that's it. I know your father!'

'How would you know Dad?' I ask, intrigued by this revelation.

'I went to his sixtieth birthday party,' Harry explains. 'The company I used to work for before I went out on my own did a lot of business with your father and I was one of the token industry guests that night. I seem to remember you were very late getting there that evening, weren't you?' He raises an accusing eyebrow at me.

'Yes, well. It's one of the very few times I've been late in my life, I can assure you,' I reply haughtily. 'Usually I'm a very good timekeeper. My time is very precious to me so I use what little I have wisely.'

'I'm sure you do,' Harry says, appearing to nod in agreement, but I get the feeling he's mocking me. 'But that's definitely the place I remember you from, that party.' He smiles.

I think back to the party. No, I don't remember Harry being there that night, but he obviously remembers me – how strange. I guess I wasn't there that long, but even so . . .

'Anyway,' Harry announces, 'don't let me take up any more of your time. Which, as you kindly pointed out, is very precious to you. I've just popped in at George's request to browse his stock again and have a little chat.' He turns to George. 'We'll catch up in a bit, I'm in no hurry, I've got *all day* . . .' He says this easily, but I'm pretty sure he's aiming his comments at me. 'Do continue with whatever you were doing before I rudely interrupted you.' He smiles again, turns his back on us, and begins to thumb through a pile of seventies punk albums.

I look at George, who just grins at me.

'So, George,' I say, opening up his accounts book. 'As I was telling you before we were *interrupted* a few moments ago, you've managed to turn over a healthy profit this year.'

George nods. 'I never doubted I would,' he says, standing up and stretching. 'This shop's been in business fifty years this year, and we've never turned in a loss in all that time.'

'That's pretty amazing,' Harry says, turning around again. 'Fifty years without a loss. How'd you manage that?'

I sigh, but George just taps the side of his nose. 'Wouldn't you like to know, Mr Hot-Shot Businessman?'

'Ha, I'm hardly that,' Harry says, sliding the record he's holding back into the rack. 'I struggle to make my accounts look as healthy as yours from week to week, let alone year to year.'

'Maybe you should get Jo-Jo to take a look at them?' George suggests. 'She's very good with numbers.' He turns and winks at me so Harry can't see.

Good grief, is that what this is about? Is he trying to set me up with this guy? Has George orchestrated this whole meeting today to get us to go on a date together?

'That's not a bad idea,' Harry says, to my horror. 'What about it, Jo-Jo? Shall we meet up some time and discuss my figures? And just for now, here's a few to be going on with.' And to my absolute disbelief he cheesily passes me a business card with his contact details on.

18

I stare down at it.

'Er ... I'm actually quite busy right now,' I reply hastily. 'But I can get one of my associates to give you a call if you like?'

I'm quite surprised when Harry looks disappointed.

'Sure, yeah, that would be great. If you could.' He turns and immediately goes back to his examination of a Sex Pistols album.

For a split second I quite feel sorry for him.

'So, anyway,' I say to George, 'I think we're probably finished now.' I quickly finish off the last of my tea, suddenly desperate to make a swift exit. I don't get chatted up very often – if that's what just happened – and now I feel seriously awkward. 'It's been lovely to see you again, George, as always.' I stand up.

'Jo-Jo, do you have to go already?' George asks, looking over at Harry who's still thumbing through records.

'I'm afraid so. I'll try and call again soon, though.' I put my mug down on the counter and turn to leave.

'Nice meeting you, Jo-Jo,' Harry says, turning his head to look at me.

'Yes, likewise,' I reply politely. 'You never know, maybe we'll meet in George's shop again.'

'Oh, I'm sure of it,' Harry says, and I see him exchange a quick glance with George.

'Right ...' I quickly make a move for the door before either of them has time to say anything else. 'Goodbye, George,' I call before I exit. 'Look after yourself.'

'Don't you be worrying about me, Jo-Jo. I'm not the one that needs looking after any more,' George says peculiarly.

'Watch how you go, young lady. I've a feeling I'll be seeing you sooner than you think.'

'Perhaps,' I smile. 'Like I said, I'll try.'

George simply nods, and finally I'm able to escape back outside on to the King's Road.

I breathe a sigh of relief as I walk back along the pavement towards the crossing. I know George is getting on a bit, but he was behaving very strangely today. And as for trying to set me up with that guy Harry? What was he *thinking*?

I allow my thoughts to linger on Harry for a moment. Harry *was* very good-looking and his thick brown hair and sapphire blue eyes are certainly my type – if I actually have a type. I've always been a sucker for a pair of very blue eyes for as long as I can remember. But I certainly don't want a relationship in my life right now. Relationships are always so complicated, and they take up so much time.

No. I shake my head, it isn't going to happen. And anyway, what are the chances of me bumping into Harry again? About as likely as all this traffic coming to an immediate halt the minute I step on to the zebra crossing I'm about to arrive at.

As I stand at the edge of the same crossing I walked over earlier, waiting for the orange beacons to do their stuff, I suddenly feel a hand on my arm and I jump.

'Sorry,' Harry says as I turn towards the hand, 'it's just you left this back in George's shop.' He holds up my iPhone.

'How on earth did I manage to do that?'

'Perhaps you put it down with George's accounts earlier?' Harry suggests.

'Yes … maybe.' But I don't remember taking it from my bag.

'Anyway, you have it back now.' He turns to leave.

'Thank you,' I say, 'it was good of you to chase after me.'

Harry turns back and I get a flash of just how blue his eyes are now in the bright afternoon sunshine. 'Any time.'

I turn and look at the traffic. Is it ever going to stop for me?

'How I asked you out before ...' Harry says, suddenly aware that any moment I'm going to step out on to the crossing and it'll be too late. 'That wasn't really me. I'm just not very good at asking women out, especially attractive ones.' His cheeks flush a little and his gaze drops down to the ground. 'And it was the first thing that came into my head.'

I smile at him; he's actually quite sweet.

'And I'm guessing it wasn't the best chat-up line you've ever heard?' he continues, grimacing, as he looks up at me again.

'No,' I say, omitting to mention it's been a long time since I've heard any sort of a chat-up line, let alone a bad one, so he really shouldn't be asking my opinion. 'Perhaps you'd do better just being yourself.'

'Myself?' he says as if he's considering this. 'I'm never too sure who that is. Are you?'

'How do you mean?'

'Our personalities seem to come from so many diverse places. From different experiences we have in life, and people we meet, which means it's often hard to define ourselves as just one person.'

I wasn't quite expecting *that* answer! 'Yes, I suppose you could be right,' I manage.

'It's usually when we confine ourselves to just one aspect of our life that we become regimented and rigid in our ways.'

'Have you been talking to George?' I ask, suddenly realising where all this is heading again. 'Has he sent you after me?'

Harry looks surprised. 'No, I just came to bring you your phone.'

'Good. Well, thank you for doing that, but I really have to be going now.'

'I've arsed up again, haven't I?'

'No, no, really, it's fine. But I have another appointment I have to get to.' I tap the pocket of my suit where I tucked his card a few minutes ago. 'Look, I have your card now, so maybe I'll give you a call some time.'

'Great,' Harry says. 'I'd like that. I hope I'll see you soon, Jo-Jo.'

The constant onslaught of London traffic suddenly ceases and, very unusually for the King's Road at this time of day, there appear to be no cars, buses or taxis in either direction. So I step confidently out on to the black and white stripes of the crossing.

It's when I'm about halfway across, and I decide to look back to see if Harry is still there, that I first notice it out of the corner of my eye. It's as I fully turn to face the white sports car that's careering towards me, that everything suddenly turns cold . . .

Ticket to Ride

Two

As I open my eyes the first thing I see is sky, blue sky with wispy white clouds floating by. Then I become aware of faces in my line of vision too. For a few moments I think they're part of the clouds. Then I realise they're not, they're real faces attached to real bodies, which are peering down at me. And it's then I also notice that although I feel incredibly warm right now, I'm lying down on something hard and cold. So I sit bolt upright.

'Whoah, steady on there, gal,' a man's voice says next to me. 'You'd best wait until the ambulance gets here.'

'What ambulance?' I ask, looking at the ground below and seeing black and white stripes. I appear to be sitting on a zebra crossing.

'The ambulance that's coming to take you to hospital,' a woman with a bright pink patent leather handbag says. 'You've been hit by a car, lovey, and you'd best lie down.'

I look up at her face. Her make-up is very bold: black, thick, heavy eyeliner and the palest of lipsticks. I shake my head. 'But I'm fine,' I insist. 'Let me stand up.' I struggle to my feet and a few hands are thrust out to help me. 'Really, I'm fine. Look ...' I demonstrate this by brushing my clothes down and moving my limbs around. That's odd. I don't remember putting on a bright red figure-hugging pencil skirt today; I thought I was in my grey suit earlier? 'See, absolutely fine. Not a scratch on me.'

'Jo-Jo, are you OK?' I hear a male voice ask as it arrives beside my concerned entourage. 'I just heard what happened.'

I look across and recognise Harry from George's shop.

'Yeah, I'm fine, thanks,' I tell him, grateful to see a familiar face. 'I keep trying to tell everyone,' I insist, 'but they won't listen.'

'How can you be fine?' Pink-handbag woman asks. 'You were hit by a car – I saw it with my own eyes, I did.'

'Well, I am. I don't know how, but it can't have been that bad or I wouldn't be standing here, now would I?'

'I suppose ...' the woman admits slowly, looking me up and down. 'But the way you bounced off that bonnet, it was like something from *The Avengers*, so it was. Honor Blackman couldn't have done it any better herself.'

I stare hard at her. What on earth is she talking about? Who's Honor Blackman? I don't think I'm the one in need of help ...

'I've read about this,' Harry says confidently. 'Apparently some people just go soft when the body goes into shock. Like a self-defence mechanism. Perhaps you saw the car coming and automatically went into soft-mode.'

I stare at him now. *Soft-mode?* I've never heard anything so ridiculous in all my life. I'm about to tell him so, when he winks.

'She's probably in shock, too,' he continues. 'I think the best thing we can do is take her somewhere for a sit down and a cup of tea.'

There are murmurs of approval at the tea suggestion.

'I'll take her to George's shop – it's just back there,' he says, pointing. 'Groovy Records, it's called.'

'Oh, the new place,' one of the older men in my entourage says. 'A record store – how long does he think that will last down here?'

'My daughter goes in there a lot,' another woman pipes up. 'She says the owner is lovely and very helpful. Lets her put the records aside when she can't afford them. Then she pays a bit on tick when she can until she's paid enough to take the record home. I think that's lovely in this day and age.'

The others nod their approval, and Harry puts his arm through mine, and I notice then as I see my sleeve that I'm also wearing a black wool coat with big black buttons. 'I'll take it from here then, folks,' Harry says with assurance, guiding me away. 'Don't worry, she'll be fine with George and me.'

The crowd finally stands back and I'm allowed to leave the zebra crossing, letting the traffic begin flowing freely across it again.

As I allow Harry to guide me back along the King's Road, I notice that the long queue of cars that have backed up along the street appear to be vintage vehicles. Great, not only have I created a scene on a zebra crossing in the middle of central London, I've held up a car rally too.

'Are you OK?' Harry asks as we walk back along the road, me still with my arm through his. 'You must have had quite a shock.'

27

'Yes, I still feel a bit woozy – some of the things people back there were saying didn't really make sense. But I seem to be in one piece, physically.'

Harry pauses for a moment to look at me. 'You do look a little pale, but George will soon sort you out with a cup of tea.'

'You were serious about the tea?' I ask in surprise. 'I thought that was just a ruse to get me away.'

'It was, partly. But I've never seen a problem George couldn't sort with a cuppa.'

As we arrive back at the shop, I'm struck by the exterior. It looks different, somehow. Newer. Fresher. Like it's just had a lick of paint. I shake my head. Perhaps I'm more affected than I realise.

'George?' Harry calls as we enter the shop and the bell rings above us. 'Are you there?'

'Right here.' A man appears from the back of the shop wearing a black turtleneck sweater, grey drainpipe trousers and a grey single-breasted jacket. 'What's up, Harry? Whoa, Jo-Jo! What happened to you?'

I look at the man standing in front of me. *He does look familiar. He almost looks a little bit like … No, it can't be! It just can't.* I glance over to where I sat a little while ago drinking tea with George, and to my relief I see the wooden seat is still there. 'Can I … can I just sit down,' I manage to stutter. 'I feel a little light-headed.'

'Sure,' the man says, as Harry helps me over to the seat. 'I'll stick the kettle on. Just serve this customer, Harry, will you?' he adds, gesturing to a man brandishing a record at the cash desk. 'I'll be back in a mo.'

As he disappears out to the back of the shop, I try to run my hands through my hair in exasperation – and find that for some reason I've so much hairspray in it that I can't. I settle for rubbing at my forehead instead. *What is going on here? How come that man who answers to George looks so much like a younger version of my George and sounds exactly like him? And why am I wearing this ridiculously tight skirt – I don't even own a red skirt, for heavens sake!* I look up now at the walls surrounding me. Where have all the posters gone that I looked at a few minutes ago? They've all been replaced with glass-framed black and white photos of the Beatles, Elvis Presley – and is that Cliff Richard grinning down at me? In fact the whole shop looks different, the only thing that remains the same is the bell above the door, the vase of sunflowers on the counter next to the till, and the old wooden mantle clock ticking away behind it. But even that doesn't look so old any more.

'Are you OK?' Harry asks as the customer, happy with his purchase, leaves the shop. 'You still look awfully pale. I know that's the fashion make-up-wise right now, but I've a feeling that's your actual colour.'

For the first time I notice Harry's clothes. That wasn't what he was wearing a few minutes ago when we met here in the shop, was it? I try to remember. No, he was wearing a single-breasted, dark charcoal suit with a white shirt. He's still wearing a grey suit, but it's pale grey with no lapel or collar, now. He has it buttoned right up too, so all I can see is a tight white shirt peeping out of the top, with a thin black tie. He reminds me of someone … I know I've seen that look somewhere before. I glance at the wall opposite and see a picture of the Beatles.

'You're dressed exactly like they are!' I exclaim, pointing at the photo.

Harry looks at the picture. 'Why, thank you, yes I was trying to model my look on them. My suit isn't quite the quality of theirs, or even the price. But I'm glad you like it.'

'But a few minutes ago you were wearing something different, weren't you?' I ask aghast, staring at his clothes.

'Nope, don't think so,' Harry says. He bends down to look at me. 'Maybe you've had more of a bump to your head than you think? Follow my finger.' He moves a finger from side to side in front of my face.

'Harry, leave the poor girl alone,' George Mark II comes out from the back of the shop carrying two china cups balancing on saucers. 'I've made you some too, Harry,' he says, sitting down on the chair next to me and handing me my tea. 'Can you go and collect it?'

Harry sighs good naturedly, and departs to fetch his own tea.

I look at this doppelganger George. 'How come you look so young?' I ask, staring at him.

He laughs. 'Must be all the tea I drink. Take a sip of yours, Jo-Jo, I've made it extra sweet. It will help with the shock.'

I lift my cup and drink the hot tea while I continue to watch him. He's right, it is extremely sweet.

Harry returns with his own cup and saucer. What has happened to the mugs we were using earlier that George has always used before?

I look up at the two of them. 'What's going on here? Where's the joke?' I ask.

'What do you mean?' Harry asks.

'I mean, how come *you're* dressed all funny?' I demand, pointing my finger at him. 'And why does *this* George looks like he does?' I swivel round in my chair and thrust my face into George's. 'Is it some sort of television trickery? Have you had prosthetic make-up? Where's the hidden camera? This isn't live, is it?' I twist my head around trying to spot hidden cameras and tiny microphones dotted around the shop.

'You couldn't hide one of those huge TV cameras in here!' Harry laughs. 'Massive great things on wheels, aren't they?'

Another customer, a woman this time, enters the shop. She's wearing a bright green coat, black gloves and hat, and she carries a black patent handbag that matches her very pointy court shoes. 'Would you mind again, Harry?' George asks, nodding in her direction.

Harry sighs. 'Anyone would think I worked here!'

'I'd employ you if I could,' George says, grinning at him. 'I wouldn't be able to pay you as much as that music company you supposedly work for. But then you wouldn't need the sharp suit, so you'd save money there, I suppose.' He winks at me.

Harry, laughing, goes over to assist the woman.

Young George sits down next to me. 'It's happened again, hasn't it?' he whispers, not looking directly at me.

'What has?' I ask, turning towards him. I still can't get over how young he looks. This George is actually quite handsome.

'You got hit by the car, didn't you? I didn't think it would happen so soon.'

'What are you talking about? You didn't think *what* would happen?'

'What year are we in?' George asks, turning to face me.

'2013,' I reply with confidence. 'I didn't get hit so badly I can't remember that!'

George nods knowingly. 'When I tell you something in a

31

moment, Jo-Jo, I want you to keep very calm. You mustn't shriek or scream or draw attention to yourself.'

'What are you talking about, why would I do that?'

'Remember, Jo-Jo, you must keep calm.'

'And Carry On, Drink Tea, Eat Chocolate or something else hilarious they haven't thought of yet to put on a tea towel or a mug?' I ask, rolling my eyes.

George shakes his head, clearly not understanding my attempt at a joke. 'No, just keep very calm.' He takes a deep breath. 'Jo-Jo, you're not in 2013 any more.'

I want to laugh. George might as well have said: 'Dorothy, you're not in Kansas any more.'

'I'm not?' I ask slowly, indulging him. This is getting weirder by the second. Why is George talking in riddles? It's getting more and more like some strange game show. What do I need to do, work out the clues and then I'll win a prize when the TV cameras are revealed and the smarmy host jumps out from behind a screen? God, I hope it's a holiday. I could do with a change of scene!

'No, Jo-Jo, you're not. You're in *1963*.'

'Yep,' I say, grinning at him. 'And?'

'And that's it. At this very moment you're sitting in my record shop in the King's Road, London, in November 1963.'

I eye George, disbelieving. He's mad!

'Here,' he says, reaching behind the shop counter for a newspaper, 'look.'

And I do. And the date at the top of *The Times* newspaper is, just as George has said, *November 1963*.

'What!' I shout, jumping to my feet. 'How can this be?'

Harry and his customer glance round at me for a moment before returning to their record discussion.

'Calm, Jo-Jo,' George reminds me, tugging on my arm to get me to sit down again. 'Remain calm. You really must.'

'But what do you mean, telling me I'm in 1963,' I hiss. 'Are you mad? Have I been drugged? Am I hallucinating?'

'No, not any of those,' George says quietly. 'And *I'm* not mad, either.'

'Am I, then?' I ask in a strangled voice. 'Is this what this is, the start of insanity, or a mental breakdown? I know I've been working hard recently, but—'

'Jo-Jo . . . ' George places a reassuring hand on my arm. He looks to where Harry is still trying to persuade the customer into choosing an album by Bob Dylan instead of her preferred Frank Sinatra. He lowers his voice even further. 'You're not going mad, you've just travelled back in time.'

I open my eyes wide. 'Oh well, that makes it all right then! What do you mean, I've travelled in time? How can I have? Don't be so ridiculous.'

'Like I said, I've seen it happen before. You're not the first, you know. It must have been when you got hit on the crossing – you probably hit a time portal.'

'A *what*? Whatever do you mean, time portal? You only get those in sci-fi films and TV shows and I know for sure I'm not in *Dr Who*.'

'Dr what?' George asks, puzzled.

'Not Dr what, Dr *Who*. Don't tell me you haven't heard of that? I thought it began in the sixties?'

'I've seen adverts for that. It's a new TV show,' Harry joins in, as he and his customer make their way over to the till with both albums, which Harry seems to have persuaded her into buying. 'Starts next week.' He rings up her purchases on an old mechanical till with the prices popping up in a little window. 'I didn't know you were into sci-fi, Jo-Jo?'

'I'm not,' I say flatly. I glare at George now. 'Especially when it involves me.'

'Look, I can't say too much now,' George whispers, watching Harry finish up with the lady at the till. 'But you'll be absolutely fine, Jo-Jo, trust me. I've got a feeling we can work it out if you keep calm, and let it be.'

'Keep calm. Let it be? But—'

George shushes me with his hand as Harry comes over to us again.

'I think Jo-Jo is still feeling a little confused after her accident,' George says to him. 'Perhaps when you take her back to work you should keep a close eye on her, Harry.'

'Do you think she should be going back to work?' Harry asks. 'I could always let them know what happened when I go back in and she could take the afternoon off.'

'No, I think keeping everything just the same as usual will help jog Jo-Jo's slightly fuzzy memory and allow her to return to normal life much faster,' George says knowingly.

I'm about to open my mouth to protest that they're making decisions about me as though I'm not here and, more importantly, what do they mean, taking me back to work. I know where my own office is, for goodness' sake! And if I want to take the afternoon off I can do that quite easily without having to ask anyone's permission. Then I realise that if what George is saying is true, then I most probably don't know where I work and nor can I just take time off any more.

Suddenly I feel very cold, and very, very scared.

But how can this be true? Time travel simply isn't possible – it's just a fantasy. Something made up by writers and sci-fi geeks who desperately want to believe in something that can't be done. This is just complete and utter nonsense. I'm about to tell them both so, when George turns his head away from Harry and winks at me.

'You'll be fine, Jo-Jo,' he says in that same calm, reassuring voice. 'Trust me. Go with Harry. Let it Be, and everything will work out just fine. I promise you.'

Three

'So here we are,' Harry says, as we arrive outside a large building in Manchester Square. 'Time to face the music again.'

It had been the strangest journey across London with Harry. When we walked back down the King's Road the cars moving slowly along the street all appeared to be classic vehicles, the type my father would frequently stop to admire if we were out somewhere. And when we got on the tube, it was like we'd stepped into an old black and white TV show; the clothes the people were wearing looked very peculiar – retro, I guess you'd call them, all the men in smart suits, either cheap or expensive, all the women in warm coats with knee-length pencil-skirted or pleated suits, most of them wearing swept-up beehives or headbands and flicky hairdos and gloves, looking like photographs I've seen of Jackie Kennedy. What no one was wearing was casual clothes. A lot of the men wore hats, bowlers and – what did they call them? Fedoras! A few less smartphones were being tapped on – no, cancel that. There weren't any phones at all.

'Are you sure you're OK?' Harry kept asking me as I stared around me in complete bewilderment during our journey. How could something so familiar, that I use on a daily basis, suddenly become so unsettling? I'd travelled these tube lines hundreds of times before, but I'd never experienced a journey like this.

'Uhuh,' I answered. Or sometimes I'd just nod. What was happening here? Had I really gone back in time fifty years to 1963 like George had said? No, that just wasn't possible. But how could I explain what was happening around me right now – the people, the cars, the shop windows we'd passed all appearing to be selling retro goods? There was that word again – retro. Maybe this wasn't retro; maybe these were current up-to-date goods, clothes and cars I was seeing in front of me. Maybe I really was the one who was from another time, not them.

Now, as Harry and I stand outside the building that we both apparently work in, I begin to panic. If George is right and by some weird twist I have managed to travel back in time, how am I going to cope? I don't know anything about the sixties, about how you behave or what you do. I was born in 1983. What do I know, of … of mini skirts and beehive hairdos? I look down at my legs. But I'm not wearing a mini skirt, am I? I'm wearing this incredibly tight red thing that comes down to my knees. It may be tight, but thank goodness I've not got my legs out on show. Actually I hadn't seen any of the super short skirts so synonymous with the sixties since I'd arrived. Was I too early for the mini skirt to even have been invented? Exactly my point – I knew nothing about this era!

'Sure you're OK to go back?' Harry asks, looking me up and down. 'Only I've never known you to be this quiet before – and you're shaking.'

He's right. My knees are virtually knocking together in fright at what awaits me through those big glass doors. He reaches out his hands and rests them gently on my arms. I think for a split second he's going to hug me. But he just looks down into my eyes.

'You don't have to go in, you know?'

Harry's touch is strangely comforting, and I feel my legs steady. 'Yes ... I'm sure I'll be fine.' *What choice do I have? I have nowhere else to go.*

'Good.' Harry smiles at me, and then, as if he's only just realised where his hands are, he whips them away from my body and stuffs them back in to his pockets, his cheeks flushing a little. 'Right, no time like the present then, let's get you back to work.'

As we enter the building together I notice a plaque on the wall outside that reads *EMI House*, and I find myself in a large reception area filled with a magnificent desk, and behind that an impressive swivel chair. Opposite this are two red velvet chaise longues, and an enormous aspidistra plant in a wonderful brass pot. As I try to follow Harry on through the reception area and through some more glass doors, he turns around.

'Where are you going? Hadn't you better stay here and see what you've missed while you've been away? I'll let them know upstairs what's happened in case there's any trouble about you being away from your desk for so long – we're both late back from our lunch hours. But I'm sure a slight misdemeanour with an Austin-Healey will count as as good an excuse as any to take a long lunch break.'

'Yes, I'll do that.' I swivel round to look at the large desk. So, I must be the receptionist here. 'And thank you,' I say, turning back to look at Harry. 'For bringing me back and ... everything, today.'

'No problem,' Harry says. 'I'll pop down later if I can get away and check on you.' He pauses for a moment as if he's considering something. 'A gang of us were thinking of going out tonight, to catch a few bands at a local club, if you think you might feel up to it?'

'Er ... ' Oh dear, what am I supposed to say? I don't know my relationship status in the sixties. I glance down at my left hand; I don't see any rings, so assume all is well.

'You can bring that kooky flatmate of yours if you like?' Harry suggests, as if this might swing it.

I have a flatmate? 'Yes, OK then, that sounds ... groovy,' I say, hoping this might be the right lingo to use.

Harry winces at my terminology, but he looks pleased. 'Yeah, I'm sure it will be that, and hopefully much more. So I'll catch you after work to arrange details? Better be getting back myself. See you later.'

'Yes.' I give a casual wave, then hastily drop my hand again as he hurries off. 'You do that.' *What the hell was groovy all about, Jo-Jo?* I ask myself as I cringe at my choice of word. But I haven't got time to worry about that because people are beginning to find their way into the reception area, and my phone is already ringing on the desk.

Luckily the people who stop by reception in the next few minutes all have appointments, so I ask them to wait on the chaise longues while I try and figure out how I contact the office of the person they're waiting to see. I breathe a sigh of relief when I see a list of names on a clipboard followed by office extension numbers. Now, how do I work the phone? Oh God, where is the phone?

I stare around me but I can't see anything that will put me in touch with any of the many offices that I'm sure must be in this huge building. I begin to move papers and files around on the desk frantically in the hope that it will magically reveal itself to me.

'Maybe you should use the headset?' one of my 'appointments' suggests helpfully. It's the well-spoken man in the suit – a Mr Epstein, who came in asking for a Mr Maxwell. 'First day, is it?' he asks, smiling.

I nod gratefully, and look around for a headset.

'We all have to start somewhere.' He gets up and comes over to the desk while I grope about looking under more papers and books for a pair of headphones now. Jeez, they could be anywhere, I think, looking for something akin to the white set I plug into my iPhone. 'Would these be they?' he asks, holding up a huge hideous grey headset with a small microphone attached.

'Yes, I guess they would be. Thank you so much,' I say as I place them on my head. *Now what happens if I press this button here?* I wonder, looking at a console of buttons, switches, and numbers in front of me.

'Yes?' a voice booms in my ear.

'Mr Maxwell?' I ask hopefully.

'Yes?'

'This is ...' *What's my name, what's my name? Ah, it's still*

Jo-Jo, calm down, that much hasn't changed. 'This is Jo-Jo on reception. I have a Mr Epstein waiting to see you.'

'He's waiting?' the voice booms again. 'How long has he been waiting? I told you to inform me the minute he arrived, girl! I'll be down to meet him in a moment.'

The line goes dead and he's gone.

'Mr Maxwell will be with you shortly,' I announce in my best secretarial voice.

'That's absolutely fine,' Mr Epstein says, smiling at me again. 'You're doing a great job. Nothing like throwing you in at the deep end, eh?'

You have no idea! Now for the next appointment . . .

I successfully match up an extremely glamorous woman wearing a red and black suit with matching pillar-box hat and veil with her appointment in accounts. And sit back and take a deep breath for a few seconds.

Suddenly, a large, red-looking man in an ill-fitting grey suit bursts through the interior glass doors. What little hair he still retains is grey to match the suit, and he appears quite out of breath at what I expect is a fairly short journey from his office.

'Brian!' he bellows jovially at my office helper. 'How are you?'

'I'm good thank you, Walter, and yourself?'

'Excellent, excellent. I'm so sorry if this incompetent girl kept you waiting.' He glares at me.

'Not at all, Walter. She was utterly charming company.'

Walter eyes me as though he finds this hard to believe. 'Well, do come through to my office – my personal secretary will look after you now.'

They disappear through the double swing doors.

'Arse,' comments Mimi, the woman in red.

'Is he?' I enquire politely, while trying to fathom out what I'm supposed to be doing next. Lights and buttons are beginning to flash on the console in front of me like an electronic game of Battleships, and I'm afraid that if I don't do something with them, the ship we're in might explode in a few moments and sink without a trace.

'Walter Maxwell is, yes. Can't bear him myself. But Brian is lovely.'

I nod, and flick one of the switches under a lit-up red button. 'Yes, he seems like a nice guy.'

'Very influential guy.'

'Really?' I ask Mimi, but quickly realise I'm also now talking to someone on the telephone as they begin babbling into my headphones, so I hurriedly flick the switch back over.

Mimi looks surprised. 'You *are* new to this, aren't you? Good afternoon, Allan!'

Allan from accounts escorts Mimi through the double doors. Now I come to think of it, that man's name does seem a tad familiar ... Wait, it couldn't be the same Brian Epstein, could it? The Brian Epstein who was manager of the Beatles for so many years, and even called the fifth Beatle by some?

But I'm distracted by this thought by all these damn lights that keep flashing at me. It's like being in the cockpit of an aeroplane when you don't know how to fly. So I slip my headphones off again. I look back towards the doors everyone keeps disappearing through to see if I can still see anyone, but all I hear is 'Psst!' and a young girl's head suddenly pokes around the door. 'Yo, Jo-Jo, I haven't got long – if old bossy britches upstairs catches me away from me desk I'll be for the high jump.'

She looks either side of her again, and then allows the rest of her petite body to appear around the door.

'Ellie!' I exclaim, suddenly recognising the figure standing in front of me now wearing a lime green shift dress.

'Don't shout me name, you daft banana, or they'll all know I'm down here.'

'But – but what are you doing here? And – and look at your hair!'

'Do you like it?' Ellie asks, patting at her platinum blonde hair piled up in a huge beehive on top of her little head. 'I had it done in me lunch break at that salon down the road. Cost me an arm and a leg, mind, but I really think it's worth it.'

'It . . . it looks fab.'

'Doesn't it?' Ellie admires herself in the glass of the door. 'Anyways, what am I doing here? I'll tell you what I'm doing here, Jo-Jo, I've got some goss for you!'

'Goss?'

'Yeah, and I mean real good juicy goss this time, not like that nonsense about Dave and Cynthia from accounts. Apparently it was her husband's baby after all and—'

'Ellie, you said you didn't have long?' I interrupt. My Ellie is just like this, always easily distracted, and always full of the latest gossip.

'Sorry, right. Well, I was typing up this letter for 'im upstairs and he says it's to go around to all the staff at the end of the day before they leave. How I'm supposed to get it out to everyone, I don't know. What does he think I am, some sort of whirlwind? Does he know how many floors and offices there are in this building?'

'Ellie, the letter?' I prompt.

43

'Oh yeah. Well, you'll never guess what was in it . . . ' She looks at me expectantly.

'No, I won't. Perhaps you'd better just tell me to save time.'

Ellie looks a little disappointed. 'I suppose. Well . . . ' She sidles over to my desk. 'It's only a competition to meet the bloody Beatles!'

'And?'

Ellie looks at me as though I've just turned down the offer of a million pounds. 'Did you hear what I just said. I said it's a competition to—'

'Meet the Beatles, yes, I got that. How?'

'Apparently the bigwigs are going to choose an employee of the month, and they get to go to a fancy pants reception where the Beatles are receiving some plaque or other.'

'I take it you are referring to the cocktail party and luncheon on the eighteenth, Ellie, where the Beatles are to be presented with silver discs?' A tall, elegant lady in a beige skirt suit and white frilly blouse now stands behind Ellie with her arms folded.

Ellie jumps in her pink platform boots.

'Yes, of course, Miss Fields. Sorry, I was just—'

'I know what you were just doing, Ellie – gossiping as usual. Now along with you, back to your desk upstairs. You've plenty of time to talk with Jo-Jo later when the two of you get home.'

So Ellie is my flatmate? Actually the thought of that is quite comforting.

'Yes, Miss Fields,' Ellie says, turning towards the door. 'Although I don't know what time that'll be after I get all these bloomin' letters out to everyone,' she grumbles to herself.

'What did you say then?' Miss Fields asks. 'Something you'd like to share?'

Ellie turns back towards us. 'I said I don't know what time I'll get home after I've delivered all these competition letters today. Does him upstairs have any idea how many people there are working here? How am I expected to make sure they all get a letter before home time?'

The joys of email, I think, as I watch Miss Fields cast a stern eye over Ellie. If only they knew what was to come ...

'That is for you to work out, Eleanor. Sir Joseph will be expecting it of you and you know how he hates to be let down.'

'You could stand at the door as everyone leaves at the end of the day and hand them one then,' I suggest quickly. I'm kind of banking on the notion that everyone leaves at roughly the same time here. I can't imagine 'flexi-hours' have been invented yet.

'Yes, I could do that, couldn't I?' Ellie says, brightening.

'That's a very good idea, Jo-Jo,' Miss Fields says, casting her beady eye in my direction now. 'Very astute.'

'Thank you.'

'Quick then, girl, back to work,' she says to Ellie. 'Get those letters typed and printed out, so you're ready later. And I'm sure the rest of the girls in the typing pool will help you if you ask them nicely.'

'Yes, Miss Fields.' *Thank you.* Ellie mouths at me as she disappears out of the door.

'Your quick thinking has been noted, Jo-Jo,' Miss Fields says, smiling at me.

'It has?'

'In view of the competition.'

'Yes, of course, the competition.' I nod. 'Thank you.'

'Now back to work. There seem to be several lights flashing on your switchboard that need attending to.'

I look down at my desk and my switchboard is lit up like a Hollywood make-up mirror. 'Yes, I'll get right on it.'

It hasn't taken me long amongst all the chaos to figure out that I'm working for EMI, which was, until a few years ago – *my* years ago! – one of the biggest music companies in the world. I'm not too sure how big they are in the sixties, but the offices I'm in now are huge, and the amount of guests in and out of reception during one afternoon is exhausting, because I need to find out where they're going and who they're meeting with and be nice to them at all times. However, once I get the hang of the switchboard I manage to calm down a bit and sort out all the calls, get most of them through to the correct offices, and I even manage to make some visitors cups of tea and coffee while they're waiting, although it pains me to provide them with such awful-tasting instant coffee.

I have to tip mine in the aspidistra plant when I get the time to make myself a quick cup, it's that bad. I just hope it doesn't wilt. The plant, that is. Where's a Starbucks when you need one?

At last five o'clock comes and it's time to go home. I've just got myself fairly comfortable with the workings of a sixties office, so changing scenery now is suddenly very unnerving again. I hover in reception with Ellie, on the premise that I'm helping her to hand out the letters. What else can I do? I don't know my way home!

'How are you?' Harry asks as he passes us and collects his letter. 'Feeling better?'

'Much better now, thanks. A bit less dazed than earlier.'

'Good. Good. So will you and Ellie be able to make it along to the club tonight?'

I look over at Ellie who's listening keenly to every word we're saying, even though she's pretending not to. She nods frantically at me.

'Yes, yes, that would be lovely, thanks.'

Harry looks pleased. 'It's the World's End pub on the King's Road, do you know it?'

I just walked past it today ... The 2013 version. It couldn't be that different, could it?

'I know where it is,' I answer truthfully.

'Excellent, then we'll see you there, about eight-ish?'

'Yes, eight, fab!'

Harry, looking pleased, leaves the building reading his letter, along with all the other employees, and as they exit we can hear their cries of excitement wafting back through the door.

'Jo-Jo's got a da-ate! Jo-Jo's got a da-ate!' Ellie sings in my face.

'No I haven't! We're just meeting him and some mates to listen to some bands. How is that a date?'

Ellie flutters her false eyelashes at me. 'Come on, Jo-Jo, he's been after you for ages. Just a bit slow off the mark is our Harry.'

How can that be? I wonder – I've only just arrived here. Have I jumped into someone else's life and body? Like that guy on that TV show, *Quantum Leap*, used to do. No, not like that. He got into a time machine he'd built, didn't he? A bit like Dr Who and his Tardis. But Dr Who just arrives in the place as a new extra person; he doesn't have a life going on when he gets there, like I seem to have here in 1963.

'I'm sure that's not true,' I say, choosing my words carefully.

'And I'm sure it is!' Ellie says, her green eyes sparkling. 'Let's just see who's right tonight, shall we? Me or you.'

Four

The World's End Distillery in the sixties isn't really what I'd call a club, even with my limited knowledge of such establishments. It looks to me just like a pub with a stage area waiting for some bands to appear and play music on it.

But as Ellie and I arrive and manage to find Harry and a few of his pals waiting for us in amongst the crowd, there's a sense of eager excitement amongst my fellow party-goers.

So far I'd coped quite well, I thought. We'd left the offices after we'd given out all Ellie's letters and made our way back to our little flat in Fulham by bus. There we'd quickly grabbed a bite to eat – white bread sandwiches filled with cheese and pickle, which to begin with I'd turned my nose up at – I'm wholewheat all the way in 2013 – but I'd actually quite enjoyed them. We'd then spent the next couple of hours getting ready to come out tonight. And boy was that a complicated process! My hair had to be back-combed to within an inch of its life then the perfect outfit had to be chosen, and rejected, then re-chosen all over again when nothing better could be found. And then we'd spent an absolute age applying eye make-up so that we looked like Hollywood's idea of Cleopatra. I felt like a right idiot when it was all done and we were ready to leave the flat – but my look was quite tame in comparison to Ellie's golden yellow cowl-neck dress with matching gold sandals.

'Why does all this matter so much?' I'd asked her as I was trying on my fourth change of outfit.

'Why does it matter, Jo-Jo?' she'd asked, aghast. 'Because we're going out to a club where bands play, that's why! You never know who you might bump into. Anyone who's anyone hangs around down there, don't they?' Ellie had sighed with disappointment at my lack of enthusiasm and shaken her head.

I still didn't understand what was going on, but I kind of decided that I was having some sort of very vivid dream right now, and the best way to get through it was not to fight it, but to just go with the flow until I woke up and came to my senses once again.

'Hi,' Harry says, as we arrive at the bar beside him and his friends, 'glad you could make it, girls, what would you like to drink?'

'A glass of Pinot Grigio would go down a treat right now, thanks,' I say, without thinking.

'A Pinocchio what?' Harry asks, his forehead wrinkling. 'I don't think I've heard of that.'

Some of the others in our party turn to look too.

'Pinot Grigio,' I repeat. 'It's a white wine.'

'I don't think they do white wine here,' Harry says, looking anxiously behind the bar. 'Just beers and spirits. Maybe if we were in a restaurant?'

'She's joking with you, aren't you, Jo-Jo?' Ellie says happily, springing on to a bar stool that's just become free next to us. 'Don't mind her, Harry; she's been in a funny mood all day. Between you and me,' she says, leaning in towards him and whispering, 'I think she might have bumped her head a bit harder than you thought.'

I'd told her about the accident and Harry being there while we were getting ready.

'I can hear you, you know?' I say, putting my hands on my hips. 'I may have been knocked down by a car but I'm not deaf.'

'Easy, babe,' Ellie says, shushing me. 'She'll have a Babycham like she always does, Harry, and I'll have the same, thank you.'

I have to drink Babycham! This gets even worse.

I've heard of Babycham; it was this retro drink from the sixties that was marketed to look like mini bottles of champagne but was actually pear cider. Someone brought some as a joke to the office party last Christmas – apparently it was making a comeback again. But I didn't taste it then and I really didn't want to taste the original now.

Harry orders two bottles of the stuff, then pours them into two cocktail-style glasses and passes them to Ellie and I. I take a sip of mine and prepare to pretend to look like I'm enjoying it, but actually I find it isn't half as bad as I expected it to be, and while I continue to sip on the fizzy concoction I let my eyes wander around the pub.

It's not too different from how I would expect a London pub to look in 2013, except its clientele are dressed in the height of early sixties' fashion. It's a bit like being at a costume party where everyone has tried really hard, but the décor is really dated – well, it's not to everyone else drinking in the World's End pub tonight, but to me it looks very old-fashioned. But if it wasn't for the clothes and the outdated wallpaper, I really could be in any London bar right now.

'So, what do you reckon to the competition?' Harry asks me, taking a gulp from his pint of beer.

'What competition?' I ask.

'The Beatles one you and Ellie were handing out letters about earlier, of course.'

'*That* competition! Of course, yes, very exciting.'

'You don't *sound* very excited,' Harry says, watching me closely with his big blue eyes. 'It's all everyone from EMI is talking about tonight. What they're going to do to be picked as employee of the month.'

I'm not excited because I'm hoping I'm not going to be here long enough to ever find out who wins, let alone have a chance of winning it myself.

'Meeting the Beatles *would* be exciting, I suppose,' I say, choosing my words carefully. 'Perhaps I just don't expect to be picked, so I can't see any point in getting myself wound up about it?'

Harry shrugs. 'That's one way to look at it. Prevents disappointment.'

'Exactly.'

'I'm going to do some home baking,' Ellie pipes up.

52

'Baking?' Harry exclaims. 'You?'

'Yes, me, Harry Rigby, and what of it? I can bake, me mam showed me how when I was back in Liverpool.'

'Who are you going to bake for?' I ask, sipping on my Babycham again. I'm actually starting to enjoy it now.

'The bosses,' Ellie states matter-of-factly.

'Wouldn't that count as bribery, though?' I suggest gently.

Ellie huffs and folds her arms. 'Jo-Jo, why do you have to be so bloody sensible all the time?'

'She's right, though, Ellie,' Harry says. 'It might seem a bit odd if you suddenly start making cakes for those in charge of choosing the employee of the month.'

Ellie sighs. 'I know, I know – but she's always right,' she pulls a face, 'that's what's so bloody annoying about her!' Ellie looks across at me with a sour face, then she winks. 'But I still say you need to loosen up a bit. I mean, Harry, look at what she's wearing tonight, it hardly screams wild and sexy music fan when the bands come on now, does it?'

Harry looks like the proverbial rabbit caught in headlights. Except the headlights he's caught between are me and Ellie, as he examines my figure-hugging pale blue sleeveless turtle-neck sweater, and matching capri pants.

'Well ...' he attempts, clearing his throat first. 'It's not exactly Ursula Andress. However,' he hurriedly continues when Ellie smirks, 'it's not exactly Doris Day, either.'

I grin at Ellie.

'But I think you look very nice this evening, Jo-Jo,' he mumbles, before hurriedly examining the inside of his pint glass.

'Thank you, Harry,' I reply, trying not to blush like some silly schoolgirl. 'That's kind of you to say.'

Ellie nods at me in a knowing fashion.

'The bands,' she suddenly shrieks, throwing herself off her bar stool and hurtling across the floor in the direction of the small wooden stage.

Harry and I turn our heads to where she's darted off to, and sure enough a band is just setting their instruments up on the stage in preparation for their set.

'Shall we join her?' Harry asks, offering his hand to help me down off my stool.

'Why not?' I reply, taking it. *What very gentlemanly behaviour*, I think, *maybe going back in time does have some benefits after all*.

We make our way across to the stage area where everyone else is starting to gather now to wait for the first band to begin playing.

'Jo-Jo! Harry!' I hear someone call. I turn around to see George weaving his way through the crowd towards us.

'George, what are you doing here?' I ask him as he squeezes into a space next to us. I'm so glad to see George again I almost hug him. There'd been no chance of getting away earlier to go back to the shop to see him and, to be honest, I felt extremely nervous of venturing out anywhere on my own in this strange new world I found myself in, without a chaperone. But now he was here in the pub with us, perhaps he'd be able to answer some of my questions.

'I always try and pop in when they've got some local bands on,' George says, smiling. 'You never know when I might be playing their songs in my shop one day.'

'That's very true.' I look at the band setting up on the stage right now. But they don't look at all familiar, especially with my limited musical knowledge.

'Pint, George?' Harry enquires, holding up his now empty glass.

'That's very good of you, Harry – yes please, bitter.'

'Same again for you, Jo-Jo?'

I nod. 'Yes, please.'

Harry makes his way over to the bar, which is now starting to get very busy as the promise of live music about to begin swells the numbers in the pub.

'So how are you getting on?' George asks me, as a few people begin to push in front of us in their eagerness to get to the stage.

'How am I getting on? You make it sound like I've just started a new job. I'm stuck in the sixties, for goodness' sake. Wearing strange tight clothes, drinking a fizzy concoction that, for no apparent reason, is advertised by Bambi. And my *hair*,' I touch the crusty helmet that is currently masquerading as my hair, 'has been back-combed and sprayed to within an inch of its life and seems to be defying gravity at this very moment! Just what's going on, George? And more importantly, how do I make it stop?'

'Whoah, calm down,' George says. 'Let's take this one step at a time.'

'One step at a time! It's all ridiculous, and none of it makes any sense. For instance, how can I be here in 1963 with you – the same you I know from 2013, but looking so much younger? And then there's Harry, too. He looks virtually the same as he did before, but he's kind of different at the same time, and then, to make things even more complicated, Ellie is here as well!'

'Ellie?' George asks.

'Ellie – she was my PA at my accounts firm back in 2013, but she's my flatmate here in 1963. Well, a version very much like the original Ellie. What's happening to me, am I going mad, dreaming, what is it?'

George shakes his head. 'No, you're not going mad, it's difficult to explain exactly *why* this often happens. It just does. And usually for *very* good reason. It's not strange at all that Harry and Ellie are here with you again. If these people were a part of your life in 2013, there's no reason versions of them shouldn't be a similar part of your life here in 1963 too, is there?'

I try and take a step back from George as best I can on the now extremely crowded pub floor. 'I'm not sure I'm quite following you, George. You mean this really isn't a dream, that I'm not hallucinating, I just have to accept I really am living this new life in the sixties?'

'Yes, Jo-Jo, I'm afraid for now you do.'

I take another look around the pub. The band is just starting to play a medley of songs I don't know, but the sound is familiar to me from the many programmes I've caught bits of over the years, revisiting music and fashion from the fifties and sixties. In fact, suddenly it's like hopping inside one of those black and white episodes of *Top of the Pops* as the crowd begin to bob about to the music in front of me.

'But if I'm stuck here in 1963 what about my business back in 2013? I've worked too hard to let that crumble. If I'm away from it for long how will everyone cope?'

'Admirably, I expect,' George says, watching the band. 'They've had you to guide them for long enough. I'm sure you do them a disservice if you think they'll run your business into the ground in a few weeks.'

'A few weeks? So there is a chance I could return home again?'

'It's possible,' George says, nodding, partly at me, partly in time to the music.

'Only *possible*!'

'It depends.'

'On?'

'Two pints and a Babycham,' Harry says, arriving back beside us again. 'Now what have you two been talking about while I've been gone?'

'Not much,' George says, his foot tapping in time to the music. 'Bit difficult to have a decent conversation now the bands have started playing, isn't it, Jo-Jo? Why don't you pop in and see me at the shop tomorrow in your lunch break? Maybe I'll have what you're looking for then?' He gives me a knowing look.

Is he kidding me? I need answers *now*. 'Sure, George,' I sigh, knowing I have little choice. 'I'll do that. I really hope you do have what I want, though.'

A way for me to get back home. And fast.

Five

This morning I asked Miss Fields if I could take an extra half-hour for lunch, promising that I'll make it up tomorrow, and luckily she agreed. So right now I'm hurrying over to George's shop as fast as I can in my extended lunch break.

Today as I'm travelling along the King's Road I'm taking in everything and everyone as I walk along. It's weird, when you see old photos or footage of people and places from the past, they're either in black and white, or shot on old cine film where the colours are worn and faded over time. But actually being here like this, living and breathing the era, I can experience just how vividly real everything is. The colours, the designs, and especially the people; they may look odd to me with their unusual clothes and peculiar hairstyles, but they're living, breathing human beings, simply going about their day-to-day business, just like I am this lunchtime on my way to see George.

Watching the bands last night had been quite good fun in

the end, and I was really starting to enjoy some of their music by the end of the night. Harry and his friend Derek had walked Ellie and I to our bus stop after we left the pub, which I found very quaint, though very chivalrous of them, but I was secretly quite pleased when that's as far as it went. So as we leapt up on to the back of the bright red London bus that was going to take us home, and held on to the conductor's pole, I'd waved happily to Harry as the bus disappeared along the King's Road. Much as I liked him, I had more important things to deal with right now than a blossoming romance between a version of myself and a Harry that I wasn't really even sure existed.

This lunchtime as I arrive at George's shop and push open the door, the little bell rings above my head, just as it always does.

'Jo-Jo,' George says, looking up from the counter where he's browsing a music catalogue. 'You managed to survive to see another day, then?'

'Just,' I say, flopping down on to the wooden chair where I sat yesterday. 'It's so hard keeping up this pretence, though. I keep sticking my foot in it by mentioning things that no one even knows about yet.'

'Such as?'

'Like when Ellie and I were getting ready for work this morning I asked if she had any hair straighteners I could borrow. When I explained what they were, she suggested I used the iron.'

George laughs.

'And just now, before I came away from work, someone was moaning about a file that they'd lost in the office, so I asked them if they'd backed it up on a flash stick. They looked at me like I was some sort of pervert!'

'You'll get used to it,' George says. 'I've just put the kettle on. Tea?'

'Yes, please. But I don't want to get used to it,' I call to him as he disappears out the back. 'I want to go back home.'

'And you will do,' George says, sticking his head back around the door, 'just as soon as we find out what the best route is to get you there. Excuse me a moment,' he apologises, as a phone rings out the back and he disappears again.

A man comes into the shop with a young boy. He nods at me, so I smile at him.

'I'm looking for a birthday present for my son,' he says, mistaking me for an assistant. 'He loves his music, and so I thought I'd bring him down here to the King's Road to buy him a gift, something a bit different. Can you recommend anything he might like?'

I stand up slowly, desperately trawling my brain for bands from the sixties, but only the obvious springs to mind. 'The Beatles?'

'Nah, he has everything they've done, don't you, son?'

The boy nods.

'I think he'd like something a bit different.'

I look desperately to the back of the shop; the sound of the ticking clock, usually so calming, suddenly becomes painfully loud. *Oh, please hurry up, George!* 'Let's see now …' I say, stalling for time. 'Erm, how about The Kinks, perhaps … Or maybe The Who? They're great sixties bands, aren't they?'

'I don't know,' the man says, looking at me oddly, 'you're supposed to be the expert!'

'How about the Rolling Stones?' I hear a knowledgeable voice behind me say. 'They're a new band, but very popular with those in the know.' He comes up beside me and taps the side of his nose, then he winks at the young boy.

'I haven't heard of them, have you, Richard?'

His son nods. 'I have actually, and I'd love a record by them. What do you have, sir?' he asks, looking keenly at George.

George grins and pulls a couple of 45 records from a display.

I sit back down on my chair. Apparently I know as much about sixties music as I do about living in the sixties, and that isn't a lot.

The father and his son eventually find something they're happy with and pay for their purchases. George has managed to sell them a few other bits while they're here, too, and Richard is looking more than a bit pleased with his collection of birthday gifts. George shuts his till happy with his latest sale, and bids them farewell.

'Goodbye, Richard,' he waves as they open the door to leave the shop.

'Thanks, sir,' Richard says happily. 'You know, one day I think I'd like to own a record shop just like this one.'

'That's a fine ambition to have,' George smiles, 'and I hope you achieve it, young man. Goodbye, Mr Branson,' he says to Richard's father. 'Do call again, won't you?'

I stare with disbelief at the departing figures. Then I shake my head. Hold on just one minute, have we just sold records to a young Richard Branson – the future multi-millionaire and owner of the Virgin group?

'Do you know who that was, George?' I ask, still staring at the closed door.

'Of course, Mr Branson and his son Richard – he left me his card.'

I turn and look at George. He returns my look with one of complete innocence.

'I'll get that tea now, shall I?' he asks.

George returns with our tea and sits down next to me.

'I'm sorry about before,' I say apologetically, 'with the bands. I obviously know nothing about music.'

George grins. 'Actually both those groups you suggested would have been great recommendations for the young boy, but you're about a year too early, Jo-Jo, they were both formed in 1964.'

'Ah! Bit difficult for you to sell their records then, eh?' I grin. 'Seems like I'm ahead of my time, George! Unlike now ...' Then my smile fades. 'Wait, how do you know about those bands if they're not together yet? In fact, how come you seem to know so much about what's happening to me?'

'I don't know that much. Not really. I just know that for you to return to your time you need to find the one thing that links you back to the future.'

'Like the movie?'

'How do you mean?' George looks at me with a puzzled expression.

Argh! George is so infuriating. One minute he seems to know so much about what is going on, and the next he appears to know nothing.

'Never mind that now. What sort of a link?'

'A link that will help you find what it is you need to know,' George replies even more cryptically. 'We know that part of your link to the future is the zebra crossing because that's where you arrived from the first time it happened, but we don't know why or when your link might appear again.'

'Can't I just step out on to the crossing again in front of a car?' I suggest hopefully.

'Unless you want to die a very painful death here in 1963, I wouldn't recommend it, no.'

I somehow knew it wouldn't be that easy. 'So what do I have to do, then?'

'I don't know exactly. It's always very vague. Different for everyone that comes.'

'What do you mean, *everyone*? Do you mean there are more people like me wandering about here?'

'Not here necessarily; most go back.'

'Most?'

George takes a sip of his tea. 'Like I say, it depends on whether they figure it all out.'

'Yes, but figure *what* out?'

'The reason they're here.'

I shake my head. This is all just madness. And George seems to be the only person who knows anything about it. And that doesn't appear to be much.

I open my mouth to question him further, but another customer enters the shop.

'Hadn't you better be getting back to your office?' George asks as he stands up to greet the lady. 'You've been here for half an hour – you're going to be very late back.'

I glance at the clock on the wall. 'Damn, you're right! I'll be back again soon, George, I promise.'

'I know you will, Jo-Jo,' George nods, as I dash out of the door and up the King's Road, the shop's bell still ringing in my ears. 'Of that I have no doubt.'

Six

I throw myself out of the doors of the train at my tube stop, and I'm so glad I'm wearing flat black boots, not high heels, with my pink and black Jackie Kennedy-inspired suit, as I run back towards the office, glancing at my watch every few paces. I haven't lost my hatred of tardiness during time travel, and arriving back at work fifteen minutes late from lunch – an extended lunch too – simply isn't acceptable for me.

There's no one in reception as I enter the building, so I quickly hang my jacket behind my chair, shove my bag in one of the deep drawers in my desk, and flatten down my wayward hair while I assume my position on my swivel chair, ready to begin receiving visitors again.

'Long lunch, Miss McKenzie?' a voice enquires through the double doors.

'Mr Maxwell!' I jump. 'What can I do for you?'

'You can tell me why you were away from your desk for so long, that's what you can do.'

'I thought Vera was covering my lunch break.' I'm trying to speak normally but I'm still out of breath.

'She was for your allotted hour and a half that Miss Field gave you. But then she had work of her own to attend to, so I sent her back to her desk.'

'I'm very sorry I'm late back, Mr Maxwell, but I had to go all the way over to the King's Road, and ... there was a hold-up on the way back on the tube.'

Mr Maxwell eyes me suspiciously. 'What sort of a hold-up? Whenever I travel by tube train, which, thank heaven, isn't too often, they always run frequently and on time.'

'Leaves on the line!' I improvise.

'How can there be leaves on an underground line?'

'I'm not too sure myself, but that's what the announcement said. Maybe there was a strong wind and it blew them down the tunnel?'

Mr Maxwell's face contorts, and I wonder if he's about to have a fit or something. But I suddenly realise he's trying to smile.

'Young lady, that has to be the best excuse for being late I've come across since I've been working here.' His smile fades with much more ease than it appeared. 'Don't let it happen again, though.'

'I won't, Mr Maxwell. Thank you, Mr Maxwell.'

He turns around and is about to head through the glass doors again, when he turns back. 'Out of interest, what took you all the way over to the King's Road in your lunch break?'

'I have a friend who owns a record shop over there. I – I needed to go and see him about something.'

'Would that be George's shop you're talking about?' Mr Maxwell asks.

'Yes, it is, Groovy Records. Do you know George, then?'

Mr Maxwell nods. 'Yes, we've met once or twice.'

I'm about to ask when and how, but he backs towards the doors again. 'No more chit-chat. Back to work immediately, young lady, before I have to dock your wages.'

That sounds more like the usual Mr Maxwell. I pull my headphones on and put all thoughts of George and his shop aside for now.

The afternoon is a quiet one, thank goodness, and I manage to cope fairly easily with the demands of being a 1963 receptionist.

In a way it's actually quite nice being on this side of things for a change, without all the hassles of being the boss. I could never have imagined taking a step back down the career ladder would be so enjoyable back in 2013 – the thought of such a thing would have horrified me – but it's really good fun to be in contact with the many interesting and diverse people that pass through the reception of EMI House on a daily basis, and I'm quite enjoying it.

When I leave the office at the end of my second day there, at an incredibly early time of day for me to finish work, I head home with Ellie. I thought about trying to dash back over to George's shop, but decided he'd probably be closed for the day now, and Ellie had seemed in a bit of a flap when we left the office, and I wanted to find out why.

'So,' I ask her as we travel on the bus together. 'What are we up to tonight?' Finishing work so early gives me much more spare time in the evenings than I'm used to; I never had this luxury back in 2013. I'm not too sure what sort of things I'm supposed to get up to in the sixties, but I'm eager to find out.

'I don't know about you, Jo-Jo, but I'm baking tonight.'

'Baking? For us?'

'Nooo, for the bosses – I said I was going to, didn't I?'

'You're still going to do that?'

'Yep, I'm going to bake them lots of cakes and take them in tomorrow – I bought all the stuff at lunchtime in Marylebone High Street.' She holds up a bag stuffed full of groceries. 'I haven't got much time, have I, if I want to win this competition. The fancy lunch is next Monday.'

'No, I suppose you haven't.'

'What are you going to do?' Ellie asks as she pulls a cookery book from her bag. As she opens it, I notice it's a library edition.

'I don't know, just chill out, I guess.'

Ellie pulls a face. 'Chill out? It's November, aren't you cold enough already?'

'I mean relax, watch a bit of TV, that kind of thing.'

'Oh, I see. What are you going to watch, *Coronation Street* or that dreadful Hancock man? Oh, hey, isn't it a *Dr Kildare* night tonight? I might join you for a spot of Richard Chamberlain if I get my baking done in time – if he was my doctor I'd be ill all the time, I reckon!'

'Perhaps I'll just read a book, then,' I say, thinking this doesn't sound all that enthralling. 'Did you go to the library to get that out at lunchtime?' I ask, looking down at her book.

'Yes, I don't have any cookbooks, but this,' she holds up a blue *Good Housekeeping* cookery book, 'this will help me turn out perfect cakes. The woman in the library says she swears by it.'

'Must be good then. *Good Housekeeping* is a household

name, so I'm sure they'll see you right – they've been going for years.'

'Have they?' Ellie asks absentmindedly, as she pores over the pages again. 'Maybe this is the book me mam uses, too. Can't say I remember.'

We arrive back home, quickly get changed out of our work gear and make sandwiches again. Ellie is keen to get on with her evening's baking, and doesn't want the tiny kitchen in our little flat to be congested with mundane stuff like pots and pans and plates from making a proper dinner. I don't actually think Ellie and I ever really cook that much for ourselves anyway, which is why this idea of hers is a bit worrying.

While Ellie gets busy with her cakes, I go into the little lounge and flick between the two channels we have on our black and white TV. Not with a remote control, though – I have to press buttons on the TV itself! Ellie's right; there isn't much on, and the picture quality is pretty dire. I try and watch a news report about the Beatlemania that's sweeping the nation, and I smile as I watch the screaming, hysterical girls, going mad for the Fab Four. What have you guys started? I ask them through the screen, as I think about all the boy bands that will be screamed at in the future by young girls at concerts and at airports: they have you to thank for this. Then I switch the TV off and take a look through the pile of records that sit next to a suitcase on the sideboard.

Golly, what a choice! Cliff Richard, the Beach Boys, Elvis Presley – there's even a Doris Day LP. I sigh. It's a toss up between Elvis and the Beatles, but I plump for the Fab Four – really they're the only thing worth listening to in this collection. And for me that's really saying something. Ellie has quite a few

Beatles records to choose from; lots of singles, but only the one album, *Please Please Me*. I wonder why this is, then suddenly realise it's because we're in November 1963, and they've only released one album up until now.

'Ellie,' I call through to the kitchen, 'where has the record player gone?'

'What do you mean?' Ellie asks, sounding flustered as she pokes her head around the door. There's flour on her nose and cheek. 'It's right where it always is, on the sideboard next to the records. Stop messing around with me, Jo-Jo, I haven't got time for this tonight.'

She disappears back into the kitchen, while I look at the thing that looks like a small suitcase sitting next to the records. Is this the record player? I wonder, gently lifting up the lid – and sure enough, inside the case there is a fully functioning record player with a turntable, needle and arm.

This is actually quite a cool little gadget, I think as I attempt to load a record on to the turntable; in a way it could actually be the prototype for the first iPod – it's portable music!

I smile to myself as the arm of the record player drops into the groove of the record and a song begins to play. If only you knew what's to come for you all, I think, as familiar Beatles' songs such as 'Love Me Do', 'I Saw Her Standing There' and 'Do You Want to Know a Secret?' fill the room. I find myself humming and then singing along to each one as they remind me of my parents and all the times spent listening to the Beatles with them, either recently or as a child.

The Ellie of 2013 had told me on the phone the day I got hit by the car that I should speak to my mother, and I'd foolishly said there was plenty of time. But what if I never got a chance to speak to my parents again? What if I'm stuck here in 1963 for ever, except it won't be for ever, will it? My life will continue from this point onwards, because I'm now living in a different timeline. That's what this must be, an alternative lifetime running parallel to my own back in 2013. How else can I explain what's going on right now if this isn't a dream? I wonder what's happened to the other me back in 2013. Am I lying injured in a hospital somewhere, or am I missing altogether because I'm now living here in the sixties? There's so many things I don't understand, so many questions I need answering. And all I know for definite at the moment is I have to get back, and to do that I have to find the – what had George called it? The link that will help me learn what I need to know. Even that was cryptic.

Deciding I've heard enough music for now, I lift the needle on the record player, replace the Beatles record in its sleeve, and head into the kitchen to see how Ellie is getting on.

The scene that greets me is somewhat chaotic.

There are mixing bowls, wooden spoons and empty packets everywhere. Lying on the kitchen counter, there's an upturned set of kitchen scales that Ellie borrowed from one of our neighbours before she began, and a cloud of white dust floats over the whole kitchen, which could either be flour or icing sugar.

'How's it going?' I ask casually, leaning against the doorframe.

'Bloody awful,' Ellie moans, turning to face me. 'Look.' She waves her hand in the direction of two trays of fairy cakes. At least, I think that's what they are. The contents of one tray are so black it looks as if Ellie has commanded a dragon to breathe fire across it in order to bake the cakes. On the second tray, the cakes are a much more edible golden brown colour, but there appear to be large craters in the centre of every one.

'Oh,' I say, pulling a face.

'It's a disaster, Jo-Jo, a 100 per cent, no-holds-barred disaster!'

'It can't be that bad,' I try to reassure her, moving into the kitchen to fully inspect the cakes. 'Oh,' I repeat, as I view the full extent of the catastrophe in front of me. 'Apparently it can.'

'Aw,' Ellie wails, 'what am I gonna do? This was me only chance of impressing the bosses. It's not like anyone notices me at work, is it? I'm just a typist; I'm like all the other typists in the pool, I'm never goin' to stand out. And I *want* to win that prize. I *want* to meet the Beatles! It's me one chance to do something exciting!'

'Right,' I say, taking charge. 'For one thing, don't let me ever hear you say that again. You, Ellie, are an individual. You're unique. No one else is like you, and don't you ever forget it. You can do anything you want to if you put your mind to it, just you wait and see.'

Ellie's big green eyes open wide in her flour-covered face.

'And secondly,' I continue, as I reach for a flowery apron hanging on a hook in the kitchen, 'you happen to be sharing your flat with the best cake maker since Jane Asher!'

'Jane Asher?' Ellie wrinkles her nose. 'Do you mean Paul McCartney's girlfriend? Does she cook, then?'

'I don't know about now,' I say hastily, as I reach for a clean mixing bowl and a new packet of flour, 'but I'm pretty sure she'll be very good at it in the future.'

We spend the rest of the evening creating perfect-looking cupcakes, although Ellie insists on calling them *mahoosive* fairy cakes. Luckily our neighbour, Martha, is a keen cook, and lends us a few more items than just her scales, after we visit her begging for supplies. Martha, who I find to be an enchanting little old lady, delights in finding us the perfect items for our baking session. She confesses she doesn't bake as often as she used to since her husband's death, and she's more than happy for her equipment to be put to good use. So we return to our flat with piping bags, cake decorations, food colouring – the lot, with a promise to let Martha taste some of our first batch when we've finished baking for the evening.

I wonder if Martha might be a bit lonely, living on her own next door, and it seems such a shame she never gets to use any of her baking equipment any more. So while I'm working away, I decide I'll ask her to bake Ellie and I one of her own favourite cakes if she'd like to, when we return with our own efforts, and we'll pop in and have tea with her one day.

In our own kitchen we quickly get a routine going between the two of us, and soon we are producing dozens of beautifully browned and perfectly risen cupcakes. But it's when I start to decorate them with various types of coloured icing that Ellie gets really excited.

'Where on earth did you learn to do this, Jo-Jo?' she asks. 'Have you been taking lessons from that Fanny Cradock?'

I assume Fanny Cradock must be the sixties TV equivalent of Mary Berry or Jamie Oliver. 'Er, no, my granny taught me how to bake when I was little, and my sisters and I used to go and stay with her in the holidays. But these,' I say proudly, scanning my hand across the plates of finished cupcakes, 'these are almost as good as the ones that the Hummingbird Bakery make, aren't they?'

'The what bakery?' Ellie asks, looking puzzled.

'The Hummingbird,' I say without thinking, as I now concentrate on piping out some pink icing on to a row of cakes. 'The place you go and get cakes from when it's someone's birthday in the office.'

'Have you breathed in too much icing sugar? We don't celebrate birthdays at work, do we? It's not allowed. Let alone going out to buy cakes from a bakery!'

'Maybe they should start then,' I suggest quickly. Damn, I need to be more careful. It was so easy to relax and forget. 'So what do you think?' I ask her, standing back to admire my work.

'They look fantastic, Jo-Jo, never seen fairy cakes like them before in me life!'

'Cupcakes,' I remind her.

'Cakes for giant fairies!' she grins.

'I don't care what you call them, when you hand them out tomorrow I'm sure everyone will love them.' I flop down on to a chair. Gosh that was hard work, but I really enjoyed it. I can't remember the last time I had a chance to do some home baking. Something else I used to really enjoy, but haven't had the time for in years.

'I can't take all the credit for these little beauties,' Ellie says, still admiring the cakes. 'You made them, you must hand them out. They can be your attempt to win employee of the month.'

'No way! I did this to help you. You were part of the baking process, I didn't do it all myself. Plus, I'm not bothered about winning the prize.'

Ellie looks stunned. Her pert little mouth forms a big round O. 'How can you even say that, Jo-Jo?' she asks in shock. 'It's the *Beatles*, everyone wants to meet the Beatles!'

I shrug. 'Not me. Can't see what all the fuss is about.'

Ellie shakes her head, and a curl of her blonde hair falls down from where she has it pinned up on the top of her head. 'Jo-Jo, you've changed,' she says, a tinge of sadness in her voice. 'I dunno what it is about you, it's almost like . . .'

'Like what?' I ask, suddenly afraid she's going to make some incredible guess as to what's going on.

'Like you've lost some of your spark.'

'What do you mean, my spark?'

Ellie shrugs now. 'I'm not sure really, you're just so down about everything, so serious these days. You've no enthusiasm for life like you used to have, and you never have any fun. In fact, making these cakes tonight is the happiest I've seen you in ages!'

'Don't be silly, Ellie,' I say lightly. 'Of course I'm happy. I just don't show it quite as visually as you. I was happy when we went out with Harry and his friends last night.'

'Yes, I have to give you that. Harry certainly seems to put a skip in your step,' she winks.

'See?' I grin to keep her happy. But beneath my smile I realise the Jo-Jo she's describing is exactly the Jo-Jo of the future.

Maybe that's why I'm here? To try and regain some of my spark? I've already realised in the short time I've been here that I must make time when I get back to find some fun outside of work. I enjoyed being out with Harry at the World's End, and I loved making cakes with Ellie tonight. For a few precious minutes I'd forgotten all about time travel and working out how to get back home. I simply enjoyed being in the moment – and that was something I never did, now or in the future.

But I get the feeling it's not going to be as easy as simply discovering how to enjoy having fun again. Life, whatever life you're living in, never is.

Seven

'Have you tasted Ellie's fairy cakes yet?' Harry asks, bounding into the reception area at EMI. He's carrying some files and a large cupcake with blue icing and green and pink Smarties on top. 'They're delicious!'

'I have, actually,' I smile as he puts the files down and takes a big bite out of his cake. 'They're excellent.'

'They can't get enough of them upstairs,' Harry mumbles with a full mouth. 'I could barely get a look-in. I bet she's get-ting plenty of Brownie points.'

'Good. I mean good they're popular, not good you nearly didn't get one. So ...' I ask, looking at him as he brushes crumbs off the front of his white shirt. 'What are *you* going to do?'

Harry swallows. 'How do you mean?'

'About the competition, what are you going to try and do to win it?'

'I really don't know. Everyone is trying everything to get in

77

the bosses' good books. People are licking up closer to them than they are to Ellie's icing right now.'

I laugh. 'But you want to go, right? To the luncheon? You want to go and meet the Beatles?'

'Too right I do! It's the chance of a lifetime, isn't it? But the thing is, I don't do anything special here, I just shuffle papers around all day, and I sure as hell can't bake cakes, so what chance do I have of winning?'

Why do they all seem to think their existence is pointless? 'There must be something you can do?' I ask him hopefully. 'Something special. What do you like doing when you're not at work, what are you good at?'

Harry looks down at his shoes and pretends to wipe an imaginary speck of dirt off the toe by rubbing it on his trouser leg. 'Nothing, I just like my music.'

'That's all you do, listen to music?'

Harry's head snaps up. 'And what's wrong with that? God, Jo-Jo, you're starting to sound just like my dad before I moved out.'

The irony. 'Calm down, I didn't say there was anything wrong with that, did I? So, do you just listen to music, or do you play anything? Like an instrument?'

Harry fiddles with the lapel of his grey jacket now. 'I've been known to play a bit of guitar, on occasion.'

'Really? Are you any good?'

'No. Look, I gotta be going, I only popped down to deliver these files and eat my cake quickly. I'll catch you later, Jo-Jo.' And before I can say anything else he spins around and disappears through the double doors.

I sigh; I was only trying to help.

I gather up the files Harry's left on the desk and sort them into the piles waiting to be collected by Mr Maxwell and Sir Joseph Lockwood's secretaries. Sir Joseph is the managing director and I'm not sure why all these files have to be delivered here to me at reception first, but apparently that's what's always happened, so I arrange them as neatly as possible into two piles on my desk.

My telephone buzzes.

'Have you all the files yet, girl?' Mr Maxwell barks down the line at me.

'Yes, they're right here, Mr Maxwell, I'm just waiting for Prudence to come down and collect them.'

'Prudence has gone home. Her son, or her daughter, or was it her dog? – I don't know, something equally inconvenient to me – has been taken ill.'

'I'm sorry to hear that.'

'Yes, well, it means I need you to bring the files up to me as soon as reception is free for you to do so.'

'OK . . . I mean, yes sir, I'll do that sir, just as soon as I can, sir.'

'Hmm . . . ' I hear before the line goes dead.

As soon as reception is empty I scoop the files up from the desk and head up to the top floor.

When I reach Mr Maxwell's office, Prudence's desk is indeed vacated, so I rest the files on it, freeing up my hand to knock on the big wooden door that leads into Mr Maxwell's private office.

But as I go to do this I notice the door is already slightly ajar, so I take a little peek inside.

Walter Maxwell is standing by his desk gazing down at a

small silver photo frame in his hand and, as he turns his head a little in my direction, his desperately sad expression makes me gasp.

His head snaps up. 'Who's there?' he hisses, thrusting the frame down on to the desk.

'It's me, Mr Maxwell,' I say, gently pushing the door open. 'I've brought the files as you requested.'

'Oh ... right, I see.' He clears his throat. 'Well, bring them in! Bring them in!' He quickly turns his face away.

I hurry back out to Prudence's desk and pick up the files. When I return to the office Walter Maxwell is sitting at his desk, blowing his nose hard on a blue handkerchief.

'Don't just stand there, girl,' he says, stuffing the hankie back in his top pocket. 'Put them down on the desk!'

I do this, quickly glancing at the photo in the frame as I place the files down next to him.

It's a photo of a younger-looking Mr Maxwell, with a woman and two children leaning up against a brand new car. Mr Maxwell is holding some keys and they all look very happy and relaxed.

'Is this your family?' I ask bravely, expecting my head to be bitten off for such a personal question.

Walter Maxwell looks for a brief moment as if he's going to do more than just bite my head off; he looks like he's going to chew my arms and legs off one by one too. Then his face softens.

'They were,' he says, looking towards the frame again. And I notice his eyes glisten under the harsh fluorescent lighting of the office. Was he crying when I disturbed him just now?

'Were?' I venture again. 'Did something happen? Have you and your wife separated?'

80

He shakes his head.

'Worse?' I ask again, hardly wanting to know the answer. What happened to them? Were they killed in a car accident? Bludgeoned to death by a mass murderer? This was the sixties; what horrible criminals were around then? The Yorkshire Ripper? No I think he was the seventies, or was it the eighties? The great train robbers? They were the sixties, weren't they? But they were hardly likely to have murdered Mr Maxwell's family!

'Let's just say we're not together any more and leave it at that,' he says sadly, his gaze returning to the photo again.

'Yes, of course. Well, you all looked very happy in that photo. I'm sure you had some lovely times together.'

I feel like slapping myself in the face. *Shut up, Jo-Jo! That's not going to help, now is it?*

'We were,' he replies to my surprise. 'We'd just bought a new car with a little win I'd had on the lottery. It was a great day. But, sadly, no more.'

'I'm so sorry,' I say, genuinely meaning it. 'It's awful to be parted from your family.'

'Don't let it happen to you, Jo-Jo,' he says, looking directly at me for the first time since I came into the room.

'Don't let what happen, Mr Maxwell?' I'm surprised he actually remembers my name.

'Don't become old and lonely like me. Do something about it while you can. Loneliness is a very sad place to find yourself in.'

'You're not old, Mr Maxwell,' I say lightly, trying to lift his mood. 'I'm sure there's someone out there for you.'

'Yes, there is, Jo-Jo – I just can't get back to them any more.'

I'm about to ask him what he means when there's a delicate knock on the door, and Cynthia from accounts timidly pokes her head through the opening.

'I have this month's figures, Mr Maxwell,' she says nervously, as she glances at me standing next to the desk. 'If it's a bad time I can come back?'

'No, Cynthia, that won't be necessary. Jo-Jo is just leaving. Thank you, Jo-Jo,' he nods at me. 'And remember what I said. Yes?'

'Yes, Mr Maxwell, and thank you.' I smile at him, and turn to leave the office, passing Cynthia on her way in.

'You must have the magic touch!' she whispers as I pass.

'I heard that, Cynthia!' The booming voice echoes across the office as Walter Maxwell reverts to his usual role. 'And I can assure you that David Nixon himself wouldn't have the magic touch on me!'

As I wink at Cynthia and hurry out of the office, I wonder who David Nixon could be. But as I make my way down to reception again something doesn't feel right. What was it about that meeting with Walter Maxwell that's unsettling me? I think about the conversation we just had, and then suddenly stop dead in my tracks in the middle of the corridor.

He said the lottery. He said he'd won the money to buy his new car on the lottery. There were football pools in this country in the sixties – I know that because my grandad had won some money on them once. He was always telling us about it, and how he'd paid for the first proper family holiday abroad with the money. But there wasn't a lottery in the sixties for sure – that didn't exist until 1994.

Damn! I stamp my foot in frustration. Why didn't I notice

that when he said it just now? I look back towards the office, wondering if I should go back. Then something else hits me in the face. Something so obvious I can't believe I didn't notice it before. The car that Walter Maxwell and his family were pictured standing in front of in the silver-framed photo wasn't a classic sixties Ford Anglia, Volkswagen Beetle or brand new Mini, as it should have been if they'd just bought a new car in the sixties. No, the car they were all standing next to, smiling happily at their win on the lottery, was an extremely expensive-looking, top-of-the-range, bright red BMW.

Eight

I stand completely still in the corridor for a few moments, trying to take in the enormity of what I've just discovered.

Walter Maxwell's car is most probably from the mid-nineties. I know this because my dad had driven one just like it as his company car, and I remember us all scrambling to get our favourite seats in the back for family outings.

But if that *is* the case, and Walter's car *is* from the nineties, then is he also? Is Walter like me? Is he one of the people George hinted at who is stuck here from another time and unable to return? And if that is the case, how has he got a photo of his former life with him back here in 1963? Can our possessions travel with us too?

I'm about to head back up to his office to confront him and ask him further questions, when I hear the faint sound of a guitar playing, and someone singing in a low voice. I look round; it's coming from the room I'm standing outside. The melody is soothing and gentle, and the voice, although quiet, is rich and warm in tone. I push the door, which is already slightly ajar, open a tad more to see who it is playing.

And the person sitting on a chair with his back to me isn't a sixties musician strumming his latest tune on a guitar while his manager and roadies look on, but someone that looks remarkably like Harry.

I listen to him sing gently and quite beautifully along with his guitar. When he finishes I feel like I should applaud, and I'm about to say something when a voice behind me makes me jump.

'What are you doing up here, Jo-Jo?' Miss Fields asks.

In the room Harry jumps too and turns around to see me peeking through the door. He glares at me.

I quickly turn around and step away from the door.

'I was just on my way back from Mr Maxwell's office,' I reply smartly. 'Actually, I'm pleased I've seen you, Miss Fields, I have some files for you on my desk downstairs. If you'd be so good as to follow me I can pass them on to you.'

I begin to walk down the corridor, praying that Miss Fields will follow me. Luckily she does, because I'm pretty sure Harry isn't supposed to be practising his guitar during work hours, let alone in one of the upstairs offices as I've just found him doing all on his own.

Reception is so busy during the afternoon, there's no chance of me returning to see Mr Maxwell, or even getting the time to pop up to Harry's office to apologise for listening in on him earlier.

When it's finally time to go home, Mr Maxwell has left early for a business dinner, but I manage to catch Harry on his way out of the office.

'I'm sorry,' I pant, almost running down the street as I try and keep up with his big lolloping strides. 'About earlier. I didn't mean to eavesdrop. But you're very good, you know, with the guitar and the singing?'

'I don't like people listening to me play,' Harry says, still walking and looking ahead.

'Why were you doing it at work then? You must have known someone would overhear you!'

'I walked past the room just like you did,' Harry says, looking across at me and slowing down to my pace. 'And I saw the guitar all set up with a stand and a chair and everything. It must have been for someone they were going to listen to for a demo. You know, to see if they want to offer them a contract?'

I nod.

'I just couldn't help myself; I had to have a go. Pretend it was me for a few minutes.'

'Is that what you'd like to do one day, sing professionally?'

Harry shrugs. 'Maybe. Write songs mainly, because that's what I love to do best.'

'You should give it a go then.'

Harry stops walking now and looks at me. 'And just how am I supposed to do that, Jo-Jo? I work in the advertising department of a record company and I'm just a junior office boy, so no one notices me. No one's going to stand up one day and shout "open auditions for a new talent show, anyone welcome. We'll make you an overnight superstar".'

No, but they will one day, I think. *You just need to wait a few decades ...*

86

'Maybe not, but there must be some way of you getting heard by the right people.'

Harry smiles down at me. 'Very determined, aren't you?' he says gently, his eyes tracing their way slowly over my eager face. 'Does anything ever stop you from getting what you want?'

'Not often,' I reply, looking back up at him. 'I believe that if you really want something you should go for it. Don't let anything stand in your way.'

Harry smiles thoughtfully. 'I'll remember that. There's ... things that I really want. But I'm not sure how to go about getting them.'

I wonder what he means. 'If it's something your heart feels strongly about then you should go for it.'

'Really?' Harry says, his voice low.

'Yes, really. That's what I did with my business.'

'Your *business*?' Harry replies, his voice swiftly returning to normal. 'What business is that then?'

'Oh – nothing. Just a few ideas I have for the future. I don't want to work as a receptionist for ever, do I?'

'Obviously not.' Harry turns his face away and studies the passing traffic. 'Look, Jo-Jo, don't worry about me. I sing for my own amusement and write songs for my own pleasure, and I'm happy that way.'

'But, Harry, if—'

'I'll see you tomorrow, unless you're coming down the pub tonight?' he asks tersely, glancing back at me.

'I'm not sure what we're up to yet.' I'm confused. What did I do wrong?

'Well, I'll be there if you feel like coming down.'

'I'm sure Ellie and I could pop in for a while,' I say and smile at him.

Harry briefly returns my smile, then I watch as he walks off down the street. How odd. He was fine one moment, and then the next ...

I shake my head; and I thought travelling back in time was confusing! But there must be something I can do to help Harry, because he sang so beautifully earlier, and if there was such a thing as the *X Factor* now, and Harry went to the open auditions, he'd sail though to the live shows with a voice like that.

I stop abruptly on the pavement as an idea begins to form in my head, an idea that could just work ... And rather than hurrying away from the EMI building with everyone else, I think I might just work a bit later at the office tonight.

'It's very dull down here this evening,' I pretend to complain later when we're all sitting around a table drinking beer, and my new favourite tipple, Babycham. 'We need to liven this place up tonight if there are no bands on.'

'Ooh, what do you have in mind, Jo-Jo?' Ellie asks with a giggle. Ellie is now known at work as the cake lady, after her cupcakes went down an absolute storm today. She even promised to bring some more in tomorrow, and we spent nearly all our time before coming out tonight knocking up another few dozen, with Ellie doing much more of the baking this time, under my guidance. I was also insisting Ellie should charge people for the cakes in the future, which she thought I was mad to suggest, but I didn't think it would take much more persuasion to change her mind, if I kept banging on about it.

'Karaoke,' I announce, standing up and heading towards the bar.

'What the bloomin' 'eck is karaoke?' I hear Ellie call to my departing figure. But I don't answer. I'm now in negotiations with Tony the barman on whether we can use his mic and speakers to create some 'entertainment' tonight.

After a bit of persuasion he agrees, and we're away. However, karaoke isn't one of my favourite pastimes, I usually avoid it the way I do *Jeremy Kyle* back in 2013. So I'm in pretty deep water before I even begin trying to ad lib my way through explaining what's supposed to happen to the regulars of this 1963 pub, along with another slightly more worrying issue – I don't actually have any backing tracks for anyone to sing to.

Then I spy a jukebox in the corner of the pub.

'The jukebox,' I call euphorically across the bar. 'We can use the jukebox. We can pop some tunes on, turn the sound down a bit, and then whoever is up here can sing along with them so that we hear them more than the record.'

'You first then, Jo-Jo,' one of Harry's mates shouts. 'You show us how it's done, then we'll know when it's our go!'

I hadn't banked on actually having to perform myself. Singing really isn't one of my strong points, and what songs am I going to know the words to now?

'Yes, yes, you sing, Jo-Jo!' Ellie calls, rushing to the jukebox. 'I know just the one!'

Ellie, no, at least let me choose my own song!

The opening bars to the Beatles classic 'Do You Want to Know a Secret?' come wafting though the pub. *If only Ellie knew how appropriate these lyrics are for me at the moment!*

Standing on the stage, wearing a black and white floral print shift dress with leather knee-length boots, I again feel like I'm in that old black and white episode of *Top of the Pops* as I do my best to keep up with George Harrison's vocal and sing the Beatles song to the best of my ability. For once I'm grateful to my parents for these familiar lyrics being as much a part of my childhood as nursery rhymes should have been. But I'm stunned, at the end of the song, when I get a round of applause and even a few whoops from the crowd, and even more surprised when some of the others then seem keen to join in and have a go on the little stage.

A number of songs later, with the World's End hearing some good, bad and truly awful performances within its four walls, the karaoke is turning into a real success, and people are now clambering to get on stage, eager to sing along with the sounds of the sixties. So that's part one of my plan achieved. Now for part two; I need to get Harry up there. But of course he's reticent.

'Nah, not my thing,' he says, drinking from his pint glass.

Harry has been fine with me tonight in the pub. I still can't quite work out what the problem was earlier but then I've had quite a bit to think about since our conversation on the pavement.

'But why, when you sing so beautifully,' I encourage.

'My songs perhaps, not other peoples'.'

'So sing one of yours, then.'

'Are you kidding, Jo-Jo? I'm not standing up there singing one of my songs to this lot.' He gestures with his glass around the table at his work colleagues. 'I'd never hear the end of it.'

'Please, Harry, I'll do anything you want if you just sing up there tonight.'

Harry almost spits his mouthful of beer back into his glass, but he manages to calm himself, swallow his beer, and respond as casually as he can. 'You *really* shouldn't say things like that you know, Jo-Jo, it could be misconstrued by the wrong ears.'

'You know what I mean, Harry. *Please* . . .' I plead, smiling at him and virtually fluttering the false eyelashes that Ellie has made me wear tonight.

'Why, why is this so important to you?' he asks, resting his beer on the table.

'Because it is. Just do this one little thing for me, pretty purrlease?'

Harry looks at me as if he's considering the matter; his deep blue eyes trace their way over my eager face. 'Oh, all right, if it means that much to you, but I want something in return, mind.'

'What?' I clap my hands excitedly. 'Name it.'

'One, more fairy cakes. Ellie told me you helped her make them, and the fun the two of you had doing it. Not only are they delicious, Jo-Jo, but you should do more of that kind of thing if you enjoy it.'

'Absolutely. No problem at all.' I look excitedly up towards the stage. The latest singer is just finishing his rendition of 'Devil in Disguise' with Elvis Presley accompanying him on the jukebox.

'And two,' Harry continues, then he hesitates, so I look back across at him.

'What? What's two? Just name it.'

Harry looks down into his lap for a moment, then back up

at me sitting next to him. 'If you're not too busy planning your new business, I'd like to take you out on a proper date some time?'

I sit bolt upright in my seat. I hadn't been expecting *that*. 'Sure, yes of course, that would be lovely. We'll arrange something.' I smile shyly at him.

'For the cakes or the date?' He grins at me now.

'Both,' I assure him. 'Now go and sing before someone else grabs that microphone!'

Harry jumps up from his seat and hurries on to the stage. 'Can I use that guitar?' he asks Tony, pointing to a guitar behind the bar, which I 'borrowed' from work earlier and planted behind the bar in case this all worked out. I just hope no one misses it before tomorrow!

'Sure,' Tony says, and the guitar is quickly passed to Harry. He looks at it for a moment, recognising it as the one he was playing earlier today when I caught him singing. He gives me a 'how on earth is this here?' look.

I smile sweetly back at him with an innocent expression.

Harry begins to strum his guitar and sing. In the time it's taken to get him on the stage and his guitar all set up, the noise level in the pub has risen again, so I can barely hear him to begin with, but as more people start to listen to him play, it gets quieter and quieter in the pub until there's only the sound of Harry and his guitar filling the place. It's the tune I heard him play earlier today at work, and Harry's voice seems to have the same hypnotic effect on all these people here tonight as it did on me earlier in the office.

When he comes to the end of his song, there's just silence for a moment, before a deafening round of applause breaks out, interspersed with a few whistles, cheers and shouts of 'more!'

Harry smiles, raises his hand, and then begins to play a second song, while I, happy that all is going well now I've got him up on the stage, go over to a table in the corner where a tall, slim, smartly dressed man, with dark hair smoothed into shape with Brylcreem, sits, a newspaper in front of him. There's a photo on the front page of President John F. Kennedy, and something pings in my brain; I can't put my finger on why right now, because I'm too busy thinking about Harry, but I put that thought aside to deal with later.

The man lowers his newspaper as I approach.

'What do you think?' I ask breathlessly, hardly daring to hear his reply.

'Ah, Jo-Jo,' he says, smiling at me. 'He's not quite Paul or John, but he's definitely got something there with his song-writing, and his singing is not too shabby either.'

'So?' I ask hopefully, 'Do you think you might be able to work with him?'

George Martin smiles at me. 'With a little work, yes.'

I nearly punch the air in a "Yes" fashion. But quickly realise that wouldn't be ladylike behaviour for the sixties. 'That's fantastic! Thank you so much for coming along tonight, George, I mean Mr Martin,' I hastily correct myself.

'No, thank *you*, Jo-Jo, for asking me. Well perhaps I should say, *twisting my arm* to come,' he winks. 'There's not many people who can persuade me to come down the King's Road on a Thursday evening and sit in a pub listening to, what did you call it?'

'Karaoke.'

93

'Interesting. Tell your friend to call my secretary tomorrow morning, and we'll try and make an appointment for a demo on Monday.'

'Wow! I will, I will, and thank you again.'

'Not a problem,' he says, standing up now. 'Just don't forget those cakes you promised me – I'll expect them up on my desk first thing tomorrow morning. The ones I had today at the office were delicious. You and your friend should be commended on them.'

'Don't you worry, Mr Martin, I won't forget. It's Ellie that does most of the baking, I'm just her – publicist, I guess you'd call me.'

George Martin smiles. 'And a fine job you do of it too. It's been noted, Jo-Jo. It's been noted. Have a good rest of your evening. I'll look forward to the cakes, and thank you once again.'

George Martin stands up to leave. He raises his hand casually to Harry who has just finished his second song, and is insisting to his eager crowd that that is it for him for tonight.

He comes rushing over just as George leaves the pub.

'Was that George Martin you were talking to then?' he asks breathlessly.

'Yep.'

'What on earth was he doing here tonight?'

'I asked him to come.'

'*You* did? Why?'

'I asked him to come and listen to you play,' I say, sitting down in the seat George Martin has just vacated.

Harry's mouth drops open and he rubs his forehead with his hands. 'Oh my lord! I just auditioned for George Martin and

I didn't know!' He stares down at me, sheer panic and trepidation in his eyes. 'And what did he think? Did he say anything to you?'

'Relax, Harry, he thinks you're fab, and he wants you to come and sing for him on Monday.'

Harry just stares at me again. Then he flops down on to the seat next to me. 'Jo-Jo, you do know George was the one who signed the Beatles to Parlophone at EMI, don't you?' He shakes his head in disbelief. 'Of course you do, sorry; I'm just in a state of shock. George Martin, music producer extraordinaire, has asked to see me!' And without having time to feel awkward or nervous, he leans across, wraps his arms around me and kisses me on the cheek. 'You're bloody fantastic, do you know that!'

'Yes, I have been told once or twice,' I say, grinning, as I hug him back. This is starting to be fun, helping people out here in 1963. Maybe it isn't so bad after all. And as I rest my head on Harry's shoulder and hold him close to me, I spy the other George sitting across the pub, even more tucked away than George Martin was. He winks at me and mouths the words: 'Nearly there.'

Nine

'Welcome,' Walter Maxwell says, looking out into the foyer of EMI House, where right now as many employees as humanly possible are squeezed in. 'I hope you can all hear me at the back.'

There are a few murmurs of acknowledgment, and Walter continues.

'The time has come to announce the winner of the tickets to the gala lunch with the Beatles, and,' he adds with a flourish, 'I'm pleased to say that the winner and guest will now have the morning off and receive free transport from their home in a Rolls-Royce Silver Cloud, kindly donated by Abbey Car Hire.'

Oohs and aahs fill the room.

I look at Walter Maxwell standing slightly raised up on a little footstool that someone has found for him to balance on. I haven't had a chance to go back to his office and question him more about his photo, or the reason for him being here, or any of the hundred other questions I have for him, because he's been out on business all day and has only just come back in time to make the big announcement. I'm determined to try and catch him tonight, though, after everyone leaves, and before he goes home himself.

It's Friday night and we're all gathered to find out who will win employee of the month, and, more importantly it would seem to everyone else, also win the 'golden ticket' to ride in the Rolls-Royce to the gala lunch and meet the Beatles. I smile at my choice of words. 'Ticket to Ride' – another Beatles song, but not quite out yet if my memory serves me correctly. Gosh, I really do know far too much about the Beatles – my parents have a lot to answer for.

'So without further ado,' Mr Maxwell says, 'and in the best award ceremony style, I'm going to read you a shortlist of the top nominees, and we're honoured that Sir Joseph has joined us to announce the winner.'

A friendly-looking man with thinning wispy hair raises his hand from the chair he waits patiently on. Ah, this must be the famous Sir Joseph Lockwood, MD of EMI. I've only heard about him; I've never actually seen him around the building.

I look back at Walter Maxwell again. *Can't you get this over with quickly?* I implore him silently. *I need to ask you some questions.*

'Cynthia Roper, for her sterling work in accounts this month. It's been a busy month, and there have been many staff shortages with the measles epidemic that we experienced through a few departments, so we think you've coped admirably, Cynthia.'

Cynthia smiles and blushes profusely behind her tortoise-shell spectacles.

'James Pepper in publicity for his latest campaign for Cliff Richard. A fantastic job in conjunction with the *Summer Holiday* film, I think we'll all agree.'

'Bloody great job,' Harry murmurs, standing next to me. 'Why would you release a summer movie in February? Jimmy had to sweat blood to counterbalance that.'

I think about the incredibly detailed thought process that will go into every inch of a publicity campaign in the future. Releasing a summer movie in the winter? It just wouldn't happen.

'Ellie Williams for her beautiful and incredibly tasty cakes that she generously baked for us all. A kind gesture, and one I understand you're going to continue, Ellie, am I correct?' Mr Maxwell looks around the room for Ellie.

I see a petite hand waving from beneath the sea of people. They part a little so Ellie can be seen.

Ellie, bright red, looks eagerly back at Mr Maxwell. 'Yes, Mr Maxwell, of course, Mr Maxwell.'

'But with recompense,' Sir Joseph murmurs from his seat. 'I hope you'll be charging us all a small amount for your cakes in future, Ellie? I certainly won't mind paying for them.'

'You tried one, Sir Joseph?' Ellie asks, stunned.

'I certainly did and it was delicious.' He smiles at Ellie. 'I'll take two dozen next week if you can manage it, Ellie – it's my niece's birthday on Tuesday.'

'Yes, yes, of course, Sir Joseph. You just let me know when and where.' She grins at me.

'Our next nominee is Harry Rigby.'

Harry, usually so relaxed, stands bolt upright, like an iron rod has just been dropped down the back of his suit.

'You've made the shortlist at the insistence of Mr Martin,' Mr Maxwell says, almost begrudgingly. 'It isn't for your work here that you've been nominated, Harry, but Mr Martin insists that you have a raw musical talent that we rarely see, and therefore that makes you a unique EMI employee, eligible for this award, and a particularly suitable candidate for the prize.'

'Wow!' is all Harry can mutter.

'And that completes the list of nominees. Now I'd like to hand over to Sir Joseph to announce the winner.'

Sir Joseph Lockwood stands and Mr Maxwell steps down from his stool to make way for him. But Sir Joseph waves a dismissive hand at it.

'I think you'll agree, everyone mentioned thus far has contributed to the company in very different and very special ways of late. But our winner has gone above and beyond all of the other nominees' achievements. Not because they've made a significant difference to the company's profits, nor have they done something out of the ordinary. No, they've simply helped and assisted everyone else, quietly and without fuss. It's those people that we need to recognise more in life, and the sort of person who we at EMI House would like to recognise today.' He pauses for a moment just to make sure he has everyone's full attention. 'So, the winner of employee of the month and the person who will be going to the gala lunch with the Beatles is ...' He looks between all the nominees. Then his glance falls on me. 'Jo-Jo McKenzie.'

I stare at him for a few seconds before my voice eventually stutters into action. 'What? How . . . I mean, why me?'

'Because you, Jo-Jo, keep this company moving at the grass roots level. You're the person our clients see when they first come into our building, and we've had some very favourable reports about you recently. But more importantly than that, I believe you helped out Cynthia when she was struggling up in accounts one day with some strategies about how she could make her department run that little bit more productively, am I correct?'

I nod. Last night when I'd come back for the guitar, I'd gone upstairs to deliver some files before going home, and found Cynthia getting herself in a complete state about how she was going to cope with half her staff off sick, so I'd suggested a few ways an accounts department might run a little more smoothly. But it wasn't a big deal – accounts were my speciality.

'And if I'm not mistaken,' Sir Joseph continues, 'you were also the person who helped Ellie bake the first of her cakes?'

I shoot a quick glance at Ellie. She always did have a big mouth.

I nod again.

'*And* you were the person responsible for making sure Harry was discovered by Mr Martin the other evening. Am I correct, Jo-Jo?'

Blushing furiously now, I look up at Sir Joseph. 'Yes, yes you are. But I didn't do it for any credit, really I didn't.' I glance around the room. 'I didn't help James with Cliff Richard, did I?' *No way am I taking any blame for anything Cliff Richard does now or in the future.*

'No, indeed you didn't,' Sir Joseph agrees. 'But your efforts with the other three, and with the rest of the staff and clients in the company recently, haven't gone unnoticed, and as a result, Jo-Jo, have earned you the title employee of the month and the prize that goes with it. So, everyone, I think that deserves a round of applause.'

Clapping, interspersed with the odd cheer breaks out in the foyer of EMI House.

'Who are you going to take with you, Jo-Jo?' someone shouts across the room. 'Who will be your special guest at the luncheon on Monday?'

I look from Ellie to Harry. How on earth am I going to choose between them?

But luckily I don't have to answer that question right then because both Sir Joseph and Mr Maxwell come over to congratulate me.

'Well done, Jo-Jo,' they say as the foyer begins to empty and the others begin to filter back upstairs to their offices. 'Congratulations.'

'Thank you,' I say, shaking their hands. 'I'm sure I don't deserve it, though.'

'Well, we're sure you do,' Walter Maxwell says. 'In fact, I know you deserve it. Chances like this don't come around more than once in a lifetime, you know.' He nods knowingly at me, and gives my hand a little squeeze before letting it go.

I look at him. There are so many questions I want to ask him right now, but I can't, I need to get him on his own.

'So, do you know who you'll take with you?' Sir Joseph asks. 'I hope you know someone who's a huge Beatles fan?'

I'm about to ask them if it might be possible to have two tickets because there's no way I'll be able to choose between Ellie and Harry, when I stop.

'You know something, I know just the person . . .'

Ten

As I hurry along the King's Road, my mind is whizzing as fast as my legs. I haven't got long; George will be shutting up his shop soon. He always stays open a bit later on a Friday night to try and catch keen music buyers on their way home from work with their weekly pay packets clutched in their hot little hands. He's been doing it for years, he once told me. It was one of the best things he ever did when he first started up, and he's been doing it ever since.

I can see now how George has kept that shop running for so long; he was way ahead of his time even back then – by which I mean now. Oh, this time travel thing is still confusing me, and I've been living in 1963 for nearly a week.

When I told Ellie and Harry what I was going to do with my spare ticket they were fully behind me. As Harry pointed out, he'd have enough excitement on Monday auditioning for George Martin without anything else happening, and Ellie's response was much the same.

'Jo-Jo, I'll be up to me neck in flour and icing sugar on Sunday making these cakes for Sir Joseph's niece on Tuesday. What sort of state would I be in for meeting the Beatles? You go and take George with you. He'll really enjoy himself – you know what a huge fan he is.'

So here I am, hurrying towards Groovy Records. But there's something else bothering me too as I walk. I've seen another newspaper with a photo of John F. Kennedy on the front, and I've worked out why this bothered me in the pub last night. 1963 was the year JFK was assassinated. I knew this because I'd had to do a project on American history at school and dates always stuck in my head. They're numbers, aren't they? And I've never had a problem remembering numbers. This event that will shape US history, probably world history, is going to happen a week today, on the twenty-second of November; in fact, the same day the second Beatles album is released. Is there anything I can do to prevent the assassination happening? And more to the point *should* I do something? Every time travel TV show or movie I've ever watched has always warned against changing the future. But now I'm here it seems different. Can I live with myself, knowing that something of that magnitude is about to occur, and not at least *trying* to do something to prevent it?

As I arrive at the zebra crossing opposite the World's End pub, my mind is racing with this new dilemma. There's already a mother pushing a big old-fashioned pram over the crossing in front of me. She's managing to do this with one hand, because her other one is gripping tightly to the small hand of a young boy wearing school uniform. He's wriggling and squirming as they cross, and just as they're about to reach the other side I notice the boy has dropped something on the crossing.

I see him try to wrestle himself from his mother's grip, so he can go back and retrieve it, and to prevent this I take a quick look either side of me and step out confidently on to the stripes, quickly picking up the dropped item as I cross. As I lift it up I'm surprised to see it's an issue of the *Beano* comic. I wave it in the air for the little boy to see, and shout to his mother to wait.

But as they stand on the pavement watching me, it's not joy that I've rescued their possession for them that I see in their faces, but looks of horror.

So I turn my face to see the cause of their dismay.

And as the white car hits me at full speed, everything goes cold. Again.

Lady Madonna

Eleven

I can feel warmth again, so I open my eyes to see the sun shining down from a bright blue sky, with fluffy white clouds floating gently across it.

Breaking my lovely view is a sea of faces hovering above me, looking with concern at my prostrate body lying strewn over the zebra crossing once more.

I turn my head to the side; there's an extremely high, platform-soled boot placed right next to my face. Turning it to the other side I see a pair of flared tartan trousers.

I sit bolt upright.

'Careful, love,' a woman wearing a floaty kaftan-style dress says with concern. 'You've had a bit of an accident.'

'Yes, no sudden movements.'

I turn to the man who's now speaking. He's wearing flared trousers too, only they're denim this time. He has on a tight yellow shirt with a long collar. And his hair is long and scruffy with big sideburns extending down both cheeks.

'I'm fine,' I mumble, trying to stand up. 'Really, see?' I jiggle my limbs around a bit on the ground, and as I do so it sounds like I'm a one-man percussion band. I look down at my wrists and they're covered in bangles and beads.

'I don't know how you can be,' the woman says again. 'The way you bounced off that car, it was like something from *The Professionals*.'

'Have you seen that?' another woman joins in now. 'It's great, isn't it? That Martin Shaw is *gorgeous*.'

'Yes,' the kaftan woman coos. 'He can screech to a halt and slide over his bonnet towards me any day.'

'Ahem!' I clear my throat. 'If you can just help me up, I'm on my way to the record shop.'

'You mean George's place?' the man asks.

'Yes.'

'He's shut early today – I've just come from there.'

'Why?' I demand. 'Why would he shut early?'

'I don't know, the sign just says personal reasons. I was over there just now trying to buy an Abba album for my wife's birthday.'

'A – Abba? But they're not around yet, are they?'

The assembled crowd look at each other suspiciously. 'You sure you're all right, love?' the man asks, bending down to take a closer look at me. 'Maybe we should call that ambulance after all.'

'No, no don't do that,' I insist. 'Really, I'm fine. Just give me a minute.' *Oh lord – this isn't the sixties, is it?* I suddenly realise. The clothes, the things they're talking about, it's more like the—

'Jo-Jo! What the bloody hell happened to you?' A small

figure pushes its way through the crowd and I see a familiar face at last – Ellie.

Except this Ellie isn't wearing the striped dress I last saw her in. Neither has she got her long blonde hair all piled up in a beehive on top of her head.

No, this much younger-looking Ellie is wearing tartan from head to toe, and her long hair is arranged in soft curls around her face. She's taller than I remember, too. Possibly because she's balancing precariously on top of some enormous silver platform-soled boots.

'Car accident, apparently.' I shrug. 'But I'm fine. Help me up, Ellie.'

Ellie holds out her hand and tries to pull me up, but she doesn't have very good balance in her skyscraper boots, and nearly topples over on top of me herself.

There are loud guffaws and sniggers from the pavement; I look towards them to see a small crowd of scruffy-looking yobs standing around on the side of the road. They're wearing an assortment of jeans, leather trousers and T-shirts, all of which seem to be torn or ripped in some way.

'Ah, you can just bugger off,' Ellie shouts at them, 'if you can't do better than laugh and jeer when you see a lady in distress.'

'You ain't no lady, Ellie Williams,' one of the boys with shocking green spikes all over his head shouts back. 'I've seen ya behind the bike sheds when we was at school.'

Ellie snarls at him, then she holds her hand out to me again. 'Come on, Jo-Jo,' she says. 'Let's get out of here, if you're sure you're OK?'

'Yes, really, I'm fine.' I take her hand and haul myself to my feet. 'Thank you,' I say to the other people as they stand back to let us past. 'I'll be fine now my friend is here.'

As we cross over to the pavement, the gang smirk at us. Ellie juts out her chin and ignores them, but I can't help taking a quick glance at their outfits. They really are quite intricate, not simply scruffy, as I'd assumed on first sight. Chains and leather bind the rips in their clothes, and a number of them have Union Jacks as added embellishment to their outfits; some of the flags are plain, and some have pictures of the Queen. I could almost be back in our jubilant summer of 2012 with this much patriotism about. I think for a brief moment. But then I notice the Queen's face is blotted out on the prints, and I suddenly realise they're not royalists at all, but punks, and of course this isn't 2012, but is very definitely the seventies.

It has to be; it all makes sense now – the punks, the platforms, the flared trousers. I'm just about to ask Ellie what year we're in, when one of the punks steps forward.

'Are you OK, Jo-Jo?' he asks in a much gentler voice than I would have expected.

His voice sounds familiar, but I don't see anyone I recognise. Then he speaks again.

'Only I was waiting outside a shop when you got hit by the car and I saw the whole thing. It looked pretty bad.'

It's Harry again! But not Harry in any guise I'd know him in. The Harry I've met before has always been suited and booted, both in the future *and* in the past. But this Harry is a fully-fledged seventies punk rocker, with pierced ears, a mostly shaved head and a blue Mohican on top of his head that any parrot would be proud of. And he's much younger.

'H – Harry?' I stutter. 'Is that *you*?'

'Ooh Harry, is that you-oo?' the others mock, looking at Harry with derision.

'Of course it's me,' he whispers, pretending to adjust the collar of his battered leather jacket. 'What do you think to the hair? Me mum'll go up the wall when she sees it. But I think it's far out.'

I stare at the bright blue comb on top of his head. 'It's ... different.'

'You don't like it, do you?' He folds his arms. 'I knew you wouldn't.'

I glance at myself in the shop window opposite. Apart from looking incredibly young, I'm wearing navy flared cotton trousers, a white smock top and sandals, and I have a truly vast quantity of beads and bangles hanging all over my arms. My long hair hangs loosely around my shoulders, save for two thin braids which are pulled tightly back to the side of my head.

'I'm a hippy!' I exclaim, voicing my thoughts aloud.

'Exactly,' Harry agrees. 'Which is precisely why you don't appreciate this new look of mine.'

'Come on, Harry,' one of the other lads shouts now. 'We've stuff to do. Leave the flower power reject and her wee tartan friend alone.'

Ellie makes an angry move towards them, but I put my hand out to her. 'Just leave it, Ellie.'

'I'd better go,' Harry says. 'I'll see you both later.'

'Yeah,' Ellie smirks. 'We'll be hearing your mam all the way down the street when she sees your hair like that.'

Harry fires a scornful look in her direction then heads back to his pals.

'Come on,' Ellie says, linking her arm through mine. 'I think we've had enough fun on the King's Road for one day. Let's go home.'

I look briefly in the direction of George's shop, wondering if, even though he's closed, he might be in there stocktaking or something. But what excuse could I possibly find to remove myself from Ellie's grasp and head over there? Besides, if I don't go with Ellie now I won't know what I'm doing, or where I'm going in this decade, will I? And desperate as I am to see George again and find out what's going on this time, he won't be able to speak to me with Ellie there. No, I'll have to wait until I'm alone again.

We catch a bus to Lambeth, not Fulham, this time. While I sit quietly staring out of the window at the passing London scenery, desperately trying to think about what's going on now, Ellie babbles about the Bay City Rollers and their latest song. That explains the tartan then, I think, glancing across at her while she's off in her Les McKeown dream world. The Bay City Rollers were a Scottish glam-rock band from the seventies, and their lead singer, Les McKeown, was a teenage pin-up back then. I happen to know all this because we used to look after his accounts at the firm when I was a junior, and some of the older ladies in the office would come over all of a fluster when he popped into the office occasionally.

I think about the office and wonder what's going on there while I'm away, if everything's functioning successfully without me. I've never left it alone for more than a day since I've been in charge. The place will surely fall apart – won't it?

Oh, why didn't I go back home to 2013 when I was hit by the car again? Why have I moved on into the seventies? I wish

I could have caught up with George before we left the King's Road. He's the only one who seems to know anything about what's happening to me. All I know is I've time travelled again, and into a new decade. But, incredibly, Ellie and Harry are with me again, albeit in very different guises. Yes, I definitely need to speak to George as soon as I possibly can to find out just what's going on. But until then I'll just have to follow Ellie's lead in this new world I find myself in.

'Righty-ho, then,' Ellie says as we alight from the bus, walk down a long street of Victorian terraced houses, then stop outside one with a blue painted door. 'I'll see you later,' she says, pulling a face. 'For the meeting.'

'Yeah,' I say, wondering what 'the meeting' is.

'I wonder what me mam'll have me signed up to this time. I've only just finished making miles of bunting and if I never see another red, white or blue triangle it will be too soon!'

Bunting? What might we be celebrating?

'The Jubilee!' I exclaim. 'The Queen's Silver Jubilee. It's 1977, isn't it?'

Ellie looks at me oddly. 'You sure you didn't bang your head on that crossing? Maybe you'd better lie down for a while when you get inside.'

'Yes, perhaps I'll do that.'

'See ya later then,' she calls, and I watch as she skips across the road and disappears into a similar-looking house to this one, but with a green door.

'Right then,' I say, turning towards my own blue door. 'I wonder what awaits me behind you?'

Twelve

Gingerly I push open the blue door and step inside the house.

'Jo-Jo, is that you?' I hear my name called from a room at the bottom of a messy hallway.

'Yes, it is,' I reply carefully. I make my way down the narrow hall, skilfully avoiding stepping on the pieces of Lego and half-naked Barbie dolls that lie in my path.

The door at the end of the hall is partly ajar, so I push it a little further open and find a woman sitting at a kitchen table bottle-feeding a baby.

'There you are, sweetie,' the woman, who I'm guessing is in her mid-forties, says, smiling at me. 'Could you be an absolute angel and pick the twins up from school for me today? Bonnie hasn't settled all afternoon and I'm exhausted.'

She certainly looks tired. Beneath her mop of bleached blonde hair, there are big dark circles underneath her brown eyes. She heaves the large baby on to her shoulder, and tries to wind her.

'Yes – yes of course.'

'You all right, Jo?' she asks, looking at me with concern. 'You look a little pale.'

'Yes, I'm fine. I had a slight accident this afternoon, that's all. But I wasn't hurt, so nothing to worry about.'

'Nothing to worry about?' The woman leaps up out of her chair with the baby still on her shoulder and comes rushing over. She puts her hand on my forehead. 'You're my daughter, I'll decide if you're hurt or not!'

Whoah, just hold on a moment! This woman is claiming to be my mother? This is just too weird. I may be feeling a bit woozy from my latest jump through time, but I know this woman standing in front of me isn't my mother. Besides, I wasn't even born until 1983! Calm down, Jo-Jo, this is the 1977 Jo-Jo's mum, of course it is.

'Really, M – Mum,' I mumble, backing away from her hand, 'I'm just fine.'

She stares into my eyes, narrowing her own at the same time. 'No, you're not, there's something different about you; a mother can tell these things.'

I turn my face away. 'I'm fine, really.'

She sighs. 'You've not been the same since you turned sixteen. I think it's working in that weird shop you've got yourself involved in.'

A shop? How bad can that be? Let's hope it's not some salacious sex shop, or an early version of Ann Summers.

'I *like* the shop,' I venture. 'It's fun working there.'

Please don't let it be something incredibly dull like a supermarket, or grotesque like a butchers.

'Hmm,' my new mother huffs. 'What good is a shop selling

117

all this hippy nonsense? It'll be another passing fad like all this computer stuff will probably turn out to be.' She gestures towards the table where there's a magazine lying open, and on the page there's a photo of a man with a beard, demonstrating a large, cumbersome computer.

I go over to the table and pick up the magazine. 'That's Steve Jobs,' I smile. 'Wow, look at the size of that Mac!'

'What are you talking about, Jo-Jo? The man isn't wearing a mac; he's wearing a shirt and tie. I just read that article. And how do *you* know his name?'

'I just saw it on the page,' I say hurriedly. I fold over the front cover of the magazine. '*BusinessWeek*?' I look at my mother in surprise; she doesn't look the sort of person who reads *BusinessWeek* as a rule.

'I just picked it up at the hairdresser's,' she says casually, taking the baby off her shoulder; it looks suspiciously up at me from her arms. 'They were busy and didn't have anything else to flick through.'

'Ah, OK.'

She glances up at a clock on the kitchen wall. 'The twins, Jo-Jo! Quick, or you'll be late! I'll try and get Bonnie settled while you're gone.'

The mere mention of the word late jolts me into action. 'Don't worry, I'm on it!'

I turn and head back down the hall, hesitating for a moment on the front doorstep. In theory I could escape now and go and see George, it's the perfect moment, but I can't exactly leave two kids standing all alone outside a school, can I? And will he even be open? No, my need to see George is going to have to wait again.

I look down the street figuring I'll just ask someone where the local primary school is, but luckily I don't have to, as I step out on to the pavement and see a steady stream of mums, buggies and prams all heading in one direction. So I follow them.

While I walk I eavesdrop on some of their conversations. They're much like any group of mothers I've ever heard as they flock to collect their young from school, except instead of chatting about what was being discussed on *Loose Women* at lunchtime today, they're talking about the guests on a programme called *Pebble Mill at One*, and whereas a group of 2013 mothers might be debating the pros and cons of their latest smartphone, these mums are discussing the latest in hair styling – the merits of a Braun electric curling iron against their favoured Carmen Rollers.

Eventually we all arrive outside some school gates, so I stand with the other mothers, waiting for my charges to come pouring through the gates with their fellow pupils, desperate to escape their day's schooling. My mother said 'the twins'; I don't know whether to expect twin girls, boys, or one of each, so I just have to hope they recognise me first.

While I have a few minutes, I think about what's happening to me this time.

It's pretty clear I've time travelled again, to the seventies. And it happened when a car hit me on the exact same zebra crossing on the King's Road where it occurred the first time. There must be a link there of sorts, right outside that World's End pub. The World's End . . . I wonder if that's relevant? It's quite an apt name, considering. And then there's Harry and Ellie again. They're here with me, which is quite comforting

119

in one way, but weird in another, because they've changed personas again, as I have. And we're all so young this time, teenagers, which is incredibly odd. I want to work it out, to know why. I don't like unanswered questions and unsolved puzzles. They unsettle me, almost more than the actual time travelling itself.

I really, really need to see George.

'All right, Jo-Jo?' a young woman standing next to me remarks. 'You're deep in thought this afternoon.'

'Not really,' I reply. 'Just waiting for the twins.'

'How's your mum doing?' the woman, who is wearing the most hideously patterned purple blouse and orange flared trousers continues. 'She still holding out?'

'Yes ... I think so.' *Here we go again; I have no idea what I'm supposed to reply*.

'She's a brave one, is Penny. That's all I can say. Single mum. Four kids. You'd think she'd snap the council's hand off, being offered a brand new home out in the country.'

'But she's not snapping their hand off?' I ask in surprise.

'No, you're right, she's not. She's got her pride, that one. And good on her for sticking to it. More than I'd do in her position, but they don't wanna knock down the shithole I'm livin' in, more's the pity!'

Just then the familiar sound of a school bell rings, and suddenly doors burst open and children rush euphorically out on to the playground and through the school gate.

I look helplessly at the children swarming around us now. Twins ... there must be some twins here somewhere, I think, looking all around me at the schoolbags being swung in the air, and the newly painted pictures being thrust proudly under mothers' noses. Suddenly I feel tugging at my top. I look down to see a young girl of about ten standing quietly next me.

'Hi,' I say, presuming this must be one of the twins. 'Good day at school?'

'Yeah, not bad, Sean's just coming – he forgot his PE kit and went back for it.'

So there's a girl and a boy, I know that much now.

'Good, good.'

Turning her head side to side, she looks up at me suspiciously, and her long chocolate brown plaits move up and down her shoulders. 'You look different.'

'Do I?' *Here we go* …

'What have you done to your hair? I know, you've got it braided up at the sides. Did Ellie do that for you?'

'Erm, yeah.'

She screws up her face. 'I want a friend like Ellie! The girls here are so dull and she wears such great clothes.'

I think of Ellie in all her tartan today.

'And she listens to great music too.'

I smile even more now. The Bay City Rollers make great music?

'You'll find your own way when it's your time,' I say, surprising myself by sounding so wise. 'You'll have your own clothes and your own music in the eighties. You won't need to borrow someone else's taste.'

'I don't know about taste, but I think someone's borrowed me PE kit,' a young boy, looking exactly like the girl but with a messy mop of brown wavy hair, says now. 'I can't find it anywhere.' *Ah, this must be Sean then* …

121

'Mum will kill you if you've lost that!' the girl says. 'Your new football boots were in that kit.'

'Shut up, Sally,' Sean says, giving her a shove. 'Just cos you're Miss Perfect.'

'I ain't!' Sally pushes Sean now too. 'I'm just not stupid enough to lose my PE kit like you all the time.'

'OK, OK!' I say putting my hands out to hold them apart. 'That's enough. Let's get you two home.'

We set off in the direction I've just come from while Sally and Sean continue their bickering behind me as we walk.

'Can we get sweets, Jo-Jo?' Sally asks as we pass a little corner shop at the top of the road.

'Yeah, please, Jo-Jo,' Sean joins in. 'You said the other day we could have some if we were good when Mum went out, but then you rushed off and never got us any.'

Did I? I look inside the large cotton patchwork bag I've been carrying across my body for the first time since I've arrived here in the seventies, to see if I've got any money on me, and I'm surprised to find, in amongst the odd bits of make-up and a comb, a small rolled-up magazine, or is it a newspaper? It feels more like that type of paper as I pull it from my bag.

'Why have you got a copy of the *Beano*?' Sean asks, looking at it in my hand. 'It's an old one too, by the looks of that front cover.'

'I ... I'm not sure.' I look at the comic; it must be the one I picked up on the zebra crossing before the car hit me. But how could that be here with me now? Did it come with me like Walter Maxwell's photo did with him?

'Can I have it?' Sean asks, reaching for the comic. 'It might be old but I bet Dennis the Menace is still the same.'

122

'No!' I snatch it away from him. 'I mean,' I say a little more gently, 'I'm just looking after it for someone, so you can't.' Quickly I shove the comic back in my bag and retrieve my purse. 'Let's get you some sweets now. Luckily for you both, I have a *little* bit of money on me.'

We finally leave the sweetshop after Sally and Sean have spent a great deal of time and deliberation choosing their confectionery. Sean has a Marathon – which looks very much like a Snickers bar to me – and Sally has a packet of Spangles, some sort of brightly coloured fruit-flavoured sweets.

It's quite interesting just how many of the sweets from the seventies I recognised in the shop. Their packaging may have evolved a little differently by the time they reach 2013, but children and adults here are enjoying the same delicious contents in 1977 as they will be in the future.

Sally and Sean clatter and crash their way back into the house when we arrive home, immediately abandoning their schoolbags on the hall floor in favour of their sweets.

'I'm in here, kids,' Penny calls.

We all go through another door into a living room this time, and I feel as if I've stepped on to the set of a seventies TV sitcom. One of the four walls is papered in a bright, bold wallpaper, patterned with big swirly orange and brown circles. The other three are plain, but are still painted a vibrant orange. Nearly all the furniture is brown, except for an olive green beanbag sitting in front of a large, boxy TV, which is currently showing some type of children's TV programme, with a Humpty Dumpty, a teddy bear and some dolls sitting in various different shaped windows.

'Mum, are you watching *Play School* again?' Sean asks as he jumps on to the settee.

'Bonnie likes it and it gets her off to sleep,' she says. 'She's only just gone off.'

'What's on today?' Sally asks, settling down next to him. 'Is it *Take Hart*? Do you think my picture might be shown on the gallery today, Mum? Do you?'

Sean laughs. 'What, that mess of dried lentils you sent in? I hardly think so. You'd have been better sending it to that cookery woman Mum likes.'

'Delia Smith,' Penny says. 'Yes, it might be, Sally, you never know.'

'Well, I wanna watch *The Red Hand Gang*,' Sean says. 'That's definitely on today.'

'More American rubbish.' Penny shakes her head. 'So much of it on our TV these days.' She sighs. 'But if it keeps you quiet ...'

I watch them all arguing over the television, and I'm taken forward to a time in my own past, when my own sisters and I will be doing something similar. Except we'll be arguing over whether to watch Ant and Dec in *Byker Grove* on the BBC or David Jason voicing *Danger Mouse* on ITV.

'What are you doing?' Sally demands as Sean leaps off the sofa in the direction of the television.

'*Jamie and the Magic Torch* is on!' Sean says, pressing a button on the TV, then settling back down on to the sofa, channel changed.

'You're such a baby,' Sally teases.

'It's just to pass the time until something better comes on.'

At least they don't have a remote control to fight over yet! I think.

'Are you OK, love?' Penny asks, watching me as I stand in the doorway. 'You're very quiet.'

'I'm fine. Do you guys want anything?' I ask, looking at the children now completely engrossed in the TV. 'I'm just going to get myself a drink from the kitchen.'

'Don't you be waiting on them hand and foot, Jo-Jo,' Penny says dismissively, 'they'll get something when they're ready.'

'Right, so it's OK if I head up to my room then?' I ask, hoping I actually have my own room.

'Sure, love, whatever you like. I'll give you a shout later and I've got your favourite in for tea tonight!'

'You have?'

'Yes, that new pot noodly stuff! I know how you love them, and since we're gonna be in a hurry tonight, what with the Jubilee meeting 'n' all, I thought we'd have something quick. I'll do fish fingers for the kids though – I think Pot Noodle is a bit adventurous for them!'

'Yes, that's … great, Mum, thanks.' First Babycham, now Pot Noodle; time travel is sure turning into a culinary experience – of sorts – if nothing else.

In the kitchen I pour myself a glass of water, and then I head back through the hall and up the narrow staircase. I pause as I reach the top of the stairs. Now which room might be mine?

I open one door and know immediately it's the twins' room. There are Sindy dolls and Action Men abandoned on the beds in mid play, a space hopper over in the corner of the room, and a half-finished game of Mousetrap lies in the middle of the floor.

I close the door quietly and open the one next to it, assuming I'll probably find Bonnie's nursery, or Penny's room, but I don't, it's my room.

I know this must be mine, because the dressing table is covered in make-up and jewellery and there are clothes left all over the bed where I obviously had many changes of mind as well as outfit before I left the house this morning. More importantly, covering every inch of my walls are posters; posters of boys. Actually, on closer inspection I realise they're posters of pop, film and television stars.

Staring back at me I recognise TV cops Starsky and Hutch, film star Sylvester Stallone, pop star Donny Osmond, the *Six Million Dollar Man* Lee Majors, and the original cast of *Charlie's Angels*.

Great, this will make it easy to drop off at night with all these eyes staring down at me! I had posters up on my wall as a teen in my own time, of course, but somehow Boyzone and Take That seemed much more innocent than these testosterone-filled, hairy men – the 'Angels' and Donny Osmond being the exception.

I push some of the clothes out of the way and sit down on the bed.

So I'm a teenage girl in 1977 this time, with a mother who serves Pot Noodle and fish fingers for dinner, TV addict twins for siblings, and a baby sister who – well, Bonnie doesn't seem too much trouble, right now, but I don't want to rule her out just yet. There's obviously not a father around; the woman outside the school said Penny was a single mum. So maybe I'm being a bit harsh criticising. Penny's doing well to keep us all together with a roof over our heads and food in our mouths. I'm not too sure about the benefit system in 1977, but I bet it isn't great.

Once I can get over to see George on the King's Road maybe he'll be able to shed some light on why I'm here this time. I'll definitely go tomorrow.

Right then, I sigh to myself, I'm just going to have to make the best of it. Now what did teenagers do in the seventies? I look around the room. Jo-Jo from 1977 doesn't seem to do much apart from try on clothes and put on make-up. I get up and wander over to the half-open window.

'Yo, Jo-Jo!' a voice calls, and I see Ellie waving at me from the bedroom window opposite. 'Check it out!' She points down the street and I see Harry walking along casually with his hands in his pockets.

Ellie puts her finger to her lips in a shushing fashion as we watch him go into a house a few doors down from mine.

Then Ellie cups her hand to her ear. 'Wait for it,' she mouths from her window.

Suddenly shrieked from the house we hear: 'Harry! What the bloody hell have you done to your hair? You look like one of your grandad's parakeets!'

Ellie laughs. 'Serves him right for mocking us,' she calls across the gap. 'I knew his mam would go mental when she saw him.'

I continue to listen at the window. But it all goes quiet. Then the front door opens again and Harry comes storming out.

'Shove it then, you old bag,' he shouts back through the

open doorway. 'I ain't changing me hair back and that's final. You either like me the way I am or I go!'

'Fine with me, Harry,' a voice calls back. 'One less mouth to feed!'

Harry glances back inside the house for a brief second, and even at this distance I can see hurt flicker across his eyes. Then he shrugs and slams the door hard.

'What are you two gawping at?' he calls, looking up at us peering out of our windows. 'Shouldn't you be drooling over a pop star or something equally useful?'

Ellie tosses her hair back. 'I'm not the one making a scene of myself in the street, am I?'

Harry ignores her and looks across at me. 'Nothing to add, Jo-Jo?'

I shake my head.

'Good. Then I'm going for a fag,' he announces, strutting off down the street.

'Idiot,' Ellie says, looking across at me again. 'No wonder his mam wants shot of him. Look, I gotta go, Jo-Jo, cos I said I'd help me mam with the tea tonight. But I'll see you later at this meeting, yeah?'

'Yes,' I reply, but I'm half watching which direction Harry is heading in. 'Yes, I'll see you later.'

I pull myself in from the window, and hurry back downstairs again.

'Mum, I'm just going out, OK?' I say, popping my head around the living room door. 'I'll be back for tea, though.'

'Yeah, sure, Jo-Jo,' Penny mumbles, as engrossed in little plasticine Morph's adventures on *Take Hart* as the children are. 'Can you get some milk, please, while you're out? Take some money from my purse, it's on the table in the hall next to the phone.'

'Sure.' I'd hoped to slip out immediately, but I run into the hall and pick up a red purse that sits next to a purple Trimphone on a small hall table. I pull out a few coins ... how much was milk in 1977 anyway? I have no idea. As I'm trying to do the purse up again, a card jams in the zip, so I have to pull it out to get it back in the purse evenly. I glance at the wording on the front: *Lambeth College Evening School*. So Penny goes to evening classes, does she? That's good, I think as I ram the card back in the purse, then dash down the hall and out of the front door. I vaguely hear Penny calling something about tea, and being back in time for the Jubilee meeting, as I slam the door closed behind me.

Now which way did Harry go?

I hurry down the road and find that Harry hasn't gone too far. He's leaning up against a wall at the end of the street, smoking his cigarette.

'What do you want?' he asks as I approach.

'To see if you're OK.'

He looks at me suspiciously. 'Why?'

'Probably for the same reason you came over to see if I was all right this afternoon after my accident.'

He surveys me for a moment through narrowed eyes surrounded by black eyeliner. Then he shrugs. 'Fair enough.'

'Are you OK then? I heard what your mother said.'

'Old bag,' Harry states, taking a long drag of his cigarette. 'She's said it before. She'll say it again no doubt. Wouldn't be the first time I've been thrown out.'

'But why?'

'Don't fit in here, do I, Jo-Jo? You know me. Always the outcast.'

'I'm hardly the archetypal teenager myself dressed like this, am I?' I gesture at my white smock top.

Harry looks me up and down. 'Sixties reject!' he says, grinning at me.

If only you knew ...

'At least you don't dress like a packet of shortbread, like that lunatic friend of yours,' he adds, waiting for my reaction.

'Ellie? She's OK. Nothing wrong with the Bay City Rollers, is there?'

Harry drops his cigarette on the ground and stubs it out with his foot. 'Nothing wrong with the Bay City Rollers?' he exclaims. 'You're asking someone with hair like mine that question?'

We both look at each other for a moment, then burst out laughing.

'Come on,' Harry says. 'Let's get out of here for a bit.'

We walk together along the road towards a park where a few boys are playing on some swings and a slide. As we approach they glance across at us, take one look at Harry, and immediately mount their Chopper bikes and scarper.

'Don't you mind having that effect on people?' I ask him as we sit companionably next to each other on the deserted swings.

'How do you mean?' Harry asks, lighting up another cigarette.

'Scaring them away like you just did, those kids?'

Harry shrugs. 'Not really. Part of the image, ain't it?'

'Is putting yourself in an early grave part of it too?' I nod at the cigarette.

'What's with you tonight, Jo-Jo? You're normally a bit goody two shoes, but you're even more weird today.'

'Nothing wrong with me. I just don't see you as a punk, that's all.'

'Why not?'

'You're too nice.'

Harry laughs. 'Punks can be nice too. We're just different, that's all. Anti-establishment.'

'Anti most things, aren't you?'

'I won't be going to this Jubilee meeting tonight, that's for sure.'

'I guess it's not really your thing. Although it would be pretty funny to see the reactions to you turning up in a Sex Pistols God Save the Queen T-shirt.' I wink at him.

Harry fakes astonishment. 'Jo-Jo, that's not like you! You'll be throwing away your incense sticks and piercing your nose next!'

'I hardly think so. But you don't have to dress like you to be brave and daring. There are other ways of doing it.'

'Like attending Peace rallies and Love-ins?'

'Perhaps.'

'I suppose you think them guys on those American cop shows like *Starsky and Hutch* are all brave with their fast cars and big muscles?'

'Hardly,' I say, stifling a giggle as I think of my poster boys up on my wall.

'What *do* you like, then?' Harry asks, pushing himself back on the swings and allowing his boots to scuff along the ground as he moves back and forth.

'Do you mean in a man?' I ask, forgetting for a moment I'm only a sixteen-year-old teenager.

'Oh, so it's *men* you go for,' Harry says, studying the pattern the toe of his boot is now making on the dust below him.

'No, I didn't mean that, I meant . . .' *Oh, what did I mean!* 'I meant I like someone who's prepared to be themselves, to stand up for what they believe in, who's punctual – and, most importantly, who can make me laugh.'

Harry looks up at me now. 'Laugh? Really?'

'Yeah,' I say, nodding, surprised at myself for listing this. It isn't something I would have thought would have been a high priority for me.

'Interesting,' Harry says. 'I'm not too good with jokes, so does that count against me?'

'How do you mean?'

'I hope I might be better at this . . .' Harry leans across the space between the two swings and I suddenly realise he's about to kiss me. I recoil in surprise and Harry, not having anywhere to rest his lips, tips off balance, and lands on his knees on the ground below.

'Oi, oi, Harry!' a voice calls across the park. 'What you up to?'

We both look up to see the gang of punks that Harry was hanging out with before making their way across the park towards us.

'Harry, I'm sorry,' I whisper as the boys get closer. 'I didn't realise what you were about to do.'

'I wasn't doing nuffin',' Harry says, red-faced. 'Was only

132

trying to make you laugh. Looks like I failed at that too,' he mumbles as he stands up and brushes himself down.

'Trying it on with Miss Flower Power here, were ya?' one of the gang, who has green spikes covering his shaven head and just as many metal piercings to match, continues. 'If ya gonna go for that type, she ain't a bad choice, I suppose.' He looks me up and down. 'Wouldn't mind havin' a crack meself.'

I regard him with derision. 'I hardly think so.'

'Ooh, hark at you, ya snotty cow – who d'you think you are? Royalty?'

'Leave it, Stu,' Harry says quietly. 'Jo-Jo's OK.'

I smile at Harry.

'Harry Rigby, you wouldn't be picking one of them sort over us, would ya?' Stu snarls, his top lip beginning to curl. 'Cos that might prove to be a very costly decision.' He punches his fist into his hand and some of the other boys begin to form a threatening semi-circle behind him.

'I ain't picking no one over nobody,' Harry says, 'Just let it be, Stu.'

'Shit, Harry!' Stu almost explodes. 'You're even quoting namby-pamby peace-lovin' Lennon now! She's really got to you, hasn't she?'

I don't like the look of this at all. It may just be an exchange of bravado, big words from little boys right now, but it's likely to deteriorate into something more physical. So I step in.

'Nobody has got to anyone. If you must know, Harry was smoking here alone on the swings when I came along and sat down next to him. So if anything it was *me* bothering *him*. But,' I sniff and pretend to look upset, 'Harry has made it quite clear he's not interested, haven't you, Harry?' I turn towards him

133

with my back to the others. 'I should have known you wouldn't be interested in someone like me. I guess we're just too different. So I'm going to make it very easy for you now, and leave.' I try and wink at him, so the others don't see. 'He's all yours,' I announce to the rest of the gang as I turn around. 'You're welcome to him.' Then I march off across the park, to jeers and shouts. But I don't look back; I just hope I've done enough to let Harry off the hook with his mates.

Everyone's watching *Blue Peter* in front of the TV when I get back to the house, eating their dinner off trays balanced precariously on their laps.

'Jo-Jo, the kettle's not long boiled if you want to do your Pot Noodle,' Penny says, barely taking her eyes away from the screen. 'I'll have to nip upstairs in a minute and get ready for this meeting. Damn it, I'll miss *The Good Life* tonight.'

'Can't you record it?' I say without thinking.

'What, love?' my mother says, distracted by John Noakes sticking two washing-up liquid bottles together on the screen.

'I was just thinking it would be handy if you could record TV programmes on tape, like you can songs from the radio. Then you could watch them whenever you wanted to.' I wait for their reactions.

'That would be brilliant!' Sally says, shovelling a large forkful of fish finger into her mouth.

'Ah, that'll never happen,' Sean says. 'How would you record pictures and sound together?'

'They do at the cinema,' Sally mumbles while chewing. 'How do they do that?'

'What would be really cool,' I say, thinking I'll play with

them a bit more, 'would be if you could pause live TV and rewind it in case you missed something, or if your phone rang in the middle of a programme.'

They all turn to look at me now.

'I think you've been spending too much time breathing in all the incense they burn in that shop of yours, Jo-Jo,' Penny says, raising one of her pencilled-on eyebrows. 'Next thing you'll be telling me we'll have hundreds of channels instead of just the three to choose from. There was some lunatic babbling on about that happening in the future in a magazine I was reading in the hairdresser's one day.'

Penny seemed to read a lot in magazines at the hairdresser's ... I open my mouth to respond, but decide to leave it. 'Yeah, it'll never happen. Bit like us having a female prime minister,' I grin as I leave the room, and go and re-boil the kettle for my gourmet dinner.

Thirteen

The next morning I wake up to *Starsky and Hutch*'s David Soul smirking down at me from the wall next to my bed.

'Aargh!' I cry, covering my face with the sheet again. 'Stop staring at me!'

But seeing him reminds me of Harry, and our few minutes together on the swings yesterday.

I wonder if he was OK after I left the park? I didn't see him again last night because we were kept busy all evening with the neighbourhood meeting for the Queen's Silver Jubilee. An eclectic mix of the many residents of the street had all packed into the small church hall to finalise preparations for our own celebrations. We were having a street party – like so many communities had done in 1977, and the majority of the evening seemed to have been taken up deciding who was bringing what type of sandwich, and which type of cake. The residents were also trying to get a band to play some music during the festivities "to keep the younger ones amused", but weren't having much luck in persuading anyone to come along and play on what little budget they could muster.

I felt genuine empathy for the younger members of the audience – obviously forced to attend by well-meaning parents, they all looked thoroughly fed up during the evening; not only due to the fact that they were spending their night in a drab church hall discussing cakes and bunting, but at the thought of the actual Silver Jubilee festivities themselves. My own mother was a very active and keen member of the Women's Institute, and in my younger days, when my older sisters weren't available to babysit me, I'd been dragged along to many a church hall meeting, where I'd been forced into selling jumble or partaking in some random craft activity. So I could genuinely feel their pain at being forced to sit through this.

I peel back the sheet while at the same time trying to avert my eyes from Sylvester Stallone's exposed chest. Rocky was a fine figure of a man back here in 1977, but I really didn't need to see this much of him first thing in the morning!

I go over to my window and pull my curtains back. Right, let's see what today brings forth. And whatever else happens I *must* get over to George's shop.

After breakfast, which I'm pleased to find doesn't consist of re-hydrated noodles, but Cornflakes, Rice Krispies and toast, Penny takes the twins to school while I head off to work.

During the course of breakfast I managed to find out, with a few carefully worded questions, exactly where the holistic shop I worked in was situated – on the King's Road, not that far, luckily, from George's record shop. So as soon as I got a chance today I knew exactly where I'd be headed.

Ellie and I get off the bus at the top of the King's Road.

Today Ellie is dressed more soberly than her Bay City Rollers tartan of yesterday, but she's still sporting high fashion – a purple catsuit and black platform boots – to work in the boutique where she has a part-time job.

Apparently we both left school without really knowing what we wanted to do, and while we await the fate of our O-levels, we've both managed to find part-time jobs for the summer. It's amazing what information you can discover in the course of conversation without actually asking direct questions. I'm starting to become quite good at it.

'See ya later, then,' Ellie says, opening the door of the boutique she works in. 'Dunno what time me lunch will be, but I can meet ya if ya like?'

'No!' I reply a bit too sharply. 'I mean, I know I'm on a late lunch today, so there's not much point in you trying.' I just have to see George alone.

'Ah, OK then,' Ellie says, not appearing to notice anything strange in my behaviour. 'See ya at home time then. Have a good day!'

I leave Ellie and walk down the road towards the shop I'm supposed to work in. I know it's called Tranquillity, and I don't have to go too far before I stumble across it, more by accident than expert detective work. It's a funny little place, quite hidden away amongst all the other shops lining this side of the street. Its tiny window display has Buddha statues, dreamcatchers, crystals and meditation tools crammed into it. I'm used to seeing odd little shops like this scattered about back in 2013 – holistic healing and alternative health is quite the norm by then, but I'm guessing that back here in 1977 it's still looked on as a quirky oddity.

'Hi,' I call as I push the door open and a bell rings – just like in George's shop.

'Good morning, Jo-Jo,' floats a voice from the back of the shop. 'How are you today?'

'Fine, thank you,' I reply, following the voice to its owner.

'Good, I'm pleased to hear it.' An elderly lady wearing a kaftan, several strings of beads and a peace symbol around her neck is sitting at the back of the shop. 'Put the kettle on, love, will you?' she asks. 'Old Rita here is parched.'

'Sure.' I look around for the kettle and see it standing in a tiny kitchen just behind where the woman sits, sorting some coloured candles.

I fill the kettle while I watch her surreptitiously from behind. She must be about seventy, I guess, but she has a thick lustrous mane of long grey hair tied loosely in a plait that hangs down the length of her back.

Aware I'm watching her, she turns around.

'Are you OK, Jo-Jo, love?' she asks. 'You seem a bit jumpy this morning.'

'Yes ... yes, I'm fine,' I try and reassure her. 'Just too much caffeine, probably. Shouldn't have stopped for that venti cappuccino on the way here!' *Damn!* I chide myself, turning my head away, *I must be more careful!*

Hesitantly I look back at her to see if she's noticed. Her deep blue eyes flicker momentarily, but she makes no comment and carries on with what she's doing, carefully sorting the coloured candles into individual boxes.

'So,' I say, hurriedly changing the subject. 'What should I do today?'

'We'll just do what we normally do, shall we, sweetie?

139

Muddle along and see where the day takes us,' she says, looking up and smiling at me. 'That's the best way, I've always found.'

'Sure,' I agree, to be amiable. Really, running a successful company takes organisation and planning, not simply 'muddling along'. I should know. But who am I to argue. I'm not even supposed to be here.

Surprisingly, the morning goes incredibly quickly, and there's a steady stream of customers into Rita's little shop. They range from aging hippies looking a bit like Rita with long grey hair either tied back in plaits or wildly cascading around their frail bodies, to young free spirits looking to find spiritual enlightenment in the products Rita keeps in her shop. But when Rita finally says it's time for my lunch break, I can't get out of there fast enough.

'Say hello to George for me,' she says, placing some joss sticks in a jar on the counter.

'Yes, I will!' I call back as I'm exiting the shop.

Wait, I think, pausing on the doorstep for a moment. How does she know where I'm going? I didn't say. I look back at Rita, but she just smiles serenely.

I don't have time to worry about that now, I think, leaving the shop and sprinting along the pavement towards Groovy Records, praying that George is open today. *Hurrah, you are!* I celebrate silently as I push open the door and the bell rings above my head.

'George!' I call, wincing as a barrage of heavy punk music assaults my ears. As I enter the shop I glance at the familiar surroundings. The sunflowers are in their usual spot and the wooden clock ticks steadily away, even though I can't actually hear it today. There are a few new posters up replacing the framed photos of the sixties, but it's still Groovy Records. 'George, are you here?' I call again.

'No, but I am,' Harry says as the music ceases and he appears from the back of the shop.

'What – what are *you* doing here?' I stutter.

'Work here, don't I?' Harry says, curling up his lip. 'What else would I be doing?'

'But where's George?'

'On his lunch break, why?'

'I just needed to see him, that's all.' I stare hard at a poster of Freddie Mercury and Queen on the wall in front of me and try not to look too disappointed. Then I glance at Harry again. 'He lets you work here like that?' I look up at his hair; he's so tall it almost touches the ceiling of the little shop, like a big blue brush sweeping for cobwebs.

'He wasn't best pleased when I came in this morning looking like this, no.'

'I bet. So, was everything OK after I left the park last night? With the others, I mean?'

'Ask a lot of questions these days, don't you?' Harry says, folding his white arms across his ripped, sleeveless black T-shirt. I notice he has quite well-toned biceps.

'Perhaps. I just wanted to know you were all right.'

Harry shrugs. 'Yeah, why shouldn't I be?'

Gosh, he was being particularly awkward today. 'It's just things were getting a bit heated, and I thought it might be best if I said what I did and just left.'

'I'm here in one piece, ain't I?' Harry shrugs. 'What's up, Jo-Jo? Bit late to be worried about me, isn't it?'

141

He's a teenager, Jo-Jo, I remind myself. Try and remember what it feels like to have hormones surging through you, tipping you off kilter all the time.

'You know I only said what I did to get you out of a tight spot with your mates.'

'Really?'

'Yeah, of course.'

Some of the hostility drains from Harry's face, and is replaced with a sense of hope.

'I see,' Harry replies, and looks about him shiftily.

What's he up to now?

'It's just that I was wondering, Jo-Jo . . .'

'Yes?'

He clears his throat. 'I was wondering if you might like *Star Wars* at all?'

Star Wars – *where was this heading?* 'It's OK. I've seen it a few times, why?'

Harry looks stunned. 'You've been already?'

'Yeah, why do you ask?' I think hurriedly. Star Wars – Star Wars. *Is that only just out?*

'It's just I was going to ask if you'd like to go and see it some time, with me like, but if you've already been, it's fine, don't worry about it.' He hurriedly begins rearranging some Rolling Stones records.

Oh boy!

'What I meant was, I've seen it *advertised* lots of times and I've seen the trailers!' I improvise. 'Of course I'd love to go and see it with you.'

Harry swivels around as fast as his DM boots will allow, a broad grin covering his face. 'Really?' His voice is an octave higher than it usually is. 'I mean, that's cool,' he says in a gruffer voice.

'What's cool?' The door of the shop opens and George comes through it carrying a couple of paper bags. 'Jo-Jo! How wonderful to see you again. I knew you'd be back.'

I stare at George. He's wearing black flared trousers with a thin tan belt, a black T-shirt, and the same tan leather safari jacket he wore in the sixties. His brown hair now hangs messily around his shoulders and he has long sideburns down each cheek with a thick brown moustache to match. He removes his gold aviator-style sunglasses and smiles at me. 'How have you been?'

I'm not sure if this George is asking about the 1977 me, or the time-travelling one. 'I'm well, thanks, George.' I reply cautiously, unable to take my eyes off this new version of him.

'Did you come in for something in particular?' he asks, putting the paper bags down on the counter. 'Only I'm just about to eat my lunch, and you're welcome to join me if you like – I have plenty.'

'Thanks, that would be good.' I glance at Harry.

'Harry, do you want to take your lunch break now?' George asks. 'You won't eat what I've got in here, not enough grease and chip fat.'

'Have you been to that god-awful veggie place again?'

George nods.

'Yeah, I'm definitely outta here then,' Harry says, his indifferent manner returning. 'Time me, man,' he says, pointing to the wooden clock behind the counter. 'I won't be late. Never am, am I?' He turns and winks at me. 'Catch you later, Jo-Jo, and we'll sort out a date for that ... thing.'

'Sure, Harry,' I smile, 'let's do that.'

Harry and his blue hair disappear out of the door and I'm left with George. I look at him, wondering if I should say anything, but luckily I don't have to.

'So, you're back again, then?' George asks. 'You obviously didn't do everything you needed to in 1963.'

'Thank goodness you know,' I sigh with relief. 'I wasn't sure.'

'Of course I know! I remember you back in the sixties – it wasn't that long ago,' he winks. 'So the most important question: have I aged well?' he asks, holding out the sides of his jacket and posing like a catalogue model.

I have to grin. 'Yes, you have, actually. You look very … smart!'

George grins. 'You don't need to lie. But right now what I'm wearing is considered the height of fashion for men. So, you're a teenager this time?'

I nod. 'And it's not easy. If there's one time I wouldn't want to go back to, it's my teenage years.'

'Why?' George asks thoughtfully. 'Particularly difficult time for you, was it?'

'No more than most teenagers, I expect. We were travelling a lot back then with my father's job and we didn't stay anywhere too long.'

'So you must have found it difficult to make friends?'

I think about this. 'Maybe, sometimes I guess. Depends on where we were. I try not to think about it too much, though.'

'Hmm,' George nods knowingly.

'Hmm, what?'

'Just thinking.'

'I can see that. Thinking about what?'

'Why you're here again.' He still has the same contemplative look on his face.

'And?'

'I'm not sure yet. But I'll work it out,' he finishes brightly.

'Great! So until then?'

'Just do your best to fit in,' George says helpfully. 'Make sure you don't do anything to upset things in the future too much.'

'How do you mean?'

'Oh, Jo-Jo,' George sighs. 'Do you know nothing of the rules of time travel?'

'Not really, but I'm having to learn pretty fast.'

'Let me put the kettle on, make us a nice cup of tea, and I'll tell you all about it, while we munch on my peanut butter sandwiches and flapjack.'

Fourteen

George makes us both a cup of tea, and while I eat a piece of flapjack (I pass on the peanut butter) he tells me all he knows about time travel. Which isn't that much considering George is the only person I've got to help me out on this – I'd call it an adventure if I was actually enjoying it, but really it's more like a bad dream. It's not quite bad enough to be classed as a nightmare – yet.

' . . . so if I change something back here it could affect what goes on in the future?' I repeat while George takes a sip from his mug of tea. I'm pleased to see the mugs are back, even if the one I'm holding has The Bee Gees on it, and George's a very fetching photo of Noddy Holder and Slade.

'Uh-huh. And that could be a very bad thing. But, it might also be a good one too,' he adds unhelpfully.

'But how will I know?'

'You won't.'

'But what if I do something that majorly changes mankind in some way?' I ask, my mind beginning to race.

George smiles. 'No offence, Jo-Jo, but I don't think you're likely to influence any world leaders while you're here, now are you?'

'You never know. When I was back in the sixties, it was just before JFK was shot. It felt odd knowing that was going to happen. Like I should do something to try and prevent it.'

George nods. 'Exactly. That's just the sort of event you must stay away from. You would create too many waves that would rock and wreck too many ships in the future if you even *tried* to prevent world events of that magnitude from occurring.'

All the terrible disasters that will happen both in this country and abroad suddenly flash through my mind. I know many of the dates and the times they will occur, so how can I just stand by and let them happen? Surely I should at least *try* and do something to prevent them? But who would listen to one person spouting off about some terrible event that was going to take place, like a bomb going off on the underground, an assassination attempt, or even something as devastating as 911? There are always people trying to warn us of events like this. More often than not they're dismissed as loonies and freaks; they're laughed at, ridiculed, or even worse, locked up. I wonder if they're people like me, caught up in some strange time-travelling nightmare, doing their best to try and help.

George rests his hand on mine. 'You look as if you've suddenly got the weight of the world resting on your shoulders, Jo-Jo. Please don't fret about this. There *are* those that are here to affect world events, but there are many more who are here to affect their own journey in life and that of those around them.'

'How do you mean?'

'Take for instance the Ellie and Harry of the sixties. In the years after you left Ellie went on to become a famous baker and entrepreneur – she owned eight cake shops in London alone.'

'Ellie did?' I ask in surprise.

'Yes, pretty impressive, eh? And there's Harry, too. After you got him that audition for George Martin, EMI employed him as a songwriter, and he went on to write some very well-loved tunes for some very big stars – some of which are still played well into the future.'

I think about this.

'But that doesn't make sense. How can they both exist in the sixties, and then in the seventies as different people? Surely the sixties version would just age? Are there two of them here now in 1977? And what about the Ellie and Harry of the future from 2013? How does it all work, George, how?'

George sighs. 'So many questions, Jo-Jo. I didn't say I had all the answers, did I?'

'No, but you must at least have some, George?' I plead. 'I'm not good with all this let it be, see what pans out, trust it will all be fine stuff. I'm an accountant. I deal in figures and if the sums don't add up you keep redoing them until the books balance.'

George nods. 'Perhaps I can explain it in a way you might understand, then. Hmm, let me see . . . ' He strokes his moustache thoughtfully. 'Let's try this: imagine if you were doing someone's accounts, and they'd mislaid a whole page of figures, what would happen?'

'That's easy, their books wouldn't balance,' I say with certainty.

'Exactly, but those missing transactions would have still taken place whether you could see them written down or not.'

'Yes . . .' I say hesitantly, not really knowing where George is going with this.

'That's a bit like what's happening to you right now. Instead of a page of your yearly account book that's missing, it's a page of your life account book. Once you find that again, everything else will balance. But until you do, you just have to believe in those missing transactions until you can fit them back into their rightful place.'

I stare dubiously at George. 'What you just said shouldn't make any sense at all. But strangely it does . . .'

George smiles. 'Life is often like that, Jo-Jo; it doesn't always have to balance, but just because it doesn't, it doesn't stop it from happening.'

'But if all that's true, how do I find the missing page?' I ask, thinking aloud. George's accountancy analogy has struck a chord.

'When I said I didn't have all the answers, I meant it. I'm sorry, Jo-Jo, I didn't say time travel would be easy or simple to work out.'

'No one ever said it was possible either, but look at me now!' I say, the realisation truly dawning that I'm not suddenly going to wake from a dream, or a coma, like in that TV show, the police one when she went back in time. *Ashes to Ashes* it was called. That character went back to the eighties, but was never quite sure if it was all in her subconscious mind. Apparently this wasn't, according to George – it was actually happening to me right here and right now.

'Yes, look at you now,' George says proudly. 'You're coping incredibly well with everything that's being thrown at you.'

'Really?'

'Definitely. As I've mentioned before, you're not the first to do this. And no doubt you won't be the last either. But you *can* do this; you're strong, and bright and capable. Otherwise you wouldn't be here.'

I'm touched by George's compliments. 'You make it sound like I've been specially selected. Like this isn't just random?'

George looks down into his now virtually empty mug and thoughtfully swills the last of his tea around in the bottom.

'Wait, are you saying I have been?' I demand. 'What about these others you've mentioned before? I think I might have met someone else like me back in 1963. Are there many of us doing this?'

George opens his mouth, but I hear Harry's voice.

'Would you like fries with your Donna Summer album?' he calls, piling back through the door carrying a takeaway bag with the Wimpy logo on it.

'If you fuel your insides with junk, your outsides will look like it too!' George says knowingly, getting up from where we've been sitting next to each other on the now-familiar wooden chairs.

'Yeah, yeah,' Harry says, pulling a greasy-looking burger from his bag. 'If it's good enough for the Yanks, it's good enough for me! Listen, you'll never guess who I just saw walking along the King's Road? Only Malcolm bloomin' McLaren!'

'Was he heading towards SEX?' George asks.

'Yeah, off to see Vivienne, no doubt. God, I'd love some stuff from their shop. No way on my wages, though. Any chance of a rise, George?' He winks at George and offers him a chip.

'Ditch the Sex Pistols hairdo, start selling some more records, and I'll think about it!' George smiles, turning down his offer.

I look hopefully across at George, in case we might be able to continue our conversation. But with Harry back I know that's going to be impossible in the tiny shop.

'I guess I'd better be getting back to Rita then,' I announce, casting one hopeful last glance in George's direction.

'Yes,' George agrees, collecting up our empty mugs and the remains of his lunch. 'Return to Rita, Jo-Jo. I'm sure an afternoon spent in her company will be most enlightening for you.' His piercing blue eyes look directly into mine. '*Most* enlightening.'

Fifteen

I leave George and Harry to their various lunches and head back towards Tranquillity and Rita.

'Good lunch?' she asks as I re-enter the shop.

'Yes, not bad, thanks.'

'And what did George have to say for himself today?'

Rita is sitting behind the counter arranging some beaded jewellery on a display stand.

'Not too much – wait, I meant to ask you before: how did you know I was going to see George earlier?'

Rita lifts her head and her bright blue eyes stare intently back at me. 'Sit down, child,' she says, gesturing to a high-backed wooden stool in front of the counter. 'Now, if I could have your hand?' she asks as I pull myself up to sit in front of her.

I hold out my hand and she turns it over, clasping it in hers, palm upwards.

'Ahh . . . ' Rita says, examining the lines on my hand. 'That makes perfect sense. I understand now.'

'What do you understand?'

'This,' she says, running her finger along a line on the heel of my palm, 'is your lifeline. On most people it's a fairly solid line, broken occasionally to represent any traumas in their life or major events.'

I look down at my hand.

'But yours,' she says, running her finger up and down, 'is solid to here, see, then it breaks off into many different lines.'

I pull my hand away to take a closer look at my palm. She's right, there's a strong indent, which further down suddenly branches off like a tree into many other lines.

'You know, don't you?' I ask her. 'You know I'm not the real Jo-Jo.'

'You're the real Jo-Jo, all right,' she says, smiling serenely. 'Just from another line.'

'But ...'

She takes hold of my hand again. 'This is your heartline,' she says, again tracing her finger along my hand. 'See how it's strong, yet it breaks off occasionally in the middle, then forms a strong line again at the end. It shows you will care many times, but truly fall in love only once.'

'Sure,' I mutter, dismissing this. The last thing I need to know about at the moment is my love life. 'But back to the lifeline, you just said—'

'And your headline just here,' she points to a different line on my hand. 'That shows me you're a very practical, analytical person, that you need black and white answers, no grey areas.'

'Yes. Yes, that's exactly right, I do need answers. I need to find the missing page. Can *you* help me find it, Rita?'

Rita studies me carefully across the desk. 'I don't need to, Jo-Jo, the answers you need are all in here.' She turns my hand over and places it on to my heart.

'But, that's no good!' I cry, jumping off the stool. 'I need to know why I'm doing this! You know, don't you?' I desperately search Rita's calm face. It gives nothing away. 'Is there going to be more when I'm finished here? Is there?'

'Calm down, child.' Rita takes a deep, almost meditating breath. 'Now take a seat again,' she says, gesturing to the stool. 'I can't help you if you're leaping about the place.'

'What *can* you tell me then?' I ask, pulling myself back on to the seat. 'You obviously know something, I'm not stupid.'

'No, you're definitely not that, Jo-Jo,' she smiles. 'I know that you can be very demanding at times, and you always want to know what's going on right at this very minute, and you're not good at letting things be and waiting for answers to arrive at their own pace.'

She's right. That is one of my faults. I'm not very good when it comes to waiting. In fact, it's amazing I've been able to be so patient this far. Maybe my brain has been more addled by the process of time travel than I realise.

'You're also a very determined person, and once you set your heart on something nothing will prevent you from getting it.'

I nod at this. Also true.

'This has helped you in your life so far, in your career especially.'

'Yes, you're right. I'm very determined when it comes to my job.'

'But for all your success you're very lonely too.'

'Of course I'm lonely. At the moment I'm being thrust into all sorts of random time zones with complete strangers most of the time. It doesn't take a genius to work that one out!'

Rita regards me with another patient, yet knowing look.

'I mean you're lonely back in 2013.'

'I am not,' I answer without thinking. 'I have plenty of friends, colleagues and family. I see them all the time.'

'Do you, Jo-Jo? Really?'

'Yes,' I answer firmly. 'I do.'

'You may see them, but are you close to them?' Rita may only be looking into my eyes as she asks her question, but it feels as if she's burrowing deep into my soul. 'Aren't most of them more casual acquaintances than close friends? What people do you have in your life who you could share your every thought and desire with?'

'Maybe I don't want to share my every thought and desire with people,' I respond huffily. 'Maybe I prefer keeping them to myself.'

'But why is that?'

'I don't know, do I?' I rub at my forehead, and I'm surprised to find tiny beads of sweat there. I wipe them away. 'It's just easier if you keep things to yourself.'

'Why?' Rita's eyes blink innocently back at me. 'Surely the more you share with people the easier life becomes? A problem halved and all that?'

'But it doesn't work like that, does it? When you share with people you can't keep things ordered; you don't know what you're doing. Humans are too unreliable, in my experience. Life is so much easier when it's just you. You're in complete control.'

'Ah …' Rita says, nodding. 'Now we're getting some-where.'

'I'm sorry, but I don't think we are. Look, are you going to help me discover why I'm travelling through time, or are you just going to sit there and judge me and my choice of lifestyle?'

'Jo-Jo, you will discover all you need to know in time. I can promise you that. And when that time comes this journey will truly be worthwhile for you.'

I sigh. How frustrating this all is. First George and now Rita. They obviously know more than they're letting on, but they won't tell me.

'Why don't you take the rest of the day off?' Rita suggests. 'I think your time would be better spent elsewhere while you're here than in my shop, don't you?'

'Will it make me leave here any quicker?'

'Have patience. All things are difficult before they become easy.'

I have to smile. 'You may be very infuriating, Rita, but you're very wise.'

'Sadly not one of my own,' she says, gesturing to a book of quotations on the shelf. 'But there are some very wise words in there if you'd like to read it some time. Take it.'

I lift the book down off the shelf. 'You're sure?'

'Jo-Jo, I'm never wrong. Trust me.'

So, still feeling a little frustrated, but with new reading material under my arm, I leave Tranquillity early and walk back down the King's Road. I pass the World's End pub, which doesn't seem to have changed much since the sixties, and carry on along the high street, stopping occasionally to look in shop windows at the weird and wonderful assortment of goods on sale in 1977. In an electrical store I see a cassette tape recorder being advertised as the latest must-have gadget and I can't help but pause outside a hairdresser's window to stare at all the tight poodle-like perms being applied to lovely locks of straight hair.

'Want to come in, love?' one of the hairdressers mouths at me through the window.

I shake my head ferociously. Perming my long hair is the last thing I want to do to it. I think I'd rather have it cut like Harry's.

I think about this version of Harry as I carry on down the street. He's a strange mix again – in some ways very mature for his sixteen years, even with that silly haircut. It's like he doesn't quite fit in, but is also desperately trying anything to do so. There is something very endearing about him that seems to transcend all the times we've met. It never feels like I'm meeting him for the first time. It's as if I've always known him.

'Watch it!' a raucous voice calls, barging into me as it exits the newsagents I'm just passing.

'I think you'll find you should be the one watching it!' I snap, swivelling around to find Stu, Harry's punk mate glaring at me.

'I should have know it would be you, dreaming your way down the road,' Stu says, lighting up a cigarette from his newly purchased packet.

'I was not dreaming my way down the road, I was—' I stop myself. Actually, I had been daydreaming; I'd been thinking about Harry.

Stu sniggers. 'I thought as much. All you lot do is dream your way through life, ain't it?'

'What do you mean, "my lot"?'

'The flower-power brigade. Heads in the clouds. No idea of what's going on here in the real world. Blip on society, that's what you are, if you ask me.'

I look at Stu leaning up against the shop wall, with his shaven head of green spikes and his upper lip formed into a permanent snarl.

'*I'm* a blip on society? Look at you!'

Stu regards his look in the window of the shop by strutting to and fro along the pavement. 'Yeah, and your point is? Nothing wrong with the way *I* look,' he says, holding out his hands. 'I stand out. I don't try and blend into the background like all them other morons.' He gestures across the road at the shoppers bustling up and down the street – who are by no means your dullest-looking Londoners. This is the King's Road, mecca to all things and all people wanting to be hip and trendy. But he's right; they don't make anywhere near the statement Stu did.

'But you look aggressive dressed like that. People are scared of you, afraid to approach you.'

'And so?' he shrugs. 'That's a good thing far as I'm concerned. Don't want people approaching me. Not them sort of people anyway.' He shudders.

I look at him again. And suddenly I see something different behind all his bravado. I see a streak of vulnerability.

'What you staring at now?' he demands. 'You're weird, you.'

'You're scared, aren't you?' I ask in a quiet voice.

'I ain't scared of nothing, me.' He raises his face up to the sky and blows a plume of smoke casually in the air.

'What are you scared of?' I continue. 'All people? Or just these sort of people? People who conform to life?'

Stu throws his cigarette to the ground and stubs it out viciously on the pavement with his boot. Then he turns to me, pushes me up against the wall and presses himself up against my chest so his face is centimetres from mine. 'Listen, you. You don't know nothing about me and who I am. So don't you go spreading any nasty rumours, or you'll find out just how *not* scared I really am! Of you, them, or anything in this lifetime.'

Then as quickly as he's pinned me up against the wall, I'm released, and he's strutting off down the street, lighting up yet another cigarette.

I stand in the middle of the pavement staring after him, pedestrians brushing against me as they try to get past along the busy street. As scared as I'd been for that split second when Stu had had me pressed against the wall, when he'd looked directly into my eyes, I'd seen something. Something I'd seen somewhere before, but where? And on whom?

Sixteen

'You all right, love?' Penny calls as I come back through the door. 'You're home early today, ain't ya?'

'Rita let me away early because we were quiet,' I lie, heading straight through to the kitchen to get a drink. I know it will have to be a Tizer or a Panda Pops or something equally sugary and horrid. Right now, after my encounter with Stu, I could do with a nice chilled glass of Pinot Grigio, but I have to remember I'm only sixteen, and I don't think Penny is likely to allow that, or even likely to have any in the house for me to drink in any case.

I find her at the kitchen table, hurriedly gathering up the books that cover it. She looks a bit jittery.

'What's wrong?' I ask her as I go straight to the fridge and pull open the door. Even worse, I think as I view the contents, only full-sugar Pepsi. Still, the sugar hit might help quell my shakes.

'Nothing, I was just doing a bit of light reading.'

I stroll over to the table and pick up one of the books. '*Accounting for Beginners*?'

'Yes!' she says, snatching it back. 'I just borrowed it from – from the library.'

I pick up another. '*Running Your Own Business the Easy Way*.' I flick open the front cover. 'But there's no library ticket in here and it's virtually brand new.' I look at Penny again; she's now flushed bright red. 'What are you doing?'

She sighs and rolls her eyes. 'You had to come home early, didn't you? I was trying to keep it quiet. I'm doing some night school courses, that's all. That's where I've been going every Monday and Wednesday when I said I was going over to Maggie's to watch *Coronation Street* with her.'

'So?' I say, perching on the edge of the table to take a sip of my Pepsi – *blimey it's sweet!* 'What's wrong with that?'

Penny looks surprised. 'I – I didn't think you'd understand.' 'Why?'

'Well, your mum going back to school when you can't wait to get away from the place.' She begins arranging the books into a neat pile now. 'I didn't think you'd think I was clever enough to do it, either.'

'And are you?' I ask. 'Clever enough, I mean. How are you getting on?'

Again Penny looks surprised by my question. 'Very well, actually. And I'm enjoying it too.'

'Then that's all that matters. Go for it, I say.'

I wish my own mother had been more proactive in creating a full life for herself before my sisters and I left home. She spent so long travelling the world with my father and his job that she never seemed to do anything for herself, except the

Women's Institute which she threw herself into every time we were based in England for a bit. Maybe if she had made a proper career for herself she'd spend less time trying to meddle in *my* life.

Although right now, hearing my mother's composed, calm voice trying to control this current mess I've found myself in, would actually be very welcome.

Penny, as if sensing this, stands up, walks round to the other side of the table and wraps her arms around me.

'My girl,' she says, hugging me tightly. 'That's what you are. *My best girl.*' Then she stands back to look at me. 'You're changing, though.' She looks me over.

'How do you mean?' I ask, trying to remain casual, but inside I feel very touched by this stranger's tender gesture, just when I most needed it.

'You're more mature. Like you've grown up suddenly. Maybe working in that shop is doing you some good after all.'

'Yes, maybe it is. So,' I ask, changing the subject before she has time to consider this apparent change too long, 'what are you going to do with all these new qualifications when you get them?'

'Nothing, I expect,' she says, moving back around the table again. 'This college stuff is just a bit of fun really, something to pass the time in between my odd shift at the factory and looking after you lot.'

I stare at her. 'Don't be daft! You have to do something with what you've learnt or else it's just a waste of time.'

'Jo-Jo, I'm a widowed mother of four, lucky to be living in the council house whose lease she inherited from her mother because your dad and I chose to live here and look after her.

I'm hardly going to wake up one morning and start up my own business, now am I?'

Penny's widowed? I assumed her marriage had broken down and her husband had left her. My resolve to help her becomes even greater.

'Why not? Plenty of single women run very successful businesses and still cope with having a family. Why not you?'

'Like who?' she demands. 'Name one.'

'Er ...' Now I'm struggling. My knowledge of seventies women entrepreneurs is fairly limited, to put it mildly.

'See. There aren't any.'

'So why are you doing the course then? You must want to make something more of your life than working at the factory?'

'Nothing wrong with good honest toil, Jo-Jo, you'd do well to remember that. It was good enough for your grandmother, and great-grandmother, God rest their souls.'

'But you can break the mould, Pen – Mum,' I correct myself. 'You can be the first, and set Sally a good example for the future.'

Penny considers this. 'Perhaps.'

'No perhaps, just do it!'

Penny smiles. 'That's a good slogan. I like it. Just do it. More people should *just do it*, instead of putting things off and wishing they had.'

'Yeah,' I smile. 'It's catchy, that's for sure.'

'*Just do it*,' she mutters to herself as she collects up her books from the table. 'Yes, that's what I'll do. I'll *just do it* in future.'

'Yes, you do that.' I sit down at the table with my drink and watch her.

'But now I have to go and fetch the children from school,'

she says, glancing up at the clock on the wall. 'I'll just do that first. Bonnie's down for a nap – can you listen out for her and I'll be back in a bit?'

'Sure,' I say, pleased at the thought of a few minutes' peace to collect my thoughts. 'I may have a nap myself, but I'll hear Bonnie if she wakes up.'

I listen for the click of the front door as Penny leaves the house. Then I finish off my drink, crushing the can down on the Formica table when I'm done, wishing I could pop down the road for a Starbucks or a Costa. Suddenly all the Pepsi in the world can't produce enough caffeine to get me through this weird life I'm living right now.

Exhaustion suddenly overwhelms me, so I head upstairs to take a nap.

I fall asleep quickly, and when I wake, for a split second I wonder if it's all been a really bad dream. But I soon hear the TV droning away downstairs, and Sally and Sean bickering with each other in front of it. So I lie on my bed and look at the ceiling for a few minutes – I find it's best not to look at the walls otherwise I get a bit freaked out by all the testosterone and bulging biceps.

So what next? It had seemed easier in 1963 when I felt as if I was at least working towards something, helping Ellie win the competition, getting Harry the audition. But here in 1977 I feel like I'm just treading water, not going anywhere or achieving anything. And wasting time is never a comfortable thing for me.

I think about what George said, about Harry and Ellie benefiting from me being there with them in 1963, and how I seemed to have changed their lives for the better. Maybe that's what I need to do here before I can proceed any further.

But here in 1977 Ellie and Harry are only sixteen and they don't really know what they want to do with their lives. I think wider: who else? Penny, perhaps? But how can I persuade Penny that there's more to life than looking after Sally, Sean, and Bonnie? I can't just magic up something to transform her evening classes into a practical business opportunity that would benefit her and her family.

Or can I?

Seventeen

'Would you like some popcorn?' Harry asks as we wait in a long line to buy tickets for *Star Wars*.

'No, you're OK. Pen – I mean Mum – cooked for me before I came out.'

I say cooked. She poured water on some Smash potato granules and grilled us some sausages, which might as well have been vegetarian for all the meat they had in them. Although I moan about my nomadic childhood, my mother always made sure we ate right. We always had a proper dinner every night, whatever country we were in. Even if my parents were entertaining clients at some fancy dinner, we'd still be fed properly before we were put to bed, and we almost always had a bedtime story read to us too. Perhaps my mother wasn't so bad, I think; maybe I've just let years of distant memories cloud my judgement of her. Living with Penny, the twins and Bonnie was certainly making me think a lot about my own childhood again. Something I usually avoided.

'You OK?' Harry asks. 'You seem a bit distracted tonight.' He looks longingly at the machine where fluffy pieces of popcorn are flying around waiting to be dropped into a cone. 'Do you mind if I get some when we've got our tickets? Only I didn't get any dinner and I'm starving.'

'No of course not, go for it, and I'm fine, really. Few things on my mind, that's all.'

We finally reach the booth, and Harry insists on paying for my ticket. We then move across the foyer to another queue for food and drink, and when we reach the front of that one, in addition to his popcorn and my drink, Harry buys a Mars Bar, two Cadbury Flakes, and a Kit Kat.

'You really are hungry!' I remark, glancing at his stash as we walk towards the screen together. This is a small cinema in comparison to the multiplexes I'm used to back home; it only has two screens.

'Yeah, haven't eaten since that Wimpy at lunchtime; nothing in the house when I got in from work tonight.'

'Where was your mum?'

'Out, thank God.'

'Have you two settled your differences yet?' I pass my ticket to the usherette who rips it in half.

'Nah, not really. But I won't be there much longer anyway. Where do you want to sit?' Harry asks, looking up at the rows of seats filling fast.

'Up there will do.' I point to a couple of seats in the middle rows. 'Why won't you be? Living there, I mean.'

'Mum is moving out to new housing. The council have been after her house for ages and she was holding out like your mum, but they kept pestering her, offering her more and more incentives to move, and finally she's decided to give in.'

'Does she want to move?' I ask, settling into my seat. I look for the cup holder to put my drink in, but quickly realise there isn't one in the velvet armrest.

'Nah, she's lived there all her life, but she's weak, my mum; the promise of a fitted carpet and a fridge freezer and she's anyone's. Your mum's done well holding out, can't see anyone moving her. It was your gran's house originally, wasn't it?'

I nod. 'Yes. Harry, has your mum signed anything yet?' I ask, my brain beginning to race.

'Don't think so. Difficult to tell, we only communicate through shouting most of the time these days.'

I feel a pang of sorrow. I'm not sure if it's for Harry's problematic relationship with his mum, or for mine with my own mother.

'Stop her,' I say urgently, turning towards Harry, my hand on his arm. 'Just make sure you stop her.'

Harry smiles at me. 'What's got into you?'

'Nothing. I just think your mum would be better staying in her house than moving to some grotty estate, that's all.'

Harry stares at me now. 'How do you know it's a grotty estate? It looks OK in the brochures they've sent her. Yes, she's gonna be a few floors up in the air, but at least she'll have a view.'

'It will look OK now; in fact, it will seem great. But in a few years it will be completely run down, with graffiti all over the walls, and gangs doing drugs and—'

'Now it's your turn to stop!' Harry says, holding his hand up in front of my face. 'You sound like someone that's been on the drugs, Jo-Jo. How on earth could you know all this?'

I know it because I caught the end of a documentary all about the seventies on TV the other night while I was waiting for a film to start on BBC2.

'I read something about how all these new estates they're building might not be such great things in the future,' I improvise, 'and how the tower blocks will become like prisons for many, especially the elderly and women living alone.'

Harry still stares at me. But it's a different kind of stare now; it's more a fascinated gaze. 'You might be right, I suppose,' he says thoughtfully. 'It's a lot of people to be living in one place.'

'Try and put her off if you can?' I ask him again. 'Just for a while, anyway.'

'Why, what are you going to do?'

'I'm not sure, but I might just have a plan,' I whisper, as the lights in the cinema suddenly dim. 'I'll tell you about it later, after we've enjoyed the film.'

'How do you know you're gonna like it?' Harry whispers back, sending a strange shiver of excitement down my spine as I feel his warm breath on my ear. 'It might be rubbish.'

'Trust me,' I say, sounding like George now. 'We'll like it.'

I do genuinely enjoy watching *Star Wars* again, especially on the big screen. All the stuff about letting 'the force be with you' resonates tonight in a way it's never done before when I've watched it on TV. The audience in the little cinema in Lambeth love it. Although two people behind us do complain at one point that they can't see because of Harry's hair, and an usherette has to come along and move them by torchlight during the film, which is a little embarrassing. But apart from that, all goes well.

Harry's been the perfect date so far; he bought my ticket, provided interesting and thoughtful conversation, and didn't try to grope me once during the movie. In a way I'm a little disappointed – oh, not by the lack of groping, but I'd half expected a yawn halfway through the film, followed by an arm casually draped around my shoulders. In fact, his behaviour wasn't really in keeping with a sixteen-year-old boy at all – really, it would have been much more suited to a man twice his age.

As we stroll back home towards our street, again I wonder about him. To look at he's quite obviously a teenage punk, there's no doubting that. But I can't help feeling there's more to him, that he's hiding something ...

'Jo-Jo,' Harry says, suddenly pausing under a street lamp for a moment and turning towards me. 'We've known each other a fair while now, haven't we?'

'Yes ... ' I reply hesitantly.

Harry takes hold of my hand. 'Since primary school, when I used to steal your Jelly Tots from your lunch box, and later when you used to come round to my house and listen to my Beatles albums on my old box record player.'

The Beatles again! I feel like they're following me.

'And we've always been friends, haven't we? Right through secondary school, and even when you started going through your weird peace-loving phase.'

I'm going through a phase! I think, looking up at Harry's Mohican. But I just nod.

'But lately, Jo-Jo, circumstances have conspired to allow me to appreciate what an attractive person you really are.'

I stare at up him. The words coming from his mouth just aren't matching up with the image that's standing in front of me. Do sixteen-year-old boys really say this sort of thing? Not any I've ever met before.

'You might not have noticed, but I'm usually not that good when it comes to expressing how I truly feel ...'

I don't know, you're doing a pretty good job of it right now!

'But if I don't tell you this now I'm not sure when I'll get the chance again.' Harry looks down at me, and there's something very familiar about the blue eyes that gaze back into mine.

'Harry?' I murmur, not seeing his outer shell of teenage angst for a few seconds, but something much deeper. 'What's going on here?'

Harry leans in towards me, and for a split second I think we might actually kiss this time, but then I hear Stu's raucous voice reverberating down the street.

'Oi, oi! You two again! What you up to this time?'

Harry's head drops forward and his blue spikes brush my face.

'Not now!' he moans under his breath. He drops my hand and turns towards the oncoming gang.

As we're surrounded by denim, leather, chains and spikes of all varieties from coloured ones formed from hair, to silver ones sewn on to clothes, I'm surprised to see tartan in amongst them.

'Ellie, what on earth are you doing with *them*?' I ask, shocked at seeing her little frame tottering along in red patent platforms in the middle of the gang.

'She's with me,' Stu says, grabbing hold of Ellie's hand. 'Aint ya?'

Ellie juts out her chest in defiance. 'Steady, Spike, I only agreed to come out with ya because she was going out with Harry tonight, and it was better than spending the evening at home on me own. Don't think you own me or nothing.'

I expect Stu to go mental, but instead he just grins. 'She's got spirit, this one – I like that in a girl.' He puts his arm around Ellie and turns his attention to Harry. 'Harry,' he says steadily, watching him.

'All right, Stu,' Harry replies equally calmly. 'What's up?'

'Shouldn't I be asking you that?' Stu smirks, looking down at Harry's crotch. 'Been having fun?'

I screw up my face in disdain.

'What's wrong with you, little Miss Perfect?' Stu sneers. 'Never seen a hard-on before? You should be flattered, it's for your benefit.'

Harry suddenly lunges at Stu, and before I know what's happening they're rolling around on the pavement, lashing out at each other with punches, kicks and whatever else they can hurt each other with.

'Stop it!' I cry. 'Stop it, both of you!'

But either they don't hear me, or they choose not respond. I look desperately at the other gang members who stand observing this brawl with much amusement.

'Do something!' I implore them. 'You have to stop them or someone will get hurt.'

'Are you kidding? Most entertainment we've had all week,' one of them says, grinning at me.

'Ellie,' I ask, 'what shall we do?'

'Let them fight it out, Jo-Jo,' she says matter-of-factly.

'Seems like the pair of them have been spoiling for this for a while.'

I look down at the two boys, still trying to beat each other to a pulp on the ground. If it wasn't so serious it would actually look quite funny, because with Harry's blue hair and Stu's green, they resemble two birds of paradise scuffling over seed on the pavement. Stu suddenly does some sort of flipping motion and leaps to his feet where he strikes an attacking pose. 'Jean-Claude Van Damme taught me everything I know,' he jeers at Harry, who's still floored.

'Claude Van who?' Harry asks, slightly winded, as he lifts himself up off the pavement. 'More like Van Gogh!'

Stu releases an almighty roar and tries to launch himself full on into Harry with a series of flying kicks and punches. But Harry manages to dodge most of them, leaving Stu red-faced and breathless.

'Enough now, the pair of you!' I shout. 'This is getting you nowhere.'

'Why should I listen to you, little Miss Gandhi,' Stu snarls, preparing himself for another onslaught. 'What do you know? This is how we sort things here.'

'But it's not how you sort things where *you* come from, is it, Stu?' I ask him before he has time to throw any more punches. 'I know about Jean-Claude Van Damme. I know where he's from, which means I know where you're from too.'

Stu swivels around, and for one awful moment I think he's going to start on me, but he doesn't. His hands drop down from their attacking pose to hang limply by his side, and all his bravado and venom vanishes. He stands like an empty shell on the side of the pavement, his hollow eyes staring at me.

Harry sees his opportunity to strike back. But I position myself between him and Stu.

'No, Harry, you mustn't.'

Harry looks at me in exasperation. 'Jo-Jo?'

'Please?'

Harry sighs and nods his agreement.

'What's up, Stu, lost ya bottle?' one of the other punks jeers.

'Shut up, Knitting Nancy,' Ellie says, putting him and his silver spikes in his place. 'Let Jo-Jo deal with this.'

'I think you should all just let him be,' I suggest quietly. 'I've seen this before,' I improvise. 'He could have concussion if he banged his head in the fight. Stu?' I go over to him. 'Are you OK?'

'How do you know?' Stu whispers. He looks at me with guarded eyes. 'How could you possibly know the truth?'

'Because I'm one of them too,' I whisper. 'Look, come back to my house and we can talk about it.'

Harry comes over.

'What's going on?' he asks. 'Why are you two whispering together? Is there something I should know?' He looks at me questioningly.

'No, Harry, it's nothing. I'm just checking Stu is OK, that's all.'

'Shouldn't you be checking *I'm* OK?' he asks. He puts his hand to his nose, and for the first time I notice it's bleeding.

'Here,' I reach into my bag and pull out a tissue, 'let's all go back to mine and I'll try and sort *both* of you out.'

Thank goodness I decided to take part in that first aid

course we ran last year at the office, I think, as Ellie and I walk the two injured boys back to my house. Although I'm pretty sure it didn't cover how to treat two seventies punk rockers; one for a nosebleed and the other for extreme shock.

Eighteen

When we get back to the house it's quiet. The children would have gone to bed ages ago, and Penny, exhausted as always, wouldn't have been much after.

While Ellie, Harry and Stu make themselves at home in the kitchen, I dash upstairs to find some sort of first aid kit. But all I can find in the bathroom cabinet are some plasters, cotton wool and a bottle of Dettol. That will have to do, I think, shoving the plasters in my pocket and hurrying back downstairs in case Harry and Stu are trying to kill each other again.

But as I arrive back in the kitchen I find all is well, and they're sitting with Ellie, calmly drinking cans of Pepsi together.

'Everything OK?' I ask, looking between the two of them.

'Good as gold,' Ellie says, winking at me.

'Yeah, we're OK,' Harry says. 'Me and Stu never stay angry at each other for long. Do we, Stu?'

Stu, still looking a little pale, nods. 'Nah, life's too short for holding grudges.'

'The boys have just been talking about starting up their band again,' Ellie says. 'I think it's a great idea.'

'That's good,' I say, looking at the pair of them while I dilute some Dettol in a bowl. 'I didn't know the two of you had a band.' Now this was more like the behaviour of teens; one minute they hate each other with a passion, and the next they're best buddies again.

'Yes, you did,' Harry says. 'You and Ellie used to moan about the noise we were making when we were practising in my mum's front room last summer with the windows open.'

'Oh, *that* band. Yes of course, how could I forget?' I exchange a look with Stu. 'Ellie, do you think your mum will have any plasters?' I ask. 'We seem to be out of them.'

'Yeah, probably. Do you want me to go get some?'

'If you could. Harry, would you go with Ellie, please, while I clean Stu up?' I sit down in front of Stu with the cotton wool and the bowl of Dettol.

'But it's just over the road,' Harry moans. 'And she's hardly going to get attacked wearing that, is she,' he gestures at Ellie's scarlet tartan dungarees. 'One look and it would scare them away.'

'As would your hair,' I say. 'So please, go with her, just to keep me happy?' I smile imploringly at him.

'Oh, all right,' Harry says with a shrug of his shoulders. 'Me nose has stopped bleeding now, and I guess Stu's in a worse state than me.'

'Oi!' Stu protests.

'Come on you,' Harry says to Ellie, 'let's go.'

So Ellie and Harry leave us alone in the kitchen.

*

177

'Right, what do you know?' Stu demands as soon as they go.

'Hardly anything,' I reply. 'I just knew, as soon as you mentioned Jean-Claude Van Damme, that you couldn't be from this era. No one knows about him yet, and they're certainly not trying to emulate his kick-boxing moves.'

'But who *are* you?' Stu asks.

'I'm Jo-Jo from 2013. I got hit by a car on a zebra crossing and found myself in 1963, then it happened again on the same zebra crossing and I found myself here in 1977.'

'Whoah!' Stu exclaims, looking impressed. 'I've only ever been here in this decade, nowhere else. I'm really Stuart from 1985 and I used to be roadie for a band. I was backstage, helping out at this huge outdoor gig at Wembley, massive it was at the time, and someone asked me to plug this cable into an amp. Usually I'd always check everything myself, but I didn't on this occasion because it wasn't us setting up the equipment. There was a fault – and boom! Next thing I know I find myself here, acting out life as this damn boy who thinks he's cool and hard cos he's got a daft haircut.'

'God, how awful! How long ago was that?'

Stu thinks. 'About six months ago, I guess. Do you think that's what I need to do, Jo-Jo, get electrified again, then I'll go back? You used the same method to time travel twice, so maybe I need to.'

'I don't know about that.' I'm pretty sure I shouldn't advise someone to try electrocuting themselves. 'I think mine was just a coincidence. Besides, you might just move on to another time zone, like me.'

'True, but it'd be worth a shot – I bloody hate this life I'm in now.'

'Then change it. Who says you have to continue being the anarchic punk, Stu? Be whatever it makes you happy to be.'

'Ya think?'

'Yes. You only get one life. Although in our case that's not strictly true . . . '

Stu grins. 'You know what, I might just do that. You've given me some hope, Jo-Jo. If I do change, maybe I'll get to go back one day.'

'Perhaps . . . '

'You know that dude Harry works for in the record shop? He told me something similar once – about being who I needed to be. I remember thinking at the time he was babbling about nothing. But it's got to be worth a shot.' His grin fades now. 'I'm so lonely living here, Jo-Jo. I miss my friends and family back in 1985 so much.'

I think of Walter Maxwell back at EMI House; that's just what he said to me. All these lonely people living like this in the wrong time zone – it's very sad. But as much as I want to return to 2013, to continue living my life and not someone else's, it isn't because I'm lonely here in 1977, or even that I was lonely in 1963. Quite the opposite, in fact. I've probably been more 'social' during the time I've been travelling than when I was at home. Back there I was always working and, even though I was in a busy office, I spent much of that time alone. But I miss the familiarity of my life; my family, and the few friends I have – however much I might have neglected them.

'Well, it might help,' I tell Stu, trying to sound positive. 'Changing your ways for the better never does any harm.' I hear my mother in my voice as I say this. My *real* mother, that is. Perhaps she did talk some sense on occasion.

'Plasters,' Harry says, throwing a box on the table as he and Ellie appear in the kitchen again. I was so deep in conversation with Stu I didn't even hear the front door. Harry looks at Stu and I sitting close together at the table, Dettol and cotton wool untouched. 'Everything OK?' he asks steadily.

'Yes,' I nod. 'Yes, everything is just fine. I think Stu and I are going to be good friends from now on. He'll be a changed man, after this evening.'

'Really?' Harry says sceptically.

'What ya do to him, Jo-Jo? Hypnotise him?' Ellie asks with a wink. 'Has that Rita been teaching you some of her weirdo ways?'

'Something like that. I've just been passing on some of my knowledge, haven't I, Stu?'

Stu nods.

'They say miracles can happen,' Harry announces. 'Maybe we're seeing one right here in front of us. Perhaps we just have to trust Jo-Jo.' He puts his hand on my shoulder; it feels strong, and oddly comforting.

'Anything is possible, Harry,' I reply, looking up at him. 'Sometimes you just have to believe in the unbelievable.'

Nineteen

'I wish I'd never agreed to organise this street party,' Penny moans as she stands over a long row of trestle tables, trying to sort out what's going where and who's going to be sitting next to who. Every now and then one of the team of neighbours who are helping out with the setting up comes over for further instruction from Penny, or to ask for her approval on whatever task they've just undertaken.

'You're doing a great job,' I reassure her. 'It takes a lot to be able to organise an event like this and motivate all these people successfully. The sort of skills you would need to run a successful business, in fact.'

Penny laughs as she rolls out a long paper tablecloth. 'I hardly think organising a little street party for a few folk is the same as running a big business, now is it, Jo-Jo?'

'You'd be surprised at what skills are required. There are organisational skills, and people skills, and this isn't just a *little* street party. It's a party for nearly a hundred people, with food and drink and entertainment.'

'I only agreed to do it because that Maggie dropped out. What sort of an excuse is her dad passing on up in Manchester, and her havin' to go to the funeral?' Penny looks at me out of the corner of her eye. 'All right, a pretty good one, I guess.'

'It makes no difference how you came to be doing it. The fact is you *are*. And you're doing it very well.'

Penny looks pleased at my praise. 'I just hope Maggie doesn't stay on up there once the funeral's done with, and the will has been read. Otherwise we'll lose another one.'

'Another one?'

'What do you want me to do with these things, Mrs Lane?' Ellie asks, tottering towards us on massive knee-length red platform boots that match her red tartan waistcoat and skirt combination.

'Ah, Ellie, I was wondering where the ribbon was,' Penny says, taking three rolls of red, white and blue ribbon from her and rolling it out along the white cloth. 'Now, if you and Jo-Jo can decorate the tables with it, that would be lovely. I want it to go in bands all along the tables like this.' And she begins to demonstrate.

'Mum, what did you mean, another one?' I remind her.

'Jo-Jo, do we have to discuss this now?' she asks. 'I've so much to do.'

'Yes, Mum – Ellie and I have got this ribbon thing sewn up. Haven't we, Ellie?'

Ellie ceases tying strips of the ribbon in her hair. 'What? Yeah, we'll do it, Mrs L, no worries.'

Penny looks doubtful. 'Yes, Maggie is another one,' she

continues, as I catch hold of some of the red ribbon and begin cutting it with Ellie. 'She's another one like me who is desperately trying to hold on to their house against those sharks at the council who want to take everything from under our feet.'

'So how many of you are there?' I ask. 'Like you and Maggie and Harry's mum?'

'Carol?' Penny looks away from Ellie. 'Does she want to stay as well?'

'Apparently, according to Harry, but she's on the verge of signing her house away too.'

'My mam doesn't want to go either, really,' Ellie pipes up. 'She said she'd much rather stay here where she knows everyone, than go somewhere with a load of strangers.'

'Then we must stop them both from signing anything,' Penny says urgently. 'If there are more of us standing firm against this, the greater the power we have to stand up to the authorities.'

I'm impressed. 'Where did you get that from?' I ask. 'Wait, let me guess: a magazine at the hairdresser's?'

Penny smiles. 'Probably, I don't remember.'

'Why don't you form a syndicate, all of you in the street that don't want to move on to these new flats. Like you said, there's always strength in numbers.'

Penny thinks about this. 'That's not a bad idea. But how will it help? The council will just get their own way, they always do. Money always wins out in the end.'

'Not always, you just need to show them it would be better for them if you all stayed on. At least think about it, Mum, please. I know you're made for more than just the factory. This could lead to something.'

'Yes, lead me into not having this lot ready for this afternoon if I allow you to keep distracting me and I don't get a shift on! Now, all this fancy talk from you is good and fine, but what time is that band of yours getting here? And they better be good.'

Harry and Stu, in their new spirit of friendship, have started up their band again as they said they would, and I persuaded Penny to let them play this afternoon – her only stipulation being that they didn't play any of their hard-core punk songs. This won't be too difficult, because since the night of the cinema fight Stu really has changed. 'Gone soft' is what the other gang members are calling it. Stu is just calling it a 'change of direction' for himself and his music.

'They are good, Mrs Lane,' Ellie calls from down the table. 'I've heard them. They're no Bay City Rollers, mind, but they'll do.'

'Hi!' I call happily, as Stu, Harry and the rest come trooping down the bunting-clad street carrying an assortment of guitars, amps and a drum kit.

'Ya made it then?' I ask as I lead them to the 'stage', an area of the street that's been marked off with blackboard chalk, and they begin setting up their equipment.

'Last-minute dress rehearsal,' Stu says. 'We want everything to go just right.' He winks at me, and I wonder why.

'Jo-Jo, can I have a quick word,' Harry asks, taking my arm and leading me out of earshot of the others.

'Sure, what's up?'

'We haven't spoken that much since the night of the cinema and I just wanted to know if you're angry with me because of what happened with Stu? I know, with your hippy peace stuff, you don't like fighting.'

'No, I don't like physical violence in any form, but I'm not angry with you, Harry. Actually, I thought you might be a bit cross with me.'

'Why?'

'You seemed a bit ... jealous, of me helping Stu out that night.'

'I was a bit,' Harry says, and his pale cheeks flush a little. He looks down at his boots, then he looks back up at me. 'I was trying to tell you the other night: I really like you, Jo-Jo, you must know that by now?'

'I kinda got that feeling.'

'But every time I try and tell you, it just comes out wrong or we get interrupted or—'

'Or what?'

It's very odd, but as I have this very teenage conversation with Harry, I don't see the sixteen-year-old punk with strange blue hair standing in front of me, but the man I'm sure he will become in the future. And I like that vision. I like it a lot.

Harry shakes his head. 'Nothing. It can wait. But I'm not sure this can.' His face leans in towards mine.

Boom!

'What the hell was that?' Harry asks, his face turning away just before our lips meet.

We both look in the direction the noise burst from.

'Sounds like it came from where the band are setting up!'

Harry grabs my hand and we hurry back over to the stage area to find Stu trying to sit up from where he's lying on the ground. He looks shocked and stunned.

'What the hell happened?' Harry asks, looking wildly at the others gawping at Stu on the ground.

'Stu was just plugging his guitar into the amp and it exploded,' one of the other boys replies. 'It shot him right through the air! Bloody hell, Harry, he's lucky he's still alive!'

We all look down at Stu. His face is grey and he looks very pale.

'But I checked all the equipment this morning,' Harry says, shaking his head. He looks around him, baffled. 'It was all fine then. How can this have happened?' He looks down at Stu now. 'I'm really sorry, mate.'

Stu pushes himself up on to his elbows. He looks up at Harry, then across at me. He looks like he's about to cry.

God, he didn't, did he? He didn't try to electrocute himself in the hope he'd go back home?

But the look of desperation on Stu's face tells me that's exactly what he did.

'You're lucky to be alive, Stu,' I say, crouching down next to him, 'let alone still conscious. Have you unplugged the power supply?' I ask the others, my first-aid training kicking into action. The last thing we want is for the current to still be running through Stu, and one of us to touch him.

'The plug was yanked right out of the wall, the force was so great,' one of the other boys says, his eyes wide with shock. 'No chance of any power still coming through there, Jo-Jo.'

'Good.' I look at Stu more closely. 'Are you OK?' I ask him gently.

He nods resignedly.

'Then I suggest you rest here for now. Perhaps we can get one of the neighbours to make you a cup of tea and get you a blanket. And I think we should probably call an ambulance too, just to be on the safe side.'

'No, no ambulance,' Stu says, speaking for the first time. 'Sadly, I'll be just fine.'

'Jo-Jo, none of the equipment is working,' Harry says, examining it. 'The explosion must have blown more than just the fuses in the main amp. We can't play like this, we'll have to call it off.'

'But you can't!'

Penny has put so much into this event. I just can't allow things to go wrong now as it might affect her future, and if good things don't happen for Penny, I might not move on again – hopefully to my own time.

'Hello, boys,' Penny says, walking towards us carrying Bonnie. 'How's it all going? I just popped back to the house to get a few things and we heard this bloody loud bang. I hope everything's OK?'

I look at the boys who have moved in front of Stu on the ground, and then back at Penny.

'Yes, Mum,' I reassure her, leading her and Bonnie away. 'Everything is going to be just fine. Don't you worry; I'll make sure this event runs smoothly. Just as if my life depends on it.'

Twenty

'Are you sure about this?' Harry asks as we dash along the King's Road towards George's shop. 'Will he really lend us records to play this afternoon?'

'Of course he will.' At least, I hope he will, I think, as I hurry along next to Harry, who has the most enormous great lolloping strides. How I miss having a mobile phone at times like this!

When it became clear that Harry and Stu's band were not going to be able to provide the entertainment for the Jubilee celebration, I racked my brains and came up with the idea of us raiding George's shop – with his permission! – and playing pop music on record players.

Penny is putting the word out on the neighbourhood grapevine and hopefully, with some good will from our friends and neighbours, when Harry and I return we will have enough players for music to be heard up and down the street all afternoon.

The traffic's been horrendous trying to get here. Half the streets of London seem to be closed off for the Jubilee parade, and all buses are taking alternative routes. We tried to get the tube, but the stations were packed with tourists waving union jacks and brimming over with Silver Jubilee spirit.

'But won't he be closed for the parade?' Harry says, turning around to speak to me as I try and keep up with him.

'Yes, I think he will, but he lives above the shop so hopefully he should be up there watching the celebrations on TV.'

That word *hopefully* again. I seem to be *living* on hope these days.

Somehow I don't think George will be one of the crowd surging down the Mall to Buckingham Palace to see the Queen on the balcony today. I wouldn't think it's his thing. But then, how well do I actually know this George? I suddenly wonder as my mind begins to race. And did they even do the whole balcony thing in 1977? Or did the people all just stand politely on the parade route waving flags at the Queen as she passed sedately by in her carriage?

Suddenly I'm filled with a pang of longing for my own life, and the year 2012. It only seems like yesterday since I watched the Queen celebrate her Diamond Jubilee. I wonder if anyone realises today just how long she will reign over our country for, and all the changes her family will see in that time.

'You better hope so,' Harry says, still talking about George, 'or you'll be the one singing as entertainment!'

'No, I don't do singing,' I pant breathlessly, finally catching up with him. 'Well, maybe the odd bit of karaoke,' I say, thinking of 1963.

'What's karaoke?'

'You'll find out soon enough. Here we are, then.'

As we suspected, the shop is indeed closed for the bank holiday. So we bang hard on the door and shout up at the window above.

'George! George, we need your help.'

After a minute or so, George appears at the window. 'Jo-Jo, Harry, what can I do for you?'

'Can we borrow some records, George?' I plead, looking up at him desperately. 'It's an emergency. Of sorts.'

George comes downstairs and lets us into his shop, and is more than happy for us to borrow some music for the afternoon.

'On one condition,' he says. 'That I get to come to the party.'

'But how are we going to get all this stuff back over there?' Harry asks as we stand back looking at the boxes of albums and singles we've chosen between the three of us as suitable party songs. 'We can't take it on the tube or the bus, there's too much to carry.'

'I have a car,' George says, to my relief. 'But unfortunately it's a sports car, so it only has two seats, and one of those will need to be filled with boxes because the boot is going to be overflowing as well.'

Look's like it's public transport for us again then.

'Don't worry, George, that's great. We'll help you load it all into the car, then Harry and I will get the bus back.'

We help George pack his little white Triumph Spitfire with all the music and give him directions to our street in Lambeth.

'I'll see you two back at your house, then,' George says. 'I almost forgot, Jo-Jo, you'll be needing these.' He reaches into the passenger footwell of the car and passes me a pair of children's football boots.

'What would I be needing these for?' I ask, holding the boots up by their laces in front of my face. 'I've no time for a kick-about today!'

'They're for Sean, silly. The other night at our evening class your mum mentioned he was missing a pair, and I noticed these in a second-hand shop down the road. I think you'll find they're his size.'

I look at the boots again. And then I look suspiciously at George. 'You go to the same evening classes as Penny?'

George nods casually and jumps into the driver's seat of his car without opening the door. He starts up the engine.

'I'll see you guys in a bit!' he calls as he pulls out from the kerb and moves off down the street.

'But how did you know his size!' I call after him, the boots still dangling from my fingers. 'How did he know his size?' I ask a bemused Harry who is standing by my side.

Harry shrugs. 'Dunno. Come on, though, we've no time to be worrying about that now – we've a party to get to!'

I'm still thinking about George and the boots as we walk, well march, along.

How did he know Sean's size? Penny wouldn't have mentioned that casually in a conversation about her son's boots going missing at school. And more to the point, how come George was taking evening classes at all, especially ones with Penny?

'Come on, Jo-Jo,' Harry urges from the other side of the zebra crossing as I hesitate outside the World's End pub. 'Stop daydreaming or you'll never get back!'

I look at him and shake my head. Yes, he's right. I have to make this party work or Penny might not realise how successful she can be if she tries. Without thinking about it, I step blindly out on to the crossing.

It's in the split second I hear the shriek of a car's tyres, and I see the same white sports car hurtling towards me, that I realise I won't be eating any of the Jubilee jelly that Penny's made, or singing any celebration songs this afternoon with the others . . . as it all goes cold once more.

Can't Buy Me Love

Twenty-One

Slowly I open one eye. There's the sky, that's one thing that never changes, and as always it's bright blue. As I open the other eye and watch the white clouds float slowly by for a few seconds, I realise that, as always, I feel warm too. And now the all-too-familiar stranger's face bending over me, with the usual look of great concern in their eyes, appears in my line of vision. When they see me open *my* eyes the concern changes to relief.

'She's alive!' this one calls. 'Her eyes are open.'

'Thank the Lord for that,' another voice says.

I look up at them both. They don't look too weird this time. The man is wearing jeans, maybe a little on the tight side, though, and at the angle I'm viewing them, a tad short too. The young woman who stands next to him has on ankle-length suede pixie boots, and a short skirt full of ruffles.

Hmm ... I've seen a skirt like that somewhere before. But now is not the time to be thinking about fashion.

'Yes, I'm fine,' I say, sitting up.

'Be careful, you hit that car pretty hard!' the man says. 'Like something from *Dempsey and Makepeace* you were, rolling off that bonnet. Bloody hit-and-run drivers.'

'Never mind TV detectives. Has anyone called the real police?' the girl asks. 'I think there's a phone box down the road.'

So I can't be back in 2013, or at least four people would have pulled iPhones from their pocket, dialled 999, then probably Tweeted photos of my accident by now!

'I have a phone,' a calm voice says from the back of the usual mob that's assembled to see whether I live or die on the zebra crossing.

Through the sea of legs I spy a pair of black leather shoes, so shiny the sun is virtually glinting off them as they walk towards me. My eyes follow the shoes up a charcoal-grey trouser leg, to a white shirt, a red tie, and a face that looks remarkably like Harry's.

'Harry! You're here,' I say with relief.

Harry looks down at me in surprise.

'I'm sorry, young lady, do I know you?' he asks, lifting a huge monstrosity of a phone from his pocket. He pulls the aerial of the phone up and prepares to make his call. The phone looks more like one of those huge two-way radios you see cops in US TV shows using.

'No, stop, I don't need the police calling, or an ambulance or anything. I'm fine, really.' I look up at Harry again. Does he not know me this time? Actually, I hardly recognise him either. He's wearing a sharp charcoal-grey suit and his hair is slicked back with gel. He's much older this time, too. I hazard a guess at thirty, maybe?

'If you're sure,' he says, his dark brow furrowing. He puts his phone back in his jacket pocket, which is a ridiculous place to keep something so big, and holds his hand out. 'Let me help you up, though.'

I take his hand and look him in the eyes as I become level with him, but there's still not a flicker of recognition, and I'm quite disappointed.

Harry lets go of my hand immediately.

'Here, I believe these are yours too,' he says, passing me up a pair of football boots. Why have these come with me again, just like the *Beano* did last time? 'So if you're OK,' Harry continues, as I still stare at the boots hanging in my hand, 'I'll be on my way.' He pulls a black Filofax from his other jacket pocket and begins to walk towards the pavement.

'We're in the eighties!' I suddenly exclaim.

Harry stops and looks up at the sky. 'It is pretty warm today, yes. I'm not sure it's quite eighty degrees though.' He gives me a terse nod, and turns away again to examine the pages of his Filofax.

'Is George still in the record shop down the road?' I call to him. The others are beginning to move away now, to continue with their own business, and I'm aware I'm holding up the traffic by standing in the middle of the zebra crossing. So I wave my hand up at the waiting cars by way of apology, and follow Harry to the pavement.

'What?' he snaps.

'George. Do you know if he owns the record shop down the road – Groovy Records, it used to be called.'

Harry thinks about this for a moment.

'I used to spend a lot of time in that shop when I was

younger,' he says, sounding a little wistful. 'But I have no idea if it's still there now.'

'I'm sure it will be – George's been in that same shop for fifty years.'

Harry's eyes narrow a little as he studies me. 'Are you sure you're OK? That would make George about seventy at least and the last time I saw him he couldn't have been more than forty-something.'

'Yes,' I say hastily, 'I must have got a little confused there. Maybe it *was* the accident ...' And then I do something I never do. I feign weakness in front of a man to get what I want, and I rock a little from side to side.

'Hey, careful!' He holds out his hand to steady me. 'Look, would you like me to walk you there? I think I remember roughly where it is.'

'Would you?' I continue, still in eyelash-fluttering mode. 'That would be very kind.'

'Of course,' Harry says in a matter-of-fact way, as though rescuing damsels in distress is part of his everyday life. 'What sort of gentleman would I be if I didn't?'

Together we walk slowly towards George's shop.

'So, you're sure you're all right after your accident?' Harry asks after a few moments of silence. 'No injuries whatsoever?'

'Yes, perfectly all right. I don't think the car can have hit me that hard.'

'Do you think?' Harry asks in a mocking voice.

'You know what I mean. Maybe I just fainted or something when I saw it coming so close, and it didn't actually touch me?'

'It's possible, I suppose,' he says. But he doesn't look very

198

convinced. 'I didn't actually see the accident. I'd just come out of a shop when I saw all the commotion in the middle of the road, so I wandered over to see if I could be of assistance.'

'Ah, I see. Thanks.'

'Not a problem,' Harry says, not looking at me.

'So why did you stop going to George's shop all those years ago?' I ask, forgetting that Harry and I don't know each other at all this time. The trouble is he seems so familiar to me now, and I feel so comfortable with him, even though he looks so different again. Twice before Harry was wearing a suit when we first met, but he does seem much more formal this time.

'Is it any of your business?' Harry replies abruptly.

'Sorry, I didn't mean to pry.'

As we continue walking together in silence, Harry uneasily adjusts his red tie, and places it back down on his shirt in exactly the same place it was resting before.

'I'm the one who should apologise,' he says at last in a stiff voice. 'I snapped at you, and for that I'm sorry.'

'That's OK, I'm just a bit too nosey for my own good some-times.'

'Yes, indeed,' he agrees. 'Here, is this the place?'

I look up at the shop we've paused outside, and yes, it's Groovy Records. It never seems to change that much: except for the window displays and the music on sale inside, the shop always looks as if it's just jumped from one time zone to another. A bit like me I guess – the heart of us both remains the same whatever year we're in, it's just external influences that change the way we appear to others.

Talking of which, I take a look at my reflection in the window. *Oh my days, what do I look like?* I'm wearing a turquoise green jumpsuit with huge shoulder pads, purple wool leg warmers, and, like the woman at the crossing, tiny ankle-length pixie boots. But where hers were black leather, mine are purple suede. And my hair – it's just so *big*! It's cut in a long bob to my shoulders, but it's blow-dried to within an inch of its life to enable it to permanently flick back at the sides.

'Bloody hell, I look like Krystle Carrington,' I exclaim. I had a flatmate once who was obsessed with the TV show *Dynasty*, and watched all the re-runs on one of the cable channels constantly. Actually, he was obsessed with *everything* eighties and I was glad when he moved out to live with his boyfriend – Wham, Bananarama and Culture Club on repeat twenty-four hours a day was not good for my mental health.

There's a chuckle next to me.

'Sorry,' Harry says, trying not to smirk. 'But I think I'd know if I was standing next to Linda Evans right now. And you,' he says, looking down at my jumpsuit, 'are definitely not her.'

'Are you coming in?' I ask tersely. I'm not warming to this version of Harry much. I'm trying to, really I am. It's Harry, and I've got used to him being around me over the last couple of decades and I kind of like it now. But this version of him ... he's beginning to be quite irritating.

Harry hesitates and looks up at the shop front. 'I guess it couldn't hurt.'

I push open the door and, as always, the bell rings above my head.

'George, are you there?' I call.

'Well, hello again, Jo-Jo,' George says, appearing from the back of the shop. 'I wondered when you'd be back. And you've brought a friend, this time.'

George is wearing a loose-fitting pale grey suit, and a baby pink T-shirt. He has the sleeves of the jacket rolled up to his elbows so you can see the lining, and a pair of sunglasses protrudes casually from his top pocket. On his feet are strange white cotton slip-on shoes with hessian fabric soles. Are those what they call espadrilles? I wonder, trying not to laugh at this *Miami Vice*-inspired vision that stands before me.

I know all about the American TV programme *Miami Vice* from my flatmate's obsession. He used to wear something similar to what George is in now when he went to his eighties theme nights. He thought he looked just like Don Johnson, one of the lead actors in that show, which I guess he did a bit, until he got his moped and put on his bright pink crash helmet, then the effect was somewhat lost.

'Good afternoon, George,' Harry says uneasily from behind me. 'It's – it's good to see you again.'

'Well, well, if it isn't Harry Rigby,' George says, without a hint of awkwardness. 'I didn't think I'd see you in here again. How have you been?'

'I'm well thank you, George, and yourself?'

'Never better. So what brings you back?'

Harry looks at me. 'Just giving this lady directions. She wasn't sure where your shop was. Perhaps you should make her one of your infamous cups of tea though, she had a bit of a shock earlier.'

'I'll do just that. Will you stay for one too?' George asks hopefully.

'I won't, no. But thank you,' Harry adds when George looks disappointed. 'Perhaps another time – I have some urgent appointments to get to.' He goes to leave the shop but pauses for a moment and picks up a record. '*Sergeant Pepper*?' he asks, looking back at George. 'An original?'

'Hardly! Do you know how much one of those things is worth these days?'

'Always worth a shot.' Harry smiles briefly at George.

'Indeed,' George agrees.

Harry turns to me. 'Goodbye, it was nice meeting you.'

'Yes, likewise, I hope we meet again.'

Harry looks surprised at this. 'Perhaps we shall. You never know.' He inclines his head towards George. 'It was good to see you again.'

George nods and watches as Harry leaves the shop, closing the door behind him.

'I'm back again!' I announce, without formalities this time. 'Why am I, George? And why doesn't Harry know me this time? It's weird.'

'Tea,' George simply says. 'We need tea.'

Twenty-Two

I sip from George's *Choose Life* mug and listen to the clock behind the counter tick steadily on.

'So, what's the story this time, George?' I ask as we sit on the wooden chairs once more.

George shrugs. 'Your guess is as good as mine, Jo-Jo.'

I roll my eyes. *Great.*

'It can't be like the other times; Harry doesn't know who I am. *I* don't know who I am, even, where I live, or what I do.' I'm panic-stricken for a moment. This is what it must feel like to wake up from a coma and have lost your memory. Except at least you normally wake up in the same decade. And if you've been unconscious so long it's not the same decade when you awake, at least time has moved forward, not back.

'Just relax, Jo-Jo,' George says calmly.

'I know we're in the eighties, George. But I think I

preferred it when you quoted the Beatles, not Frankie Goes to Hollywood.'

George smiles at my attempt at a joke. 'What do you have there?' he asks, noticing the football boots lying on the floor beside me.

'Those! Ah yes, I forgot to tell you last time so much else was going on, but I travelled from the sixties to the seventies with a *Beano* comic too.' I open up the huge clutch bag that I was passed after the accident and, as I suspected, there's the *Beano* tucked away inside. 'Why would I bring it with me again, and why the boots too, this time?'

George examines the comic, and then the football boots. 'Who gave them to you?' he asks.

'You did! The boots, anyway. The comic I picked up off the crossing just before I got hit in 1963.'

'When did I give you the boots?'

'Just before you left for the Silver Jubilee street party in your car.'

'And what happened after?'

'Harry and I had to walk back because you only had a two-seater sports car— look, don't you remember any of this?'

George shakes his head. 'It's hazy.'

'I don't remember anything else because then I got hit by the white car and bam! woke up here in – what year *are* we in, by the way? I'm guessing it's the eighties because of the horrendous fashions and the big phones.'

'1985,' George says, still thinking. 'So you always get given these items just before you get hit by the car?'

'Yes, it would appear so.' But I'm thinking now too. '1985,

you say? That means there's a little me running around the place somewhere. I was born in 1983.'

'Maybe, on another page,' George reminds me.

'What do you mean?'

'The missing page we talked about last time? All these new lives you keep finding yourself in, they're like pages from different stories, but they're being bound together right now into one new book. Some of the characters are the same – they just don't always fit in with the way we want the story to be.'

I look at George for a few seconds, then I shake my head.

'One,' I point out, 'last time you said it was a page of figures I'd lost from an accountancy book, and this time you're saying it's a novel. And two, how come you remember telling me that, but you don't remember giving me the boots?'

'Ah, my memory isn't what it used to be,' George says, rubbing at his forehead.

'George,' I growl, 'you can't keep doing this!' I'm about to press him further when the shop door flies open, and in bursts a whirlwind of lace, net skirts, beads and bangles. Topping it all off is a big floppy black bow holding back a mass of blonde curls. And underneath it all is Ellie.

'There you are, Jo-Jo,' she pants. 'You'll never guess who I just saw walking up the road, only Neil bloody Tennant!'

I stare at her blankly. For two reasons; one, I can't place the name Neil Tennant. It seems familiar, but nothing is instantly springing to mind, and two, I'm trying desperately to think who Ellie reminds me of.

'Madonna!' I suddenly exclaim.

'Where?' Ellie says, darting to the window. She pulls a

camera from her bag as she does so. 'She's not in the country, is she? Bloody hell, I thought the Neil Tennant spot was good.'

'No, I mean you look like Madonna. Your outfit does.'

Ellie turns away from the window. 'Oh,' she says, sounding disappointed. 'I mean thanks 'n' all. But getting a shot of Her Greatness would have been terrific to go back into the office with tomorrow morning. Still, Neil Tennant's not bad, although both the Pet Shop Boys together out on the King's Road would have been better, but no one ever knows what the other fella looks like, do they?'

Ah, that's why I knew the name.

'He's often in here,' George says, 'that Neil Tennant. Nice fella; I think he has a flat along here somewhere.'

But Ellie's lost interest already. 'So, do you have anything we can hand in?' she demands, looking at me. '*Any* juicy gossip?'

'Er . . .'

'I thought not. We'll have to dream something up if we don't find a story before our deadline.' She sighs impatiently. 'What have you been doing all afternoon anyway?'

'She got hit by a car,' George says. 'Give her a break.'

'What!' Ellie cries, rushing over. 'Are you OK? What happened?'

'It's nothing. I don't actually think it hit me anyway. It's possible I just fainted in the road.'

'How did you get here, then?' Ellie asks.

'A guy called Harry brought me. Didn't he, George?'

George nods.

'Ah, OK,' Ellie says, accepting this. 'Wait! You don't mean that bastard Harry Rigby, do you? I just bumped into him outside Peter Jones and he nearly bit my head off, and I don't mean verbally.'

'Yes, that was him,' I say quietly. 'Why, what's wrong with Harry? He seemed OK to me.'

'Jo-Jo McKenzie, have you lost your mind? You *must* have been hit by that car. Harry Rigby is the biggest pain in the ass since that curry house down the road had an epidemic of food poisoning!'

'Nice analogy,' I say, screwing up my face. 'But why have you got a problem with Harry?'

Ellie shakes her head. 'George, tell her.'

George opens his mouth to speak but Ellie continues. 'Actually, no, I'll tell you, otherwise George will only soft-soap it. He has a tendency to see the best in everyone, don't you, George?'

'You say that like it's a bad thing, Ellie,' George says, dis-approvingly, as if he's scolding a small child.

Ellie raises her blonde eyebrows at him. 'I like to remain sceptical about folk, that's all. Comes with the territory.' She raises her camera. 'That's why I wouldn't trust that Harry Rigby as far as his red braces would fire him.'

Of course, Harry is a yuppie! I didn't realise it before. He's a 'young upwardly mobile professional person' – a very common expression in the eighties.

'But what's he done?' I ask again. 'You still haven't told me.'

Ellie glances at George. He nods.

'Harry owns a music distribution company – you know, the people that send the tapes and discs out to the music stores from the record companies?'

I nod at her. I think I know what she means.

'Harry decided about a year ago that George here wasn't worth supplying to. This little shop we're standing in now wasn't worthy to sell the crappy music that Harry's company provides. Isn't that right, George?'

'It's not quite that simple, Ellie—' George begins, but Ellie hushes him.

'Yes it is, George. Don't you go defending him now.'

'I wasn't going to. I was simply going to explain the facts for Jo-Jo's benefit.'

Ellie folds her arms huffily. 'Go on then. But don't go easy on the bastard.'

'Ellie!' George raises his eyebrows, which I notice are just starting to fleck with the odd grey hair.

'Well, what would you call him, then? Shifty, no good, son of a—'

'Enough now,' George says sternly. 'Jo-Jo's only been here five minutes; let her make up her own mind.'

I stare hard at George. *Yes, but Ellie doesn't know that, does she?*

'Fair dos, George,' Ellie says, shrugging. 'I guess she's new to the area 'n' all. I should probably let her find her own way.'

So I'm new around here?

'But I have to tell you, working as a journo in the big smoke is a bit different than out in the middle of nowhere.'

'Ellie, I hardly think Norfolk is the middle of nowhere,' George says reprovingly.

'As good as. I come from Liverpool and moving to London was a big enough shock to my system when I did it. God knows how Jo-Jo is coping.'

They both look at me.

'I'm doing all right,' is all I can think to reply.

'Well, I gotta go!' Ellie suddenly announces. 'I got a hot date tonight with a dancer.' She winks at us. 'And they're usually very agile!'

'Indeed,' George replies. 'Don't let us keep you. I'm sure you have lots of preparations to make for your night out.'

'What preparations?' Ellie asks, looking concerned. 'I'm going like this.'

'Oh,' George says. He looks at me and pulls a face. 'I see.'

'Maybe you should tone down the Madonna stuff just a tad for the date?' I suggest. 'Is it your first with him?'

Ellie nods.

'Definitely, then.'

Ellie looks down at her clothes. 'Yikes, I really had better go then if I need to magic myself into Lady Di in an hour. See you guys tomorrow. I'll pick you up on the way as always, Jo-Jo.'

'Sure.' I manage a smile, but I still haven't found out where I live and with whom this time. 'That'd be great.'

And with the bell tinkling above her head she's gone.

'But pick me up from where?' I ask George now Ellie has left us alone once more. 'Where do I live in 1985?'

'You live here, Jo-Jo,' George says. 'With me.'

Twenty-Three

I don't exactly *live* with George. But I do live in the flat above his shop. Apparently just before the housing boom of the mid-eighties George bought property and now owns a couple of little houses down the road in Chelsea; one he rents out, and the other he lives in himself. So his flat, which he lived in for twenty years, is also rented – by me.

George shows me upstairs and makes me familiar with everything. Which makes a change: usually I have to guess my way around my new surroundings.

'Will you be OK now?' he asks when he's shown me around. 'Only I have to get back. I have a little dog now – she usually comes to the shop with me, but she's expecting puppies any day so I've left her at home, and my neighbour is keeping an eye on her.'

'Of course it is,' I reassure him, 'I'll be fine. Compared to some of them, this time seems easy.' I think for a moment.

'What is it?' George asks.

'It's easy except for Harry. I don't like this nasty streak you're all suggesting he has.'

'I'm not suggesting anything, Jo-Jo, it was Ellie that said those things, not me.'

'But what he did to your shop?'

George shrugs. 'It's in the past. I cope, and the majority of the big labels still supply to me. Just not the ones Harry handles.'

'Hmm,' I say.

'Hmm, what?'

'Nothing, just thinking ...'

'Plotting, more like, if I know you. Seriously, Jo-Jo, just leave it. Really, it's old news now. Ha ha, get it? Old news?'

I don't. I look at George with a puzzled expression. Then I do get it. 'Because this time I'm a journalist? Ah yes, very good.'

'I'll obviously have to work on my comedic skills,' George grins. 'Right, I'm off to see how Dakota is doing. I'll be back in tomorrow bright and early to see how you're getting on. You'll be OK, yes?'

'Of course. Like I said just now, this is easy compared to the last two times. I'm on my own, no family or flatmate to try and convince I'm from their time. What happened to them?' I ask, suddenly remembering. 'The people from the seventies, what happened to Penny and Harry and Stu?'

'Ah,' George says mysteriously. 'I wondered when you'd get around to that. Let's see ... Harry and his mother made up their differences and they continued to live together, until Harry left home and went to university.'

'How'd he do that?'

211

'Harry actually did quite well at school; it was only when he got into the wrong crowd that he started to go off the rails. He went back to college, did A-levels, then went on to do a business degree in Liverpool.'

'Gosh, he really did change when I left.'

'Your influence put him back on course again.'

'It did?'

George nods as if it was never in doubt.

'Is that why I was there, do you think – for Harry?'

'Not just Harry. Penny changed too. She formed an alliance with her other neighbours who didn't want to move out to the new estate. They managed to take on the council and keep their houses, which the council had wanted to sell to a developer who would have knocked them down and built blocks of upmarket flats instead. Funnily enough, Penny ended up forming her own property company, acquiring properties that she could lease at a sum that was competitive with council rents and still make her a profit while providing decent accommodation. She was very successful at it too.'

'I knew it!' I exclaim, punching the air. 'I knew she could do it. Wow, I really am making a difference, George. Maybe this is what my travelling is all about, putting people back on course for a better life. And what about Stu?' I ask, looking keenly at him.

'Ah . . .'

'Ah what?' I don't like George's tone. His expression has changed too.

'Sadly, Stu passed away a couple of years after you left.'

'No!' I gasp in horror, my hand shooting up to my mouth. 'Did he try and electrocute himself again?'

'Many times, I'm afraid. So many that he was institution-alised for his own safety. He passed away inside the hospital.'

I feel my legs wobble, so I put my hand out to the first thing I find to steady myself; it's the arm of the settee so I sit down on it.

'Poor Stu! Was that my fault?'

'Did you tell him to try to electrocute himself again?'

'No, but I told him that every time I travelled in time it was always the same way as I'd got here in the first place. It's the zebra crossing for me, isn't it?'

George sighs. 'Like I said before, you need to be careful what you say and do, Jo-Jo. You know so much in some respects, and yet so little in others.'

I nod sadly, then suddenly I have a thought, 'Wait! How do we know he didn't jump back to his own future again from the hospital? He might have done, he might have—'

'No,' George says, stopping me; he holds his hand up in front of my face to supress my sudden rush of optimism. 'No, he didn't, Jo-Jo. He died of an overdose. It was the end for him, that day. And I mean *the end*.'

There's silence in the little flat above George's shop as we both contemplate what this means.

'That could happen to me, couldn't it?' I say, voicing what I know George is thinking.

'Not necessarily, every case is different.'

'What do you mean, "every case"? These people are just like me, George, stuck in times they're not supposed to be in, desperately wanting to return home again.'

'You're not stuck in one time though, are you?' George points out. 'You keep moving.'

213

'Yes, that's true I suppose, I do. Why is that, do you think?'

George studies my face for a few seconds, then he sits down next to me on the settee and takes a deep breath.

'Do you think you have control issues?' he asks.

'What?'

'Control issues. Do you need to feel in control of your life at all times to feel happy?'

Even though I know the answer to this, I try and act ambivalent.

'Possibly. But who likes to feel out of control? To not know what's happening next, or who's going to be doing what and when? That would just make you feel as if you had no foundation in life. Everyone needs a firm base to function from.'

George nods in that knowing way he has.

'What? What now?'

'You mentioned once before that your parents travelled a lot when you were younger.'

'Yes – and so?'

'Did that make you feel out of control at all? As if you didn't have that firm base on which to function from?'

I think about this. Yes, it was true; I didn't always appreciate us moving from country to country all the time. I'd just feel settled in one place, make a friend if I was lucky, and then we'd move again. But I really didn't see what that had to do with ...

I look at George. 'Are you saying this is why I'm time travelling? That it works like some sort of aversion therapy for a childhood of constant house moves?'

'I think it might go a bit deeper than that, Jo-Jo,' George says, re-rolling his jacket sleeve up. 'But I do think we're beginning to make some progress down the *why* road at last. Now, I really do have to go and check on Dakota. We'll continue this next time.'

I feel like George has just ended a session of counselling with me.

'You have a peaceful evening,' he says, taking the pair of sunglasses from his pocket and balancing them at a jaunty angle on his nose. He bids me farewell, 'And I'll be back in the morning.' He heads off down the stairs that lead past the shop and out on to the King's Road. I hear the front door shut behind him, and the engine of a sports car roar as it races off down the road, and I wonder if he still has his little white car from the seventies.

Could this really be why I'm travelling through time? To cleanse myself of some childhood trauma I'm still suffering from because my parents took us travelling around the world when I was growing up? There must be more to it than that. Surely?

I shake my head. 'I'll need real therapy to get over all this when I'm finished,' I say aloud, taking another look around my new home. 'But for now I'm just going to have to roll with it again. So, just what sort of person am I in this decade? And what will I need to do to move on this time?'

It appears, after a thorough investigation of the flat, that this time I'm a fairly normal young woman of the eighties. Yes, I seem to have many bright, flamboyant – sometimes bordering on weird – clothes filling my wardrobe, but from what I know of the fashion of the time, they're probably quite tame. There's lots of shoulder pads in my tops and jackets, a few

215

pairs of leg warmers in my sock drawer, some nasty stone-washed jeans in my wardrobe – some oversized and baggy, and some skintight. But it's only when I come across the pink puff-ball skirt that I let out a gasp of horror.

'No way, Jo-Jo!' I promise myself. 'If there's one thing I can guarantee while I'm here, this version of you definitely won't be wearing that monstrosity!'

My taste in music seems to be quite varied. On my shelf of cassette tapes I have some pure pop: Duran Duran, Wham, and Madonna – Ellie would be proud – mixed with Rock Gods Bruce Springsteen, U2 and Simple Minds. I'm just about to put one of the cassette tapes into the player in the kitchen when a phone rings somewhere. Now where did I see it? Yes, in the little hallway at the top of the stairs. The little phone ringing merrily on the hall table is red, with push buttons. At least we've moved on from the old-fashioned Trimphone that Penny owned in 1977. I watched her dialling on it a number of times, and wondered how anyone had the inclination to actually speak by the time they eventually got through, after turning the dial ninety degrees after each digit.

'Hello?' I say hesitantly into the receiver.

'Jo-Jo!' the spritely voice sings. 'It's me. Make sure your ass is looking good and down at the bottom of your stairs in fifteen minutes sharp! We've got a story – I'm picking you up!'

'But I thought you had a date tonight, Ellie? With a hot dancer?'

'Sod the dancer! This is an even hotter story, and me and you are gonna get the scoop!'

216

Twenty-Four

I quickly freshen up, wondering just what sort of a story Ellie has for us, and also, what she's picking me up in. I'm assuming a car, but what sort? Knowing Ellie it will be something small, zippy and immensely colourful.

Waiting on the pavement downstairs, I watch all the people passing by, most of them on their way home from work at this time of the evening. The eighties really weren't the best for fashion, I decide, looking at the mixed appearances as they walk by along the street. The hair, the make-up (on both sexes now!) and the clothes add up to a strange mix. It's as if people are undefined about who they are in this time of change for the country. Androgynously dressed individuals walk along next to men defined by their sharp suits and power-dressing women defined by the size of their shoulder pads and hair, where big always appears to be better.

'Yo, Jo-Jo!' Ellie shouts, screeching to a halt.

I'd expected many things, but Ellie on a motorbike wasn't

one of them. 'Here,' she calls, holding out a helmet. 'Shove it on quick, we gotta dash.'

I pull on the red helmet, and climb on to the purple and silver motorbike behind Ellie, glad I've changed into a black jumpsuit with a thin red belt and matching heels and shoulder bag, rather than the white and gold dress I was eyeing up in my wardrobe a few minutes previously.

'Where are we going?' I shout, grabbing hold of her and holding on for dear life as she pulls out into the traffic.

'A private bar in Soho. Tip-off. They reckon Phil Collins is gonna meet Bob Geldolf and Midge Ure there to talk about Live Aid.'

Right, it's 1985, so Live Aid was this summer. The music industry would be buzzing with gossip about who was going to appear at the concert, and what they were going to sing.

'Yeah, Phil Collins performs in both London *and* Philadelphia on the day,' I reply without thinking. 'He gets Concorde over during the concert.'

'What did you say?' Ellie shouts over the noise of the traffic as we whizz along the street. 'Couldn't quite catch it, something about Concorde?'

'Doesn't matter,' I call back, relieved. 'Tell you another time.'

We arrive at the Karma club in Soho, whip off our helmets and try and shake out our hair in that glamorous way they do in movies. It doesn't work, so we quickly pull out hairbrushes to rectify our helmet hair.

'Where do we have to go?' I ask as we dash down some steps and in through a doorway to a darkened club.

A large burly chap with a bushy, overgrown moustache

suddenly appears to block our way. 'Can I help you, ladies?' he enquires.

'We'd like to get into the club, please,' I ask politely.

'Are you members?' he growls.

I look helplessly at Ellie.

'Is Ringo here?' she demands.

The man looks suspiciously at her. 'He might be. Why, who are you?'

'Just tell him Ellie is here.'

'Ringo is busy.'

'Look, Boyd,' Ellie says, her eyes darting towards the bouncer's name embroidered in purple on his suit lapel, 'we're not going anywhere until you've spoken to Ringo, so you may as well just take your pet rat there,' she gestures to his moustache, 'and go tell him right now. It will save us all a lot of bother in the long run.' Ellie thrusts her hands on her hips, and all five foot of her is suddenly a mighty force I wouldn't want to mess with, and by the look of Boyd he feels the same.

'All right,' Boyd grumbles under his moustache. 'I'll see what he's got to say about it.'

'Who's Ringo?' I ask as we stand in the foyer waiting.

'The owner. I know him from old because he used to be mates with me dad up in Liverpool.'

'Ellie, it's not *the* Ringo, is it? As in Starr?' This really would be taking my Beatles suspicions to the extreme.

Ellie laughs. 'Course not! Ringo is his nickname. The lads round here called him that when he first came in the sixties because of his accent, and I guess it stuck. I don't know what his real name is, actually.'

'Ellie, love!' A large bald man with a hairy chest appears

from the depths of the club. 'It's great to see you again, but what you doing standing there on the doorstep? Come on in!'

Ellie tosses her hair at Boyd, who has now reappeared at the door, and marches through.

'Thank you,' I say to him as I pass. 'We appreciate it.'

He nods at me, and his moustache gives an approving wiggle.

'What can I do for you two girls?' Ringo asks us, looking me up and down appraisingly with a pair of jet black eyes. 'Have we met before?'

'No, Jo-Jo is new to the newspaper, she's just moved here from Norwich.'

'Ah, country girl, eh?' Ringo says, showing a shark-like set of teeth when he smiles.

'Norwich is hardly country,' I begin, but Ellie interrupts.

'Ringo, have you got Bob Geldof in here tonight?' she demands.

'Ellie, you know I can't divulge information about my private clientele,' Ringo says, raising a bushy black eyebrow at her.

'What about Phil Collins, then, or Midge Ure? Please, Ringo, it's important.'

Ringo looks over his shoulder, from side to side, then leans in towards us. 'Ellie, I would be absolutely delighted to entertain all the aforementioned parties in my establishment. But I'm afraid that sadly, no, I do not.'

Ellie bangs her fist into her other hand. 'Damn!'

'Have you been thrown what my American clients would call a curve ball, by any chance?'

'Spun a pack of bloody lies, more like, to put me off the proper scent! Getting any scoops on anything to do with Live

Aid is like trying to break through the Berlin Wall. It just ain't gonna happen.'

'Never say never, Ellie,' I suggest knowingly. 'You just never know what's going to happen in the future.'

'I know what will happen in my future if we don't get some decent celebrity scoops soon – I'll be out of a job.'

'Aw, I'm sure that's not the case,' Ringo says kindly. 'Look, why don't the two of you stay, now you're here – we've got some entertainment on this evening you might enjoy.'

Ellie, still sulking, makes a sort of humphing sound.

'What sort of entertainment?' I ask.

'A cabaret – of sorts. Stay, please, my treat,' he insists.

'Free drinks?' Ellie asks brightening.

'*One* free drink,' Ringo says wisely. 'Or I'll have your father to answer to.'

'Deal!' Ellie sings, already taking her jacket off.

We follow Ringo into the club proper, and I find myself inside what seems like, from what little I know of them, a swanky-looking gentlemen's club. It has a mostly black interior, with the odd dash of purple here and there on things like the plush velvet seat covers, and the luxurious black and purple flocked wallpaper.

'Here we go, ladies,' Ringo says, showing us to a small booth tucked away in the corner of the club. 'I'll send Lucy over in a moment and she'll take care of you this evening.'

'Thanks, Ringo,' Ellie says, 'we really appreciate it. This is *cool*,' she whistles, turning to me as Ringo wanders across to another table to talk to one of his customers. She snuggles down on the velvet settee. 'I bet I can get more than one free drink out of Ringo if I sweet talk him, too.'

221

I look round the club at our fellow drinkers. They're mostly older men in dinner jackets drinking spirits and smoking a mixture of cigarettes and cigars, either surrounded by similar-looking men, or accompanied by their trophy wives and girlfriends, who all look bored stiff by their company.

'Good evening,' our waitress says as she arrives at our table. 'What can I get for you ladies tonight?'

I look up at the young girl who has come to take our order. She's in her late teens, I'd guess, but it's hard to tell because she's wearing so much make-up. She has black, bobbed hair and is wearing a very low-cut, short black dress, with black high heels and a tiny purple apron.

'I'll have a peach schnapps, please,' Ellie says. 'Jo-Jo?'

Here we go, what did they drink in the eighties?

'A glass of wine would be lovely,' I venture, thinking I'll be on safe territory with that.

'Red or white, miss?'

'Red?'

'Beaujolais Nouveau, miss?'

Of course, the classic wine of the eighties. 'Yes, that would be lovely, thank you – Lucy, isn't it?'

'That's right, miss.' Lucy lifts her heavily made-up eyes to look at me properly for the first time. 'I'll be back in a few minutes with your order.'

Lucy disappears to fetch our drinks.

'Bit sleazy this place, isn't it?' I whisper.

'Nah, these types of places are just like that, aren't they?' Ellie says, fiddling with one of the black plastic coasters. 'Ringo's above board 'n' all that. Me dad knew him for years.'

'Ah, all right then,' I say, but I'm not too sure. There's something not quite right about the place.

Lucy quickly returns with our drinks. 'Here we are, a peach schnapps,' she says, placing a glass down in front of Ellie, 'and a large glass of the Nouveau for you,' she continues, smiling at me. 'Just give me a call when you're ready for a top-up. I know Ringo said just the one free drink, but I'm sure he won't notice – we're pretty busy in here tonight.' She winks at us. Loud, raucous laughter suddenly spills over from a large group of men filling two tables at the far side of the club. Lucy leans in towards us. 'Just between the three of us, they're a huge pain in my arse tonight,' she says, looking over in their direction. 'But I gotta make them think they're the bee's knees, that's the job!'

'Waitress!' we hear bellowed across the room. 'More drinks over here, now!'

Lucy rolls a pair of very pretty brown eyes underneath her heavy black fringe. 'Back in a bit,' she says.

Ellie starts downing her peach schnapps far too quickly, while I sip cautiously at my wine.

'Great this, innit?' Ellie says, helping herself from a bowl of peanuts sitting on the table. 'I wonder what time the entertainment comes on?'

'Do you know how many germs there are in a bowl of peanuts like that?' I ask her, looking with disdain at the free snacks.

'What?' Ellie asks, still munching.

'They've done tests on bowls like that in bars like this, and found more germs on them than on the inside of a toilet. It's when people go to the loo and then don't wash their—'

'OK, OK!' Ellie says, spitting out the peanuts into the napkin her drink was served on. 'When did you become Dr Death? I've never heard that one before.'

'I think I only read it myself quite recently,' I say truthfully.

'It's disgusting! Who would have thought an innocent peanut could do all that harm?'

'Indeed, but I believe it's true. Look,' I say, pointing to a small stage in the corner of the club, 'apparently our entertainment is about to begin.'

We both look towards the stage and see Ringo standing under a small spotlight with a microphone in his hand.

'Gentlemen and Ladies,' he says, smiling at the few women in the bar in that leery way he has about him. 'I would like to welcome to the Karma club this evening a new act that I'm sure you're going to enjoy. They're a bit shy,' he winks purposefully, 'so please give them a very warm welcome. I give you – Strawberry Fields.'

While the stage lights dim and Ringo exits, I roll my eyes. *Bloody Beatles, here they are again.* When the lights come up there are five women with their backs to us now on the stage. I can already see they're not wearing an awful lot. But what little fabric does cover them is fashioned into a black silk corset with a single strawberry stitched pertinently in the centre of each of their pert little behinds. As they swivel around on their high heels and begin to gyrate to the music that pounds through the club's speaker system, I see they have two more matching strawberries placed very prominently on each breast.

I turn to Ellie whose eyes are wide open.

'See,' I hiss. 'I told you this place was sleazy.'

'Bloody hell, I didn't know Ringo had strippers here.'

'They're not stripping . . . yet,' I point out, giving them the benefit of the doubt. 'Maybe they just dance?'

But no, within a couple of minutes, long black gloves are being removed in unison, and then somehow corset tops manage to disappear, while strawberries remain intact, and soon the same thing happens with their lower strawberries too. I would actually be quite impressed by the complexity of it all, if I weren't too busy being appalled.

Eventually they reach the end of their – even I have to admit – quite artistic routine, and disappear, strawberry-less, into the darkness with only their heels still on.

Enthusiastic cheers break out around the club and Ringo appears back on the stage.

'Thank you! Thank you!' he calls, taking the plaudits of the crowd as though he had performed himself. 'I know the girls are thrilled at your appreciation. My girls are a very talented bunch as you've just seen, but their individual talents extend far beyond dancing . . . ' He raises his black bushy eyebrows suggestively. 'If you'd like to find out anything further about any of them then please don't hesitate to contact me and I will be happy to set up a private meeting for you backstage. But for now, enjoy your evening, gentlemen.'

'What did he just say?' I turn to Ellie, who's nearly emptied her glass of peach schnapps already.

'Something about meeting the girls backstage, but why would you want their autographs? They're hardly famous, are they?'

I continue to stare hard at Ellie.

'Oh!' she says as the penny begins to drop. 'You don't think . . . '

225

'I damn well do think!'

'... Ringo's running a knocking shop?' she asks, her green eyes wide.

'I wouldn't have put it quite like that. But yes, a call girl service maybe, that kind of thing.'

Ellie screws up her face. 'Disgusting.'

'More drinks, ladies?' Lucy asks, arriving at our table again.

Ellie and I look at each other.

'It's on the house,' Lucy adds. 'Officially like. Ringo just said.'

'Definitely then,' I say, smiling at her. 'I think we'll make it champagne this time, if Ringo is paying.'

'Nice one,' Lucy grins. 'I'll make sure I find you a bottle of the good stuff!'

'What'd you do that for?' Ellie asks after Lucy has gone. 'I'd have thought you'd have wanted to be well shot of here if that sort of thing is going on.'

'If Ringo *is* running that kind of game, Ellie, he'll be making an absolute mint, so I think we should sting him for all we can. He deserves it. Besides,' I say taking a sideways glance at Lucy at the bar, 'there are a few things in here I'd like to investigate a little bit further.'

Twenty-Five

The evening continues to flow, as do the drinks to our table. After our bottle of very fine champagne, Ellie's now moved on to Malibu and Coke, which seem to keep appearing just as Ellie empties the last drop from her previous glass.

'Steady on,' I warn her at one stage, 'I don't want to have to carry you home tonight.'

'Ah, I'm fine,' she says, waving her hand casually in my face. 'You just stick with ya boring old wine, and leave the exciting stuff to me.'

Lucy waited on us brilliantly all evening, and when sensible conversation with Ellie started to become nigh on impossible, I managed to have a few quick chats with Lucy in between rounds. She seemed like a bright, intelligent girl, and I couldn't quite figure out why she was working in a place like this.

'How do you put up with this, night after night?' I ask her, after I've witnessed a particularly bad bout of her trying to avoid her bum being pinched, and having her chest constantly ogled. Just watching it from a distance is bad enough.

She shrugs. 'Beats being stuck at home on my own, I guess.'

'Don't you have any friends?' I ask. 'Any family?'

'Not really. I work two jobs, see, this one at night and another in a packing department in the day. No time for mates, and my family . . . well, they live far away now.'

I feel a bit sorry for her. 'After the way you've looked after us tonight, Ellie and I are certainly your friends from now on if you'll have us.'

Lucy looks at Ellie gently swaying next to me on the plush sofa we're sitting on. 'Do I have to prop her up?' she asks, grinning.

I laugh. 'Sometimes, but she's so small you'll hardly notice.'

'Deal then,' Lucy says, winking at me. Then she hurries off across the club as another table requires her services.

Suddenly there's a kerfuffle at one of the tables across the room, and a few of the people around it push back their chairs and stand up.

'What's going on there?' I ask Ellie, trying to lean around her so I can see better.

'I dunno, probably one of them don't know how to hold his drink – talking of which, I think I might just need to visit the ladies' room meself.' Ellie leaps to her feet and hurries in the direction of the ladies' toilet.

I watch her go, and then turn my attention back to the other table. Several of the occupants are looking panicky now and keep looking anxiously around them as if to try and summon help. But I still can't see properly what's going on because the people standing around it keep masking the table.

Ringo appears to find out what's going on, and he emerges from the huddle that's building around the table looking fearful.

'Ladies and gentlemen,' he calls, 'do we have a doctor in the house at all?' He looks desperately around him. 'Lucy, call an ambulance!' he shouts at Lucy, who's standing by the bar about to collect another round of drinks. 'And tell them to make it snappy!'

One of the men who's been blocking my view moves out of the way and as he stands back to loosen his tie and get some air, I see another man still sitting at the table being comforted by a woman in a sparkling turquoise green dress. Except the man doesn't look very comforted at all; he looks extremely *un*comfortable, and as if he's having difficulty breathing. His face seems to be swelling up and he's holding his throat.

I leap to my feet and rush over to the table.

'What did he eat?' I demand, looking at the others standing helplessly around the distressed man.

They shrug, and look back at me with furrowed brows and puzzled expressions as if I'm asking the most complicated question in the world.

'Did he eat some of these?' I demand of them again, lifting a half-empty bowl of peanuts from the table.

'Yes,' the woman in the green dress says. 'Yes, he did, just a handful, though. But Rocky didn't choke or anything, he was talking to me for a few minutes after.'

'He's allergic,' I say, my outer voice belying my inner feelings of panic as I see Rocky's having even more trouble breathing. He's beginning to turn more of a burgundy colour now, rather than simply tomato red. 'He has a nut allergy, that's what's causing this reaction.'

'You're the one with the nut problem,' one of the men says. 'Nutcase, that's what you are! Never heard such a lot of shite.'

'It's not shite! I've seen it before because someone in my office has the same thing. Has anyone got an EpiPen?' I ask them, then realise that it's probably too early for such a thing when they look at me with even more derision. I think hard. 'What about an anti-allergy medication, then? Like hay fever tablets?'

They all just stare at me like I'm mad.

'I've got medicine,' a voice suddenly pipes up. 'I take it because I'm allergic to animal fur.'

I look around at Lucy. 'Perfect. Have you got it here by any chance?'

She nods. 'In my locker. I'll run and get it!'

Lucy dashes off, and is replaced in the circle now gathering around Rocky and I by Ellie.

'What are you doing, Jo-Jo?' she hisses. 'Let the ambulance people do their job when they get here.'

'If we wait for them,' I say, looking at Rocky, 'he might not make it.'

'Here,' Lucy says, returning with a bottle of medicine, 'what should I do?'

'Loosen his tie,' I tell her, sliding on to the seat next to a now almost-blue Rocky. 'Could you move over, please?' I ask green dress woman. 'This just might save his life.'

While Lucy loosens Rocky's bow tie and shirt, I shake up the bottle. There's no time to find a spoon. So I simply remove the lid.

'I know this is going to be difficult for you,' I tell him, lifting the bottle so it's right in front of his face, 'but I need you to drink some of this. It will help, I promise.'

At least I hope it will. We have a girl in the office back home who is allergic to peanuts and she carries an EpiPen everywhere now. She discovered her allergy one Christmas when she had an attack during an office lunch. Some bright spark realised what her problem was and dashed along to the local chemist and bought a bottle of Benadryl to calm her throat, which was just beginning to tighten. It was so successful she didn't even need to go to hospital, but simply made an appointment to see her doctor the next morning.

Rocky manages a weak nod. By the look of him he doesn't usually do anything weakly. He's a big, broad man. Not fat, but not slim. Muscly, I'm guessing, by the way his white shirt is pulling across his chest right now, but that might be more to do with him gasping for each and every breath.

I lift the bottle of medicine to his lips and he weakly attempts to sip from it.

'That's it,' I encourage him, 'nice and gently.'

Very slowly, in tiny drips, he manages to swallow some of the liquid down.

'Where's that bloody ambulance?' I hear Ringo call behind me. 'I can see me getting sued here for every penny I own, if this goes wrong.'

But as Rocky sips more and more of the allergy medication, his breathing starts to become easier, and then his swollen face begins to reduce in size.

'It's working!' green-dress woman shouts. 'Look, my Rocky's getting better.'

'She's right,' one of the men agrees. 'I think the girl has done it.'

Two paramedics arrive then, and I'm pleased to see that's what they are, not just ambulance drivers as they might have been in my previous re-incarnations.

'Everyone stand back,' they call. 'We'll take over now.'

They look with horror at me still feeding Rocky medicine. 'What have you been giving him?' the older of the two men demands.

'It's an antihistamine medication,' I explain quickly. 'I think Rocky may have had an allergic reaction to nuts.' I gesture towards the peanut bowl.

The paramedic stares at me for a moment. 'We'll be the judge of that,' he says as I stand up and move out of the way to let him deal with Rocky.

'Are you all right?' Ellie asks as I walk slowly back over towards her. 'You look very white.'

'Yeah, I'm fine. It was a bit stressful for a few minutes back then, that's all.'

'Saving lives usually is!' Ellie says and she winks. 'You did great, babe. How'd you know all that stuff?'

'Someone at my – my old work suffered in the same way. When she had an attack we treated her with the same type of medicine.'

'Who'd have thought peanuts could be so dangerous,' Ellie says, wrinkling up her nose. 'What with this and your toilet story earlier, I'm never touching them again!'

The younger paramedic comes over towards us. 'You proba-bly saved his life, you know,' he says, nodding at me approvingly. 'That was quick thinking – the antihistamine medication.'

'Thanks, just pleased I could help.'

'But how did you know? I've only seen a few cases like that, and that's doing the job I do.'

'I bet you're gonna see a whole lot more over the next few years,' I say knowingly as I spy Ringo heading this way now. 'You'd better get prepared.'

'Jo-Jo!' he says, beaming at me, his shark-like teeth fully on display. 'It seems I owe you a big favour. You appear to have saved the life of one of my most important clients.'

'It's fine, Ringo, really, you don't owe me anything,' I reply as I watch Rocky being wheeled away with an oxygen mask over his face.

'Yes, I do,' Ringo continues. 'Anything I can do for you and Ellie *ever*, you just let me know, OK?'

'Sure, Ringo,' I say, but I'm distracted by Rocky who is attempting to pull the oxygen mask away from his face. He whispers to the paramedic on his right, who then beckons me over.

'He wants to thank you,' the paramedic says as I arrive by their side.

Rocky pulls the mask away again. 'Rocky owes you,' he says in a raspy voice. 'Anything you want, you just come and see Rocky, OK?'

I nod at him. And, happy I've understood the gratitude his message implies, he allows the mask to return to his face, and the paramedics to escort him and his lady out of the club to the waiting ambulance.

'I have to give it to you,' Ellie says, coming up to me. 'You country girls are quick workers.'

'What do you mean?' I ask, taking the glass of wine Ellie

is holding out for me, and gulping a large mouthful of it.

'In one evening you've managed to not only get the owner of one of the trendiest clubs this side of London eating out of your hand, but one of the biggest gangsters, too. You've only been here five minutes, Jo-Jo, what are you gonna get up to next?'

Twenty-Six

The next morning, fresh from my exploits at the club, I'm standing in front of the mirror in the ladies' toilet at the office of the newspaper where Ellie and I work – apparently as 'showbiz' reporters, although from what I gather, it appears our job description may delve a bit deeper into the realms of generalised gossip-mongering.

'Ready to rumble?' Ellie asks as she emerges from the toilet cubicle and begins washing her hands at the sink.

'Yes, but are you sure about this so-called tip-off?'

Ellie shakes her hands and pulls some green paper towel from a container. 'Of course – Zak is one of my best sources.'

'If you're sure – but something doesn't feel right about it.'

'What's up?' Ellie asks, tossing the paper towel into the bin. 'You still bothered about rogue Rigby's reputation?'

'No,' I insist as we leave the toilets. 'I just don't want to storm in accusing someone of something if it's not true, that's all.'

'We're not going to storm in anywhere. Far from it. We need to find out what's going on first, then we can break the story . . . '

As I ride along on the back of Ellie's bike, I think about what Zak, Ellie's source, has told her. He said he suspected Harry was involved in trafficking drugs. There was a 'strong rumour', he said, from those in the know, that Harry was using his record company as a cover to ship and supply all sorts of illegal substances to the UK, and that was how he'd made his money. It seemed that Harry was catering to the public's tastes, but it wasn't exactly their ears that were benefiting from his shipments.

I couldn't believe that any of this was true. It just didn't sound like Harry at all. Well, not the Harry I knew. But how could this version of him be so different from the others? Had something happened to him to make him this way?

Eventually we pull up outside a large modern building situated behind some black railings. There's a security guard sitting in a wooden booth at the gates.

'Now what do we do?' I whisper to Ellie as we park the bike and remove our helmets. 'We have no reason to be here, he's not going to just let us in.'

'Use your initiative!' Ellie hisses. 'Didn't you learn anything in Norwich?'

'Hello . . . ' I sidle up to the booth and smile sweetly at the security guard. 'I'm here to see Mr Rigby.'

'Name,' he demands flatly.

'Jo-Jo,' I say without thinking.

'Surname?'

'McKenzie.'

The security guard scans the list in front of him. 'Your name isn't on the list,' he says, looking up at me expressionless.

'That's because I don't *have* an appointment,' I point out, to his immediate annoyance. 'I just wondered if I could see him.'

'Mr Rigby is a very busy man,' the security guard sighs. 'He doesn't see just anyone at the drop of a hat.' He looks me up and down. *Especially the likes of you*, he may as well have added.

I look across at Ellie and pull a 'help me' face.

'But Jo-Jo isn't just *anyone*,' Ellie says, emerging from the side of the wooden booth, so the security guard can see her beneath his hatch. 'Mr Rigby virtually saved her life the other day down on the King's Road. He'll want to see her, I'm sure of it.'

The security guard looks suspiciously at Ellie.

'Honestly!' Ellie insists. 'Didn't he, Jo-Jo?'

'In a way, I guess . . .'

'There you go! So hadn't you better check, just to be on the safe side?' Ellie insists.

The security guard, more to get a peaceful life than to help us, I think, decides to pick up his phone and call through to the main building.

'Harry won't let us in if the guard tells him that story,' I whisper to Ellie. 'Why did you say that?'

'It's not that far from the truth, and if you don't ask you don't get. Plus we *need* to get inside that building!'

'Mr Rigby will see you,' the guard suddenly announces.

'What? I mean, that's great. Thank you,' I say, smiling gratefully at him, as Ellie spins jubilantly around next to me.

'You'll need these,' the guard says, handing us two lanyards with visitor passes dangling at the bottom of them. 'Wear them at all times, and report to reception when you get inside.'

'Thank you!' Ellie calls to the guard, as she hangs the pass around her neck. 'You've been fandabbydozy!'

I stare after Ellie as she rushes through the opening electronic gates. Of course! It's the eighties, The Krankies would be big right now. Well, as big as the little one was ever going to get.

'Come on, Jo-Jo!' she calls. 'Stop daydreaming and get your ass in here!'

We rush across the car park to the main building and into reception.

'Just sign in here, ladies, please,' the receptionist says. 'You're expected.'

We quickly sign our names and the receptionist asks us to wait on some red leather settees while she informs Harry we're here.

I have to smile as I look around the reception area of Beat Music – the décor is just so eighties! It's all red, black and chrome – just like I've seen in interior magazines when they've talked about going retro. It's very harsh and unforgiving, I guess a bit like the times. It's all about money now, isn't it? And lots of it.

'When he gets here you distract him and I'll slip away and go in search of some evidence with my camera,' Ellie says, patting her bag.

'What do you mean distract him?' I ask in horror. 'How?'

Ellie nods at my legs. I'm wearing a short red batwing sleeve dress and opaque black tights. 'Use what God gave you!' she suggests.

'Yeah, like that will work,' I laugh.

'You'd be surprised!' she says, winking. 'Plus it's all we've got right now!'

'Jo-Jo,' Harry says as he enters the reception area. 'What a pleasant surprise to see you so soon. What can I do for you?'

Oops, we haven't thought of a reason to be here yet. We really are useless at this. Well, I am.

'Hello, Harry,' I say, suddenly feeling a little shy. 'Can I introduce my colleague, Ellie Williams?'

'Good morning, Mr Rigby,' Ellie says confidently, standing up to greet him. She walks over to shake his hand in a very accomplished, non-Ellie way. I'd wondered why she'd toned down the Madonna look today, and had erred more towards the Maggie Thatcher in a two-piece blue suit. She has more pearls slung round her neck and wrists than I'm sure Maggie owns, but it's a very fine attempt on Ellie's part to look sleek and sophisticated. 'It's a professional visit, I'm afraid.'

'Is it now?' Harry asks, looking amused. 'And please, call me Harry.'

'Certainly,' Ellie gushes. 'Well, Harry, Jo-Jo is writing a feature on the most eligible bachelors in the music industry, and we'd like to do a feature on you.'

Harry's amusement turns to shock. He looks as surprised by this news as I am. 'I – I'm sure we could arrange an interview some time,' he stutters. 'If you'd like, you can make an appointment with my secretary.'

'Why not now?' Ellie demands. 'Since we're here. It won't take long. Jo-Jo can ask you a few questions and I'll just take a few snaps, if that's OK? Some of you and then some of your office, that kind of thing?'

Harry, looking flustered, glances at his watch. 'I guess I could give you half an hour or so ... ' he says hesitantly.

'Great!' Ellie says, grabbing her chance. 'Let's go!'

Harry leads us up to his office. Unlike the reception area and foyer, it's not at all flash and modern. It's very warm and quite cosy, with a large walnut desk and soft brown leather seats.

'Would you like a drink?' he asks as we sit down on two of the leather seats in front of his desk. 'Tea, coffee?'

'I'm fine, thanks, Harry,' Ellie says as she begins unpacking her camera from her bag. 'You two just carry on and I'll start snapping some casual shots.'

'Jo-Jo?' Harry asks. 'Can I get you anything? We have a very good coffee machine here. Top of the range.'

As Harry stands there in his grey suit, crisp white shirt and red and grey striped tie, I have a sudden flash of him as his former self with blue hair, and I'm distracted.

'Ooh, I could murder a caramel macchiato right now, if it does one?'

Harry stares at me. 'Er, I don't think I've come across that one before ...'

'Oh sorry, I went on holiday to Italy recently, they're quite advanced with their coffee over there. Sometimes I forget.'

'Fancy,' Harry says, eyeing me suspiciously. 'Sorry, we just have plain filter here, but it is good. Will a cup of that do?'

'Yes, of course. That would be lovely.'

Harry presses a buzzer on his desk, speaks to his secretary and asks for two coffees.

'Now,' he says, sitting down behind his desk and giving Ellie a pained glance as she darts round his desk, flashing her camera in his face. 'What would you like to ask me?'

'Ah, yes ...' I root about in my bag and, in amongst all the other junk I seem to carry around, I find a notebook and pen. I take it out and carefully turn to a new page.

Harry watches me do this with an impatient expression on his face.

'So, Harry, have you had many girlfriends?' I ask him.

Ellie, who happens to be standing behind Harry's desk, grins in amusement.

'A few, thank you,' Harry says, leaning back in his leather chair; he casually links his hands together in his lap.

'Good, good, and did you think any of them would ever make good wives?'

Ellie makes a snorting noise, which she swiftly turns into a cough.

I glare at her. *What was I supposed to ask?*

'Maybe you'd like to go and take some photos around the building, Ellie?' Harry suggests, turning around to look at her. 'I'm sure Michelle will be delighted to show you around when she brings our coffees.'

'Yes, Ellie,' I agree, 'perhaps you should go for a while.'

'Yeah, yeah, I get it, you two – three's a crowd and all that!'

'Hardly,' Harry mutters. 'I'm just sick of you flashing that thing in my face.'

Ellie struggles to bite her tongue as Harry's secretary appears through the door with two cups of coffee on a glass tray.

'Thank you, Michelle,' Harry says, smiling at her. 'Would you be good enough to show Ellie around the offices? She'd like to flash somewhere else other than at me for a while.'

Ellie and Harry give each other similar looks of disdain as Ellie leaves the office with Michelle.

Harry watches them go and then turns his attention to me.

'So, what are you really doing here?' he asks, looking directly at me with his deep blue eyes, which never change, however much the rest of him does.

'A story . . . ' I respond weakly, holding up my pad as if it's evidence.

'Oh really?'

'Yes, really.'

'Go on then,' he says, sitting back in his high-backed leather chair, sipping casually on his coffee. 'Ask away.'

I think for a moment.

'Do you think being a rich, successful businessman helps or hinders you in your love life?' I ask a bit bluntly.

Harry nods. 'Good question. Direct. I like that.' He thinks now. 'That depends,' he says.

'On?'

'On whether I'm looking for a permanent relationship or just a bit of fun?'

'Define your answer,' I say, trying to keep it short and to the point. I'm sensing he prefers this approach.

'Do I need to?' He raises an eyebrow again, but in a suggestive way this time instead of a cross one.

'What do you prefer, then?' I try to do the same. But I fear all I look like is someone with a nervous tic.

'Well, I'm not wearing a gold band,' he says, holding up his left hand.

'I see . . . ' I pretend to scribble something down on my pad. Is he flirting with me? I *knew* I should have worn a longer skirt. Harry as an office boy and a teenager I could cope with, but this Harry just seems much more . . . dangerous.

'And neither are you,' he continues, 'so perhaps you prefer the same?'

I pull awkwardly at the hem of my dress. Now I feel like a gawky teenager. My cheeks are flushing too, I notice, as I feel them begin to burn.

Harry just watches me steadily as I suffer under his intense gaze.

'But we're here to discuss your availability as a bachelor, not mine,' I recover eventually, 'so, sadly, that information must remain under wraps for now.'

'For now, eh?' Harry says, smiling at me. 'That suggests I'm going to see you again, Jo-Jo.'

I turn over the pages of my pad, even though I've only scribbled a couple of words down so far, and in my haste knock it to the floor.

'Perhaps,' I respond, as I pick it up again. 'It depends on how well you answer my questions today, doesn't it?'

Harry grins now. 'I'm only winding you up. The truth is I'm pretty rubbish at relationships, actually. That's why I don't have a ring yet. Always too busy working.'

Now that sounds more like a scenario I'm familiar with.

I'm about to ask him another question but I'm prevented by an urgent hammering on Harry's office door. Suddenly it's thrust open and Michelle bursts through.

'I'm so sorry to disturb you,' she says to Harry, her eyes flickering in an irritated fashion in my direction. 'But the other girl seems to have gone missing.'

'What do you mean, missing?' Harry asks, standing up behind his desk. He looks suspiciously at me.

'She was with me for a while,' Michelle explains, 'and then

243

she asked to go to the toilet. I waited for a bit while she visited the ladies'. But when she'd been in there over five minutes I thought I'd better check on her.'

'And?' Harry asks impatiently.

'And she was gone. No one was in there. I've looked for her everywhere, but I simply can't find her. I'm terribly sorry, Harry.'

I like how Harry's staff call him by his first name; it's very friendly and informal. But I don't like how Harry is looking at me now.

'Do you know anything about this?' he demands.

'Me? No, why would I?'

'She's your colleague.'

'Ellie is a law unto herself. I can't be held accountable for her actions.' I rearrange my pad and pen in my lap.

'Really?' Harry says, still looking at me doubtfully. 'You'd better inform security, Michelle, and when they find her, tell them to remove her from the building immediately.'

'Yes, sir,' Michelle says, retreating out of the door. 'And once again, I'm sorry.'

'I don't hold you responsible in any way whatsoever, Michelle!' Harry calls to her departing figure. 'But I do you!' he says accusingly, pointing at me.

'Me! How am I to blame?'

'Eligible bachelors! I'm as much likely to make a list for most eligible bachelor as you are for the Pulitzer Prize. Now, why are you really here and where is your friend?'

'I'm right here,' Ellie says, walking calmly through the door with Michelle hurrying along behind her. 'I simply got a bit lost, that's all. It's quite a building you have here, Harry.'

'Mr Rigby to you, thank you,' Harry says, glaring at her. 'I'm only Harry to friends and people I trust.'

Ellie narrows her eyes and is about to open her mouth when I jump to my feet.

'I think we'd better be going now,' I say hurriedly. 'Thank you for your time, Harry – er – Mr Rigby.'

'I'd say it was a pleasure.' Harry takes his eyes away from Ellie for a moment and allows them to rest on me. 'But now I'm not so sure.'

We are unceremoniously escorted out of the building by a big burly security guard, and firmly ejected back through the black gates and on to the pavement outside.

'That was definitely worth getting thrown out for!' Ellie says, her bright green eyes shining with excitement as we make our way back over to her motorbike.

'Do you think?' I ask, glancing back through the railings at the Beat Music building.

'Yup, I learnt some *very* interesting stuff about our Mr Rigby while I was there.'

'You and me both,' I reply, deep in thought, as I think about my last few minutes with Harry. '*Interesting* it's definitely going to be this time. That's for sure.'

Twenty-Seven

We're sitting in a local café sipping on two weak, non-syrup filled coffees, discussing what Ellie discovered on her travels around Harry's offices, while I wish I had anything with a shot of caramel or vanilla inside my cup, or at least a big green mermaid on the outside keeping it warm ...

'... so when I'd finally given Michelle the slip,' Ellie continues, her eyes lighting up.

'Just how did you do that?' I interrupt. 'I mean, you're many things, but Houdini's not one of them.' I nearly use Dynamo as my magician of choice, but I'm getting better at remembering to think before I speak.

'Toilet window,' Ellie says, grinning. 'One of the perks of being tiny. The toilets are on the ground floor and I waited until all the cubicles were free then climbed up on the sinks and squeezed out of the window. It led out on to a sort of patio area.'

'Then what happened?' I ask, amazed at her ingenuity.

'Then you'll never guess who appeared for a break in the sun with a packet of ciggies and a desperate look in her eye?'

'Who?'

'Only Lucy.'

'Lucy?' I rack my brains for a few seconds. 'Do you mean Lucy from the club?'

'Yeah, that Lucy.'

'But what's she doing in Harry's work?'

'It seems Lucy works at the Beat Music building in the day, and the Karma club at night.'

'She told me she worked in the packing department of a firm. But how is there a link between that and what we're trying to prove, though? I say we, but I still find it hard to believe that Harry is involved in anything like this.'

Ellie smiles. 'Aw, Jo-Jo, you spent a few minutes in his office earlier and you know him inside out now, do you? That's good going.'

'No, of course not. But ...' I need to phrase this carefully 'you can tell a lot about a person in half an hour, and I'm certain that Harry wouldn't knowingly be involved with drugs. But look, we're getting off track. What did you find out from Lucy?'

Ellie leans in towards me across the table. 'Well, I didn't have long, but she definitely *hinted* that Harry was involved.'

'Hinted, Ellie? This is *drugs* we're talking about. Hinted isn't enough to take this any further.'

'Shush,' Ellie hisses, looking on either side of her. 'We don't want it getting out.'

'What *exactly* did she say?' I whisper. 'Word for word.'

Ellie takes a maddening sip of her coffee before replying. I get the feeling she's enjoying this little drama.

'After I told her what we were really doing there today, she said it was possible that drugs could be coming in through the company. Apparently there are packages that come in that they aren't allowed to open down in the unloading bay. *Special deliveries* she called them, said they all go straight up to Harry's office.'

'And so?' I ask her, wide-eyed. 'That proves nothing.'

'No, it doesn't have to ... yet. But, she also told me something we didn't know.'

I lift my cup of coffee and wait, not prepared to add to her dramatics.

'That Harry and Ringo are big buddies.'

'What?' I exclaim, slamming the cup back down on the saucer.

'Apparently, Harry is often in Karma and has private meetings with Ringo – she's seen them both.'

I let this information digest for a few moments.

'Are you suggesting that Harry is supplying Ringo with drugs for the Karma club?' I ask eventually.

Ellie nods. 'What other explanation is there?'

I think again.

'I don't know,' I reply carefully, 'but if there is one I'm damn well going to find it. Either way, I'm going to uncover the truth.'

Twenty-Eight

It's later that afternoon and I'm sitting in my flat above George's record shop, thinking.

Ellie and I sat in the café and talked for ages about what we should do next. Ellie was only used to dealing in celebrity gossip and I, well, I wasn't used to dealing with any sort of information like this, big or small. We were like the proverbial fish out of water, flailing about on the bank for air, except in our case it was our next lead, or bright idea.

In the end we decided our only option was to return to Ringo's club, to see if we could find out anything more for ourselves. So we headed home with the intention of taking a quick nap, knowing that tonight was probably going to be another late and fairly boozy one.

But as hard as I try, I just can't nod off, so instead I'm lying flicking through the TV channels until it's time to get ready to go out. But the stations are full of kids' TV programmes, and after I've done a few minutes of *Grange Hill* and *Blockbusters*,

I decide to turn on the little portable radio that sits on a table next to the sofa. I recognise the DJ's voice immediately: it's Steve Wright, a DJ I know from 2013. He's on Radio 2 in my future, but back now in 1985 he's on peak time Radio 1 in the afternoon.

He plays 'Crazy for You' by Madonna, and then 'The Power of Love' by Huey Lewis and the News, and he goes on to talk about a brand new movie about to open in cinemas called *Back to the Future*.

I have to smile. That's one of my favourite eighties movies. Michael J. Fox and Christopher Lloyd fighting to get Marty McFly – Michael's time-travelling alter-ego – to return to his life in 1985 when he accidentally travels back in time to 1955.

It seems great fun in the movies, all these time-travelling adventures. But when you're doing it for real, it's a very different story. At least I didn't travel back as far as the fifties, I only went back to 1963, and since then I appear to be moving steadily forward. If I keep jumping in time like this, I'll make it back to 2013 in no time. If that's how it works.

How it works – that's the question that keeps bothering me. It's the thing that keeps me awake at night, the thing that unsettles me more than anything. It's not the constant change of decade, the bed I sleep in, the clothes I wear, or the company I keep on a daily basis that disturbs me most. It's why. *Why* is this happening to me? And how can I prevent it happening over and over again, instead of returning home?

I sit up on the sofa and bury my head in my hands. I need answers, and the only person who can give them to me is downstairs, selling records.

*

'Hi, Jo-Jo,' George says as the bell rings above my head and I enter the shop. 'I thought you were resting?'

'I can't settle, George, I need to know,' I say, flopping into one of the wooden chairs.

'Need to know what?' George asks calmly, as he continues to arrange some new sunflowers in the vase that always stands on the shop counter.

'Why I'm here.'

'Ah! Well, that's a question we'd all like to know the answer to,' George says, not looking up. He puts the final flower in the vase and takes a sniff before pushing them forward on the counter. 'Indeed, why are we all here?'

I'm really not in the mood for George's vagueness today. 'No, I mean why am I – *I* – here specifically? You said we could discuss this further yesterday.'

The shop bell rings as a young man enters.

'And we will, Jo-Jo, but for now, can you just excuse me for a minute?' George says as he walks over to greet his customer.

I sigh wearily; will I ever get to the bottom of this? I gaze out of the window, not taking much notice of the man George is dealing with, but as he speaks there's something about his voice I recognise.

'Yeah, it's gonna be great,' he says excitedly, 'the band are really up for it. Which is madness really, because they've played so many huge gigs in their time, but this is the one everyone wants to say they were there for.'

'I'm really looking forward to watching it on TV,' George replies. 'It'll be one of those days about which people will ask in the future: "Where were you and what were you doing during Live Aid?".'

I turn and stare hard at the man George is talking to. It can't be, can it? It sounds just like him, but he has his back to me so I can't see him properly to decide for sure.

'I might be able to do better than that for you, George. How do you fancy actually being there and seeing the gig live?'

'And how am I going to do that?' George asks. 'Tickets are like gold dust.'

'Not when you're a roadie to one of the bands performing, they're not. Let me see what I can do for you, buddy.'

'Really?' George asks, a huge smile spreading across his face. 'That's very kind of you.'

'Come on, George, you've always been good to me here. Where else would I be able to indulge in my fetish for rare and eclectic punk records? I can't get them anywhere else and I know that if I mention your name in the right ears it'll always be heard favourably. Everyone knows George from Groovy Records.'

'Stu?' I exclaim, standing up. 'Is that you?'

The blond head in front of me turns around, and the face that looks quizzically back at me is maybe older, without anger, and is no longer framed with green spikes, but there's no doubting it's Stu from 1977.

'My name is Stuart, yes,' he replies. 'I'm sorry, but do I know you?'

'I – I'm Jo-Jo,' I stutter. 'We – we met a long time ago, when we were younger.'

Stu looks at me with interest. 'Really? I'm sure I would have remembered *you*. I'm not great with names, but faces I'm usually very good at recalling. Especially really pretty ones.'

I can't do anything but smile. I'm not sure how I'm supp-osed to respond because I have no idea what's happening now. How can Stu be here?

'It was at a party,' I improvise. 'It was quite dark and I think you were a little drunk.'

Stu looks a tad embarrassed. 'There are a lot of parties in the business I'm in. You meet a lot of people . . .'

'It's fine,' I say hastily. 'I understand completely.'

'Listen, if you're not doing anything later,' he says, 'me and a few friends are heading down to a little club in Soho called Karma. Maybe you'd like to join us?'

Stu from 1977 is hitting on me now? This is just getting too weird!

'Actually, I'm already heading there tonight with a friend. We know the owner.'

'You know Ringo?' Stu asks, looking surprised.

'My friend does.'

Stu nods. 'Makes more sense.'

I'm about to ask him why, when George interrupts.

'Shall I just leave you two to your arrangements? I have things to be doing around the shop.'

'No, George, I'll just take this,' Stu says, holding up a Sex Pistols album. 'I don't have this one any more. I lent it to a dancer on one of my tours and never saw it again.' He turns to me. 'So, Jo-Jo, if you're at Ringo's place tonight maybe we'll catch-up again.'

'Maybe we will,' I say, trying to sound casual.

Stu pays for his album and, promising he'll be in touch with George about Live Aid, he leaves the shop.

I immediately turn towards George.

'What the hell was that all about?' I ask with my hands held aloft.

'The Live Aid tickets?' George asks with wide eyes.

'George!'

'Sorry. It would seem that a few of the pages of your book are starting to stick together a little. Some of the characters we thought we'd left behind are reappearing in a new chapter.'

'George, enough of the book analogies!'

'All right, some of your time travel wires are very definitely becoming crossed, and before you ask, no, I don't know why.'

George sits down on one of the wooden seats. He does look a little bemused by the situation this time, so perhaps he doesn't have all the answers.

I run my hands through my hair and pace about the shop.

'This is the first time this has happened. I've never met the exact same person twice, have I? This must be the Stu that jumped back to 1977. He told me he was a roadie with a band, that's how he got electrocuted on stage, and . . .' my voice trails off as I stop pacing and stare at George.

His face tells me everything I need to know.

'No, Jo-Jo,' he says, shaking his head, 'you can't mess with the future, it's one of the golden rules.'

'Rules are made to be broken, George,' I say calmly, as I think through what I need to do. 'It's my fault that Stu from 1977 didn't ever return to his future. So this time I'm going to make sure he never goes back to the past.'

Twenty-Nine

The Karma club is packed when we arrive, and Ellie and I can barely find space to stand, let alone a booth. Boyd is on the door again and he lets us straight in this time.

We end up squeezing on to a couple of stools at the bar, and while we wait to order I look around to see if I can see Stu, but there just appears to be the usual bunch of suited, booted and incredibly loud businessmen and their 'adornments' taking up the tables, chairs and booths.

'Looking for our friend?' Ellie asks, leaning in towards me so I've a chance of hearing her – it really is incredibly loud in here tonight.

'Who do you mean?' I ask, jumping a little on my stool.

'Easy, I meant Harry. He could well show up here at some point, couldn't he, if he's in cahoots with Ringo.'

'Yes, I suppose he could,' I reply almost in relief. With Stu turning up in George's shop this afternoon, I'd almost forgotten about the Harry and Ringo situation.

'Why, who did you think I meant?' Ellie asks, her eyes narrowing. 'Do you know something I don't, Jo-Jo?'

'No, of course not. Sorry, I'm just on edge tonight, that's all. This whole story doesn't sit easy with me.'

'I bet nothing sits easy with you in that skirt,' Ellie says, nodding at my black leather mini skirt. 'Blimey, Jo-Jo, I never thought you had it in you – black leather and red stilettos? They'll be thinking you're one of them.' She nods towards one of the girls carrying drinks.

'Don't be silly, Ellie, we don't know that's going on here for sure, we're just guessing. Until we get some firm leads, everything we're doing right now is simply guesswork.'

'You make us sound like cops.' Ellie's green eyes sparkle. 'Looking for leads and on such a serious subject too. I've never done anything like this before. We're like ... ' She pauses for inspiration. 'I know: those female cops in *Cagney & Lacey*!'

I stifle a grin. This situation with Harry is far from an amusing one, but the thought of Ellie and I as the female crime-fighting duo is. 'Bagsy I'm the blonde one then,' I wink.

Ellie screws up her face. 'Aw, I want to be Christine; I have the right colour hair and everything. You're much more a Mary-Beth.'

I don't know that much about *Cagney & Lacey*, but the little I do says that Mary-Beth was definitely the frumpier one of the two. 'Why would you say that? I'm not dull.'

'No, I don't mean that. I mean you're just more sensible, that's all. Whereas I'm more flirty and outgoing.'

'Oh, really?'

'Yes, really.'

'We'll see about that,' I say with determination. 'I'll show you who's *sensible*!'

I sit up on my bar stool and cross my legs so my black leather skirt slides up a bit higher. Immediately the barman, who's been ignoring us up until now, pops up ready to take our order.

'Tequila slammers, please,' I request. 'Two of them!'

'Slammers, eh?' Ellie says with approval. 'You *are* living dangerously; you might make detective Christine Cagney yet.'

The barman brings us our first slammers and we bang them on the counter to make the liquid fizz and bubble in the glass, then we down them as fast as we can.

'Another,' I gesture to the barman when he catches my eye.

'You don't have to prove anything to me, you know,' Ellie says, trying to catch my eye now too. 'I was only joking.'

'I'm not. I just feel like having a drink tonight, that's all.' And I do. I'm suddenly sick of all this time-travelling nonsense. Of trying to figure out not only what's happening to me, but what's happening to everyone else around me too.

We're on our third slammer, and just waiting for a fourth, when I spot Harry at the other side of the bar. He's sitting on his own, sipping from a glass of whisky. I'm about to wave and shout hi, when he looks across at us. And the look he fires at me is filled with such disapproval that its intensity alone almost knocks me from my stool.

My head drops towards my chest in shame; I don't want Harry seeing me getting drunk on shots. Then I reconsider that thought. Why should it matter to me what Harry thinks? This Harry anyway – I don't really know him. Plus, what right does he have to judge my behaviour, especially if Ellie and Lucy are right about him?

'Excuse me for a moment, Ellie,' I announce, climbing carefully down from my stool and rearranging my skirt. 'I have something to do.'

Ellie doesn't take a lot of notice of me – she's too busy right now, fending off the advances of a rather large and sweaty city banker who's introduced himself as Rudolph. Rudolph, unfortunately for him, sports an alcohol-induced red nose to match his rather unfortunate name.

As I approach him, Harry's just left his seat at the bar and is making his way towards a door marked *Private*, in front of which is a burly bouncer. But this doesn't stop me. I don't drink much usually – a couple of glasses of wine are typically my limit. In fact, since I've been time travelling I've probably taken in more alcohol of varying sorts than I have ever done before, so three slammers in the short space of time we've downed them in are making me feel very confident about life.

Tottering slowly across the shiny club floor in my red heels means I don't quite reach Harry before he disappears through the door, and the bouncer steps in front of it again.

'Jo-Jo, hi,' a voice in the crowd calls, and I see Lucy expertly weaving her way towards me. She carries a tray with some glasses and an ice bucket chilling a bottle of Bollinger champagne.

'Hello again,' I call over the noise in the club; I glance towards the closed door where Harry has just gone.

'What are you doing here so soon?' she asks, leaning in towards my ear so I can hear her. 'Guests of Ringo again?'

'No, we're just here for . . . pleasure,' I improvise.

She looks surprised. 'Really? I didn't think this would be the sort of place you'd come out of choice. Your friend Ellie told me what you do when we met the other day, so I know why you're here.' She nods her head towards the closed door. 'You after him?'

I look at Lucy, and wonder whether I should trust her. 'Yes,' I say, deciding to.

'What's Ringo done?'

Ah, so that must be Ringo's office? 'I'm not sure yet.'

'Ringo's all right. It's that Harry you wanna watch.'

What's Harry done to everyone?

'Really?'

'Yeah,' she nods. 'He's trouble. Look, I gotta go; that lot will be wanting this in a minute. She tosses her head in the direction of a rowdy bunch of city types over in the corner who're downing champagne as if it was water. 'Watch out for yourself, Jo-Jo. There're some nasty people about.' And she begins weaving her away across the club again, the tray held above her head.

Damn! I'm torn about whether to go after Lucy and ask her more, or to try and pursue my original prey, Harry. My decision is made when a scuffle suddenly breaks out in front of me, as two city men argue about whose eighties haircut is the silliest, or something equally unimportant, and the bouncer guarding the private door Harry went through a few minutes ago moves forward to break up the fight. So I grab my chance, quickly side-step around them, and slip quietly through the door.

As the door closes behind me I find myself in a dim corridor lit only by an occasional spotlight mounted on the purple and black flock-papered wall. Maybe this wasn't such a great idea after all, I think, my earlier bravado ebbing away fast. But then I hear voices coming from a room at the end of the corridor. It's Harry, and he's talking to Ringo.

I creep down the corridor closer to the room and pause at the half-open doorway.

'... and you think this makes it acceptable?' I hear Harry say, as I press myself against the wall as close to the door as I can get without being seen. 'When I provide you with the goods I expect them to be looked after, not stashed away in some damp old basement. This is top-of-the-range merchandise, Ringo.'

'Harry, Harry,' I hear Ringo say now in that gravelly voice of his. 'What I do with the goods once you provide them is up to me. It's no longer your concern then. You've done your bit in getting them to me, and a damn fine job you do too, if I may say. My clients have been very happy with what we've provided just lately, very happy indeed. I've had no complaints.' Then Ringo laughs in a way that sends a cold shiver down my spine.

I cover my mouth with my hand to prevent a gasp escaping. So Ellie was right, Harry and Ringo *are* involved in drugs trafficking. Harry's providing Ringo with the drugs, and Ringo's selling them on to his clients.

I turn away from the door and hurry back down the corridor, but I forget I'm in ridiculously high heels, so I stumble and bang my hand into the wall as I try to keep myself balanced. I flick off my heels, pick them up and dash the final few metres to the door, but just as I get my hand on the handle I hear: 'Jo-Jo, what are you doing in here?' behind me.

Slowly I turn around.

'Harry,' I reply lightly. 'I must have taken a wrong turning – I thought this was the door for the ladies'.'

'No,' Harry says, eyeing me curiously. 'And I don't believe the word *Private* looks anything like *Ladies*.'

'Didn't see that! Really *must* have had a few too many slammers earlier if I can't read now, eh?'

Ringo, who has been standing behind Harry puffing on his cigar, blows a big plume of smoke into the corridor. 'I do hope you weren't snooping, Jo-Jo,' he says as the security guard, fresh from breaking up his fight, comes through the door behind me. 'Because there's nothing I hate more than a journalist nosing into things she shouldn't.'

'What would I have to snoop about, Ringo?' I ask, looking him directly in the eye. 'If everything you do here is perfectly legal and above board?'

Ringo appears to lunge towards me, but Harry holds him back by putting his arm out.

'Steady, Ringo, she's only lost her way.'

Ringo, still growling, eyes me suspiciously.

'If you'll just let me pass, I'll be on my way,' I say, turning to the guard behind me. 'I don't want any trouble. It was a simple mistake.'

'Ringo?' he enquires of his boss, looking over my head.

'Let her pass, Brian,' Ringo says eventually. 'But make sure she's escorted from the premises immediately.'

'Charming!' I say, flashing my eyes at him.

'Don't push it, sweetheart; I don't take kindly to finding people trespassing on private property. The only reason I'm being lenient with you is because you helped me out the

261

other night with Rocky, and I owe you. But that debt is paid now,' he adds. 'So, I don't want to see you in here ever again.'

'Don't worry, Ringo, I wouldn't lower myself.'

'I suggest you just leave, Jo-Jo,' Harry interrupts quickly, before Ringo can speak. He walks down the corridor towards me. 'Just let it be,' he whispers, looking me in the eye. 'Please, just go. It's for your own good.'

I look at Harry, and I'm about to reply, but there's something about the look in his eyes that tells me not to.

Don't think you've got away with it though, Harry. You can wait until later.

I slip on my shoes while the security guard opens the door, then he steps back to let me pass and follows me through when I do. 'This way, miss,' he says, guiding me by the arm towards the main exit of the club.

My cheeks are burning with embarrassment as we make our way through the busy club.

'Hey, stop!' I hear as I'm about to be shown the door. 'Is that you, Jo-Jo?'

Brian and I turn towards the voice exiting from the gents' toilet. It's Rocky from the other night, although I barely recognise him without his purplish hue of then.

'What's going on?' he asks, looking at Brian's hand on my arm. 'Why are you manhandling this lady when she saved my life the other evening?'

'Boss's orders, Mr R,' Brian mumbles.

'I think not,' Rocky says, removing my arm from Brian's big paw and looping it through his own. 'She's *my* guest now, and any guest of mine is never unwelcome in Ringo's club.' He gives Brian a meaningful glare. 'If Ringo has a problem with that, just you send him over to speak to me, OK?'

'Yes, Mr Rockwell, whatever you say, Mr Rockwell,' Brian mutters, scuttling away. Which, when you're way over six foot, isn't an easy thing to do.

'Thanks for that,' I say, as Rocky guides me towards one of the private booths across the other side of the room.

'No problem. Anyone that saves my life is my permanent special guest. Sadie will be made up to see you again.'

'Sadie?' I enquire, wondering who I'm going to encounter now.

'Yes, Sadie, my fiancée.'

'Is she the woman in the green dress from the other night?'

'Yup, that's my Sadie. It's her birthday, so we've a few friends in with us tonight, celebrating.'

'I don't want to intrude,' I say, pretty sure Sadie won't be too pleased to have me gatecrashing her birthday celebrations, but we're already at the table, kept slightly private from the rest of the club by the addition of an ornate black net curtain circling the outside of the purple velvet seats.

Rocky pulls back the curtain and I'm surprised to see in amongst the guests enjoying champagne and cocktails not one but two familiar faces: Sadie, wearing a red satin dress so tight I can hardly believe she can breathe in it, let alone bend to sit down, and, sitting a bit further around the table from Sadie – Stu.

I'm not sure who looks more shocked to see me standing with my arm locked with Rocky's, Sadie or Stu.

'Doll face, look who I found!' Rocky bellows, oblivious to their expressions. 'It's my guardian angel.'

'Darling,' Sadie gushes at me, recovering her momentarily lost composure. She fixes a tight smile to her lips. 'How wonderful to see you again. Won't you join us?'

'Thank you, and happy birthday – I'm so sorry for gatecrashing your party,' I smile nervously.

'You're not gatecrashing, darling, anyone that saves my Rocky's life is welcome at any family gathering.'

It's family! That makes it even worse. I cast a quick glance in Stu's direction. What is he, her brother? *Getting too weird now* ... but he just smiles back.

I'm found a seat, thrust a glass of champagne, and I sit down, glad that no one else seems bothered by my presence. They all just continue with their conversations and their drinking. Rocky and Sadie become the perfect hosts again, mingling with everyone.

'How do you know Rocky?' Stu asks, leaning across the table towards me. 'I thought it was Ringo you were in with. Quite the dark horse, aren't you?'

'No, not at all. I don't know him that well really. Unless you call saving his life, knowing him, I guess?'

Stu looks confused. 'Is that what he meant about you being his guardian angel just now? Care to explain further?' Stu slides his chair around the table so it's closer to mine, but no one seems to care, and I begin to tell him all about the peanut incident.

'Impressive,' he says when I've finished. 'How'd you know to do that?'

'Saw it happen at a Christmas party. So,' I ask, keen to move the subject away from my future knowledge. 'How do *you* know Rocky?'

'He's involved with the band I roadie for.'

'Is he, how?'

'He finances them, basically, shoves money into them when they need a bit extra for tours and the like.'

'Is he a big music fan then?' I look at Rocky standing with his arm around another man, drinking whisky and laughing. Rocky looks many things but a fan of pop music isn't one of them.

Stu laughs. 'Not really. It's Sadie – her brother is one of the band members, so Rocky does it for her.'

Now it makes sense.

'And Sadie is my cousin, so that's how I got the gig working with them originally. Been doing it for years, now. Got to know them all quite well, and it's not a bad job, gets me out and about, seeing things I wouldn't if I were stuck in an office all day. I've pretty much travelled the world.'

'There you are!' Ellie comes tottering over to us on her bright yellow high heels. 'I wondered where you'd got to. You left me all alone at the bar.'

'I bet you weren't alone long, though?' Stu says to her, casting an admiring eye over her short black dress.

'*Hello*, and who might you be?' Ellie asks, putting her hand out.

'Your lucky day,' Stu says, standing up to take her hand.

I roll my eyes. 'Stuart, meet Ellie, my friend and work colleague,' I cast my hand in Ellie's direction, 'Ellie, meet Stuart. We met earlier today in George's shop.'

'You like music then, Stuart?' Ellie asks.

'Yeah, I'm embarrassed to say I have a sad addiction to obscure seventies punk music, which George feeds nicely for me.'

265

'That's not so bad,' Ellie says, smiling at him. 'Just between the two of us I like a bit of the Bay City Rollers when I'm all alone of an evening. Now *that's* embarrassing!'

'Yes, it is,' Stu says seriously, and then he grins. 'Are you here all alone tonight?'

'Yes,' Ellie says without hesitation, her eyes not wavering from Stu's.

I clear my throat.

'Well, I came with Jo-Jo but she doesn't really count.'

'Thanks a bunch!'

'You know what I mean, Jo!' She winks at me. *Needs must!* she mouths so Stu can't see.

I look at the pair of them, gazing at each other above me while I perch on the seat below.

'Why don't you two just go and have some fun together?' I suggest. 'I'll be fine here with Rocky and his pals.'

'Are you sure?' Ellie asks, barely looking at me.

'Yes, just go,' I say, waving my hand dismissively at them. 'I'll catch you later. By the way, I've got some info for us,' I say as Ellie and Stu wander off still gazing at each other, but I don't think Ellie even hears me.

I pick up my champagne from the table and take a long consolatory gulp.

So, it looks like I'm all on my own again.

But isn't that how I'm supposed to prefer it?

As I sip my champagne I ponder how, even in the middle of a noisy club like this, you can feel so alone. How when sitting at a table of people, all chattering away and enjoying themselves, you can still manage to feel lonely.

But that's just how I feel now that Stu has gone off with Ellie and I don't really know anyone. It's odd, I should have felt like this before in all the unfamiliar situations I've found myself in, but I haven't; I've always felt fine before, able to cope, so why has it suddenly hit me now in the middle of all this noise and merriment, how utterly alone I actually feel in all this?

'What are you still doing here?' someone hisses in my ear.

I turn around to find Harry bending over my shoulder.

'If Ringo catches you still in his club you'll be for more than the high jump.'

'I'm having a drink with Rocky – he invited me to stay as his guest,' I reply haughtily, turning away from him and facing forward again.

'Did he now?' Harry says, sounding surprised. 'And how might you know Rocky?'

Not this one again.

'It's complicated,' I reply, to make it easier.

'I bet it is if Rocky is anything to do with it. I wish you luck if you're involved in any of his shady dealings.'

I swivel around in my chair. 'You're a fine one to talk!'

'What do you mean?' Harry asks. His face is right next to mine as I stare indignantly into his deep blue eyes.

Damn! I didn't mean to say anything until I spoke to Ellie first. But now I have I'm not backing down.

'I mean about you and Ringo.'

'What about me and Ringo?' Harry asks, looking right back into my eyes without blinking. 'What do you know? Or should I say what do you *think* you know!'

'I know enough.'

'Enlighten me?' Harry's eyes flicker with danger now.

'Here? You want me to say it here in front of everyone?'

'Let's go elsewhere then,' Harry suggests quietly.

'I'm not going somewhere with you! I hardly know you and after earlier in the corridor, why would I?'

It was true; I didn't really know this version of Harry. I might think I did because of all the other times I'd met him, but it might be different this time: he really could be dangerous.

Harry sighs. 'Are you suggesting that I might harm you in some way?'

I look at Harry in his smart black suit and blue shirt as he squats down next to my chair now. No, I have to admit he doesn't look very dangerous. But an expensive designer suit doesn't mean anything. Then I glance into his eyes again. But a pair of kind eyes does mean something. And Harry has some of the kindest, loveliest eyes I've ever seen.

'No,' I say quietly. 'But you're a virtual stranger to me. I'm not going just anywhere with a stranger.'

Harry's face softens. 'There's a bar down the road from here. Well, it's more of a pub really, but you have to call them bars these days. We'll go there and you can explain to me just why you think I might be anything like Ringo, Rocky and anyone else with the initial R you can think of.'

The Angel's Wings is indeed more of a traditional pub than a trendy eighties bar, and while I find us a seat, Harry gets us both a drink. I've asked for an orange juice – I think I've had enough alcohol for one night!

While I settle at a small wooden table in the corner of the

pub and wait for Harry to bring our drinks over, I glance around me. The pub seems very quiet. There are a few people drinking at the bar and a couple of young guys playing on a Pac-Man game next to a fruit machine, and as I check the time on my watch I realise it's nearly time for last orders.

'One orange juice,' Harry says, putting a glass down on the table in front of me. 'I'm surprised you ordered that.'

'Why?' I ask before taking a sip.

'The way you were knocking back the shots earlier, I didn't think you'd entertain anything non-alcoholic this evening.'

'That was just for show.'

'Was it now?' Harry says, looking amused. 'To show who what?'

'To show Ellie I wasn't dull and boring.'

Harry laughs now. 'Oh, really? Well, I think you've managed that tonight: first you get thrown out of the club by Ringo, then you sneak back in again via Rocky and gatecrash his wife's birthday party.'

'His fiancée actually, and the truth is Rocky rescued me before I got to the exit and invited me along to the party. So, technically, I didn't do any of those things.'

'Nit-picking details.' Harry takes a long slow sip from his pint of beer. 'Ah ... A hundred times better than that slop they serve at Karma.'

'Why do you go there then?'

'Necessity. Ringo is my business partner, so I need to on occasion. Which brings me around to your earlier allegations. Would you like to enlighten me?'

I look across the table at Harry. Should I tell him?

'I heard you,' I blurt out before my brain has a chance to

consult with my mouth on the best course of action. 'I heard you talking to Ringo when I was in the corridor before.'

'I see,' Harry says, nodding calmly. 'And what *exactly* did you hear?'

'I heard you discussing the illegal drugs you provide him with for the club.'

Harry's face doesn't change as he appears to think over what I've just said. He looks over the table at me with a completely neutral expression. 'And what else did you hear – anything?'

'Isn't that enough?'

Harry nods again and contemplates his beer for a moment. 'Yes, I would think running an illegal drugs operation is a pretty big allegation to make against anyone.' He looks up at me now, his expression sending shivers down my spine. Not because it's menacing or fearsome, but because of the disappointment it contains, as if I've wounded him with my accusations. 'And that's exactly what you heard me say – word for word? I was providing Ringo with drugs for the club?'

I think about this.

'Maybe not exactly word for word, no, but what else could you have been discussing? You're not exactly denying it, are you?' As I sit here defending my actions, I'm starting to wish I'd listened to my original gut instinct, and not so much to Ellie. This wasn't going as I planned. But that's exactly the problem; I didn't *plan* anything. I allowed myself to get carried away with the moment, allowed myself to rely on someone else's judgement. And now it feels as if it's all going horribly wrong, spiralling out of my control. And I hate that.

Harry takes another sip of his beer, but his eyes don't leave mine. 'These are pretty serious allegations, Jo-Jo,' he says, resting his glass back down on the table.

I swallow hard. But I hold his intense gaze.

'They are, Harry.'

'Not the type that one friend makes against another.' Harry pushes his beer away from him across the table and stands up. 'Goodbye, Jo-Jo,' he says, to my surprise. The disappointment in his blue eyes as he looks down at me feels like a dagger stabbing me in the heart. 'I'd say it's been nice knowing you, but I'm not so sure.' Then he turns and heads for the door.

I'm stunned for a moment; I didn't expect that reaction from him at all. 'Wait!' I shout, pushing my chair back across the tiled floor. 'Harry, wait up!'

I chase after him through the pub doors and out on to the pavement.

'I'm sorry if I got it wrong,' I call, as I see him marching away down the dimly lit street. 'Won't you at least explain?'

Harry stops walking. He stands under the yellow glow of a street lamp but doesn't turn around. I wait, my heart beating fast in my chest to see what he does next.

Passers by on the London street barely give me a glance as they hurry along home. It's started to rain now, and I can feel large drips of water on my head as I stand there waiting for Harry to do something. Anything.

Finally he turns around and walks back towards me.

'It's raining,' he announces. 'I think you'd better come with me.'

Thirty

I sit in the back seat of the car Harry summoned on his huge brick of a mobile phone and wonder where we're going.

I suppose most people would think I'm taking a bit of a risk getting into a chauffeur-driven car and driving off with someone I don't know, but that's the problem with Harry: whatever guise he's in I always feel I know him, and that always makes me feel safe.

We pull up outside the gates of Beat Music and Harry winds down his window to speak to the security guard in the cubicle. The guy is so shocked to see Harry, he doesn't know whether to put his cap on first or straighten his tie, so he ends up trying to do both at the same time while Harry speaks briefly to him, and then he nods hurriedly.

'Why are we here?' I ask Harry as he presses a button and the car window shoots back up again.

'I want to show you something,' Harry answers without further detail.

Since his car picked us up outside the pub, Harry has hardly spoken to me, except to politely enquire whether I'm warm enough, and have dried off sufficiently after the rain.

The car pulls up outside the main building, and the chauffeur hurries around to my side of the car to open the door.

I look over to Harry.

'Go on,' he says. 'I'll follow you.'

I climb out and Harry does the same.

'I won't be long, Henry,' Harry says to the chauffeur. 'If you'd just wait, please.'

'Of course, Mr Rigby,' Henry says, standing outside the car as we enter the building.

'He won't wait outside the car all the time, will he?' I ask, looking back through the glass doors at Harry's chauffeur. 'He'll get wet.'

Harry looks at me for a moment, then he smiles. 'No, of course not. Don't worry about Henry; he'll be fine. He's been chauffeuring for my family for years – he worked for my father before he worked for me.'

'Really? Is this a family business, then?' I ask, looking around the dimly lit foyer with new eyes.

'Drug dealing?' Harry asks.

I wince. But then I see a twinkle in his eye.

'Whatever it is you *really* do here.'

'No,' Harry smiles, 'Beat Music isn't a family business – I built it myself from scratch. And if you come with me now I'll show it to you.'

We take the lift down, as opposed to travelling up as we did when I was last in the building. When the doors open I follow Harry down the corridor silently. We pause at a large, extremely thick vault-like door and Harry inputs a few numbers on a keypad, careful to shield the code from my eyes. The door swings open and I find myself entering what looks like a storeroom.

As the vault door closes behind us I realise the room is lit only by security lighting, and I suddenly begin to wonder again if this has been a good idea, but Harry strides across the room, flicks a switch and the room is immediately flooded with light.

Looking around me I can see several long tables with columns of empty packing boxes stacked beside them, and dotted about on top of the tables are brown sticky tape machines, clipboards and pens. The walls of the room are lined with shelves filled with even more boxes – full ones, this time.

'What is this place?' I ask. Then, feeling stupid I add, 'I mean, what's in all the boxes?'

'Music,' Harry says proudly looking around him. 'Records, mainly.'

'Yes, I know you supply music,' I say, wandering over to one of the boxes. 'Everyone *knows* that's your business.'

Harry shakes his head. 'No, that's the modern stuff I distribute under the Beat Music name. This,' he lifts the flap of an unsealed box 'is vintage music, classics not in production any more. Look at this, for instance.' He puts on a pair of white cotton gloves, then carefully pulls a record from the box. It's wrapped in a white sleeve, and Harry handles it so very gently as he slips it from its protective case that I wonder if it's going to be made of gold as it slides into his hand.

But no, it just looks like a normal vinyl record to me.

'What's so special about that?' I ask, moving towards him.

Harry flinches and backs away a couple of steps as if I'm going to snatch his precious record and run away with it.

'Steady boy,' I laugh, 'I'm not going to touch!'

'This,' Harry says seriously, 'is an original copy of the Beatles' *Sergeant Pepper* album. It's so rare we're keeping the sleeve separately for security purposes.'

The Beatles again ...

'And in that box over there,' he says, gesturing towards the far wall, 'is an original copy of "Blue Suede Shoes" by Elvis Presley.'

'You're like an underground musical eBay!' I exclaim, grinning at him.

Harry doesn't get my futuristic joke.

'This is serious stuff, Jo-Jo. Collectors pay a lot of money for items like this. It's a very particular clientele I provide for. They know what they want and they're prepared to pay for it.'

'Sure,' I say, wishing now I could have time travelled with some records from the sixties and seventies instead of a copy of the *Beano* and some football boots – I'd have made a killing! 'Wait, is *that* what you were discussing with Ringo when I overheard you? Do you provide records and stuff to him?'

Harry nods. 'For his clients I do. Ringo has some very wealthy people visiting that club of his, and some of them are very into their music.'

'So the thing you didn't like being kept down in dingy cellars too long was your records?'

Harry nods. 'It doesn't do them any good to be kept in conditions like that. They're old and precious and they'll warp and bow if they get damp.'

Harry lovingly puts the Beatles album back in its box, and

removes his gloves. Then he smiles at me. 'See? The only thing I'm buying and selling is *music*.'

'Then why didn't you just say?' I ask, incredulously. 'You've nothing to be ashamed of, it's all above board, isn't it?'

'Oh yes, it's all legit. It takes us a while to source the music sometimes, and we're not keen to share our sources because of that – and the fact we do a lot of cash deals with people – but there's nothing illegal going on here.'

'So why the secrecy? Why do you keep quiet about it, make it seem like you're hiding something? It's only buying and selling old records. Ah!' I say as it suddenly dawns on me. 'I see why now. George.'

'You've got it. I don't want to rub it in his face, do I? I started out working with George, learnt everything I knew from him. Then I went out on my own and became much more successful at it than he's ever been. I didn't stop at a little shop on the King's Road, I built this small empire.' He gestures up at the floors above us.

'But George wouldn't care about that,' I protest. 'He's not like that. He'd be really pleased for you. Anyway, he loves that shop, he probably never wanted to do anything else with his life other than sell records out of it.'

'How do you know? Have you asked him?'

I think about this. 'No, I haven't, but I just know he is. And I also know he'd be so happy to learn that his love for music sparked a passion in you to produce all this.'

Harry shrugs. 'Maybe.'

'Not maybe at all, he would be. Why don't you go and visit him in the shop? I know he'd love to see you again and talk properly.'

'No,' Harry says, shaking his head. 'Too much has happened. Too many years have gone by.'

I open my mouth to protest but Harry stops me.

'No, Jo-Jo, it's not going to happen, so you might as well stop now. George and I fell out some years ago; he didn't approve of the way I was running this company at the time, and I may have stepped on his toes in a business sense a few too many times. We can't go back and change the past. It would be lovely if we could sometimes, but we can't.' He makes a move towards the big door again and beckons for me to follow him. 'I'm sorry, Jo-Jo,' he says, reaching for the light switch, 'I know you're only trying to help, but I'd appreciate it if you didn't mention this again now, thank you.'

You might not be able to change the past, Harry, I think, glancing at him as we ride silently back up in the lift together.

But I can.

Thirty-One

'Really?' Ellie asks in astonishment as we sit in a Wimpy and eat the saddest pair of burgers I think I've ever seen and tasted. It almost makes me wistful for a Big Mac and fries, something I thought I'd never feel. 'Only records? How dull.'

'Yep, and we thought we'd got the scoop of the century,' I say, giving up on the burger and laying it down on my plate – yes, plate. The joys of instantly disposable take away packaging hasn't quite reached this London burger joint in 1985.

'But what about Lucy?' Ellie asks. 'Why would she suggest that Harry was involved in drugs if he wasn't?'

'I know, that's what I've been wondering about.' I'd asked Harry about Lucy when he'd insisted Henry drive me home again, but he didn't seem to know anything about her, only that she was a member of his packing staff.

Ellie shrugs as she dips one of her fries in ketchup. 'Doesn't make any sense, does it? But if that's his story, then I guess we'd better leave it. You're sure he's telling the truth? That the record thing isn't just a cover?'

'Yes, positive. No one could pretend to be that enthusiastic about old vinyl LPs unless they genuinely meant it.'

Ellie laughs. 'I know what you mean; Stuart is the same about his punk stuff. When we went back to his flat last night—'

'Whoah there, missy!' I exclaim, holding up my hand. 'Wait just a moment! You went back to his flat?'

Ellie squirms in her chair. 'Yeah, I know, but he's so nice, Jo-Jo, and so sexy. I really, really like him.'

'Obviously!'

'Anyway, as I was saying,' Ellie continues, her cheeks flushed, 'he has this massive collection of punk memorabilia and loads of old records, too. Treats it all like it's fine wine or precious jewels.' A wistful expression appears on her face. 'I'd like to think he'll treat me like that one day if I'm lucky.'

'One night with him and you're in lurve,' I tease.

'No, I'm not! Stop it,' Ellie protests, her cheeks getting even redder. She takes a sip of her Coke. 'Have you ever been in love, Jo-Jo?' she asks. 'I mean, *really* in love? That heart-pounding, stomach-wrenching all-encompassing love that makes you think about that person all the time? And do almost anything to be with them?'

'No,' I say without having to think about it, 'I haven't. I'm not sure it really exists, does it? And if it does, I'm sure I'll never suffer from it in that way.'

'Jo-Jo, you make it sound like a nasty disease. Well, I want to believe it does exist – and I bet you'll be affected by it one day. Love does funny things to people. They say it hits you like a bolt out of the blue and you'll not know what to do with yourself when it does. What?' she asks when I don't respond. 'What are you thinking about?'

'What you just said – about love doing funny things to people. Love may not have hit me like a bolt out of the blue, but something else just has.' I push my chair back and stand up, my mind racing. 'I have to dash, I'll catch you later, OK?'

'Sure,' Ellie says, looking puzzled as I head for the door of the Wimpy. 'I have another date with Stu tonight – shall I call you later and let you know how it goes?'

'Yes, you do that,' I call back, but my mind is already elsewhere. And that place is Beat Music.

As I hurry down the street I reach for my bag as though to pull a mobile phone from it. Damn, I still can't get used to that, I think, as my hand fails to find one.

But I can't wait until tonight to talk to her at the Karma club – and anyway I'm banned from there, so I'm just going to have to try and find her at Harry's place right now.

I'm talking about Lucy, of course.

There's always been something that's bothered me about Lucy since the first time I met her, something that's familiar, and now I think I know what that something is. I also think I know why she could hate Harry so much that she's trying to tarnish his name.

Lucy has that same slightly haunted look in her eyes I'd seen before in Walter Maxwell back in 1963, and then the original Stu back in 1977. She's a loner here in 1985 because she doesn't belong. She's from another time like me, I realise that now. But in that other time had she loved and lost Harry? Had he betrayed her, or cheated on her and now she wants her revenge? Like Ellie said, love could do funny things to people, make them behave in odd ways that were quite out of character.

I manage to hail an empty taxi, and within half an hour I'm waiting outside the gates of Beat Music again. I ask the security guard on duty to tell Harry I'm here, and to my relief the gates swing open and I'm immediately let in.

The taxi sweeps up in front of the main building, looking so very different today in the daylight than it did last night, and I find Harry already waiting for me in the foyer as I step out of the door and pay the driver.

'Good afternoon,' Harry says. 'I didn't expect to see you again so soon.'

'I need to ask you a favour,' I say, smiling apologetically at him. 'And I wonder if you'd mind not asking me why.'

I wait for Lucy in the staff canteen, which, in the middle of the afternoon, is deserted.

I wonder how I'm going to ask her this. I mean, it's not every day someone comes up to you and asks the question: 'Are you from another time – just like me?'

And what if she isn't? What if I've got it all wrong? I made a mistake easily enough with Harry the other day; maybe time travelling has messed my judgement up completely. Lucy will think I'm a head case, and probably tell Harry. And oddly, as much as I don't want it to, what Harry thinks about me matters.

I think about him while I wait. He was very sweet last night after we left the vault. He took me home to my flat, and made sure I was safely in before driving off with Henry. He casually mentioned us seeing one another again – but he meant for drinks or a meal some time. Not me storming into his company and asking for favours that he wasn't allowed to ask about. But, as always, Harry was very calm and collected and did as I asked without making a fuss. He simply said, 'I guess you'll tell me when the time is right.'

Lucy walks into the canteen now. She's wearing jeans, pixie boots and a T-shirt with Duran Duran on. She has virtually no make-up on, and her black, bobbed hair is held back with a thick black Alice band. She looks completely different from the times I've seen her in the club, dressed in her mini skirts and low-cut tops and I realise now how young she actually is.

'Jo-Jo?' she asks, looking surprised as she sits down at the table opposite me. 'They said there was someone here to see me, but they didn't say it was you.'

I study Lucy's eyes for a moment, just to make sure.

'What? Why are you staring at me?' she demands. 'What's going on? Have I done something wrong?'

'Are you lonely, Lucy?' I ask.

'What sort of question is that?' she says, suddenly defensive. She folds her arms and sits back in her chair.

'Please, it's important.'

She sighs. 'I don't have a packed social calendar as you well know, working two jobs.'

'And you mentioned the other night you don't have any family here, either?'

'What is this?' she asks, looking at me suspiciously. 'Are you from the Social? I thought you were a journalist. Where's your photographer mate today?'

282

'Do you feel like you fit in?' I attempt. Can I really be wrong again?

'Yeah, I love packing bloody records up all day and serving drinks to leering fat bastards at night. Look, when they told me I was going to talk to a journalist today I was hoping for a six-page spread in *OK!* or even *Hello!* if I put a posh enough accent on!' She grins at her own joke. 'I certainly didn't expect it would be *you* asking me weird questions, Jo-Jo. I thought you were one of the all right ones.'

I sigh and lean back in my chair; this is going nowhere. Then suddenly my eyes dart back towards Lucy.

'What did you say just then?' I ask. 'About magazines?'

'Dunno,' she shrugs, her cheeks pinking a little.

'*Hello!* and *OK!* magazines aren't around yet,' I say, my eyes lighting up as my brain begins to whizz. I sit forward in my seat again. 'So I *am* right. You're one of them, aren't you? I mean, one of *us*.'

'What are you babbling on about now?' Lucy asks, opening a pack of gum with fingers that are trembling slightly. She offers me some, but I decline.

'You've travelled in time,' I whisper just in case anyone should be listening in the deserted canteen.

'What do you know about *that*?' she hisses.

'I know, because I've done it too.'

Lucy's eyes narrow. 'Why should I believe you? You're a journalist, you'll do anything if you get the whiff of a good story.'

'I'm telling you the truth, Lucy. I've been back to 1963 and 1977 and now I'm stuck here in 1985. I don't belong in any of those years, any more than you do. And I'm not a journalist, I'm an accountant from 2013.'

Lucy looks unimpressed by my plea until I mention the word 2013.

'You're from 2013?'

'Yes, that's right.'

She considers this. 'If you are, who's the president of the United States then?'

'Barack Obama, he was re-elected for a second term.'

'The prime minister of the UK?'

'David Cameron.'

She pulls a face, but nods. Then she thinks for a moment. 'Who are the judges on *The X Factor* that year?'

I stare at Lucy. 'Are you kidding me?'

She shakes her head.

'I don't know; it hadn't started when I left. But you can bet Louis Walsh is one – they can't get rid of *him*.'

Lucy grins. 'You really are from 2013, aren't you?'

'Yes, and so are you by the sound of it. What happened?'

'Hit and run,' Lucy says, grimacing. 'I'd got a job in Liverpool city centre for the day, easy money it was too, all I had to do was walk about with a stupid sandwich board strapped to my chest.' She laughs bitterly. 'Ticket to Ride bus tours they were called. Turns out it was my ticket to ride out of there that day, because when I stepped out to cross the road a car just came from nowhere and hit me.'

I swallow hard. 'That's what happened to me.'

'Really?' Lucy asks, looking surprised. 'Maybe that's how we all go.'

'No,' I shake my head, 'it varies.'

'How do you know all this?' Lucy asks 'What makes you an expert?'

'I'm no expert, believe me I wish I was, but in every decade I've visited I've met someone just like us, stuck in a time they don't want to be in.'

'Tell me about it,' Lucy rolls her eyes. 'The eighties is retro back in 2013, as you probably remember. It's cool to like the music, watch the films and wear the clothes, but it's not so much fun actually living it for real. And you say there's lots of us doing it?'

'Yes, it would appear so. I haven't quite figured out how it all works myself yet. How long have you been here?'

'Not long, a few months, so I guess I'm quite new to it all. Took me a few days to realise it wasn't some bad dream I was going to wake up from, and I was going to have to start earning some sort of living. Luckily, that's when Ringo found me and offered me the job at the club. I know you don't like him, Jo-Jo,' she says when I pull a face. 'But he saved my bacon, I was virtually living in the gutter and now at least I have a room of my own in the house that Ringo rents out to the girls at his club when they first start working for him. When I was back on my feet and I got the job here as well, I moved out into my own flat.'

I'm still not convinced by this description of Ringo as some knight in shining armour, saving damsels in distress.

'What else goes on in this house he rents out?' I ask sceptically. 'Are there many visitors to it? *Male* visitors?'

'Nah, it's not like that at all. Ringo looks after his girls, and I mean *genuinely* looks after them. I may be young, but I'm not stupid, Jo-Jo, and I wondered that myself when I took him up on his offer of a room and a job at the club. But I can 100 per cent guarantee you that no funny business goes on at that house or at the club.'

'So you're telling me he helps these young girls out of the goodness of his heart? I find that hard to believe.'

'Obviously Ringo makes money out of the club, and having pretty girls working for him is a bonus. And I'm not saying that a few shady deals haven't taken place there on occasion – Ringo isn't exactly Mother Teresa – but he's no pimp, Jo-Jo. You've got that completely wrong. He helps girls out by giving them a safe home when they're in need. In return, they work for him at the club. It's a simple arrangement that suits both parties until the former is back on their feet again and can move on. Ringo has a lot of contacts, that's how most of the girls get their new jobs, through people they meet at the club.'

I must still look sceptical, because Lucy adds, 'It's the truth, Jo-Jo – I should know, I was one of the girls on the streets. Ringo gave me a safe place to stay, and for that I'll always be grateful to him.'

'So when he offers the chance for his clients to come back-stage and *meet* the girls – that's it? He simply introduces them to prospective employers?'

'Yeah. I'm sure a lot of them think it's for something else, but Ringo makes it quite clear from the start what's what.'

I think about this for a moment. 'It's an unorthodox approach, I guess, but if it works . . .'

Lucy nods. 'It does.'

'Perhaps I did add two and two together and get five on this occasion.'

'Maths obviously not your strong point, eh?' Lucy smiles.

'Not any more, it would seem.'

Lucy thinks for a moment. 'But even though I'm fairly set-tled now, I'd do anything to go back again – I miss my family so much. It must be worse for you, though, if you keep moving around all the time. At least I'm stuck here in one decade with the same people. You can't ever know whether you're coming or going.'

'It's not easy, but I manage,' I reply, thinking about Harry and Ellie, my two constants, and then I remember George. 'Sometimes I actually prefer it to my old life.'

'Really?' Lucy asks in disbelief.

'Yes.' I'm quite surprised myself by this revelation. 'I've made some good friends throughout this journey so far, and had some fun times . . . ' I shake my head. 'Anyway, let's talk about you again, not me. This car that hit you back in 2013, it wasn't white by any chance, was it?'

'No.' Lucy vehemently shakes her head. 'Definitely not, it was black. A shiny black Audi TT.'

'You seem to remember it well.'

'Too right I do, and the driver.'

'Really, what did the driver look like?'

'That's easy – exactly like my boss.'

'Who, Ringo?'

'No, not that boss, Jo-Jo. My other boss. Harry, Harry Rigby.'

Thirty-Two

'Harry hit you with a sports car in 2013?' I exclaim, hardly able to believe my ears.

Lucy nods. 'Yep. So you can imagine how I felt when I got here and found him living in 1985 as happy as Larry, without a care in the world, when he'd wrecked mine.'

My mind rushes with thoughts faster than my brain can sift through them.

'Is that why you tried to ruin Harry's reputation, to get back at him for hitting you with his car?' So it wasn't a love-based revenge after all.

Lucy nods guiltily.

'I didn't set out to do it; I didn't even know he was my boss until a week after I started working here. But when your mate started poking her nose around and asking questions, I couldn't help myself. The man ruined my life, Jo-Jo!'

'And you could have ruined his, too. Even if the stuff about drugs wasn't true, if the papers had got hold of that rumour his business name would have been damaged for ever.'

'I know and I'm really sorry. I shouldn't have done it, I realise that now.'

Lucy does look genuinely distraught. So I decide to pursue some of the other questions that are now jostling for position in my brain. Which Harry was this in Liverpool? The Harry I'd originally met in 2013? This Harry from 1985, or a different Harry I'd not yet discovered?

'So when Harry hit you with the car, what exactly did he look like – an older version of himself?'

'No, very much like this one, only wearing cooler clothes! Sorry,' she apologises, 'I shouldn't joke about it.'

'It's fine,' I say, still thinking. 'You have to smile about this whole thing, or you'd just go mad trying to work it out sometimes. So, if it wasn't *this* Harry that hit you – that means it must be an another version of him ... '

'What do you mean?' Lucy asks. 'I've been wondering about that too: how come he hadn't aged from 1985? I know plastic surgery is good back in 2013 but it's not *that* good and we're talking twenty-eight years!'

'It's the only way to explain what's happening,' I say, looking at her across the table. 'There must be many versions of all of us existing at once. Usually our paths would never meet, but when something abnormal happens, like what's happened to the two of us, where we've jumped over from one zone into another, our paths sometimes have to cross with those we've known before.'

'I've heard of that. Don't they call it parallel universes?'

'Yes, I think they do. A friend of mine likes to describe it in book terms, though, he says it's like characters—'

'From one book crossing over into another,' Lucy chips in.

'They're not really supposed to be in that story, but they kind of fit?'

'Yes, it was something similar.'

'You must know George,' she says, nodding.

'You've met?'

'Yeah, briefly. He came into Rocky's club one day and I served him.'

'George was in Rocky's club?'

'Never seen him before or since, mind. But Rocky seemed to know him pretty well. Rocky sometimes spouts a similar type of flowery nonsense when he's trying to make a point, too.'

That's something I didn't expect to hear. George and Rocky being big pals.

'So what do you reckon, Jo-Jo?' Lucy asks. 'Do you reckon you're gonna hang around here long enough for us to be friends? It would be good to know someone who actually knew who Brad Pitt was, or the joy of a skinny vanilla latte?'

'Oh,' I sigh, 'don't talk to me about the lack of decent coffee shops. I'm desperate for a Starbucks or a Costa.'

Lucy smiles. 'There's a few Costas about in London if you search them out already. Not much choice, mind. But I tell you what,' she continues eagerly, 'when our first local Starbucks opens, we'll be its first two customers. We time travellers have to stick together, you know.'

'Not too long to wait for that skinny vanilla latte then,' I smile.

'So does that mean we're friends now?' she asks hopefully.

'Friends,' I reply taking Lucy's hand and squeezing it. 'Whatever universe or coffee shop we're in.'

*

Later, as I lie on the settee in my flat above the record shop, with the kids from *Fame* dancing away to themselves on the television in front of me, I try and fit a few more pieces of the puzzle into place.

Every decade I've been in so far has been strange in some way, but this one feels different. There are too many weird things going on this time, too many coincidences.

Like Lucy coming back from 2013 after being knocked down by a car driven by Harry. Stu being here again when I already met him in 1977, and then him and Ellie getting together too. I spoke to Lucy about paths crossing, but this is like some great big tapestry where all the threads are beginning to weave into one another – except the picture it's creating isn't a very clear one. The threads aren't making any sense. I need to untangle them and stitch them into something I can understand. But what is it?

The phone rings in the hall, so I roll up off the settee to answer it.

'Jo-Jo, guess what?' It's Ellie's excited voice, flowing at full speed down the line.

'What?' I ask, my mind still on my needlework issues.

'Stuart says he can get us all into Live Aid at the weekend. Me and you, as well as George!'

'That's great,' I reply half-heartedly, not really absorbing what Ellie is saying.

'Are you kidding me? It's gonna be mega, the music event of the decade, if not the century! And all you can say is *that's great*.'

'Sorry, of course that's absolutely fantastic! And very generous of him. But how come he can do that for so many of us?'

'The band he roadies for is playing a set, so he's gonna be

backstage with them; apparently there's tickets floating about for all those who're involved. Ooh, I can't wait! Stuart says it'll be a once-in-a-lifetime event.'

'I'm sure it will. Tell Stuart thanks, I'd love to come.'

As I put the phone back on the receiver, the phrase Ellie uttered still rings in my ears. *A once-in-a-lifetime* . . .

Of course it's once in a lifetime for Stu. It's going to be the end of one lifetime for him.

Unless . . .

Thirty-Three

It's the morning of Saturday 13 July 1985 and the whole country seems to be in the grip of Live Aid fever.

Stu, as promised, has got us all passes to get into the concert at Wembley Arena, and, at my request, has even managed to swing an extra one for Harry, too. It's my thank you to him for letting me see Lucy the other day, and also because I still feel guilty for ever doubting him in the first place.

But even though this is my way of making it up to him, his unresolved issues with George still bother me, so I've formulated a plan to try and get them together to 'talk it out'. Unfortunately, this also ties in heavily with my plan to try and help Stu, so there's an awful lot riding on this concert this afternoon, other than simply raising a lot of much-needed money for Africa. If only those bands knew ...

I've figured out, from what Stu told me back in 1977, that this must be the concert he got electrocuted at. He said it was a huge outdoor gig, and he hadn't been able to set the equipment up himself. So this must be the one – at least, I hope it is.

All I have to do is stop him from getting to the concert and plugging in the equipment, and I'll prevent him from being electrocuted. It's as simple as that. At least, it sounds that simple!

'Jo-Jo, are you nearly ready?' I hear called up the stairs. It's George. 'Public transport will be jam-packed today with all this going on.'

I look towards my TV where I've been watching the concert preparations taking place all morning, then I glance at my watch and I take a deep breath. *Here goes ...*

'Just coming, George!' I call. *Now don't you be late, Harry*, I think as I go slowly down the stairs. *I can't imagine you're ever late and today is not the time to try it out for the first time.*

'Nice outfit,' George says as I walk through the side door into the shop. I'm wearing black leather trousers, black boots, and a black and white blouse with a large pussy bow at the neck. 'Very Princess Di.'

'Am I?' I say, looking at my reflection in the window of the shop. 'I hardly think so.'

'Fine-looking woman,' George says.

'Yes, I suppose she was.'

'Was?' George questions.

I look at George. Just when I think I might have it all figured out and I know what George's part in all this is, he says something like that.

'Oh!' I say, looking out of the window at the bright red Ferrari that's just drawn up on the opposite side of the road. 'Isn't that Harry?'

Harry sits tightly in his seat, waiting for me. He doesn't look like he's going to be persuaded to move from it easily either.

'What's Harry doing here?' George asks, looking through the window. 'Is he coming too?'

'Just hold on one moment, George,' I say, opening the shop door and rushing outside.

'Why don't you come in?' I call to Harry. 'I'm not quite ready.'

'I'm fine just here, thanks,' Harry says, looking straight ahead.

Damn! This calls for drastic measures.

'Well, I'll just be a minute.'

I head back inside the shop, but no sooner have I set foot inside than I'm back out on the pavement again.

'Harry, quick, I need your help, it's George! I don't know what's wrong with him, but he's laid out on the floor and I don't think he's breathing!'

Harry's head snaps around, he casts his blue eyes quickly over me, then looks with alarm to the shop.

'Do you think it might be a heart attack?' I add, in case he needs further encouragement.

But I needn't have worried. Without bothering to open the door, Harry has already leapt from his car, and is running over the road straight past me into the shop.

'Where is he?' he demands, looking at the deserted interior.

'Where's who?' George asks, appearing from the back.

'But Jo-Jo s-said ... ' Harry stutters, looking confused.

'Sorry!' I call apologetically from the door. 'But I had to get you two talking. Now I'm even sorrier for what I'm about to do next!'

I grab the key to the shop door where George has just put it in readiness to lock up, then I pull the door shut and lock it securely from the outside.

'Jo-Jo!' Harry shouts, banging on the glass panel window. 'Open this door at once!'

'No, not until the two of you sort out your differences, or at least try and talk about them.'

Through the glass I see George shrug as Harry now rattles on the interior door that leads to the stairs up to my flat. I hold up that key in front of the glass and wave it at him.

I turn away from the shop knowing there's nothing more I can do for the moment except hope, and move my thoughts on to my other problem – Stu.

My original idea had been to do something similar to what I was doing to George and Harry right now. But I knew Stu was likely to break the door down if I tried. Live Aid was *the* event to be at today, whether you worked in the music industry or not. And there was no way Stu would miss out for the sake of a piece of plywood and some glass.

So I'd called in my favour – from Rocky.

And like the true gangster he was, he hadn't asked any questions.

So right at this minute I was praying that Stu was detained somewhere at Rocky's pleasure. I'd insisted to Rocky that 'his boys' were not to lay a finger on him, just to keep him away from the concert until it was all over, and Rocky, somewhat grudgingly to begin with, had agreed.

I sigh, and rest my head back against the cool brick wall behind me for a moment. *So far so good. Everything seems to be going to plan for once.*

'You *are* still here!' Ellie calls as a motorbike zooms up next to me with two people riding on it. She lifts her helmet and shakes out her blonde hair. 'We were ringing and ringing before we left a few minutes ago, but no one answered.'

'Yeah, there's some stuff going on in the shop, and we've been kinda tied up.'

'*You've* been tied up!' Ellie exclaims. 'What about poor Stuart? Some bloke tried to mug him earlier outside his flat.'

The passenger on the bike lifts his helmet now. It's Stu.

'They did?' I ask, looking at him in horror.

'Yeah,' Ellie continues, 'but luckily I was just pulling up on me bike. I took one of them out with my helmet, and the other I used my pepper spray on. They soon scarpered.'

'She's my hero,' Stu says, leaning across the saddle to kiss Ellie. 'Without you I might not have made it to the concert, and I'm late now already.'

'Yeah, sweetie, we'll be off in a sec,' Ellie says, looking lovingly back at him. 'I just want to make sure Jo-Jo is OK. Is that Harry's car?' she asks, looking at the red Ferrari.

'Yes,' I reply distractedly. *What am I going to do now?*

'Where is he, then?'

'Er ... he's in the shop talking to George.' *At least, I hope that's what they're doing.*

'Really? How'd you manage to get Harry Rigby to do that? Those two are sworn enemies, aren't they?'

'Ellie, sweetheart,' Stu interrupts, 'I really have to be going!'

'Sure, sorry. Look, I'll catch up with you later, Jo-Jo, we have to fly!'

'No!' I cry, thrusting my hand out to prevent her putting her helmet back on. 'I mean: you can't go yet.'

'Why?' Ellie asks, baffled. 'What's wrong?'

'I – I'm worried, that – that there might be a fight!' I improvise.

'Between Harry and George?' Ellie laughs. 'I hardly think so. Besides,' she winks, 'I wouldn't fancy Harry's chances if there was! Sorry, babe,' she pulls on her helmet properly this time, 'but we have to go! My man is an important cog in the Live Aid machine today, and I'm gonna get him there on time if it kills me!'

It won't kill you, I think, as I watch them U-turn in the road and zoom off down the street. But it probably will Stu.

'Damn!' I shout, stamping my foot on the ground in frustration. 'Damn you, Ellie, and your blasted motorbike.'

'Problem?' a voice enquires next to me.

'Ringo?' I ask in astonishment, amazed to see him out of his usual habitat – the club. 'What are you doing here?'

'Lucy told me what happened,' he says darkly. 'Is there somewhere we can go to talk?

'Um . . . ' I think about the last time Ringo and I 'talked'. 'I'd say come into the shop,' I offer, 'but there's some stuff going on in there right now.'

'A quick coffee, then?' he asks. 'Over the road? This won't take long.' He gestures to a café on the opposite side of the road a little way along from George's shop.

'Sure,' I nod. Lucy said that Ringo wasn't all bad, and as I look dejectedly in the direction of the departed motorbike, I realise there isn't much I can do now for Stu anyway – but at least I tried.

'You can't win them all,' Ringo says, after we've walked along the road a little, crossed over on the crossing and entered the café.

'What do you mean?' I ask, sitting down at a table near the window. I figure that at least if I'm in full view nothing too bad can happen to me. Whatever Lucy said, I still don't trust him.

'Two coffees, please love,' Ringo asks the waitress, who appears immediately to take our order. 'That OK with you, Jo-Jo?'

'Yes, fine thanks,' I reply, watching him. Even away from the club he's immaculately dressed as always in a sharp black suit, white shirt and tie. I almost smile. If you were to ask me to describe what a gangster looks like, Ringo would fit the bill exactly. But I don't feel much like smiling at the moment. 'What did you mean before outside? You can't win them all?'

'When you try to help people,' Ringo says, looping his big fat fingers together on the table in front of him, 'it doesn't always go right.'

I eye him suspiciously across the table. What is he getting at? I take a quick glance behind me, half expecting two big thugs to be standing in the doorway, ready to dispose of me when Ringo gives them the nod. But there's no one. The café, like so many other places today, is empty, while everyone watches the Live Aid concert. Even the waitress is watching a little portable television placed prominently on the counter.

'I try and help people all the time,' he continues. 'But they're always suspicious of my motives. People like you, for instance.'

I swallow hard. What has Lucy been telling him?

The waitress brings our coffee now. She puts two cups of brown hot liquid on the table, with a jug of milk and some sachets of sugar.

Ringo lifts the jug and pours a fair amount of the milk into his own coffee, then opens three of the sachets of sugar and tips them into his cup while I silently watch him.

'Like yours black, do you?' he asks, looking at my untouched coffee. 'Can't bear it like that myself. I'm a latte man; caramel is my favourite, gingerbread if it's available. But until that comes along, this is the best I can do.' He lifts his cup of coffee and begins to drink from it. His black eyes study me intently while I sit, open-mouthed, opposite him.

'You – you're one of us?' I whisper in amazement across the table, looking carefully around me as though the waitress might overhear us from the counter, but she's too engrossed in Status Quo's 'Rockin' All Over the World' right now. 'You must be, to know coffee like that. Only someone from the future would know about lattes and different-flavoured syrups.'

Ringo takes another sip of his coffee, then puts his cup down.

'I am indeed.'

'But why didn't you say so before?'

'I didn't know you were too until Lucy came to me with a story about how you were her new best friend and you really understood what she was going through etc, etc. I figured the rest out from there.'

'How long have you been here?' I ask 'Where are you from?'

'I've been here a long, long time, Jo-Jo,' Ringo says, not

really answering my question. 'So long, in fact, that I can't really remember what my life was like before. I help out those that I find in a similar predicament to me, and help them get back on their feet again so they can move on.'

'Like the girls in the club?' I ask. 'Although I fail to see how turning some of them into strippers is helping them.'

'Jo-Jo, don't go all holier-than-thou on me. I've had enough of that in the past. It's not ideal, I know, but the club gives them contacts, they meet people, and with my help they move on in life, get better jobs, without being taken advantage of. And stripping, although we prefer to call it exotic dancing, is as far as it goes, I can assure you.'

I think about this. 'That's what Lucy said. Is that really true, though? No funny business goes on behind the scenes?'

Ringo puts his hand on his heart. 'May Archangel Michael strike me down with his mighty sword now if I'm lying – and just between the two of us, he's one mighty fearsome dude.'

I can't figure out if Ringo is being serious now.

'But what I'm trying to tell you is, Jo-Jo, sometimes you win, and sometimes you lose at this game.'

'What do you mean?'

'Sometimes the things you do to try and help people work out for the good, and sometimes they don't. But when they don't, it's because they're not supposed to. Believe me, I know. I've been doing it long enough.'

I still look blankly at him.

'Take, for instance, your friend Stu. He was always going to get to that concert whatever you did. It's his destiny. Nothing you can do about it.'

301

I look out of the window again. 'But poor Stu – and now poor Ellie, too. She's going to suffer as well when he dies. She's besotted with him.'

'Yes, she will,' he says, nodding. 'But it will make her a stronger person for it.'

'But *why*? Why can't I just stop all this bad stuff happening to people? What's the point to all this if no good can come from it?'

'Because, if Stu doesn't plug that amp in, then someone else will. That is Stu, and now Ellie's, destiny. You can't change that. You don't need to change that. You're here to do and learn other things. Am I making any sense?'

I shrug. 'Sort of ...'

'However, if you were to look back down the road,' he says, turning his gaze out of the window towards Groovy Records, 'you'd see two old friends who should never have been parted, reunited once more. That's because of you, Jo-Jo. Apart from what you've learnt about yourself, that's what good you've done by being here in 1985.'

I look out of the window towards the shop. I can't see inside it properly from here, but as I think about George and Harry being reunited again after all this time, a deep, warm feeling spreads right through me, and I turn back towards Ringo to tell him what I've just felt, but he's gone.

What? How could he have? I look all around the café, but I'm definitely the only customer in here now, with two cups of coffee on my table, one full where I haven't touched it, and the other empty. How on earth did he leave without me hearing him? And he's left me to pay, too – charming! I'm about to get up and settle our bill, when I notice something sitting on the table in front of me; it's a tiny brooch in the shape of a four-leaf clover.

How very odd, I think, picking it up to examine it. *Why would Ringo leave me a brooch, of all things?*

I put the brooch in my purse and leave a couple of pound notes on the table for the coffees; our waitress is still too involved in the concert to even notice what I'm doing. Taking a quick glance down the road towards the shop again, I can now see Harry and George at the window, probably looking for me to come and unlock the door and let them out now they've done their part, made up and become friends again. So I hurriedly leave the shop and rush out on to the zebra crossing, confident, on this exceptionally quiet day on the King's Road, that there's unlikely to be any traffic coming.

As I get about halfway across, I can just see Harry peeking through the glass window of the shop door. He waves, so I lift my hand to wave back, and it's then that it happens. The white sports car appears from nowhere, screeching around the corner as it always does.

The last thing I see is the look of horror on Harry's face as he watches me – and then, as always, it all goes cold.

Get Back

Thirty-Four

I open my eyes, knowing what will greet me before the daylight even has time to hit my pupils.

There they all are, as always, the small crowd that has gathered above me to see whether I'm alive or dead.

The question I have to ask myself as I see the relief on their faces as they assume from my movement that I'm alive is: am I?

I mean, yes, I'm moving, breathing and living like a normal human being, but what sort of human being travels through time? Is this real? Is it a dream? Or is it my latest theory, that I'm a type of angelic being, spending a short time in people's lives, steering them back on to the right path, then moving on to another lifetime and another set of lives that need shaking up a bit?

The ice-cold water suddenly cascading down my face suggests that going with option one might be the best course of action right now. After all, how many angels get a glass of water thrown in their face?

'Sorry!' Ellie apologises. 'I thought it might help.'

'If I'd fainted, maybe it might have,' I say, wiping the water away with my hand. 'But I've been hit by a car.'

'You remember?' she asks, amazed. 'I thought you might have lost your memory in the accident, and we'd have to play Take That songs at your bedside on a twenty-four-hour loop, and maybe get the band to visit you at the hospital to try and get you to remember.'

I look up at Ellie now. She's wearing green jogging bottoms and trainers, and on her top half is a Take That tour sweatshirt with the band's faces emblazoned across the front.

'No, that won't be necessary, really. I'm fine.'

'Are you sure, love?' a man next to me asks. 'That was quite a tumble you just took. Bloody driver didn't stop, did he? I tried to get his registration, but he took off like something from that movie – *Speed*.'

'*Speed* was about a bus, not a car, you muppet,' Ellie says, shaking her head.

'I'm sorry,' I say to the man, apologising for Ellie. 'I'm fine, really. I know how to fall,' I improvise, 'I do martial arts.'

'Like Jean Claude Van Damme?' he asks.

So they know who *he* is now. 'Yeah, something like him.'

'I love his movies, I do.' The man, who's wearing a Lonsdale sweatshirt and a very tight pair of black and white stonewashed jeans, tries to do a karate kick up in the air, but fails miserably when his jeans prevent him from raising his leg over knee height.

Mmm, maybe Ellie was right about the muppet bit . . .

'Anyway . . . ' I say, making a move to stand up. Ellie grabs my arm, and I assume she's trying to help me, but then she lets go and grabs a Woolworths carrier bag that's been lying next to me on the zebra crossing. She immediately whips it open and looks inside.

'Phew,' she says, looking relieved. 'You didn't squash them.'

'Squash what?' I ask, brushing some dirt from my hooded sweatshirt. As I look down at it I notice a bright yellow double TT insignia printed on the front.

'The limited edition posters we got with the CDs this morning, dummy! Look,' she says, pulling two rolled-up tubes of paper from the bag, then to my horror she actually kisses one. 'They're still pristine!'

It's my turn to grab Ellie's arm now. 'Thanks for your concern, everyone,' I announce to the few people who have gathered on the zebra crossing. 'But I'm fine, really. Please continue with whatever you were doing.' Then I drag Ellie on to the pavement.

'What the hell are you doing?' I ask. 'Kissing a roll of paper? Have you flipped?'

She looks at me with a puzzled expression. 'Are you having me on? We've been waiting *weeks* to get these posters; the last thing we wanted was for you to flatten them. Much as I'd like to see Robbie doubled, a crease down the centre of his face splitting him in two would not look good on my wall.'

I watch her put them carefully back in the Woolworths carrier bag. Ellie doesn't look much like a teenage girl to me, the type I'd expect to be screaming at concerts and kissing posters of pop stars on her bedroom wall. She looks older than that, maybe in her late twenties, early thirties? She still has the same long blonde hair she's always had, but this time it's not curly, it's just really ... big. It's like she's gone a bit mad with the mousse, and blow-dried her hair upside down until it's as full as she can possibly make it.

I glance at myself in the reflection of the nearest shop window.

I'm hardly what you'd call a teenybopper, either. I'm a similar age to Ellie, maybe a year or two older, and in addition to my Take That hoody, I'm wearing plain black trousers and sensible flat black court shoes. I pull open my hoody at the neck and take a peek inside, nearly blinding myself at the neon that glares back up at me from a pink, blue and yellow checked black shirt.

'What are you doing?' Ellie asks. 'Have you got something stuck down there after your fall?'

'Only a bad taste in fashion,' I moan.

'Bloody hell, is that the time,' Ellie says as she glances at her watch. 'We need to get back to school, afternoon lessons will be starting in a minute and we're gonna be late.'

I'm torn by my ever-present urge to speak to George as soon as I arrive in a new decade, and by my loathing of being late for whatever it is I'm supposed to be doing right now. I take a quick look to make sure Groovy Records is still further along the street, and then at Ellie already speeding up the King's Road.

I choose to follow Ellie.

She's usually the link that helps me discover just what type of life I'm living in each new year I find myself in. Without her I haven't a clue. I'll just have to pop back later and catch up with George after I've discovered what I'm in for this time.

As we run together along the road and then duck down a couple of side streets – a short cut, Ellie insists – I wonder if I've got this all wrong. Maybe we're younger than we look? Maybe it was the fashion of the nineties to dress older? I've quickly worked out that's where I must be this time – from the fashion and Ellie's obsession with Take That. Plus it would make sense; each time when I jumped through time so far I've moved on a decade, so it ought to be. But what doesn't make sense is this age thing; if we're on our way back to school, carrying Take That posters and wearing Take That merchandise, we must be teenagers, surely? But then why aren't we wearing school uniform? Perhaps we're sixth formers – yes, that must be it.

'Afternoon, Miss Williams,' a caretaker wearing a brown overall says as we dash through the school gate. 'Cutting it a bit fine, aren't you? The bell went five minutes ago.'

'Thank you, John,' Ellie calls, pulling her sweatshirt over her head as we dash across the playground, 'we're quite aware of that!'

'Proverb 19:2,' John calls as we dash past him. '"It is not good to have zeal without knowledge, nor to be hasty and miss the way".' He gives me a meaningful look as I pass. 'It's good to see you again, Miss McKenzie.'

'Yes,' I smile. 'It's good to be back. I think.'

'Quick!' Ellie hisses as she holds open a door. 'Let's get away before he quotes the whole Bible to us. Plus we need to get to the staffroom and get changed as fast as we can – I'm supposed to be in a bloody Year 2 assembly now.'

'We're teachers?' I gasp as I follow her down a hall with a notice that clearly states 'No running' even though we are.

'I know,' she giggles. 'Doesn't set a very good example, does it?' She holds open another door and I find myself inside a teachers' staffroom. It's clear that's what it is by the copious amount of empty mugs and open packets of biscuits that are scattered in amongst the armchairs and copies of the *Guardian* and *Cosmopolitan* magazine. 'What a start to the second day of a new school year!'

Ellie runs over to some lockers, twists hers open, and pulls out a bright green and pink tracksuit top to match the jogging bottoms she's already wearing. Then, while I watch, she pulls it on, zips it up and slings a whistle round her neck. 'You're lucky,' she says, 'at least you only have to change your sweater. Why did I ever agree to teach PE this term?'

You're wearing a shell suit, Ellie! I think as I pull my hoody over my head and hang it in the locker next to hers, which luckily for me has my name on the front. *You're actually wearing a shell suit!* I try and keep a straight face while I smooth down my neon shirt, which I guess isn't that much better, turn around, and follow her as we dash out of the staffroom again.

'Catch you later,' Ellie says as we pass a classroom door and she rushes ahead. 'Lucky for you, your new lot don't look like they're causing too much aggro in there.'

I turn and look through the glass panel of the wooden door. Inside there's a classroom filled with children of about seven or eight years old sitting at and on tables. I turn back to say something to Ellie, but she's gone hurtling off in the direction of the assembly hall.

'Right then,' I say quietly to myself. 'How scary can a class of kids be?'

I take a deep breath and push open the door. And wish I had Ellie's whistle to try and restore some calm, as the wave of noise that hits me upon entering the room almost bowls me over.

'Hey!' I call into the sea of voices. 'Hey, can you all be quiet for a moment?'

It's like throwing a pebble out into the Atlantic.

So I try again. 'Quiet, you guys, *please*!'

Nothing.

I walk to the front of the classroom, picking up a metal waste paper bin as I do. Then I empty out the contents on top of my desk, turn it upside down, and bang hard on top of it, like a drum.

If David Beckham had walked into the room, he wouldn't have got a more stunned reaction than the one on the faces in front of me now. I think for a moment: is David Beckham famous yet? I'm guessing he might just have been playing for Manchester United, so he might have had less impact. I smile at the thought of a non-famous Becks.

'What's so funny, miss?' a small girl with blonde pigtails asks.

'Nothing. I'm just pleased I've got your attention, that's all. Now,' I say, walking round to the front of the desk. 'When I call for quiet in here again, I shall expect quiet, understood?'

There are murmurings of agreement from a few of the children.

'I said, *is that understood*?'

'Yes, miss!' The majority now speak up.

'Now, I'd like a volunteer to come and clear the rubbish

from my desk.' I look sternly across the room as everyone tries not to catch my eye.

A young boy with brown curly hair pushes back his chair. 'I'll do it,' he says, standing up.

'Thank you,' I say, and as he passes me I see his name is scribbled on a sticker on his sweatshirt. 'That's good of you to volunteer, Paul.'

'Now,' I announce, as Paul begins sweeping screwed up bits of paper and pencil shavings back into the metal bin, 'who can tell me what we were doing in the last lesson?'

I'm quite surprising myself at how easily I'm slipping into this new teacher role. As I look around the classroom now, the children actually seem to be listening to me.

'Them awful things with lines in the middle,' a little girl on the back table speaks up. I squint to see her name tag – thank goodness it's the beginning of term and they're wearing them, otherwise I'd have no chance.

'Can you be more specific, Beatrice?' I ask.

'The ones with numbers on the top and the bottom.'

'Do you mean fractions?'

'Yeah, them things.'

Wow, I'm teaching them maths – my specialist subject. This is great!

'Except you was talking about percentages as well,' another boy – Lee – now helps out. 'And then you said we'd talk about probably this time.'

'I said we'd talk about *probably*?'

'Yeah. That's right.'

My desk has now been cleared and Paul goes back to his seat. 'You said *probability*, not probably!' he mutters as he passes.

'Probability! That makes more sense! ' I ease myself on to the edge of my desk. 'Now, who can tell me something about probability?'

They all gaze back blankly at me.

'Let me think of an example then.' I rack my brain for something I think they'll understand. 'Imagine you have a shopping bag and in it there are three bananas and nothing else. The probability of reaching into the bag and pulling out a banana is one; that's certain because there is nothing else in the bag. But the probability of reaching into the bag and pulling out an apple is zero; it's impossible, because there are no apples in there. Does that help?'

They still stare up at me blankly. *This teaching lark might be harder than I first thought.*

'Does anyone have a coin?' I try.

They all shake their heads, so I feel around in the pocket of my trousers. I pull out a collection of coins, and in the middle of them is the four-leaf-clover brooch that Rocky gave me. So *you've* come with me this time, have you? I think, strangely unfazed this time, as I pop it safely back in my pocket, just like the *Beano* and the football boots before it.

'Now,' I say, turning my attention back to the class, 'can anyone toss a coin?'

Three hands are raised. 'Jason, would you like to come up and toss a coin for us, please?'

Jason comes up to the front of the classroom and spins a ten-pence piece high in the air, then catches it deftly on the back of his hand.

'Heads or tails, miss?' he asks.

'I'll go heads,' I choose. 'But just wait a minute before you take a look at the coin. Now, what are the chances of it being a head?'

A few hands are raised.

'Mary?'

'Half and half, miss.'

'Yes, but what's half and half expressed as a fraction?'

'A half, miss,' she answers without thinking.

'Good, now what's a half expressed as a percentage?'

Mary thinks about this one. 'Fifty per cent?'

'Yes, that's right. So if the chances of me getting a head are half or 50 per cent, what is the probability?'

Mary pulls a face.

'Yes, Stella?' I respond to the raised hand.

'One in two, miss.'

'That's right, Stella, well done. So 50 per cent, a half and one in two are all ways of describing the probability of a coin toss. What was it, out of interest, Jason?'

'A head, miss,' Jason says, lifting his hand to reveal the coin. 'Good call.' He begins to walk back to his seat.

'Jason, haven't you forgotten something?' I ask, holding out my hand.

'Sorry, miss,' he says, backing down the classroom and returning the ten pence to me.

'See, the probability of me not noticing that was zero,' I joke, smiling at him. 'Now, do we have any dice in here? We'll do some work with those next.'

I enjoy the rest of the lesson, and the children seem to catch on really quickly once I find ways of teaching the subject that make sense to them.

When the bell goes for break I'm quite surprised to find the time has gone so quickly.

'Class, gather up your things,' I call, 'and proceed in an orderly fashion outside. Remember, no running in the corridor!'

I breathe a sigh of relief as they all file out of the classroom, chattering and giggling together in anticipation of a few minutes' playtime outside in the fresh air.

'Excuse me, miss, can I just ask you a quick question?' It's Paul, the boy who helped clear my desk of rubbish.

'Yes, of course, Paul, what is it? Is there something you didn't understand in the lesson?'

'No I understood everything you said perfectly. What I was wondering is, what you thought the probability of time travel would be?'

'H – how do you mean, Paul?' I manage to reply, a little thrown by his question.

'I mean, how likely do you think it would be to take place? It's something I'm really interested in.'

'I see,' I say, playing for time. Is this kid for real? But as his innocent blue eyes stare up questioningly at me, I have to assume so. 'I don't really know the answer to that, I'm afraid. In maths we deal in facts and figures. I think time travel would be for a different subject altogether.'

'Which one would that be, then?' he asks, still looking up at me enquiringly, 'History or science maybe?'

'Science, perhaps?' I suggest, not really knowing how to answer him.

'Excellent,' he says eagerly, 'because you're teaching us that as well. I'll look forward to that lesson!'

And with that he runs off through the classroom door out into the corridor.

And all I can think to say to his departing figure is:

'Don't run!'

Thirty-Five

I flop into one of the comfy armchairs in the staffroom.

'Cup of coffee, Jo-Jo?' one of the other teachers asks. 'I'm just making one.'

'Yes, please,' I reply to a woman wearing a large floppy scarf that holds back her curly brown hair. 'That would be great, thanks.' Instant coffee hasn't killed me so far in the last three decades, so I'm sure I can cope with it again now.

The staffroom door opens again, and another teacher, carrying a huge pile of exercise books, backs through it. The pile begins to wobble, so I jump up to help him.

'Harry!' I exclaim, as he turns around and our eyes meet over the top of the books. 'I didn't expect to see you here.'

'No,' Harry says, putting the books down on a table and straightening them up, 'the job didn't work out so I'm back for another term.'

'Ah ... I'm sorry.'

I try not to stare at him too much as he goes over to the

drinks area and makes himself a cup of coffee. Unlike the Harry from the eighties who was sharply dressed in suits, shirts and ties, this Harry is wearing baggy brown corduroy trousers, a checked shirt – and is that actually a tank top?

My coffee is passed to me and I thank my fellow teacher. Taking a quick sip, I realise it's actually not that bad. I really must stop whining about my lack of expensive caffeine-based beverages – anyone would think I was addicted!

Harry comes back over to the seating area and sits down in one of the armchairs. He reaches into his pocket and puts on a pair of gold-rimmed spectacles. Gosh, now I really have seen it all – Harry as an office boy, Harry as a teen punk, Harry as a yuppie businessman and now this, Harry as a geeky teacher.

He picks up a *Guardian* and begins to read it, and I see the last part of the date on the front page – *September 1994*.

'So what happened with the other job?' I venture, hoping to find out a bit more about this version of him.

He lowers the paper. 'It didn't work out. Not my cup of tea.' He lifts his cup. 'Or coffee, in this case.'

I smile politely. 'Why?' I ask, as he's just about to lift the paper again.

A flicker of irritation crosses his face. 'Apparently I'm not the right type.'

'The right type of teacher?'

Harry blinks at me a couple of times. 'No, the right type of person.'

'To?'

He sighs now. 'To manage a tour.'

'A tour?'

'What is this, Jo-Jo, twenty questions? Yes, apparently I'm

320

not the right material to manage a rock band's tour around the UK.'

Even I could have told him that, dressed the way he is.

I take another sip of my coffee. 'Is that what you'd really like to do instead of teach? Manage bands, or rather their tours?'

Harry looks around the staffroom. 'Got to be better than this. Teaching music in a grotty London school to a bunch of kids.'

I watch him while he tries to read his paper again. This Harry, he's different to the others. He seems jaded with his life while the other versions of him, whatever their persona, always had a certain vitality about them.

'Perhaps you're good at teaching?' I suggest, trying to be positive.

Harry lowers the paper again. 'Maybe I am, but it doesn't mean I wouldn't rather *be* somewhere else, *doing* something else now does it?'

'No, I guess not.' *I can relate to that feeling.*

The bell rings to signal the end of break.

'And there's my five minutes up. Great!' he says, tossing his paper back down on the table.

'Sorry, I didn't mean to disturb you with all my questions.'

Harry smiles now for the first time.

'No, I should apologise to you, I'm in a foul mood today, I'm not the best company.' He leans in towards me as we both stand up. 'Just between the two of us, my wife was quite pleased I didn't get the job. She thought it was a stupid idea from the start. And if I'm honest, I only really wanted the job so I could get away from her for a bit.'

My eyes shoot immediately to Harry's left hand, and there it is, as clear as day, a thin gold wedding band.

'That's not good,' I say, tearing my eyes away from his hand. 'I mean her not being keen, not you wanting to get away.' *What am I supposed to say?*

'No,' Harry pulls off his glasses and eyes me a tad suspiciously. 'I guess not.'

The staffroom has all but emptied now as the other teachers head back to their classes.

'Look, we'd better go or we'll be late,' Harry says, moving towards the door which he holds open for me. 'And you can't afford to be late twice in one day. I saw you earlier, racing across the playground with Ellie.'

'Ah, that,' I say as I walk down the corridor with him. 'Yes, not the most elegant of entrances for a teacher, ripping off a sweatshirt while running across a netball court.'

'A Take That sweatshirt too,' he grins.

'Don't remind me.'

'But I thought you and Ellie were super fans? I half imagine you camping outside the band's hotel when they're in town?'

'I hardly think so!' *At least, I hope we don't do that.*

'Good. I'm glad you're not that bad!' Harry stops walking outside a classroom door. 'Would you still like a regular lift home now I'm back for another term?'

'Yes, I guess so.'

'I'll pick you up in the car park after school then, usual place.'

'Sure,' I say, as he enters his classroom and greets his pupils. *I'll find it*, I think as he smiles at me and closes the door. But all I can think, as I hurry back along to my own class of eager children, waiting for me to impart more knowledge to them is:

He's married.

This time my Harry is married . . .

Thirty-Six

The rest of day passes without too many problems, and I manage to continue the role of teacher fairly successfully, without getting myself into detention for bad behaviour.

In fact, I'm quite enjoying it.

They're a bright bunch, my lot, once you work out the best way of getting through to them, and by the end of the day we may not have quite covered everything the National Curriculum suggests, but I think they've learnt plenty.

While I'm gathering my things from my locker, Ellie comes into the staffroom to do the same.

'Fancy coming round to mine now to watch some videos?' she asks in a hushed voice.

I wonder what sort of videos she means.

'I've got *Live & Kicking* from last Saturday recorded if you want to see it?'

Wasn't Live & Kicking *a kids programme?*

'Apparently Robbie is looking really hot on it.'

Take That again.

'No, I can't tonight. Besides, Harry is giving me a lift home.'

Ellie looks surprised. 'You're not going to start that up again, are you?'

'What do you mean – start it up again? He's giving me a lift, that's all.'

'You know what happened last time when he was *giving you lifts*?'

I stare at her blankly.

'Are you still denying anything went on?' Ellie asks, her eyes wide. 'I can't believe the two of you still do that.'

'Perhaps because it's true?' I reply defensively. I have no idea what Ellie is talking about, but I bet whatever it is, her facts are wrong.

'His wife doesn't think so,' Ellie says knowingly.

'That's her problem, isn't it?' I bang my locker door shut; it's so frustrating not knowing anything all the time. 'I have to go. I'll see you tomorrow.'

'Aw, Jo-Jo,' Ellie calls to my departing figure, 'don't be like that. I didn't mean anything! Tell you what, I'll bring you that recording of the boys on *The Hit Man and Her* I've been promising you for ages to make up for it.'

'Great,' I reply, putting on a fake smile. 'You do that.'

I feel uneasy as I hurry down the school corridor. Suddenly this car journey seems like it could be fraught with difficulties. What's supposed to have happened between us? Maybe I shouldn't be accepting a lift from Harry after all.

But Harry is already waiting for me in a pale blue Fiat Uno when I arrive in the car park, so I climb into the passenger seat next to him and pull on my seat belt.

325

'How was your day?' Harry asks as we pull out of the school gates.

'Good, thanks. Not as tough as I thought it was going to be when I first arrived this morning anyway.'

Ain't that the truth!

'Yeah, Year 3 can be a tough age to teach.' Harry reaches to turn the radio on. 'Not this again,' he says as the familiar opening bars of Wet Wet Wet singing 'Love Is All Around' float through the car. 'I thought they'd banned this from being played on the radio?'

'Didn't they just stop making the record available to purchase?' I say, remembering reading something about this iconic nineties tune somewhere.

'I think they've tried everything,' Harry grumbles. 'And yet I still keep hearing it.'

'Have you seen the film it came from, *Four Weddings and a Funeral*?' I ask to make conversation.

Harry allows his eyes to flicker away from the windscreen for a moment. 'You know I have. I bumped into you and Ellie at the cinema when I was there watching it with my wife.'

'So you did! Silly me, it slipped my mind.' I quickly turn away and pretend to look out of the passenger window.

'She moaned the whole way through that movie,' Harry continues after a pause. 'I think she wanted to go and see Arnie in *True Lies* that night, but I wanted to see that one – probably why I hate the song now. Love definitely wasn't all around for us that night, that's for sure.'

I look back at him and try to nod in a sympathetic fashion.

'Things aren't too good then, between you and your wife?'

I ask hesitantly. This is so difficult – I don't know how much I'm supposed to know.

'Jo-Jo, you know they're not.' Harry doesn't look at me this time. 'Patricia and I just seem to be growing further and further apart these days.'

'I'm sorry.' I don't really know what else to say. What Ellie said before is still niggling at me, and not knowing exactly what I'm dealing with here is damned hard.

'And if she sees you in my car,' Harry says as he pulls to a halt at the end of a cul-de-sac of houses, 'life will be even more painful when I get in tonight, so is it OK if I drop you here?' he asks, nodding his head in the direction of the pavement outside.

'Yes, that's fine, thanks.' How on earth I'm supposed to find where I live is a different matter – but that's my issue.

'I'll see you Monday, then,' Harry says as I climb from the car. 'Pick you up just round the corner, in front of the phone box like we used to? I quite like these two-day weeks that end on a Friday. Joy of a new term, eh?'

I nod hesitantly.

'Are you sure you're OK?' he asks. 'About the lift? I mean if you're uncomfortable after ... well, you know? We don't have to.'

'No, I'm fine. This is fine. Lifts are fine.' I grin a bit manically, in an effort to hide my discomfort.

'Good.' Harry looks at me a bit oddly. 'Well, I'll see you Monday, then.'

'Bye,' I call as I close the door, and he drives further down into a neat and tidy close of modern brick-built semi-detached houses.

What is this thing between us? I wonder as I look around me now, and wonder which one of these houses is mine. *Did we have an affair?*

'Jo-Jo, it is you?' An elderly lady appears from her house carrying a cardboard box. 'They tried to deliver this for you earlier,' she says, hurrying down her drive, patting her white hair as she comes towards me. 'But when I told them you were out, they said it was OK to leave it with a neighbour.'

Ah, so I live in one of these houses, do I? I think, looking either side of my neighbour's house. Not bad, but how do I afford this on a teacher's salary? These houses look quite big. Do I live with someone else?

'Thank you,' I say, taking the parcel from her and wondering what it might be. 'Very kind of you.'

'No trouble, my dear. I used to do the same for your mother – God rest her soul,' she says, crossing herself. 'I still miss her, you know.'

'Yes … we all do.' My mother has passed away this time? How very sad for this Jo-Jo. I think again about my own real mother, and feel that same pull in the centre of my stomach I felt in 1977 when Penny hugged me.

'But having you here now does make up for it a little bit. It's like a small piece of her is still here with us in Apple Close.'

'That's good.'

'I'm so glad you decided to stay on in her house and not sell it. We've had some, how can I put it?' She leans in towards me. 'Less than desirable people moving into the close lately, and you being here is an added bonus.'

'Why thank you, that's kind of you to say.'

'It's no trouble, my dear. As you know, me and Mr Sullivan are here for you any time you need us.' She pats me softly on the arm. 'Talking of which, I'd best be getting back indoors, I'm cooking a nice steak and kidney pie for our tea, and then me and Mr Sullivan are going to watch a bit of *Animal Hospital* with little Rolf Harris, then *Pets Win Prizes* with that Dale Winton. Prefer him on *Supermarket Sweep* myself, but Mr Sullivan's big on animal shows.'

'Very nice,' I agree, smiling at her.

She turns to go. 'Before I forget,' she says, turning back immediately, 'Mr Sullivan says he'll come and take a look at your guttering over the weekend.' She points up at the roof of the house to her right. 'He says some of it looks a little loose and you don't want that coming adrift once the winter sets in.'

'Sure, Mrs Sullivan, that would be great. Thank you.'

'No trouble, my dear,' she says with a wave of her hand as she begins to shuffle back down her drive. 'Like I say, we're here for you any time, day or night!'

So *this* is my new home, I think, looking up at a red brick semi, with a large bay window and a navy blue front door. As I walk down the gravel drive carrying my parcel, I feel inside my bag, hoping I'll find a set of keys, and luckily I do. After a bit of trial and error when I reach the door, I manage to work out which key of the many on my *Friends* key ring will allow me to go inside.

My new home, in which I can't find any reason to suggest that I live other than alone, has a kitchen diner, a lounge, and a small cloakroom downstairs, and three bedrooms and a bathroom upstairs. It's pleasantly decorated, bright and sunny in

329

places, and seems perfectly acceptable for my usual short stay – which I'm hoping this is going to be.

I need to take a trip to see George and find out what he knows this time. I glance at my watch. His shop won't be open now, so it will have to wait until tomorrow. I look over at the parcel Mrs Sullivan has given me, still sitting unwrapped on the lounge coffee table, and I wonder what's inside? Only one way to find out, I suppose, so I go over and begin ripping off the brown packaging.

Inside, in amongst the foam packaging chips I find five more boxes, and inside them, five dolls. 'Take That dolls?' I exclaim, looking down at the boxes which proudly announce *Official Take That Merchandise*. 'Are you kidding me? Why would I order these?'

The dolls, of course, look nothing like any of the members of Take That, not unless I have a very bad memory, or I'm in a parallel universe where Take That all look like a very tanned and stoned Justin Bieber.

'Blimey, I really must be a huge fan,' I say to myself as I stare down at the dolls, all grinning back up at me from their boxes. When I was wandering around the house I saw the odd Take That poster, a few postcards pinned on the kitchen noticeboard, and obviously all their CDs stacked up near a CD player in the lounge, but I thought that was fairly mild, nothing too major I couldn't deal with. But this! I look down at the dolls again, then hurriedly put them back in the cardboard box and shut the lid. They just freak me out.

What should I do now? Just like in 2013 it doesn't seem by the look of my fridge that I'm a very adventurous cook, so I guess I'll have to go out for some supplies or get a takeaway dinner. I look out of the window; it's a bright sunny September evening, so I decide I'll take a walk.

After I wash away the schooly feeling that, even as a teacher, I still seem to have picked up, I change my clothes – and even that's quite stressful, when it appears that 80 per cent of my wardrobe consists of official Take That tour T-shirts and hood-ies. But I finally leave the blue front door again wearing baggy jeans, a plain white T-shirt and a black waistcoat, teamed with plain black lace-up Doc Marten boots, which I feel looks quite cool for the time – at least, I hope it does.

As I get to the bottom of Apple Close I realise that I have no idea where I am in London. I'm just about to step out and cross the road in the direction of the tube station I remember passing with Harry earlier when I hear a shout from across the road.

'Hey, Jo-Jo, wait-up! I was just coming over to see you.'

I look over towards the voice and see a young man in his mid-twenties with short blond hair, spiked at the front. He dashes across the road and, as he gets close to me, I realise he's got piercing blue eyes too.

'Hi,' I say cheerfully, hoping this is a suitable response. He seems very pleased to see me.

'Hey, I was just coming over to your house, babe.'

'Were you?' I look at his clothing suspiciously. He's wearing huge black baggy jeans, a pink Burberry check waistcoat, and a lime green T-shirt.

'Don't mind this,' he says, gesturing at his outfit. 'I'm just off to the World's End to do my act. I'm calling myself Billy Vanilli this time around – what do you think?'

'That's very good. Catchy.'

He narrows his eyes doubtfully. 'Anyway, I thought since you were near I'd call in on you first and discuss our plans.'

'Plans?'

'For the gigs, babe?' he says, looking shocked now. 'I've already been in touch with Ellie and she reckons we can find out where they're staying and infiltrate the hotel if we work as a team.'

I stare blankly at him.

'What is wrong with you tonight, Jo-Jo? I'd have thought you'd have been well up for this. You're usually bored once you go back to school.'

A car pulls out of the top of Apple Close now; it's Harry's, and he waves casually at me before he turns and drives off in the opposite direction from where Billy and I are standing.

'So now I see what's distracting you,' Billy says approvingly. 'Nice choice, babe, I'd quite go for him myself, but he's obviously not that way inclined if he's on *your* radar!'

'Billy! I don't know what you mean? Harry is just a teacher at my school, and he's also my neighbour.' I pray that Billy is actually his name and not simply a stage name.

'Now I know something is wrong with you.' Billy plonks his hands on his hips. 'You never ever call me Billy.'

'I don't?'

'No, you always shorten it to Bill – you say Billy sounds like one of your pupils' names.'

'Did Ellie tell you about the accident when you spoke to her?' I ask, hoping to change the subject.

'Yeah, she did say something about an incident with you

332

and a car. Oh my, are you all right, babe?' He thrusts his hand to my forehead.

'Yes, I'm fine, but maybe that's why I seem a bit off tonight.'

'Of course, babe.' He grabs me, and suddenly I find myself surrounded by pink Burberry check as Billy wraps his surprisingly strong arms around me. 'Billy is sorry. I think I'm probably a tad on edge too, what with my new set tonight.'

I ease myself gently from his grip.

'Why don't I come and listen to you then?' I ask, thinking I haven't been to the World's End in a while and it's near to where I always get hit by the white car before I jump through time; maybe it has some relevance to this whole process?

'Would you, babe? Ooh, that would be fab!' He claps his hands in glee and gives me a quick once-over. 'You're not really dressed for a night out, are you, though?' he says, looking with disdain at my waistcoat. 'But I guess you'll do!'

Thirty-Seven

The World's End pub, surprisingly, hasn't changed that much since the first time I was in it in 1963. The décor has improved somewhat, but the general layout is still the same.

While Billy heads off to get ready for his set later, I find a seat at the bar next to a tall vase of sunflowers, and wait to be served. Good, they now serve food here, I think, picking up a menu on the bar. I haven't eaten since lunchtime and I'm starving. I opt for a burger and chips, and order a Diet Coke to go with it. As I sit and look around the pub, I realise for the first time since I've been time travelling that this doesn't feel so odd; the setting, the food, the drink, it's not that different from what I'm used to at all.

I'm getting closer to home . . .

'Jo-Jo,' a familiar voice says next to me. 'I wondered when you'd be back again.'

'George!' I nearly fall off the bar stool in my rush to hug him. 'What are you doing here?'

'I've told you before, I often come in here after work to listen to music.'

'My friend Billy is singing,' I say. 'Well, at least I think that's what he's doing.'

I look at George while he heaves himself up on to the stool next to me. It's only nine years since I last saw him, but he's aged significantly. His hair is completely grey now and the clothes he's wearing are no longer up-to-the minute fashion, but much more practical items, in neutral colours and hard-wearing fabrics, like corduroy and heavy-duty cotton. He has nearly become the George I know and love from 2013.

'Ah yes, your friend Billy, I've seen him here before. He's quite something.'

'Is he? In what way?'

'You wait and see,' George grins.

'Usual, George?' the barman asks, coming over.

'Yes please, Jude.'

The barman's name is Jude? The Beatles again!

'Coming right up,' Jude says, grabbing a pint glass and pulling on the Guinness pump. 'Your food shouldn't be too long, miss,' he says, smiling at me.

'That's fine, thank you. So,' I ask eagerly, looking at George, 'what *am* I doing here this time? All I know is I appear to be the world's biggest Take That fan.' I lean in further towards him and whisper, 'I only bought the dolls, all five of them!'

George grins now. 'Keep them, they'll be worth something one day.'

'Funny! What shall I do with them, carry them with me in my magic bag where I carry all my other goodies?'

'What do you mean?'

'I have a copy of the *Beano* from the sixties, a pair of football boots from the seventies, and now I've added a four-leaf-clover brooch from 1985 to my time-travelling mementoes. I bring them with me into each new decade; they're the only things that I take with me.'

George rubs at his chin. 'Interesting . . .'

I sit back on my stool. 'So, do you have any theories about that? Or new ones as to why I'm still time travelling? Or are you going to do your usual enigmatic *I know nurthing* act.'

I see Jude's eyes flicker our way.

'Keep your voice down, Jo-Jo,' George says, leaning into me. 'Walls have ears. And barmen have even sharper ones.'

'Sorry, George.'

George waits for his Guinness to settle, then he takes a long, slow drink from his creamy pint. It's odd seeing him drink beer and not tea. Most of our conversations are over a cuppa in George's shop. At least the sunflowers on the bar are similar to the ones George always has on his counter, which in an odd way makes me feel reassured.

'Where should I begin?' he asks eventually.

'What happened between you and Harry after I left last time?' I ask, thinking quickly. 'Did you make it up properly?'

George nods slowly and he rests his pint on the bar. 'We did indeed. Thanks to you.'

'Oh, good!' I clap my hands together. 'And Stu, did he make it to the concert or did I hold him back long enough?'

'I'm afraid he did, Jo-Jo.'

'Damn!' I bang my fist on the bar loud enough so Jude looks around again. 'I tried my best to prevent that,' I whisper to George now. 'But Ringo said I couldn't do everything.

So the same thing happened when he plugged in the amp?'

George nods again. 'I've told you before, Jo-Jo, you can't always change things. And sometimes it's best not to.'

'But what's the point to all this if I can't do something positive with it. It's all just a waste of time.'

'And you hate that, don't you?' George asks. 'Wasting time.'

'Yes, I do. I can't bear it.'

'The same as you hate not being in control?'

I look at George and try to figure out where he's going with this.

'In fact,' he continues, 'if you think about it, so many of the things you've been forced to do in your time travelling are things that are completely out of your comfort zone.'

I think about this. 'Not really,' I shrug. 'I think I've coped with everything quite well so far.'

'Yes, you have,' George agrees. 'And that is exactly my point. Who would have thought you'd have enjoyed being an office junior again, or a teenager, or a journalist, for heaven's sake – they write for a living, don't they? And you hate creative writing. You're a numbers person.'

'Are you saying that this is all about me being made to do things I hate?' I ask incredulously. 'Because if it is, that sucks.'

George smiles. 'No, Jo-Jo, I'm saying it might not just be about you helping other people. It might be about *you* helping *you*.'

Thirty-Eight

I stare at George and I'm about to ask him more, when the pub lights dim a little and the small stage that I remember performing my early karaoke on in 1963 is suddenly lit by a spotlight.

'Welcome, ladies and gentlemen, to the World's End this evening,' Jude says, squinting a little into the bright light. 'May I now introduce to you our entertainment for the night, back by popular demand and with an all-new set, and an all-new name – it's Billy Vanilli!'

And on to the stage, wearing a full-length evening gown in blue sparkling sapphire, four-inch silver heels, and a long blonde wig, sways Billy.

'He's a drag artist!' I exclaim, nearly choking on a piece of gherkin from the burger that Jude has just served me.

'He said it was different,' George smiles, still looking up at Billy on the stage.

Billy's set covers hits from all the decades I've travelled

through, and he sings the songs incredibly well. When he gets to the nineties part of his show, he seems to revel in singing the Take That songs more than any of the previous medleys. Definitely another fan, I think watching him give a particularly good performance of 'Everything Changes'.

'He's good,' George remarks as we sit and watch from our place at the bar. 'I like the new songs he's added tonight, and of course his new stage persona.'

'What was he singing before?' I ask as Billy comes to the end of his set and makes an extravagant curtsey to the applauding audience.

'Mostly just Take That stuff, but that was a bit limited. It is at the moment, anyway.' George winks at me.

I'm about to enquire just how he knows this, when Billy steps elegantly down from the stage and comes tottering over to us. '*Well*, what did you think?' he asks me expectantly, his blue eyes shining with euphoria and excitement.

'You were fantastic, Bill,' I tell him truthfully.

He does a little jig on the spot, then looks across at George. 'I have no idea who you are, but did you like it too?'

'This is George, Bill,' I explain. 'He's an old friend of mine.'

'Pleased to meet you, Billy,' George says, holding out his hand for Billy to shake. 'I've seen you perform here before. Very impressive range you have.'

'Why, thank you,' Billy says, delighted. He regards George's sober attire. 'I must say my act doesn't really *look* your sort of thing.'

'Never judge a book by its cover, or a record by its sleeve,' George says knowingly.

'I like that!' Billy says playfully, punching George in the arm. 'Record by the sleeve! Very good.'

'George owns the record shop down the road,' I explain.

'Groovy Records! I've seen that little shop when I've been on my way to HMV. I must pop in some time and see you, Georgie, now I know you're a fan.'

'I am. I particularly liked your rendition of "Relight My Fire" tonight – very energetic there with the actual fire-eating in the middle.'

'Thank you,' Billy says, grinning. 'Took a bit of practice, that. Do you think I carried off "A Million Love Songs" OK, though? It's one of my favourites and I'd hate to do the great Mr Barlow a disservice by singing it badly.'

'That was very good too,' George says, smiling at him. 'I'm sure Gary would be very proud.'

Billy's face lights up with pleasure. 'Super-duper, I just wish I could sing more of their great tunes, but—' he stops abruptly.

'But, you have to sing some other bands too, I guess,' George fills in for him.

'Yes, yes that's right, I do. And it seemed to work tonight; people really seemed to enjoy it. Even the Beatles stuff, which I thought might be a bit *too* far back.'

'Never!' George says. 'The Beatles are classics, aren't they, Jo-Jo?'

'Yes, I suppose they are.' *They certainly seem to follow me everywhere I go.*

'Billy, that was great! We'd like to book you for some more dates,' Jude says, leaning over the bar with a diary. 'Have you a moment to discuss?'

'I have indeed!' Billy replies with glee. 'I'll just get my diary and check when I'm available! One moment.' He leans in towards us. 'Just between you and me I'm available all the way through to 2004 if he wants me, but he doesn't know that!' He winks. 'Back in a bit.'

I watch Billy and Jude move around to a quieter part of the bar to discuss dates.

George drains the last of the Guinness from his glass. 'That's me done for the night,' he says. 'I'm off home.'

'Where are you living now?' I ask him, wondering if he still has the house or if he's back in the flat,

'I still have my little house. I rent the flat over the shop now.'

'Ah …' I wonder to whom. It seems funny to be living there one minute, and not the next. Except it's not really a minute in reality, is it? It's a decade.

'Will you be all right getting home tonight?' he asks. 'I don't live far from you, if you'd like me to walk you back?'

I'm about to agree, always eager to get the chance to talk to George further, when I'm distracted by someone suddenly crashing through the pub doors. It's Harry, and he doesn't look happy as he makes a beeline for the bar.

'Perhaps I'll stay on for a while. You know, in case Billy wants some company.'

'Or someone else?' George says knowingly, looking across at Harry sliding on to a bar stool.

'George, Harry is married this time. You know that.'

'We all need a little help from our friends on occasion, Jo-Jo, and I think that's just what Harry needs right now.'

'Exactly. Our *friends*.'

'I'll see you very soon,' George waves as he leaves me sitting alone at the bar. 'Have fun.'

I pick up my half-empty glass and sidle over to where Harry sits waiting for his drink.

He looks up. 'Jo-Jo, what are you doing here?' he asks, looking surprised. 'I didn't know you drank in this pub?'

'I don't normally, but I was here watching my friend Billy perform earlier.' I nod in Billy's direction. Billy is now caught up talking with a bunch of new 'fans' and is having a whale of a time.

'I see.' Harry glances in Billy's direction, but I get the feeling he doesn't really see him at all. 'Cheers,' he says to Jude as he places a double whisky down on the bar in front of him. 'Can I get you something?' he asks me.

'I'm fine right now,' I say, holding up my own glass. I pull up the stool next to him. 'Mind if I sit down?'

Harry shrugs. 'No, go for it.'

'Everything OK?' I venture after a minute or two when Harry doesn't say anything, and his whisky is diminishing rapidly.

'Been better,' he replies, studying the bottom of his glass.

'I guessed that.'

'Sorry,' Harry says, looking up now. 'It's been a – a difficult evening at home.'

'Any particular reason why? Sorry, you don't need to tell me if you don't want to.'

'Just married stuff, you know, the usual.'

No, I don't really. 'So you just walked out?'

'Yeah, seemed like the best thing. It was getting a bit heated.' Harry waves his glass in Jude's direction and Jude helpfully takes it to refill.

'Ah.' I don't know what else to say. I'm not a marriage

counsellor, and to be honest I feel a bit awkward talking to Harry about his wife, considering in all our other past encounters we've been ... well, we've been heading towards more than friends, even if we never quite got there.

Harry suddenly thrusts his head into his hands. 'I hate my life! Hate it!' He turns his face towards me. 'Ask me why.'

'Why?' I ask, doing as I'm told for once.

'I'm a loser, Jo-Jo, a nowhere man.'

'No, you're not,' I reply, wondering if Harry has been drinking before he even got to the pub tonight.

'I am. I'll still be working eight days a week when I'm sixty-four, marking homework and thinking up lesson plans.'

'No you won't, not if you don't want to be doing that.'

Harry doesn't look very convinced. 'Do you want to know a secret?'

'What?' I ask, wondering where all this is heading. Although Harry is making sense, he's talking very oddly, as if he's talking in code.

'They say all you need is love, but everybody's got something to hide, Jo-Jo. Everyone. That's what screws everything up. I bet even you've got a secret?'

'Well ...'

'Do you want to know mine?' Harry has emptied his glass and is holding it up to be refilled again. 'Hey Jude,' he calls across the bar, 'another when you're ready, please.'

I stare hard at Harry. The code he's talking in. It's only bloody Beatles songs! I may not be their greatest fan, but their songs constantly being played during my childhood means I know every one.

'Tell me your secret, Harry,' I urge him, sensing there's

more to this than simply a bit of marital discord. 'What is it?'

'I want to tell you, Jo-Jo, I want to tell you so much, but I can't.'

'Yes, Harry, yes you can.'

Jude brings Harry's whisky over.

'I'll take one of those, Jude,' I tell him. 'Quick as you can, please, and make it a double.'

Jude raises his dark eyebrows, but immediately lifts a glass and turns towards the optics.

'Maybe I should just let it be,' Harry says, as he drinks from his own glass. 'It's a long and winding road we both travel along, Jo-Jo, and I'll get by with a little help from my friends.' He lifts his head and looks meaningfully at me. 'We both will.'

I look deep into Harry's blue eyes. What is it he's trying to tell me? I *know* there's something.

Jude is about to place my glass of whisky down on the bar in front of me, but before he does I grab it and rapidly down the contents, taking a few moments to recover as the first few gulps of Scotch catch the back of my throat.

'Enough with the Beatles clues, Harry,' I gasp. 'I get it. What's going on, what are you trying to tell me? Are you and George in this together? Is there something I need to know?'

Harry shakes his head before he looks at me again and this time it takes a few seconds before his eyes are able to focus properly on my face. 'I don't know what you mean.'

'All the Beatles stuff just now, it's as if you were talking in riddles.'

'Was I? Really?' He looks down at his glass. 'Maybe I've had a bit too much of this stuff. Don't do it, Jo-Jo,' he says, looking

344

at my now empty glass, 'it will ruin you.' He stands up, swaying a little from side to side, then he gently cups my face with
his hand.

'And you're too lovely to be ruined. Come on,' he says,
quickly letting go, 'I think we'd better be getting you home.'

I'd like nothing better, I think, as I watch Harry waver back
and forth across the pub floor in the direction of the door. But
if that time ever does come, I want you to be there with me.

Thirty-Nine

When I come down for breakfast, Harry is still asleep where I left him last night – on my sofa.

We took a taxi back to Apple Close last night. When we arrived Harry staggered around the outside of the cab, holding on to the door and then the boot for support while I paid the driver, so I'd suggested he come into mine and have a cup of coffee to sober up a bit before he went home. But he fell asleep on my sofa before I even had a chance to make his coffee, so I covered him up with a blanket, and left him quietly snoring away to himself.

'Harry,' I call gently to try and ease him from his sleep now. 'Harry?'

'Mmm . . .' Harry murmurs, turning over. 'What year is it this time?'

'Harry, you need to wake up,' I say, raising my voice a little.

Harry sits up with a start, staring at me. Then he looks around the room. 'Bloody hell, I'm still here! She'll kill me!'

He leaps off the sofa and pats at his clothes as if he's checking he still has them on.

'It's OK,' I say, slightly annoyed by his reaction. 'Nothing like that went on. You simply crashed out last night on the sofa. So I thought it best to just cover you up and let you sleep it off.'

'You've never been married, have you, Jo-Jo?' Harry asks, rubbing his eyes with the heels of his hands.

'No.'

'Covering me up and letting me sleep it off is not going to go down well with my wife when I try and explain where I've been all night.'

'I didn't think of that, sorry.'

Harry runs his hand through his tousled hair. He's got dark stubble on his chin this morning too, and his dishevelled appearance is making him look very sexy.

I shake my head a little. *No, Jo-Jo, now is not the time to begin developing feelings like this for Harry; you've had three decades to do that – he's married this time, remember?*

But I can't help it. I *want* this Harry. No, not just this Harry – *all* the Harrys. The Harry. Oh, it's so confusing, but I know what I mean.

'No, I'm sorry, this isn't your fault,' Harry apologises. 'I was the one who got drunk last night, then poured out my troubles to you. You were just good enough to listen.' He looks at the clock on the mantelpiece. 'Is that the correct time, 6.25?'

'Yes, I think so. Sorry, I'm up pretty early this morning.'

'No, that's good. Patricia doesn't usually wake up until around 7 so I might just be able to sneak back in without her noticing.'

We both hurry towards the front door and open it wide. Harry is about to say something to me when we both see two people talking over the low wall at the end of the garden.

It's Mrs Sullivan from next door; she's wearing a pink fluffy dressing gown and slippers, and in her hand she clutches a bottle of milk while she chats to another woman I don't recognise.

'Patti!' Harry exclaims with a gasp, looking with horror at them both.

I'm pretty sure Mrs Sullivan isn't called Patti, so I have to presume the second woman is Harry's wife. For a split second I wonder if the garden is just long enough to be out of earshot so I can whisk Harry back indoors before she hears him.

But as her head snaps around in our direction, the look of fury on her face suggests it's not.

'Patti!' Harry calls, beginning to run down my garden path. 'It's not what you think!'

'Stay right where you are, Harry,' Patti, who doesn't look anything like I expected her to – she's petite and pretty, with long auburn hair – commands. She holds out her hand like a policewoman holding back traffic. 'Don't bother coming any further. If you want to be with *her* so badly, then I suggest you stay there. Because you won't be setting foot inside our house ever again!'

Mrs Sullivan, whose grey hair is bound up in rollers, touches Patti on the arm sympathetically, then she pulls the collar of her dressing gown around her neck protectively, and looks at Harry for his response.

'Don't be silly, Patti,' Harry says impatiently, 'if you'll just let me explain—'

'Oh no! You're not talking yourself out of it this time. Mrs Sullivan here has told me everything. How you came in drunk together last night, and how your hands were all over each other as you came up the path.'

Damn! I thought I'd seen the curtains twitch next door when we came in, but I'd been so busy dealing with Harry I'd just dismissed it and forgotten about it until now.

'I don't think I quite said that, lovey,' Mrs Sullivan tries to interrupt.

'You said enough so I can figure out the rest, thank you,' Patti continues, tapping Mrs Sullivan's pink fluffy arm companionably. 'We've been here before with you two, haven't we?' she says, looking coldly at Harry and I. 'It's not like it's new ground.'

'For God's sake, woman!' Harry exclaims, rubbing at his forehead. 'I told you then, Jo-Jo is just a friend and she's still just a friend. I got drunk last night down the World's End after *we'd* argued yet again. Jo-Jo was kind enough to bring me home to try and sober me up. Unfortunately for her, I passed out on her sofa, and fortunately for me she let me stay to sleep it off.'

'Ha! A likely story,' Patti says, folding her arms. 'Anyway, you can save it. It's too late this time. She's welcome to you, Harry, she's been waiting for you long enough, and now she can have you! Goodbye!'

Patti swivels as dramatically as she can on her slippered heels and stomps off in her pyjamas back up the road.

'Shit!' Harry says, burying his head in his hands as he squats down on the path. '*That* went well.'

'I'm so sorry, Harry,' I say, tiptoeing along the gravel in my

349

bare feet to join him. 'I should have tried to wake you last night.'

'It's not your fault, Jo-Jo,' he says, standing up again, 'she's been looking for an excuse to throw me out for ages, and this is the perfect one. It's unfortunate after what happened before, but it can't be helped.'

What the bloody hell happened before? Why can't someone just spell it out? I can hardly ask, can I, because I'm supposed to have been there when whatever happened before took place.

'You know you're welcome to stay here with me until you sort things out, don't you?'

'Thanks, Jo-Jo, that's kind of you – you're sure you don't mind the gossips, though?' He glances at Mrs Sullivan still watching us from the pavement.

'Nothing I can't handle. Come on,' I say, putting my hand on his shoulder. 'Let's get you back inside. I still owe you that cup of coffee from last night, and maybe I can find some toast to go with it this morning too.'

We sit next to each other on the swirly patterned sofa in my lounge, eating biscuits now we've finished our toast, drinking coffee, and watching Andi Peters and Emma Forbes on Saturday morning television interview two of the contestants from *Gladiators*, the cast of *2 point 4 children*, and East 17 on *Live & Kicking*.

Harry hasn't said much about what happened earlier; we came back into the house and he sat very quietly for a while, just thinking, so I left him to it. I didn't know what else to do because I didn't want to appear to be interfering and, even though I was trying to be, I was hardly an impartial observer.

350

Whatever my feelings for Harry were in my previous incarnations, I was in no doubt as to what they were this time.

While Harry sits and thinks, I think too, about all the different versions of him I've encountered so far, from the first time we met in George's shop, to Harry as the gentle office junior, anarchic teenage punk, savvy businessman, and now this slightly geeky-looking teacher sitting next to me on the sofa. I realise now I had feelings for all those Harrys. It's as if his personality had been broken down into tiny building blocks, so I could encounter each part of him bit by bit, then grow to love him as a whole.

I jump at the word I've just used – *love*! Did I love Harry now?

I turn towards him on the sofa and, as he smiles at me, something pulls deep in the pit of my stomach.

I jump again, physically this time as my phone rings in the hall.

'That'll be the phone!' I cry a bit too brightly.

'Er, yes, I guess it is,' Harry says, looking at me oddly. 'They usually make that sort of noise.'

'I'll answer it then!' I leap up and dash through to the hall. My phone is white, push button and slimline this time, but it's still attached by a curly wire to the main cradle as I lift the handset to answer it. I haven't quite arrived in the cordless era yet – or at least this house hasn't.

'Hello,' I say hesitantly, half expecting it to be Patti firing a torrent of abuse in my ear.

There's a *beep beep beep* noise and then the sound of money dropping into a box.

'Yo, Jo-Jo, where are you? I'm calling from a phone box opposite the hotel. They're definitely staying there – we've seen Howard looking out of the window already!'

'Ellie, what are you talking about? Where are you?'

'The band! We're outside their hotel in Chelsea. I told you about it other day – The Conrad. Are you coming down? There's rumours they'll be out soon to sign.'

I poke my head around the lounge door. Harry is watching two puppet leprechauns in a sketch with two of the members of Boyzone.

'I'm not sure I can, Ellie, I'm a bit tied up here this morning.'

'Doing what? You never do anything on a Saturday unless it's coming shopping with me! Come on, Jo-Jo, get your butt down here now, this is Take That we're talking about, in the flesh!' *Beep beep beep*. 'Oh, that's my money running—'

And she's gone.

I replace the handset and go back into the lounge.

'Was that Ellie?' Harry asks, looking up. 'I heard you.'

'Yes, she wondered if I wanted to go out with her this morning, that's all.'

'Where – shopping?'

'Er, no, somewhere else.'

'Why don't you go then? I'll be fine here.' He picks up a packet of chocolate Hobnobs from the table and helps himself to his sixth biscuit.

'To be honest,' I say, sitting down on the sofa again, 'I don't think it's really my kind of thing.'

'Why?' Harry asks, munching his biscuit. 'What's she doing?'

'Visiting someone, at a hotel.'

Harry screws his face up. 'Why would she want you to go along to that? Oh, is she stalking Take That again? Are they in town right now?'

I sigh. Here we go again.

'Apparently, yes. For their tour.'

Harry grins. 'Ha, like you don't know! I bet you're going to every one of their London concerts?'

He was right; I'd already seen the tickets pinned up on my kitchen noticeboard. Six nights at Wembley Arena! Why on earth did I need to go six times? Were they going to do a different show every evening?

'I'm going to a few – but it's mainly to accompany Ellie.'

'Yeah, right!' Harry says, his eyes twinkling. 'I saw the dolls, you know?'

'What dolls?' I ask him innocently.

Harry raises his eyebrows. 'The Take That dolls in the box over there.' He gets up, goes over to the box still sitting in the corner of the lounge and to my horror opens it up.

'Aren't you a bit old for playing with dollies?' he laughs, lifting one of the Take That dolls up and jiggling it about in its box.

'Ah. *Those* dolls. They're for Ellie, they're a surprise.'

'Isn't *she* a bit old for dolls?'

'Look, does this really matter right now?' I ask, starting to get annoyed.

'You're in *love* aren't you, Jo-Jo?' Harry sings, gazing at the box containing Robbie.

'With who?' I snap, startled by his question.

'Take That?'

'Oh. Yeah, they're OK I guess. I like their songs, that's all.' *That was close . . .*

'Ha! I think it's a bit more than their songs you like. Who's your fave, then?' Harry digs around in the box. 'Robbie in my hand here, or Gary, or is it little Markie perhaps? Or maybe you like a man who can dance?' He pulls out the Howard and Jason dolls and begins jigging them around. Then he begins singing the lyrics to 'Relight My Fire' with the boxed dolls still held in his hand like puppets.

He looks so silly standing there performing in my lounge with a bunch of dolls that I suddenly burst out laughing.

'What's up?' Harry asks, looking perturbed.' Is my singing that bad?'

'No, but your puppet skills are.'

'Made you laugh, though,' he says, grinning. 'And that's the first time I've done that. Smile, yes, many a time. But not properly laugh. I'm guessing that's pretty important to you?'

'Yes.' I suddenly stop smiling at him and simply stare. *What did he just say?*

'Anyway,' Harry says, throwing the dolls back into the cardboard box again, 'I've had enough of sitting here moping. Why don't we go and see the real thing?'

'You want to come with me?' I ask, not only dazed by his suggestion, but by what he just said about making me laugh. 'To see Take That at a hotel? I hardly think it will be your kind of thing.'

'Ah, why not. It might be fun, and heaven knows I could do with some of that after earlier this morning.'

'OK then, if you're sure.'

'I am. And Jo-Jo?'

'Yes?'

'Before we leave, can I see that smile back on your face? You're much prettier when you smile.'

Forty

The Conrad Hotel is situated on Chelsea Harbour, just a little way away from the King's Road, and when we arrive I'm surprised to find it's quite calm and there's nowhere near as many fans as I'd expected there to be.

'Where have you been?' Ellie says, rushing over to us. 'You've missed everything! They came out, had photos taken, signed stuff and were here ages. Look,' she says, holding out a CD with a felt-tip squiggle on it. 'That's Jason's signature. And I got a photo with Robbie!'

'He came and posed next to you?' I'm quite impressed.

'Not posed, exactly. He was standing near me signing some girl's mahoosive boob that she thrust at him, and I managed to hold my camera out and take a photo, but I'm sure we'll both be in it.'

'Ah, classy,' I say, looking around. 'There aren't as many fans here as I thought there'd be.'

'No, now the band have gone over to Wembley to do

sound checks most of them have gone. They'll be back later, though.'

'Jo-Jo! Where have you been?' It's Billy, skipping across the car park towards us. 'Did Ellie tell you? I got a kiss off Gary! My life is complete!'

'You did not get a kiss off Gary,' Ellie retorts. 'He fell into you when someone shoved him from behind.'

'When he fell his lips brushed my cheek! That's good enough for me,' Billy says, grinning at me. 'Ah, I see you've brought your friend with you from last night.' Billy looks with interest at Harry. 'How are you feeling today – a little worse for wear?'

'I've felt better,' Harry says, pulling a wry smile. 'But I'll live. Ellie,' he acknowledges Ellie's piercing look. 'Still running around like a teenager, I see.'

Ellie ignores Harry's jibe, grabs me by the arm and marches me away from the others.

'What are you *doing*?' she hisses in my face. 'Why is *he* here with you, and what does Billy mean "your friend from last night"?'

'I'll try and answer your questions one at a time,' I reply, pulling my arm away from Ellie's tight grip. '*I'm* here because you asked me to come. *Harry* is here with me because he wanted to come along too. And I was at the World's End pub watching Billy perform last night, and Harry happened to be there.'

'He *happened* to be there?' Ellie asks in a tight voice. 'And did his wife *happen* to be there also?'

'No, they'd had an argument.'

Ellie's eyes open as wide as saucers. 'What about – you?'

'Don't be silly.' *But actually, Harry never did mention what the argument was about.*

'And what happened then?'

I look across at Harry, who is deep in conversation with Billy about something, heaven knows what. Billy is standing there in a Take That tour T-shirt, black jeans with fine silver glitter running right through them, and black leather boots with a silver chain and strap detailing covering the heel. Harry is wearing jeans, Nike trainers and an Oasis Live Forever T-shirt. They couldn't be more different.

'Harry had a bit too much to drink, that's all, so I took him back to mine to sober up with a coffee, but then he fell asleep on the sofa, so he stayed the night.'

'*All* night?'

'Yes, all night.'

Ellie rests her forehead on the tips of her fingers. 'Jeez, Jo-Jo, will you never learn? What will his wife say if she finds out?'

'She already knows. She saw him trying to leave early this morning.'

'Bloody hell! What happened? Did she rip your hair out?'

'No, of course not. But she told him not to come back.'

Ellie shakes her head, and a few blonde curls come cascading from the ponytail her hair is tied back in this morning. 'Poor cow, can't blame her really. Not after what happened before.'

If someone doesn't tell me soon ...

'Why does everyone keep going on about that?' I try. 'It's not like anything happened.'

Ellie raises her eyebrows. 'Hmm, I think the less said about that the better. We have more pressing matters to attend to. Where is he staying now – with you I suppose?'

I nod. *I tried.*

'And you think this is a wise move?'

'Does it really matter?'

'It might when the school finds out. The gossip will be all over the playground when the kids and the mothers find out two of their favourite teachers have hitched up together.'

'We're not *hitched* up.'

'People will think that.'

'I don't *care* what people think.'

'You might if it affects your job.' Ellie folds her arms and waits for my reaction.

'You're kidding me? This might affect our jobs?' I exclaim. 'And you standing out here like some prepubescent schoolgirl lusting after boys who are almost young enough for you to teach, *isn't* an issue?'

Ellie's bright green eyes narrow. I've committed the ultimate sin. I've criticised her beloved Take That.

'What I do in my private time is none of their business,' she says huffily. 'And you can talk – when did you become so blasé about it all?'

'Then in that case what I do in *my* private life is nothing to do with the school either!' I retort. 'And I haven't *just* become blasé; maybe I was never that bothered in the first place! *Maybe* I was just going along with all this nonsense to keep *you* company!'

I'm aware that our initial whispering has now risen to a fairly loud exchange, and some other remaining fans are beginning to glance over in our direction.

'If that's how you feel, I suggest you leave us genuine fans to it,' Ellie announces. 'We don't need hangers-on. And take lover-boy with you while you're at it!' she suggests with a flamboyant wave of her hand in Harry's direction.

'Ladies, ladies,' Harry calls, as he and Billy walk over to see what the problem is. 'What's causing all the fuss?'

'You are!' Ellie says accusingly, jabbing a finger in his direction. 'Like you did the last time Jo-Jo nearly lost her job.'

Ellie is bright red in the face, and appears to be on the verge of tears. But she's defiant in her anger as all five foot of her stands challengingly looking up at Harry's six foot plus frame.

The expression on Harry's face changes immediately from joviality to concern.

'Yes, of course. You're absolutely right, Ellie. It's admirable you're so concerned for your friend's welfare.' He turns to me. 'I'm sorry, Jo-Jo, I didn't think. I'll pick up my bits and move out just as soon as we get back.'

I look between the pair of them. *Will someone just tell me what the hell is going on?*

'Will someone please tell me for the love of Kylie what is happening here?' Billy asks to my relief. 'It's like watching an episode of *Neighbours* when you've been away on holiday for a fortnight, forgot to set the video recorder, and you haven't got the foggiest what's going on.'

Ellie hesitates. 'It's not really for me to say. That's up to Jo-Jo.'

'No, you go on, Ellie,' I say quickly, as desperate to know the answer to this one as Billy is. 'I've got nothing to hide – have you, Harry?'

Harry shakes his head. 'Nope, nothing whatsoever. But I

could do with something to eat, and maybe this isn't the best place to discuss private matters.' He nods in the direction of the other fans, still looking with much interest in our direction because we're the only form of entertainment in the hotel grounds now Take That have gone. 'Shall we head to the King's Road for lunch?'

'Yes, let's do that,' I agree. 'And then Ellie can fill you in on everything that's been going on, Bill.'

And maybe I'll discover at last what's really going on between Harry and me.

Forty-One

We find a little café on the King's Road and order some coffees and baguettes. I'm a little more hopeful of some decent coffee today when I see cappuccino listed on the hot drinks menu. I know cappuccinos have been around for some years, but sadly the food and drink establishments I've been taken to in my time travelling so far haven't been quite forward enough to be serving them yet.

'So,' Billy asks desperately, looking between the three of us once the waitress has taken our order, 'what's the goss then? What am I missing?'

Ellie looks over towards Harry and me sitting on the opposite side of the booth we're all squashed into.

'Go on, Ellie,' I encourage her, 'you're the storyteller.'

'I'd really rather one of you two told this,' she says, looking at us again. 'But if you really want me to . . . '

I nod encouragement at her.

She shrugs. 'Basically, Billy, last spring term there was an *incident* in the music room.'

'An incident?' Billy says, his eyes lighting up. 'Sounds juicy!'

'I wouldn't call it juicy, exactly. But it created quite a stir in the school at the time, didn't it?' she asks, looking at us again.

Harry and I both nod.

'Why, what happened?' Billy asks.

'One morning John the caretaker came in to unlock before school had started as he does every day, except when he got to the music room cupboard there were a couple of surprises waiting for him in there amongst all the instruments.'

Billy thinks about this for a moment. 'What – you two?' he exclaims. 'How? Why? Had you been there all night? Ooh, how naughty!'

'It wasn't quite like that,' Harry says, flapping his hand to calm Billy down. 'We'd got locked in accidentally and we had no choice but to spend the night there.'

Billy looks at us in disbelief. 'How can you get locked in a cupboard *accidentally*?'

'Very easily, apparently,' I reply, my mind racing. *So that's what happened? I thought it might have been much worse.*

'So how big was this cupboard?' Billy asks. 'Snuggle up together size? Or walk-in wardrobe?'

'It holds all my practice instruments, music stands and sheet music,' Harry explains. 'It's more like a small room than a cupboard.'

Billy nods. 'So what happened when the caretaker fella found you?'

'After he'd finished quoting the Bible at us – and boy, did

John go to town that morning! – it was all round the school by lunchtime,' Harry explains.

'And then of course it leaked out into the playground via the kids to their mothers by home time,' Ellie adds, rolling her eyes.

'Playground gossip can be so nasty,' Billy says, grimacing.

'Tell me about it,' Harry says. 'And by home time not only were we found in the cupboard together, we were apparently naked too.'

Billy's eyes light up. 'You weren't, were you?'

'Of course we weren't! But by that time it didn't matter: the damage was done. We got called into the head's office the next day, and how we didn't lose our jobs I'll never know. Enough parents were calling for it. Apparently we were a bad example to their kids.'

Maybe it was *worse than I first thought.*

'But,' Harry continues, 'Walter, who was our headmaster at the time, was in a particularly good mood that day. He'd won some money on the lottery and was in the process of getting a new car, so I think someone was looking down kindly on us when we went in to see him. He used to be a right tyrant, ran the school with a rod of iron, did Walter Maxwell.'

'Ran?' Billy asks. 'What happened to him?'

'He died, sadly. Food poisoning. It was a strange thing; everyone else who ate the same thing as him at a school awards dinner he attended was absolutely fine. Not Walter though, it got him really bad and really quickly.'

Oh my God! Walter Maxwell, my old boss from the sixties was the headmaster at the school I'm now teaching in before he travelled in time? If only I'd got here sooner ... but it hadn't

364

worked before, had it? I'd never prevented anyone like me from jumping through time. Maybe this was our destiny, to move around like this. Maybe it couldn't be prevented, however hard someone tried. Ringo had said as much. But how odd that Walter should come from this year, from the very school I'm teaching in. Could it be another link?

'Are you all right, Jo-Jo?' Ellie asks. 'You're very quiet. Are we upsetting you by bringing all this up again?'

'No, no, not at all. I'm as amazed by this as the rest of you.'

Three puzzled faces stare back at me.

'What I mean is, it's still amazing how we got locked in that cupboard at all, isn't it, Harry?'

'Er, yeah,' Harry replies, looking at me with a strange expression. 'Very odd indeed.'

After we've eaten our lunch Billy and Ellie decide to head back over to the hotel.

'Sure you don't want to come?' Ellie asks as they stand up to leave. 'Even if they don't come out and sign autographs again, you'll see them when they come back from their sound check.'

'No, you're OK, I think we'll probably head back home soon.' I look over at Harry. He nods.

'Then we'll see you tonight at the gig? We're getting there at about seven, aren't we, Billy? So we can suss out the merchandise and soak up the atmosphere.'

The tour must start tonight.

'Yes, of course, I'll be there. What time does the show actually begin?'

'I reckon they come on stage at about 8.45, but the support

band is on first,' Ellie says eagerly. 'They'll probably be rubbish, but you need to try them once, don't you?'

'I'll be sure to be there before Take That come on, don't you worry,' I assure them.

Ellie shakes her head at me. 'I don't know what's become of you,' she says, looking at me in disappointment. 'You've completely lost your sense of fun. You've gone all serious on me these days, Jo-Jo.'

Didn't another Ellie say something similar to me once before?

Then she bends down next to me. 'Just be careful,' she whispers into my ear. 'I know how much you like him. But he's married, Jo-Jo, and the two of you work together. It's doomed before it's even begun.'

'Don't worry, Ellie,' I assure her. 'I've been in worse scrapes than this. It will all work itself out, I'm certain of it this time.'

Ellie, still looking unsure, shrugs her shoulders. 'All-righty then, but don't say I didn't warn you. Come on, Billy!' she calls brightly, standing up again. 'Let's go party with Take That!'

'Shouldn't that be *Take That and Party*?' Billy says, referring to the Take That album.

'Very funny! Thinks he's a comedian as well as a singer now.' She winks at Harry and me. 'Come on Lenny Henry, let's go!'

They disappear out of the door together, laughing like a couple of schoolkids.

Next to me, Harry sighs. 'I think we just got away with that,' he says with relief.

'Away with what?'

'The getting locked in the music room story. If only they knew the truth.'

'The truth?'

Harry smiles and puts his hand over mine on the table. 'I think we both know the truth by now, Jo-Jo, don't we?'

'Another cappuccino, please!' I call urgently to the passing waitress. 'And make it a strong one this time!'

Later, when we arrive back at the house I'm still no closer to finding out what Harry meant by 'the truth'. He suddenly went all vague when I tried pressing him further on the subject, reminding me very much of George. Then we find two large holdalls sitting on the doorstep, with a note.

You can collect the rest of your stuff tomorrow when I'm out of the house visiting my mother.

Harry sighs as he reads it. 'I've really gone and blown it this time,' he says, showing me the piece of paper.

'She's angry. She'll calm down after a day or two.'

Harry lifts the bags off the step. 'Maybe I don't care whether she does or not.'

'You don't mean that,' I say as we go into the house and I close the door on the outside world once more.

'Yes, I think I do, Jo-Jo. I really think I've had enough this time. Life is too short for this sort of nonsense. I don't want to spend my life with someone I don't love any more. I want to spend it with someone I do.'

His blue eyes don't move from mine while he says this.

I look away.

Harry drops the bags on the floor and walks over to me. 'I mean it, Jo-Jo, you must know how I feel about you, and I have for a very long time.'

He gently strokes my hair away from my face, and I have to

close my eyes for a second at the intensity of feeling that surges through me at his touch.

'Getting locked in the music room was an accident, but a happy accident,' Harry whispers. 'Serendipity, some people call it. Something that was supposed to happen so something else could take place as a result – and that something was realising just how strongly I felt about you, and that I couldn't hide it any longer.'

He pulls me into his arms, and for once I don't see a Beatles look-alike, a teenage punk or a yuppie in front of me, I see the real Harry, the one I want to be with.

'And I know you feel it too,' he continues, looking down at me. 'I can feel it, Jo-Jo, right here.' He takes my hand and places it on his chest so I can feel his heart beating strong and fast. Then he puts his hand on my heart.

'We're the same, you and I,' he whispers, as we stand with our hands on each other's chests, looking deep into the other's eyes. 'The same, Jo-Jo.'

'Are we?' I ask, my own voice breathless with anticipation. 'Are we really, Harry? Do you know my secret?'

'Of course,' he whispers, leaning forward to kiss me.

The doorbell rings.

Harry's head drops forward. 'Every time!' he groans. Then he looks up at me. 'You'd better get that, I suppose.'

'Don't go anywhere!' I insist, pointing to him as I dash out to the hall and open the door.

It's Ellie and Billy, holding pizza boxes.

'We were worried you wouldn't find us tonight, or you'd be *late*!' Ellie says, pushing past me into the hall. 'So we thought we'd pop by and spend the afternoon getting in the mood for the gig.' She holds up some Take That music videos. 'That's if we're not interrupting anything?'

Billy shrugs as I hold the door open for him and he walks past me into the house. 'Sorry,' he whispers. 'She's a pretty unstoppable force when she puts her mind to something.'

'Oh, don't I know it,' I mumble as I close the door behind them. 'I've been dealing with her for over thirty years now.'

'Sorry,' I whisper to Harry later, when we're all snuggled up on the sofas, and Ellie and Billy are busy singing along to Take That and eating pizza. 'I didn't know they were coming over.'

'It's fine,' Harry says, putting his arm around me. 'At least I still get to spend some time with you.'

'That secret we were talking about earlier, what was it?' I'm still desperate to know what he was going to say.

'This, of course,' he says, gesturing at Ellie, Billy and then the television. 'Your little Take That obsession. Why, what else did you think I meant?'

Forty-Two

Everywhere I look there are girls.

Some of them are young girls. Some of them can't really be classed as girls any more but are still sporting the same uniform as their younger counterpart: Take That T-shirts, scarves, badges – in fact, anything with the Take That double TT insignia they can lay their hands on, is covering their pubescent, and in some cases menopausal, bodies.

As I look around the inside of Wembley Arena, it's not just visually that my senses are tested, it's audibly too, and even though I'm not actually in the main auditorium yet, the noise is incredible. Excited voices bounce between food kiosks and merchandise stands as females chat, gossip and scream their way through the last few minutes before showtime, and the anticipation builds for the evening's entertainment.

'Jo-Jo! Jo-Jo!' Is someone calling my name? I wonder, as I try to distinguish the lone voice in amongst the sea of noise. Then I spot Billy, madly waving at me above a forest of deely

370

boppers, glittery hairbands and baseball caps, and as he pushes his way through the crowd I spy Ellie, her tiny frame almost swamped, following in his wake.

'We thought we'd lost you in the crowd,' he gushes, hugging me.

'No, it all got a bit mad in there for me,' I reply, nodding in the direction of the main auditorium. 'But I think it's even worse out here.'

'And that's only the support act, babe. Wait until the fab five come on!'

'Ooh, let's get foam fingers!' Ellie coos, looking across at one of the merchandise stands. 'I've always wanted one of those.'

'That's only so people can see you in a crowd,' Billy jokes.

Ellie pretends to turn her nose up. 'I don't care what it's for – I want one. Back in a mo!' She skips over to one of the merchandise stalls and manages to wriggle her slim frame to the front of the table immediately, even though it's three deep with fans waiting to buy Take That pillowcases and the like.

Billy smiles at me. 'Everything OK?' he asks. 'With Harry?'

'Yeah, he's fine. He's gone to have a drink with George at the World's End so he's not on his own. This really wouldn't have been his thing.'

'We wouldn't have been able to get him a ticket anyway,' Billy says, looking around him at the ever-growing crowd. 'It's been sold out for ages.' He looks at me again. 'I'm sorry if we messed up your time with Harry earlier, but sometimes these things are for the best.'

Until now Billy's just seemed like a nice young man, if a bit over the top with his flamboyant outfits and flowery language.

But now, as we stand looking at each other in this odd setting, he seems different. Older somehow. Perhaps even wiser?

'What do you mean – for the best?'

'I think you know what I mean, Jo-Jo. It's not the right time for the two of you yet, is it?' He looks at me meaningfully now. 'I'm sure that time will come though, if you just let it be.'

'Here!' Ellie cries jubilantly, poking me with a huge pink foam finger. 'I got us all one. Bit expensive, but hey, you only live once!'

I look questioningly at Billy as I pull a blue foam finger on to my hand.

'Do we, Billy?' I ask him. 'Do we only live once?'

I enjoy the concert much more than I thought I would – when I can actually hear it, that is.

The music is almost constantly drowned out by the sound of screaming and singing girls. But when I do hear something I'm treated to a very young-looking Take That singing some of their early hits like 'Babe', 'Pray', 'Could It Be Magic' and 'Relight My Fire'.

'I *love* Gary!' Billy shouts across at me when Gary is singing 'A Million Love Songs'. 'He's gonna go through some tough times when they split, but I hope he'll pull through OK. He's destined for greater things, I know it.'

I stop swaying to the music and stare hard at Billy. Then I lean into him again.

'You mean like Robbie,' I shout into his ear, 'he'll have ups and downs, but give them both, what, say nineteen years or so, and they'll be top of their game again. Hey, they might even be married with kids, too?'

Billy nods, still looking at the stage. 'I hope so. If only they knew now what was to come in their future, they'd be able to prepare themselves.' Then he turns towards me so quickly that his foam finger, still held aloft in the air, flies off and lands in the row behind. His fearful expression tells me everything I need to know.

'You're like me, aren't you?' I whisper in his ear while he still stares at me.

'I – I don't know what you mean,' Billy says quickly. He reaches into the row behind us to retrieve his finger.

'Yes, you do,' I say as he stands upright again and begins to applaud with everyone else. 'You're from the future, aren't you?'

'Not now, Jo-Jo!' he hisses. 'In the interval.'

As the band launches into 'Everything Changes', I stand thinking about what I've just discovered. It's Billy, this time; he's the time traveller. But why didn't I spot it sooner? I look over at him again happily dancing and singing along with everyone else. He's not the same as Walter, Stu, or Lucy, he doesn't have the same look they all had. The aura they all carried was one of not quite belonging, of being an outsider – I could see it in their eyes, and I'd got good at spotting it. Billy doesn't look like that at all; he seems quite content with his life, happy even.

Why is he so different?

Forty-Three

As the boys finish their routine and the lights dim on the stage, they light up the auditorium and we all dive outside with everyone else for the interval.

'God, I'm bursting!' Ellie says, looking in anguish at the queue for the ladies' toilet. 'I'm gonna try round the back, there's more toilets there, maybe the queue is shorter. You coming, Jo-Jo?'

'No, I'm fine,' I reply, glancing across at Billy. Don't you dare disappear now, I think, looking at him. 'I'll wait here with *Bill*.'

Billy looks over at me. 'Yeah,' he says, catching my eye. 'We're not going anywhere, Ellie, you go.'

'OK, then,' Ellie says brightly. 'Back in a bit!'

I grab hold of Billy's arm and drag him towards the quietest corner I can find, away from as many hot dog stands and images of Take That as possible.

'What's going on?' I ask, getting straight to the point. 'Who are you, and where are you from originally?'

Billy looks around him before speaking. 'How do I know I can trust you?'

'Of course you can trust me! I'm like you, aren't I? From another time, stuck in a year I don't want to be.'

'See, that's just why you're *not* like me,' he says, shaking his head.

'What do you mean?'

'I'm not stuck in a year I *don't* want to be, I'm stuck in a year I *do* want to be.'

'I'm not sure I follow?'

Billy sighs. 'I'm from 2004, Jo-Jo. Back then I was a dead-end singer in a pretty poor Take That tribute band. I used to dream of seeing the band live because I never got to the first time around – let's just say I was in a difficult relationship then and he was quite controlling.' Billy closes his eyes as if trying to block out the memories. 'But anyhow,' he says, 'one day in 2004 I was involved in a nasty incident with a pair of kitchen scissors.' He winces.

'Oh my! Did you fall on them?'

'No, I was stabbed by them.'

'You were stabbed!' I exclaim. 'Bloody hell, Billy, what an awful way to go.'

Billy makes a shushing sound with his hand. 'No, it wasn't pleasant. But I don't remember much about it, to be honest. One minute I'm cooking spag bol in my kitchen, and the next, poof, I'm here!'

'Did they catch whoever did it?'

'No idea, babe, don't tell you that, do they? However, I had the last laugh over whoever did stab me because I absolutely *adore* where I am now! Don't want to go back *ever*.'

'You don't want to go back?' I ask, astounded by this admission. 'Why?'

'Because I bloody love it here amongst all this!' He holds up his hands and gesticulates at the arena. 'I get to live all this for real this time – the hype, the concerts, the TV appearances. When they break up that's it, isn't it – all gone. No more Take That.' Billy visibly deflates in front of me, as though someone has released some of his air – the air that keeps him alive.

A wonderful warm feeling rushes through me as I smile at him. 'Billy, I have some very good news for you.'

'What?' he asks, his head lifting a little.

'Take That get back together.'

Billy looks at me for a split second like I've said something in a foreign language he doesn't understand. Then, as it begins to register, his eyes narrow.

'Don't mess with me, Jo-Jo. This is important stuff to me.'

'I'm not! I'm from 2013, and not only do Take That reform in 2005 as a four-piece, and then tour twice on their own to sell-out arenas, but in 2010 they tour again with Robbie!'

Billy looks like I've just told him he's won ten million pounds on the lottery.

'No way!' He flaps his hands up and down excitedly. 'When you said in the arena you hoped things would get better for them after the split I thought you were just being optimistic. I can't believe this!'

'I'm not finished yet, it gets better.'

'It can't. It can't!' He begins to bob up and down now too,

as well as flapping his hands, so he looks like a fledgling chick trying to take off from a nest.

'Gary Barlow becomes a celebrity in his own right when he becomes a judge on a TV show called *The X Factor*.'

'Oh my days! I think I'm going to faint,' Billy says, and he actually looks as if he might. He puts his hand out to the wall behind us for support. 'That *X Factor* show had just started before I left. Is it still running?'

'Yes and it's massive. And so is Gary. He's a household name in his own right now, Billy, you've got so much to look forward to!'

'Jo-Jo, you've made my night – no, my life!' Billy gives me a big hug. 'Now what can I do for you? Are you happy to stay here in 1994, or do you want to leave?'

'I want to leave,' I reply almost immediately, then I think about Harry. 'Although this is the first time I've ever felt like I might want to stay on.'

'Harry?' Billy asks knowingly.

I nod. 'But it's not the first time I've met him . . .' and I tell Billy as quickly as I can what's been happening to me.

'How very romantic,' Billy says when I've finished. 'The two of you constantly drawn together like that over all those decades, and yet you don't know why?'

'I've absolutely no idea.'

I haven't really thought of it as romantic before. I've been so busy trying to figure out why I'm doing this, and how I'm going to get back that I haven't stopped to think that to be constantly drawn into the life of the same person is quite nice too. All right, it's more than just nice: it's pretty damn wonderful.

'You'd think there'd be something that links it all,' Billy

says. 'These sorts of occurrences are rarely completely random in my experience.'

I hesitate. 'I think there might be a Beatles link that runs through all this. Because everywhere I go they seem to show up, from their songs to their lyrics.'

'The Beatles, hmm ...' Billy says, thinking. 'That's very interesting, considering what's about to happen.'

'Why? What's relevant about tonight?'

'Come with me and you'll see in the next few minutes,' Billy says, taking my hand as Ellie now reappears, and it's time to head back into the main auditorium. 'Mr Barlow will tell us what we need to know. You just wait and see, Jo-Jo.'

As the lights dim, the screams grow louder, and a moving platform lit like a Christmas tree extends out into the audience above our heads. Then, like five blue bullets fired out of a dancing gun, Take That appear on the rooftop stage to begin the next part of their show.

They've worn some pretty snazzy stage outfits throughout the show so far, but now as they wave down at their adoring crowd, they're wearing bright blue single-breasted suits, which look extremely familiar to me.

And it's as the first few bars of their next song begin, I realise why, when I immediately recognise the Beatles hit 'I Wanna Hold Your Hand'.

'See, I told you,' Billy says, grinning at me; he waves his hand up in the air. 'Take That does the Beatles!'

I stand and watch, astonished, as they dance and sing their way through a medley of 'I Wanna Hold Your Hand', 'Hard Day's Night', 'She Loves You', and 'I Feel Fine'.

'I can't believe this!' I say out loud, forgetting that Ellie doesn't know my secret. 'I never knew Take That sang any Beatles songs on tour!'

'What do you mean?' Ellie shouts, her eyes still trained up on the stage above us. 'Not just on tour, is it? This medley is the B-side of 'Everything Changes'. How can you not know that? We played it often enough when it came out!'

'Yeah, yeah, I forgot,' I mumble, still watching the boys energetically make their way through their songs. But when Jason launches into 'Get Back', it's as if I'm the only person in the whole of Wembley listening to him.

'Hey, that's like you!' Billy shouts in my ear, while Ellie is leaping up and down on my other side. 'He's singing "Get Back", Jo-Jo, "get back to where you once belonged".'

Jason repeats this lyric over and over, as he continues his lively rendition of the song up on the stage above us. While I stand absolutely still, not moving a muscle. Even my own name is part of a Beatles lyric – of course I've realised this before, but I've just not considered it in the context of what has been happening to me lately.

It's time to get back, Jo-Jo, I repeat in my head, time to get back to where you once belonged.

It's a message.

It's time.

'Hey, where are you going?' I hear Ellie call, as I begin to push my way along the row of fans still leaping around and singing along to the songs. 'It's not over yet.'

But it is for me. It's time for me to go back. But I must find George first before I do.

*

379

I fight my way out of the noisy, packed auditorium and into the empty Wembley corridors outside. The only people milling about are stewards and a few staff still manning some of the refreshment stands. Ignoring their shouts of concern, I run past them towards the nearest exit. Then I let myself out into the fresh air, take a few deep breaths, and stop for a moment to decide on my next move.

There are a few taxis and buses arriving, ready to collect the thousands of exuberant fans that will burst forth from these same doors in a little while, and a few concerned-looking parents already beginning to hover, too, ready to retrieve their excited daughters when they eventually emerge, and take them safely back home.

'Miss McKenzie?' I jump when I hear the small voice call my name.

I turn around and have to look down to see the owner of the voice.

'Paul!' I say in surprise. 'What are you doing here?'

It's the young boy from my class, the one who helped clear up my mess, and then stayed back to ask me questions about the probability of time travel.

'We're here to collect my sister,' he explains. 'She's here with my mum.'

A man steps forward now; it's John the caretaker from the school.

'Hello, Miss McKenzie,' he says, smiling. 'Is the show over already?'

'No, I just needed to leave early, that's all.' I look between John and Paul now. There's something about the two of them that's suddenly very familiar.

380

'That's a shame,' John says. 'My wife tells me the finale is often the best part. When everything comes together, you might say.'

'Yes, indeed. Look, it's lovely to see you both, but I really have to dash—'

'Wait, I have something for you before you go,' Paul says, pulling his rucksack off his shoulders and unzipping it. He pulls out a small book and passes it to me.

'What is it?' I ask, thinking it's some homework he's forgotten to hand in. But the book is too small to be that, and the dim light outside makes it difficult for me to make out what's on the cover.

He looks up at his father, who nods his encouragement.

'My dad gave you a *Beano* many years ago, and now it's my turn to give you a gift.'

I look at Paul's face carefully now, and then at John's. Now I see what's familiar: John looks exactly like the little boy I saved from getting hit on the crossing in 1963.

'You're the boy from the zebra crossing?' I ask John in amazement.

He nods. 'You saved me that day, Jo-Jo. I didn't run back out into the road because of you, and if it wasn't for that, this little fella wouldn't be here now.' He ruffles Paul's curly hair.

'So we *can* all mix together in the same book?' I wonder out loud. 'Sometimes the pages fit together, and the words start to make sense again.' I look down at the book I now hold in my hand. 'What is this?' I ask, trying to see what it says in the light.

'It's a Bible,' Paul replies.

'Can I ask why?' I look between them, not really expecting a straight answer. I'm used to that by now.

'Just take it,' John says. 'You're on a magical mystery tour, Jo-Jo, It won't be long before you can work it out.'

I smile at them both. 'Shouldn't that be, before *we can work it out*?'

John nods. 'You will, Jo-Jo. We all do eventually.'

Suddenly the big doors behind us open, and I realise that any minute now thousands of girls and women are going to come flooding out into the area we're standing in.

I wave goodbye to John and Paul and I begin to run down Wembley Way, the long walkway that leads from Wembley Arena to the tube station; I need to get there before the station and the trains become packed out with fans. As I run, I smile to myself. John and Paul – I should have known; two of the Beatles, and some would say one of the greatest song-writing duos ever. It had to be them, didn't it?

It had been the Beatles all along. I knew that now. I'd simply refused to recognise the links because I'd chosen to continue a childhood anxiety into my adult years. It wasn't the Fab Four that I hated at all. It was their association with my youth, the years of travelling, feeling unsettled, and never being in control of my own destiny. The clues had been there all the time and I just hadn't seen them.

I climb onto a nearly empty tube train and sit and piece it all together as I travel back towards the King's Road. Apart from all the songs and lyrics that constantly kept appearing throughout my time travelling, it was John who left me the Beano comic back in 1963; George who gave me the football boots in 1977; Ringo, the four-leaf-clover brooch in 1985; and now Paul – a Bible here in 1994. All four of these funny little gifts that I carried with me through each decade have been

382

given to me by a different Beatle. So this must be it, then, I must have all the clues now; there were only four band members. So what happens now? What do I have to do before I can return to my own life back in 2013?

There is only one person who can help me.

George.

Forty-Four

Finally I'm able to exit the underground and emerge up on to the now familiar King's Road.

As I run past all the shops, I don't have time to notice anything in their windows. I've often stopped and had a giggle to myself at the fashions or the music or the latest gadgets being advertised in the windows many of the times I've travelled along this street over the last few decades. But not this time. This time I'm certain I know what I need, and I know just where I'm going to find it.

I have to wait for the traffic to pause and allow me to cross as I arrive at the zebra crossing opposite the World's End pub, and as I stand, hopping from foot to foot impatiently, I see the doors of the pub open and two figures appear, chatting to one another.

'Harry, George!' I call excitedly, waving my arm. 'It's me, Jo-Jo, over here!'

But my voice is drowned out by the noise of the traffic, so they don't appear to see or hear me.

Damn! I watch helplessly as they begin to walk away together down the road. *I need to speak to both of you.* I wait desperately for a break in the traffic. *Why is no one stopping for me tonight? What's up with these damn lights?* I look up at the big orange balls beside me.

Suddenly the road quietens, so I take my chance and dash over the crossing, still looking along the road where Harry and George are now rapidly disappearing into the distance.

But I should know better than to trust this crossing whenever it quietens suddenly. Because as quickly as my feet have made contact with the familiar black and white stripes, so does the now equally familiar white car shoot round the corner and everything goes cold . . .

The Long and
Winding Road

Forty-Five

I open my eyes and, as usual, the first thing I see is blue sky as the sun shines down, warming my horizontal body.

So I'm definitely not still in 1994, or it would be stars in the night sky I'd be seeing now, I think, as I look round, expecting to see the usual crowd of onlookers gathered to discover my fate.

But there's not a soul to be seen anywhere, just an empty zebra crossing, and me.

I sit up.

The road is deserted too. Odd, the King's Road is never clear of traffic.

Suddenly a black cab skids round the corner and screeches to a halt at the edge of the crossing.

'Oi!' the cabbie shouts, leaning out of his window. 'Do you want to get yourself killed? Get your arse up and out of the road before I drive over the top of you anyway!'

I quickly crawl to my feet, and stagger over to the side of the pavement.

'Pissed at this time of the morning, love?' he shouts as he drives slowly past me. 'You should be ashamed of yerself! Go home and get cleaned up before anyone sees ya, that's my advice. You don't look like you belong on the streets, that's for sure.'

I examine my clothes as he drives off down the road. I'm wearing a navy blue leather jacket, white T-shirt, red jeans and bright red pumps. The outfit I'd seen in the window of Peter Jones just before I visited George in his shop to deliver his accounts? But I didn't go in and look at it because I didn't think I'd be able to carry it off . . .

That means I must be back! I'm back in 2013!

'I'm back!' I shout out to the empty road, jumping up in the air. 'You told me to get back and I did! I'm here!'

I look down at my side, and I swear I've never been more pleased to see a Mulberry tote bag in my whole life. I pull it from my shoulder and thrust it open, desperately hoping my iPhone will be in there. After a few seconds of burrowing, relief floods through me. It is!

I'm about to make my first phone call, when I see the other contents of my bag: a *Beano*, a pair of football boots, a four-leaf-clover brooch and a Bible.

For just a few moments, when I was leaping up and down on the pavement, I wondered if it had all been a dream; in fact, all the time I'd been time travelling a tiny part of me had always wondered if maybe when I'd been hit by the original white car, I'd been so badly injured that I'd slipped into a coma, and my experiences were hallucinations brought on by a strong hospital medication.

But now, seeing all the items I've collected still lying in the bottom of my bag, I know it isn't a dream. It's been real. I push the screen on my iPhone.

After a few rings, there's a muffled, 'Hello?'

'Ellie? Is that you?' I ask, never so relieved to hear her Scouse accent.

'Of course it's me, Jo-Jo! What the bloody hell do you want at . . . at 5.25 in the morning?'

I'm a little taken aback. Even though a version of Ellie has been my friend through four decades, this Ellie is only my assistant, my employee.

'Is everything OK?' I ask. 'With the business?'

'What? Why on earth do you suddenly want to know that? Of course it is.' Ellie sighs at the other end of the phone. 'Look, Jo-Jo, you agreed if I took on this role of managing the business while you took a break, that you'd let me get on with it. I'm perfectly capable, you know.'

Ellie is managing my business while I take a break? No, that can't be right; I *never* take breaks.

'Yes, I'm sure you are.' I'm trying to think quickly. 'It's just . . . I worry.'

'You always have done, Jo-Jo, too much, that's why you need this time-out. You need to find a life outside the business, let someone else take control for a while. I thought we agreed on that when you first suggested it?'

I suggested this?

'And you know I'll look after the place. So just let me shoulder some of the stress for you for a while, that's what friends are for.'

I physically jump a little on the pavement when Ellie uses the word *friends*. When I left 2013 Ellie had only been working

391

for me for a few months – she was hardly a friend back then. Of course, I think of her like that now after all the adventures we've had together, but Ellie doesn't know that, does she?

'We've been through so much together, Jo-Jo,' she continues, 'and you've taught me a lot. This is my chance to prove to you just what I'm capable of, and to give you something back for all you've given to me.'

This is like a whole new Ellie I'm talking to; she's so much more confident and in control. Maybe this is an alternative 2013 I've come back to? It would explain my new clothes ... But this Ellie is definitely right about one thing: I do need a life outside of my business, my adventures have certainly taught me that. When I was in 1963 I certainly realised I was working too hard and that I needed a life away from the office.

I take a deep breath and make a decision.

Ellie will look after my business; I know she will. I trust her. She's my friend now. And she sounds so different – it's almost like she's been on a life-changing adventure herself.

'You're right, Ellie,' I say with confidence. 'I know you'll do a great job. I'm so sorry to have woken you, I didn't realise it was so early. Just go back to bed.'

'That's OK, sweetie, it wouldn't be you if you didn't worry a little bit. But it's not worth going back to sleep now. I'll just stick a bit of music on and I'll soon be awake and running!'

'Can I guess who's on your playlist?' I ask, smiling into my phone.

'If you like? Bet you don't guess many of them right, though. I have quite an eclectic taste in music.'

'I'll give it a go. Let me see now, I think there'll be a bit of Take That, for starters.'

'Yep, you know I like the boys – I've never hidden that from you.'

'Maybe some Madonna?'

'Yeah, Madge is in there too, I can't deny it.'

'The Beatles ...'

'Ooh, good going, Jo-Jo, you know me better than I thought! Yes, the Fab Four are classics, you can't go wrong with them. Bet there's one you can't get though, bit random, this.'

I'm grinning now.

'The Bay City Rollers, would it be?'

'Jo-Jo McKenzie, how the bloomin' heck do you know that? *Nobody* knows my guilty pleasure of the music world, absolutely nobody. How do you?'

'Inside info,' I laugh. 'Go back to bed, Ellie, and enjoy your iPod for a while, you deserve it!'

'Mmm, I will. Just do one thing for me, Jo-Jo, will you?'

'What's that?'

'Ring your mother about her party! She keeps badgering me about it and I can't keep putting her off!'

Some things never change.

I hang up the phone to Ellie, and stare at it for a few seconds, then I go back to Contacts. It's early, but she always used to be a dawn riser.

The phone rings a few times before an answerphone cuts in and my mother's clipped voice repeats her familiar message in my ear. Perhaps things have changed a little?

'Hi, Mum,' I say. 'I just wanted to let you know that I will be coming to your anniversary party, and yes, I'll turn up in fancy dress if that's what you both want.' A memory suddenly washes over me of the 1977 Penny hugging me in her kitchen and calling me 'her girl' as I stand all alone in the deserted street. 'And Mum, I'm sorry if I've been a pain about calling you back, or about anything else really. Especially your Beatles records. I don't really hate Paul McCartney, and if Dad goes up in the attic and looks in the big blue suitcase he'll find your copy of "Mull of Kintyre" there. Don't ask me how it got there. But that's where you'll find it.' I pause again. 'Oh, and Mum, I don't say it very often, but I do love you and Dad very much, you know, and ... well I miss you both too.'

I hang up and find I'm breathing rather heavily. But as I put my phone back in my bag, I find I'm smiling. That felt good. In fact, both those phone calls felt good. I'm starting to like this new 2013; I feel lighter, and more carefree.

As I walk along the street, I realise it's a bit early for George to be in his shop yet. Perhaps it's time, at last, to spend a few minutes enjoying my longed-for paper cup filled to the brim with sweet, frothy, syrup-filled coffee while I wait for George to arrive to open up. But as I come level with the old shop I've seen in so many lifetimes before, I have to stop and pause at the window of Groovy Records.

The display is a little more modern than I'm used to seeing in George's window. But that could be, of course, because the last few times I've looked in here it's been in a different decade. No, there *is* something unusual about this one – an artistic flair that George's displays always lacked.

I stand studying the window. There're still the same LPs and singles there always used to be; a mixture of sixties, seventies, eighties and nineties music, recorded on to vinyl, cassette tape or CD depending on the decade they were released. But they've now been joined by more modern music – CDs from bands like One Direction and The Wanted jostle for pride of place with the elder statesmen of the music industry.

'Anything you're looking for in particular?' a familiar voice asks.

I look back at the reflection in the window. *George!*

Or is it? I turn to inspect the young man standing next to me. He's wearing running clothes and trainers, and beneath his short-cropped dark brown hair, his eyes are identical to George's, the exact same shade of blue. But is it George? No, it can't be. This is younger than George ever looked, even in 1963!

'George?' I ask hesitantly.

'You're looking for my grandfather? I'm afraid he's not here any more.'

'Has he retired?'

'No,' he says and his head drops a little. 'I'm afraid he passed away a few months ago.'

My heart drops to my stomach faster than a lead weight.

'George is dead?' I repeat unnecessarily.

The young man nods. 'I'm sorry. He went peacefully, though, right here in the shop, listening to his favourite band.'

'The Beatles,' I reply, already knowing the answer.

'Yes, that's right. You obviously knew him well.'

I nod slowly, trying to take it in. I thought I'd known George well. But he never talked much about a family, let alone a grandson, so how much about George's life away from this shop did I actually know? I'd always been too busy with my own problems whenever I'd seen him.

I immediately feel bad. George was always such a great source of comfort and hope for me, wherever, or whoever, I was. And I always assumed he would be here for me at this shop with a cup of tea and some words of wisdom. I'd never considered the possibility he might not be here one day.

'Are you OK?' George's grandson asks. 'This has obviously come as a shock to you.'

'Yes … I'm fine …' But to my surprise I feel my knees buckle a little, and I hold on to the window frame for support.

'Look,' he pulls some keys from his tracksuit pocket, 'I'm not due to open up yet, but do you want to come in for a bit and take a seat and I'll make you a cuppa – you look like you could do with one.'

'Yes, thank you,' I reply gratefully. 'That would be good.'

We enter the shop together and I'm comforted to hear the little shop bell still ring above my head, and see my favourite wooden chair sitting where it's always been. The sunflowers on the counter, wilting and drooping over the edge of the vase, look as if they need changing, but apart from that, the inside looks much as it always has.

'Take a seat,' he says, disappearing around the corner, 'I won't be a minute. I'll just pop the kettle on.'

I collapse with relief onto the familiar wooden chair that I've sat and told George my problems on so many times.

I'd felt so buoyant outside, talking to Ellie, and then my mother, and now everything has been turned upside down again. I just assumed I'd be able to tell George all my news, the way I always did, and he'd give me his usual calm and considered advice. But this time he wasn't here. He was gone. Even the big wooden clock behind the counter has stopped

396

ticking, I notice, as I sit here in silence. Its hands have stopped moving at 2.13.

'That's the kettle on,' George's grandson says, returning. 'Grandad always said a cup of tea would put everything right. I'm not so sure about that myself, but it seemed to work for him for over eighty years.'

I smile as I remember all the cups of tea that George made for me in this shop.

'I'm Julian, by the way,' he says, holding out his hand.

'Jo-Jo,' I reply, shaking it.

He stops shaking my hand but still holds on to it while he stares at me.

'What?' I ask. 'What's wrong?'

'*You're* Jo-Jo?' he asks, looking dazed.

'Yes, is there a problem?' I pull my hand away.

Julian shakes his head. 'No, no, not at all. It's just that before he died Grandad told me that one day a girl called Jo-Jo would come by the shop, and when she did, I was to look after her and make her a cup of tea.'

I smile. That's so typical of George.

'I wondered at the time if he was making it up – one of his little stories. Grandad had so many of them. Used to keep us all entertained for hours, he did. I don't know how he thought of them all. But now you're actually here.'

'Yes, I am. George probably knew I'd turn up again like a bad penny. He couldn't keep me away!'

'Not at all,' Julian continues. 'Grandad talked about you with much fondness. But he also said when you returned I was to give you something, and I've been keeping it hidden under the counter ever since in case what he said was true.'

Julian goes behind the shop counter and retrieves a brown paper bag.

'What is it?' I ask, looking at the bag.

Julian hands it to me. 'Open it up and take a look. Means nothing to me. But it might to you.'

I open up the bag and pull out two black vinyl records in their slightly battered old sleeves. They're both Beatles singles – 'Eleanor Rigby' and 'All You Need Is Love'.

'Mean anything?' Julian asks.

I shrug. 'Not really.

'Maybe Grandad just wanted you to have them?' he suggests. 'He didn't say too much in his will. Only about this shop, really, and that was all a bit odd.'

'Why?' I ask, still looking at the Beatles records in my hand.

'He insisted that it should always remain as Groovy Records, that he wanted me to run it for as long as I possibly could, and that we should always welcome in anyone who seemed lost and lonely and offer them a cup of tea and a seat for a while and listen to their problems.'

I smile. Of course George would. 'Am I your problem for today, do you think?'

'No, not at all,' Julian says, smiling back. 'It's always a pleasure to meet someone who knew my grandad. And just between you and me, I've a lot more problems with this shop than a pretty lady turning up on my doorstep wanting a cup of tea.'

'Really? What?'

'It's nothing, really, you don't want me bothering you with my troubles.'

'Julian, you have no idea how many times I sat in this very

chair and bothered your grandfather with my problems. It's the least I can do.'

Julian smiles and sits down in the chair next to me. 'It's just that Grandad may have left me this shop in his will, but he didn't leave me the means to keep it going.'

'But Groovy Records always turned over a profit, although I never could understand how George did it.'

'That's the thing, it did when Grandad ran it, but since I've been in charge it's all gone downhill. We had to remain closed for five months when he first died, before I could take over, which didn't help. But running a record shop isn't really my thing, you see. I'm only doing it because it's what Grandad wanted. He seemed to have a magical touch.'

'Yes, George was a bit like that – charmed, you might call him.'

Julian nods. 'Anyway, none of this is your concern, Jo-Jo. I'll work something out.' He glances at the records I still hold in my hand. 'Should I play them for you?' he asks. 'For old times' sake? This shop hasn't heard the Beatles since Grandad passed.'

'Yes, why not?' I give them to him. 'Let's play them for George.'

Julian carefully loads one of the records on to the old player that has always stood in the corner of the shop and the familiar string introduction to 'Eleanor Rigby' begins to play, followed by the haunting vocal describing all the lonely people.

As we sit in the little shop listening to the song play, me on the little wooden chair and Julian perched on the shop counter, we're both lost for a few minutes in our memories of George.

'Any the wiser why Grandad left you that particular Beatles record?' Julian asks at the end of the song.

'Not really, no,' I reply, desperately trying to think of some link between the song and everything that's happened. I repeat the lyrics over again in my head. Where do all the lonely people come from, the Beatles asked. Where do they all belong?

'I'll play the next one,' he says, lifting 'Eleanor Rigby' away from the player and replacing it with 'All You Need Is Love'.

The memorable 'Love' intro comes wafting across the shop now, followed by the familiar lyrics.

Why did George leave me these two particular songs? There has to be some meaning to them, knowing George. It's a clue, something to help me finally find my answer.

The chorus still plays in my head as Julian lifts the second record from the turntable, places it back in its sleeve, then hands them both to me.

'I'm sorry I couldn't be of more help,' he says. 'I have no idea why Grandad left you these, only that he was very insistent that you have them.'

'It's fine,' I reply, looking down at the records in my hand. 'I'm sure I'll figure it out one day.' I look up at Julian. 'I'd like to pay my last respects to your grandfather – is there a gravestone?'

'Yes, Grandad was very specific about his whole funeral, he had the whole thing planned to a tee.' He smiles. 'We had to have this whole Beatles theme on the day, their songs, everything, and Grandad was even buried up in Liverpool.'

'In Liverpool?' I say in surprise. 'But George lived his whole life here in London.'

400

'He was actually born in Liverpool. My great-grandparents moved here when he was young, to find work I believe. I guess that's where his love of the Beatles started.'

I think about this. 'I'd still like to go some time and visit – could you tell me where it is?'

Julian reaches behind the desk for a piece of paper and a pen, then he scribbles something down. 'Here,' he says, passing it to me.

'Thank you.' I give the paper a quick glance, fold it and put it in my bag. 'I think perhaps it's time for me to go now.'

'But you haven't had your tea yet,' Julian says.

I look around the shop at the posters on the walls and the records in the racks.

'I hope you won't be offended, Julian, but it just isn't the same now your grandad isn't here. It doesn't feel right, drinking tea in here without him.'

Julian smiles. 'No offence taken. I know exactly what you mean. Besides, I'm pretty useless at making tea anyway. You'd be better getting coffee down the road at Starbucks.'

'Julian, you have no idea just how long I've been waiting for someone to say those words to me!' I stand up. 'Thank you for these,' I say, holding up the records in the bag, then quite randomly I go over and hug him. 'It was lovely to meet you. George would be very proud of you, I know he would.'

Julian looks a little surprised at the hug, but pleased at my compliment. 'I do hope so. My grandad was a very special man.'

'He was indeed, Julian. He really was, and if I can think of any way to help you with the shop I'll be in touch, I promise.'

As I leave Julian, the little shop bell tinkles above my head, and somehow I know it won't be the last time I'll hear it.

And I don't head immediately up the road to Starbucks as I originally planned. Surprisingly, as soon as I leave the shop I forget all about my need for coffee. Instead I turn in the opposite direction and start walking towards the nearest railway station. To find a train that's going to take me to Liverpool and to George.

Forty-Six

Once I get to Euston, I manage to get on a fast train up to Liverpool. But my journey still gives me plenty of time to think.

While I was waiting for my train, I used the Wi-Fi at the station to download a Beatles greatest hits album to my iPhone. So while I've been travelling, I've listened to the same two Beatles songs that George gave me, along with a few others, pretty much on repeat all the way up to Liverpool. But still nothing is any clearer.

The only things I've been able to pull from 'Eleanor Rigby' that have any meaning for me is that there's an Eleanor, of course – and Ellie was with me all the way through my time travelling. There's a Father McKenzie mentioned, which is my surname, and Eleanor's surname, Rigby, is also Harry's name, and he was with me constantly too.

I think about Harry and wonder what he's doing now. I

haven't had time to try and find out anything about him in the few hours I've been back because I've been so busy trying to work out this mystery. I thought about calling him when I was first on the train, but I placed the business card he'd given me back in the original 2013 in the pocket of my work suit and I'm certainly not wearing that now that I seem to have morphed into this new version of me, so I have no way of contacting him. But I wonder where he is right now, and more importantly if I'll ever see him again.

And the thought of never seeing Harry again is, I have to admit, a scary one.

But first things first, I must get to Liverpool, pay my respects to George, and see if the city of his and the Beatles birth might solve my time travel mystery for me once and for all.

The cemetery George is buried in is out in Woolton, a suburb of Liverpool, so as soon as my train arrives at Lime Street station I immediately head over to the taxi rank.

I'm a little surprised that the taxi driver knows the cemetery as soon as I mention its name. That's odd, I think, perhaps it's a popular church for funerals and weddings in the area? After a short journey the taxi pulls up outside a large church with a number of cars and people already milling about outside. Then I see a bride and groom climbing into a big black car a few yards down the road in front of us, and I realise there must be a wedding going on.

'Busy today,' I comment to the driver as I climb out.

'Yes, it always is,' he says. 'I come here almost every day.'

Strange, I think again. *Every day?*

'Can you wait for me?' I ask him. 'I won't be long.'

'Didn't think you would be,' he says, already opening a newspaper on top of his steering wheel. 'Yeah, love, I'll be right here.'

I close the cab door and look up at St Peter's Church in front of me; it's built in a red-brown brick, which makes a striking contrast against the bright blue of the sky on this sunny Saturday afternoon.

The wedding guests have mostly filtered away now, so I walk quietly round the back of the church clutching the sunflowers I've brought with me.

In the graveyard I walk carefully past all the new headstones until I find George's, then I pause in front of it to read the inscription.

IN LOVING MEMORY OF
GEORGE 'LENNON' McCARTNEY
1ST FEBRUARY 1933 – 3RD FEBRUARY 2013
GONE, BUT NEVER FORGOTTEN
ALWAYS IN OUR LONELY HEARTS CLUB BAND

I stand and stare at the gravestone, a deep sense of sadness suddenly engulfing me. Poor George. At least he'd just reached that magical eighty, though, before he passed away in February.

Wait, February? That can't be right. I was still here in February 2013. It was in the summer that I visited George in his shop with his accounts. The weather had been so beautiful that day, and the shops on the King's Road full of outfits ready for people's summer holidays. I'd stopped and looked

405

at some of them, and that's what had nearly made me late. *George was still alive in the summer!* I saw him. I spoke to him. He made me a cup of tea. How could this say he died in February?

I think about George, and how he always knew so much about what was going on with me. I always got the feeling he knew more but wouldn't say. Then there were those occasions he did seem to know about the future, even though he shouldn't have done.

Was George a time traveller, too? But George hadn't had that look about him that the others had; he wasn't struggling with everything that was going on. Even Billy, who'd been happy to be where he was, wasn't like George. George was always calm and serene, always knew the right thing to say, always seemed at peace with everything and everyone. He'd looked after me when I'd been in need, always been there for me when I needed guidance. He was like ... I pause. No, I don't believe in things like that. But I didn't believe in time travel before, either. Was the George that I knew a ghost? Or even ... I look round at the graveyard and see a huge stone angel on top of one of the gravestones ... My guardian angel?

'No! No ...' I protest, dropping to my knees. 'You were *real*, George, I know you were.'

'Are you all right, young lady?' a soft voice asks. 'Loss can be a very frustrating time, as well as a sad one.'

I turn to find an elderly vicar looking down at me with concern.

'Yes, I'm fine. It's just come as a shock, that's all. I had no idea he'd died until this morning.'

The vicar nods knowingly, then he looks at me with new interest. 'You wouldn't be Jo-Jo would you, by any chance?'

'Yes, yes I am. But why?'

'Ah ...' He smiles. 'He moves in mysterious ways, that's for sure,' he mutters almost under his breath. 'Wait right here, young lady, I have something for you.'

The vicar hurries back towards the church while I'm left on my knees in front of the grave wondering what's going on now. He returns quickly.

'This was left for you,' he says, thrusting a white envelope in my direction. 'It was delivered after George's funeral with the express instruction that it was to be given to a young lady of your name who would visit his grave on this day.'

I look at the envelope. It does indeed have my name on the front in an ornate black script.

'Should I open it now?' I ask, standing up to take the letter from him.

'That, my dear, is up to you,' the vicar says gently. 'Do you feel up to it?'

I look down at the envelope again; I know the letter is from George before I even open it because the two 'O's in my name have been doodled into two sunflowers. 'I'll wait, if you don't mind,' I say, looking up at him. 'I think it will be kind of personal and, as I said before, this has all been quite distressing enough today already.'

'Of course,' the vicar agrees, nodding. 'Death can be so sudden, and such a shock for us all to deal with. But I can reassure you it's not the end.' He glances at the gravestone. 'George will be up there somewhere, enjoying himself, play-

407

ing his Beatles songs. I assume he was a fan?' He inclines his head towards the stone again.

'Yes, yes he was. A big one.'

'Understandable that he wanted to be buried here, then,' the vicar says, smiling knowingly.

'What do you mean?'

'Do you not know? There's a common folktale that suggests that one of the headstones here was the one that inspired the song "Eleanor Rigby".'

My heart, which skipped a few beats when I read the inscription on George's gravestone a few moments ago, and then again when I got his letter, now almost stops beating altogether at the mention of another Beatles link. 'There is? Where?'

'Just around there,' he says, pointing. 'It's with the older headstones. You'll find it easily enough if you want to take a look. There's usually someone taking a photo or two around that area.'

'Thank you,' I say, reaching for his hand and shaking it vigorously. 'And thank you, George.' I lay my sunflowers up against his headstone. 'I don't quite know yet how you were there with me all the time, George,' I whisper to him. 'But I'm so glad you were.'

I jump to my feet again, thank the mystified-looking vicar once more, then hurry to the older part of the graveyard, where, just as the vicar had said there might be, a middle-aged couple are taking photos of a gravestone.

As I get closer they move aside to make room for me.

'Your turn now,' the man, clearly American, says smiling. 'We've got our photos.'

I look at the gravestone. The first part reads:

IN LOVING MEMORY OF
MY DEAR HUSBAND
JOHN RIGBY
WHO DEPARTED THIS LIFE
OCTOBER 4TH 1915 AGED 72 YEARS
"AT REST"

The next part then lists his wife and daughter as being buried there too, and then there it is:

ELEANOR RIGBY, GRANDDAUGHTER OF THE ABOVE,
DIED 1939.

I read the names on the grave again. Is this it? This means nothing to me. How is this going to help?

'Are you a bit disappointed?' the man asks. 'We are, aren't we, Molly? We expected something a bit more.'

'Yeah, "Eleanor Rigby" is one of my favourite Beatles songs. You'd think they'd do something a bit better than this.'

'I don't really think the gravestone was erected for the song,' I say, humouring them. 'The song might have been inspired by the name, perhaps? I think there's a few theories actually.'

'Ah ... ' they say, nodding and looking at the stone again. 'You could be right.'

'To be honest, I'm looking forward to seeing the statue more anyway,' Molly says.

'There's an Eleanor Rigby statue?' I ask. 'Where?'

'Somewhere in the centre of town, we're not exactly sure where, are we, Desmond? We were gonna go find it tomorrow after our Beatles Magical Mystery bus tour and I've read this wonderfully quaint little English tale about it.'

'What's that?' I ask, more out of politeness than interest. My mind is already working out how I'm going to find this statue.

'Apparently when the statue was erected, they buried five things underneath it to represent different facets of life.'

'I didn't know this,' Desmond says, looking at Molly with interest.

'You're not the only one who knows how to use that computer of yours, Desmond,' Molly laughs, looking up at him smugly.

'What sort of things?' I ask.

'To represent fun and humour it was a *Beano* comic – that's a British thing, right?' she asks.

'Yeah ... ' I say, my spine suddenly beginning to tingle. 'What else was there?'

'For leisure a pair of soccer boots – football, you'd call it.'

'Go on,' I encourage her.

'For luck, a four-leaf clover; for spirituality, a Bible, and for love ... this part is so romantic,' she says in delight, clasping her hands together.

'Come on, don't leave us in suspense, what is it, woman?' Desmond demands.

'Yes,' I ask quietly, hardly believing my ears. 'What is it, Molly?'

'Sonnets of love.'

'That's cool,' Desmond says, nodding. 'Do you think it could be true?' he asks, looking at me.

'I really don't know,' I answer honestly. 'I didn't even know the statue existed until Molly said. But something I've learnt recently is: you should always believe anything is possible. I'm really sorry, but I have to go now,' I apologise as I dash away from the gravestone, 'But enjoy your time in Liverpool!'

I jump back into my cab.

'Do you know where the Eleanor Rigby statue is?' I ask my taxi driver as he calmly refolds his newspaper.

'Of course I do, love. Stanley Street, right?'

'If that's where it is then that's where we're going next on this magical mystery tour.'

I smile to myself. They've even got me doing it now.

As we travel along in the taxi I open up my bag and take out George's letter. I know I've got to read it, but I'm a bit afraid of what it might say. Getting old records from someone you loved and cared about is one thing, but a personal letter, that's something else. After a few moments of staring at the envelope, I rip it open. Inside there are two pages of white paper covered in the same ornate black handwriting, and the date at the top of the first page suggests George must have written it just before he died:

28 January 2013

My Dearest Jo-Jo,

If you're reading this letter now, well done! You've discovered what you needed to learn to return successfully from your journey to an all-new and improved 2013!

Many of us have taken a life-changing journey like this before you, and, as you will have learnt, not all return. But I was

411

always confident that you would work out your clues and come back triumphant, which is why, in my last few days here on earth I have agreed to be the one to help you through this extraordinary challenge.

Everyone who is chosen to undertake this type of journey does so for a different reason, and each person's experience is unique and personal to them. The circumstances you find yourself in will help you to learn about yourself, and about others, so that your future life can be a more fruitful and happy one for you, and those around you.

I cannot rationally explain everything that you will witness, Jo-Jo, nor would I want to try; we all find our own truth when we take on a life-changing journey of this kind, and I'm sure by now you've found yours, but what I can try and answer are some of the more practical questions you may still have about what has taken place.

By the time you receive this letter in 2013, Julian will be temporarily in charge of my shop because I will have left this earth. But what you may not have realised is that when you come to visit me in the summer with my accounts before your journey even begins, I will already have moved on then as well. My role as your 'guide', shall we call it, has already begun. If you remember back to your original 2013, you have not visited the shop for some time, and neither has Harry, so neither of you will know what has happened. Please don't feel bad that you didn't know of my passing. Rest assured, Jo-Jo, it's all been carefully planned that way.

At the time of writing this letter I'm not exactly sure what role

412

I'll be playing throughout your journey, but I hope I will be helpful and comforting to you at the times when you need me most. There will be others you recognise from your own life who will be there to help you along too, and many you will meet who are on, or who have completed their own journeys and now remain to help others, but I will be your principal guide throughout.

I apologise now if at times I may seem vague or awkward when answering your questions, of which I know there will be many. This is, in part, due to the 'travelling process' which can addle even the sharpest of brains, and the fact that we are only allowed to reveal so much information to you for your own good.

But most of all, Jo-Jo, I hope with all my heart that whatever happens to us, I am a worthy choice to take you through this amazing journey of life.

Your friend, always,

George x

I read the letter through twice, then I stare out of the window at the streets of Liverpool as the taxi whizzes past, but I don't really see anything.

Now I know what George was to me. Now I understand why he was so evasive at times and at others knew so much. I find myself smiling as a warm feeling spreads right through me. George was right; I've found my truth.

I pull all the other items from my bag that I've collected on my travels, along with the records George left for me – 'Eleanor Rigby' and 'All You Need Is Love'.

413

I not only knew about George now, but I knew what all these strange little items meant too: they were all linked together by one Beatles song, 'Eleanor Rigby'. I had all the clues Molly had talked about at the graveside, all except for love. All I needed was love to complete the set.

Wait, I think ... All I need is Love. Love is all I need?

That's it! That's what George's second record is about. My final clue to help me piece together everything that has happened ...

It's love, and, hopefully, I'm going to find it at Eleanor Rigby's statue.

Forty-Seven

The busy Saturday traffic means our journey begins to slow as we get nearer to the city centre again. I wriggle about in the back seat of the taxi, desperate to get out and solve this mystery once and for all. I'm utterly convinced now that Eleanor Rigby will finally provide me with all the answers I need.

'Is it far from here?' I ask the taxi driver as we queue up at a zebra crossing. Bane of my life those things, I think, watching all the Saturday shoppers and tourists covering the crossing while the beacons flash.

'Just around the corner as the crow flies, love, ' he says, 'but by road at this speed, good few minutes yet.' He looks at me in his rear-view mirror jigging about in the back like I'm bursting for the loo. 'You'd be quicker to walk it, if yer in a hurry, like.'

'You know what, I think I'll do that,' I say, thrusting some money at him and jumping from the cab.

'Just over there,' he points through his windscreen. 'There's a Portaloo just over the road there, in case yer desperate.'

'Thanks,' I say, looking in the direction of Stanley Street. 'Thanks a lot.'

I wait at the crossing with all the other people for the beacons to begin flashing orange. When they do I step out confidently with everyone else, making sure I keep in the centre of the crowd. There is no way a runaway car is going to screech round the corner here and knock me down. It would have to take out at least five other people first.

But as I get to the centre of the crossing, something does make me want to stop, but it's not the threat of a car about to knock me flying that makes me want to turn around and go the other way, it's the sight of someone coming towards me who I recognise.

Lucy.

As she passes opposite me in the crowd of people hurrying across the black and white stripes, I turn to try and follow her, but trying to fight my way through the sea of carrier bags and Beatles T-shirts is impossible. The tide is just too strong. As the waves deliver me safely on to the far pavement, I immediately turn around to look for her, but the traffic has begun to flow again now, and she's already been swallowed up into the swarm of people moving along the pavement opposite.

I stand completely still with my mind racing, while people bump and barge into me. That was Lucy I just saw walking over the crossing. Lucy, my time-travelling friend from 1985. That was incredible enough, but what bothered me even more was that Lucy was wearing a sandwich board strapped across her chest, with the words *Ticket to Ride: Beatles Bus Tours* emblazoned across both sides.

Lucy had only worn that sandwich board for one day, she'd

told me, the day she got hit by Harry in his sports car. So if Lucy is wearing a sandwich board, and this is 2013, that means that Harry can't be too far away either.

I have to get to the statue. And fast.

I don't take a lot of notice of the many tourists and buskers as I hurry along Matthew Street and into Stanley Street; my mind is only focused on one thing, getting to the statue. This is it; I know it. Eleanor Rigby is going to answer all my questions and help me save Lucy. She has to.

As I expect, there are a few people having photos taken next to Eleanor when I arrive. The statue is a bronze figure of a woman sitting alone on a stone bench, with a tiny bronze bird resting next to her. I wait for the people to move on before I hurry forward to take a closer look.

The plaque behind her head reads:

ELEANOR RIGBY

DEDICATED TO

"ALL THE LONELY PEOPLE..."

Is this it? I wonder desperately, looking around me for something more. This is a bit like the gravestone all over again. But Eleanor's presence seems to be having a calming effect on me; I can feel my heartbeat, which has been racing at a speed it's only ever gone at when I've overdosed on caffeine before, beginning to slow as I sit down next to her on the stone bench where she rests.

I take a deep breath and reflect on the inscription behind me, think about all the different people I met on my travels into the past, remember all the people who'd been stuck in different time zones, just like me: Walter Maxwell, my over-bearing boss; Stu, my teenage punk friend; Lucy the waitress, and Billy the cross-dressing pub singer. They were all lonely in their own way, because of their attitude, their circumstance, or their own choice. Many of the other people I met had reason to be lonely too, I realise now, like Penny, the single mother; Martha, our cake-baking neighbour; even Patti, the wife Harry had fallen out of love with. So many people, so many reasons to be lonely.

And then there were my Eleanor Rigby clue-bearers. They weren't lonely necessarily, but they had the ever-present Beatles link. How had I not noticed at the time that they were called John, George, Ringo and Paul?

But what of this fifth clue, the love clue? The sonnets Desmond and Molly told me about – even those two names were from a Beatles' song, I now realise. In fact, I think, did *every* person I've come into contact with have a Beatles-related name? There are just too many to try and remember right now, but there are a few obvious ones, like Penny, Stuart, Julian, Rita, Lucy, and even the children I taught in the school.

'So, Eleanor?' I ask, looking at the faceless statue next to me. 'What do I do now? Any suggestions? I could do with a bit of help. It's quite lonely, just the two of us sitting here, isn't it?'

Then out of the corner of my eye I see a tall, slim figure walking towards us down Stanley Street. He has dark hair, and he's wearing jeans and a white cotton shirt, and, as he gets closer I can just see, in the bright afternoon sunshine, a pair of dazzling blue eyes.

I tap Eleanor on the hand. 'Thank you,' I whisper to her. 'Now I know I won't be lonely any more.'

As Harry gets closer I call out to him.

'Jo-Jo! What on earth are you doing here?' Harry looks genuinely pleased, and I'm glad he remembers me.

'Not much, just enjoying Eleanor's company for a bit,' I say truthfully.

Harry looks at the statue. 'Do you know, I've walked past here loads of times when I've been in Liverpool before and I've never noticed this statue. It's quite tucked away, isn't it?'

'Maybe she doesn't like to be noticed too often. Maybe she prefers it that way.'

'Quite possibly,' Harry agrees. 'Some people prefer to go through life unnoticed. Sometimes it's better that way.'

'Yes,' I say, considering this, 'they do, don't they? So,' I look up at him, 'what are you doing here? Are you based in Liverpool now?'

'No, I'm just here on some business.' He sits down on the bench next to me. 'Actually,' he says, 'just between the two of us that's not the only reason – it's because of this, too.' He holds up a brown envelope. 'It's all a bit odd, to be honest. This was delivered to my office in London some months ago – January, I think, and the note inside said I should come to this statue, on this very afternoon at about this time, and I should bring the contents of the envelope with me. It's all very strange.'

I look down at the envelope in his hand. It's addressed to a Mr Harrison Rigby. *Of course he's a Harrison, not just a Harry. That makes sense now as well. Harry is a Beatle too.*

'Nothing surprises me any more, Harry. I bet I can even guess what's in your envelope?'

'I bet you can't!'

'Let me see ... would there be some sonnets of love in there by any chance?'

Harry looks at me in amazement. 'How on earth do you know that? That's exactly right. The love sonnets of Shakespeare.'

'I told you, never be surprised by anything or anyone. Of all the things I've learnt recently, that's definitely one of them.'

'What do you mean?' Harry asks, looking at me quizzically. 'What's going on here?'

Before I can change my mind, and with Eleanor watching over us, I take my chance, lean forward and kiss him. And as a wonderful warm feeling spreads through my body, from my lips right down to the tips of my toes, nothing prevents us this time, this year, and this decade, from fully enjoying our moment.

'Right ...' Harry says slowly when I've finished. 'I see. I think I can definitely live with that type of surprise.' He grins. 'What's changed about you, Jo-Jo, you seem ... different?'

I'm aware my cheeks are still flushed from the kiss. 'I am. I'm a changed person. Certain recent events have taught me a lot about myself and about the person I want to be in the future. I don't want to be the person I was in the past. Hopefully, that Jo-Jo is gone for ever.'

Harry looks at me and takes my hand.

'The past isn't always a bad place,' he says seriously, 'we can learn a lot from it.'

'I know. And I have. I've learnt what's important in life – to appreciate my time, my family, my friends, and ...'

'And what?' Harry asks.

'... other things.' My cheeks flush a little again.

Harry nods approvingly. 'Good, then it was very definitely worthwhile.'

'What was?' I ask him. 'What was worthwhile, Harry, tell me?'

'Excusee, we take photo with statue now?' Some tourists interrupt us as they wait for their turn with Eleanor.

'Come on,' Harry says, standing up, still holding on to my hand, 'would you like to see the business I was talking about before? It's not far from here. It's a little shop, a bit like Groovy Records.' His face is immediately filled with sadness when he mentions George's shop.

'I know,' I say, squeezing his hand, 'I just found out myself. But George had a good life.'

'Yeah,' Harry takes hold of my other hand now, then he lifts them up in between us, 'and he brought us two together, didn't he?'

I glance at the envelope Harry now has tucked into the pocket of his trousers. He certainly did. George must have sent that clue to Harry before he died too, just like my records and my letter. He was determined to see the two of us together eventually.

'Yes, we have much to thank George for.'

'We certainly have.' Harry nods knowingly. 'I'm sure he's up there somewhere looking down on us.'

'I know he is,' I say with certainty.

'Say goodbye to Eleanor, then,' Harry says, turning back to look at the statue. 'It seems she also may have played her part in finally bringing the two of us together.'

'Yes,' I agree. 'She certainly did. Goodbye, Eleanor,' I wave at her. 'I hope you don't stay lonely too long.'

We leave the statue and walk hand in hand back down Stanley Street, then along Matthew Street, where the buskers and Beatles imitators are out in force in front of the Cavern Club on this Saturday afternoon.

'The shop isn't far from here,' Harry says. 'It's a nice little place; I think you'll like it. I could do with picking up my car, though; I really should have collected it from the parking meter by now. The time will have run out ages ago and I don't want to get a ticket.'

'No!' I insist as we stop at a zebra crossing. 'No, you mustn't drive your car this afternoon!'

Harry looks at me oddly. 'Why on earth not?'

'Because – it's a lovely day,' I say, and gesture up at the blue sky above us. 'We should make the most of this beautiful weather while we can!'

'It's OK, it's a soft-top Audi TT,' he says. 'We can have all the fresh air we like.'

'No,' I insist again. 'I really would rather we walk.'

'You are one strange cookie sometimes, Jo-Jo,' Harry says, shaking his head. 'However, I can let you off that because when you kiss,' he winks, 'you kiss like it's the last thing you'll ever do!'

I smile nervously at him. *If only you knew, Harry* ...

'In fact, maybe if you show me again now how good you are at it, I might be persuaded that walking is a good idea after all.'

I lean up and begin to kiss Harry again very slowly, and as I do, out of the corner of my eye I see a girl wearing a sandwich board stepping lightly over the zebra crossing behind us. She's texting on an iPhone while wearing a pair of earphones and listening to music, and she really isn't thinking about what she's doing at all. A car has to screech to a halt to allow her to cross safely – and Lucy doesn't even appear to notice it as she ambles over to our side of the road and continues on her way.

I pull away from Harry, my heart racing.

'Wow! My kisses have never had that much of an effect on anyone before!' he grins. 'What's wrong, Jo-Jo?' he asks, suddenly becoming serious. 'You've gone very pale.'

I've done it! At last I've actually prevented someone from being stuck in a time they didn't want to be in. I stopped Harry from hitting Lucy with his car, and I've prevented her from travelling to a year where she'd be lonely and alone. I've saved her. I've saved my friend.

'It's nothing,' I say, my words belying my euphoria. 'It's absolutely nothing.' I look up at Harry who is gazing at me with concern. 'I love you, Harry,' I say suddenly. 'I know that might seem sudden to you. But really it isn't, I've known for ages. Years. Decades even. But I've only just realised it.'

For a second I think Harry is going to run a mile; I mean, that's what he should do. Even though I've known him for ages, as far as he's concerned we've only really just met. But to my relief he doesn't, he just smiles.

'I love you too, Jo-Jo, and *I've* known for decades too.'

'You have?'

'Of course,' he says as though it was never in doubt. 'Anyone that can love me with blue hair must be all right,' he winks.

But . . .

'Come on, you,' Harry calls, stepping out onto the crossing and pulling my hand. 'There's no traffic around and we need to cross. Look, if you don't hurry up I won't let you listen to

423

any more Take That records, and that would be a real shame now, eh?' He's grinning at me now.

'But ... how could you know about that?' I ask, confused, as I allow him to lead me onto the crossing. All the times I've known Harry in the past suddenly flash through my mind, like photo-fits in a police line-up.

'I know more than you think,' Harry says. 'Trust me.'

Suddenly, as we reach the centre of the crossing, I see it hurtling towards us like it always does, the white sports car.

I brace myself, knowing what's going to happen next. I can't believe this, just when Harry and I are finally together. But instead of feeling cold the way I usually do, all I feel is a sharp pain shoot through my right arm as Harry yanks me by the hand away from the crossing towards the pavement.

Wrapped in Harry's arms I watch in shock as the white sports car continues on its way and disappears into the busy Liverpool traffic.

I didn't get hit.

I didn't go cold as the white sports car smashed into me.

Harry saved me.

'They don't always get us,' Harry says, smiling down at me. He kisses me gently on my forehead. 'It's not always our time to move on.'

'You know, don't you?' I say slowly, as the realisation of what just happened fully sinks in. 'You know what's been going on.'

Harry nods.

'How long?' I ask.

'Long enough,' he says, stroking my hair now.

'But why didn't you *say*?'

'I nearly did a couple of times, but you needed to find your

424

own way through it. Just like I did. Just like we all do. That's why we do it. That's why they make us do it.'

I take hold of Harry's hand and turn it over so I can see the palm, and there it is, his lifeline – strong and solid, but suddenly branching off into lots of new, finer lines. I turn my own palm over and hold it next to his.

'It's the same,' I whisper.

'No, Jo-Jo, *we're* the same,' Harry says, putting our palms together and linking the fingers. 'And now you've completed your journey, we need never be parted again.'

As the same warm, comforting feeling that I've felt time and time again upon waking up in the past begins to spread right through me, I know now that I'll never be alone, whatever happens to me in the future.

'Harry?' I ask him as I stand on the side of the zebra crossing wrapped in his arms.

'Yes?' he whispers, his deep blue eyes gazing back down into mine.

'You don't fancy buying a record shop on the King's Road, do you? I know a Groovy little one that's going to be up for sale soon.'

Harry grins down at me. 'Now, how might you know that?'

'Let's just say I'm very good at seeing into the future ...'

Step Back in Time ~
Back to the Beatles

A guide to all those Beatles references!
Now you've Stepped Back in Time with Jo-Jo, you'll have
hopefully enjoyed the story and picked up many of the Beatles
references and links that run through the book.

But how many of those clues did you notice as you read?

As you know now, the main characters all have names
inspired by the Beatles in some way: Jo-Jo's comes from the
song 'Get Back', Harry and George from George Harrison, and
Ellie from the song 'Eleanor Rigby'.

But here's a guide to all the Beatles links throughout the
book:

(All characters are of course purely fictional. Their names do
not have any link to a person living or dead whose name they
may share.)

Ticket to Ride 1963

- *Brian Epstein*, who passes through the foyer of EMI House, was the Beatles' manager, and *Mimi* was the name of John Lennon's mother.

- Walter *Maxwell* – from 'Maxwell's Silver Hammer'

- '*Allan* from accounts' – Allan Williams was the Beatles' first manager, before Brian Epstein.

- '*Cynthia* and *Dave* from accounts' – Cynthia Lennon was John's first wife, and Dave is from 'When I'm Sixty-Four'

- *Miss Fields* – from 'Strawberry Fields'

- *Derek*, Harry's mate – Derek Taylor was the Beatles' press officer/publicist.

- *Vera*, covering reception – from 'When I'm Sixty-Four'

- Martha, neighbour – from 'Martha My Dear'

- *Prudence*, Mr Maxwell's secretary – from 'Dear Prudence'

- *Tony* the barman – Tony Sheridan was an early collaborator and supporter of the Beatles, when they were still the Silver Beatles.

- *Abbey* Car Hire – The *Abbey Road* album, and the studios where many of the Beatles' songs were recorded.

- '*James Pepper* in publicity' – Paul McCartney's son, James, and *Sergeant Pepper's Lonely Hearts Club Band* album.

Lady Madonna 1977

- *Bonnie*, the baby – from 'My Bonnie'

- *Penny*, Jo-Jo's seventies mum – from 'Penny Lane'

- *Sally* and *Sean* – from 'Long Tall Sally' and Sean, John Lennon's son.

- Maggie, a neighbour – from 'Maggie Mae'

- *Stu*, the punk – Stuart Sutcliffe, the original bassist for the Beatles.

- *Rita*, the shop owner – from 'Lovely Rita'

- *Carol*, Harry's mum – from 'Carol'

Can't Buy Me Love 1985

- *Dakota*, George's dog – The Dakota building in New York was where John Lennon was shot in 1980.

- Zak, 'one of my [Ellie's] best sources' – Ringo Starr's son.

- *Rocky*, the gangster – from 'Rocky Raccoon'

- *Ringo*, the nightclub owner – Ringo Starr

- *Lucy*, the waitress – from 'Lucy in the Sky with Diamonds'

- *Michelle*, Harry's secretary – from 'Michelle'

- *Boyd*, the bouncer – Patti Boyd was George Harrison's first wife.

- *Brian*, the security guard – Brian Epstein, as previously mentioned.

- *Sadie*, Rocky's fiancée – from 'Sexy Sadie'

- *Henry*, Harry's chauffeur – Henry Grossman was a photographer and friend of the band.

Get Back 1994

- *John*, the caretaker and his son, *Paul* – do I need to explain those two?!

- Children in school: *Mary*, *Stella* and *Beatrice* are Paul McCartney's daughters. *Lee* and *Jason* are both Ringo Starr's sons.

- *Patricia/Patti*, Harry's wife – again Patti Boyd, George Harrison's first wife.

- *Apple* Close – Apple Corps was the name of the Beatles' own company.

- *Mrs Sullivan*, elderly neighbour – the Beatles' big break in the USA came on the Ed Sullivan TV show.

- *Billy*, the pub singer/Take That fan – from 'Bungalow Bill'

- *Jude*, the barman – from 'Hey Jude'

The Long and Winding Road 2013

- *Desmond* and *Molly*, American tourists – from 'Ob-La-Di, Ob-La-Da'

- *Julian*, George's grandson – Julian Lennon is John's son.

How many songs did you recognise in the Beatles conversation Harry has with Jo-Jo in the World's End pub?

Harry suddenly thrusts his head into his hands. 'I hate my life! Hate it!' He turns his face towards me. '**Ask me why?**'

'Why?' I ask, doing as I'm told for once.

'**I'm a loser**, Jo-Jo, a **nowhere man**.'

'No, you're not,' I reply, wondering if Harry has been drinking before he even got to the pub tonight.

'I am. I'll still be working **eight days a week when I'm sixty-four**, marking homework and thinking up lesson plans.'

'No you won't, not if you don't want to be doing that.'

Harry doesn't look very convinced. '**Do you want to know a secret?**'

'What?' I ask, wondering where all this is heading. Although Harry is making sense, he's talking very oddly, as if he's talking in code.

'They say **all you need is love**, but everybody's got something to hide, Jo-Jo. Everyone. That's what screws everything up. I bet even you've got a secret?'

'Well . . .'

'Do you want to know mine?' Harry has emptied his glass and is holding it up to be refilled again. '**Hey Jude**,' he calls across the bar, 'another when you're ready, please.'

I stare hard at Harry. The code he's talking in. It's only bloody Beatles songs! I may not be their greatest fan, but their songs constantly being played during my childhood means I know every one.

'Tell me your secret, Harry,' I urge him, sensing there's more to this than simply a bit of marital discord. 'What is it?'

'**I want to tell you**, Jo-Jo, I want to tell you so much, but I can't.'

'Yes, Harry, yes you can.'

Jude brings Harry's whisky over.

'I'll take one of those, Jude,' I tell him. 'Quick as you can, please, and make it a double.'

Jude raises his dark eyebrows, but immediately lifts a glass and turns towards the optics.

'Maybe I should just **let it be**,' Harry says, as he drinks from his own glass. 'It's a **long and winding road** we both travel along, Jo-Jo, and I'll get by **with a little help from my friends**.' He lifts his head and looks meaningfully at me. 'We both will.'

Ali McNamara 2013

Step Back in Time ~
The Step

Step on to the King's Road, London

The mysterious zebra crossing that Jo-Jo always steps onto before she travels in time is situated on the King's Road in London. This famous street in the London borough of Kensington and Chelsea derives its name from its use by Charles II as his private road to travel to Kew. It has been known throughout the world for five decades for its quirky, eccentric shops and links to the world of fashion and music.

It first became well known in the 'swinging sixties', when shops such as Mary Quant's Bazaar boutique, and the wonderfully named Granny Takes a Trip lined the street, and pop stars such as the Beatles and Eric Clapton would mingle with trendy shoppers, hoping to grab the latest individually tailored piece of clothing to distinguish them from their peers.

In the seventies, these shops were joined by the (at the time) outrageously named boutique, SEX – run by Vivienne Westwood and Malcolm McLaren – and in the eighties, bands and artists such as Madness, The Specials and George Michael visited La Rocka, to be kitted out before their live Thursday night appearances on *Top of the Pops*.

In the story, George's shop, Groovy Records, and the crossing where Jo-Jo always travels back in time are set in an area of the King's Road called World's End. In the sixties and seventies this was *the* area for the trendy bohemian set to hang out, with its mix of hippy boutiques and shops selling crafts and spiritual merchandise.

Today, just as in the story, the World's End Distillery stands proudly in the middle of all this, slightly separated from the rest of the King's Road, like a great ship floating in a sea of history. And I wondered when I went to visit the area and discovered for myself this perfect setting for my mystical story, just how many interesting tales it would have to tell us of events and people that had drunk inside its four walls over the decades.

The King's Road's past is a rich, vibrant record of popular culture, and I hope my novel of a mysterious traveller moving through its five decades of alternative bohemian thinking is a welcome addition to its magnificent history.

Ali McNamara, 2013

Step Back in Time ~ The Time

A kiss with history – why I love time travel

I've always been fascinated with time-travel stories from a young age, whether it be in the form of books, TV shows or films. I'm not sure if it's the chance to see for myself just what living in those decades might have been like, or, as is the theme of so many time-travel stories, getting a chance to put right things that went wrong the first time around ...

One of my favourite time-travel movies is *Back to the Future*. I remember as a teenager being absolutely enthralled with the adventures of Marty McFly, played by Michael J. Fox, and Dr Emmett Brown, played by Christopher Lloyd. Their comic quest to return Marty back to his own time of 1985, when he accidentally travels back thirty years to 1955 in a DeLorean car that Doc Brown has fashioned into a time machine, was a huge hit in the eighties; it spawned two sequels, and a hit single for Huey Lewis and the News with the song 'The Power of Love'.

Television has been a huge source for fuelling my love of

time travel over the years too. A US show from the nineties called *Quantum Leap* was a massive hit on both sides of the Atlantic, and won both Emmys and Golden Globes. It followed the adventures of Dr Sam Beckett, who invented his own time-travel machine, the quantum leap accelerator, but due to a malfunction (isn't there always one!) Sam was stuck leaping through time, putting right the wrongs of the world with only a wisecracking hologram, Al, to help him. I particularly liked this show as it always featured a 'kiss with history' where Sam would interact in some way with a genuine historical event, and I've added a few of these in *Step Back in Time* for Jo-Jo.

Two other favourites of mine were the British TV series *Life on Mars* and *Ashes to Ashes*, featuring TV cops DI Sam Tyler, and subsequently his counterpart DI Alex Drake, who travelled back to the seventies and the eighties. Even though they were both marketed as BBC dramas, they featured much dry humour – mainly from the lips of DCI Gene Hunt, played by Philip Glenister – and attracted a huge cult following. They used an original music soundtrack from the year that they were portraying, which added to viewers' enjoyment and the authenticity of the show.

So the enduring appeal of going back to a time that's now lost, and experiencing what we can only read about, and in some cases only watch on old newsreels, is one I've always wanted to write about – and one I'd quite like to experience for myself if I ever get the chance.

Just as long as I can always find that elusive way to get back home ...

Ali McNamara, 2013

Meet Scarlett O'Brien

'Sparky, fun and endearing' Katie Fforde

'An endearing, romantic and fun read for chick-lit (and rom com!) fans' *Closer*

'Joyous and carefree, a souffle of a book that will lift the spirits of anybody who ever daydreamed about a different, more glam life' Bernadette Strachan

'Utterly enjoyable' *Stylist*

'If you love your rom coms and know your Mark Darcy from your Daniel Cleaver then you're going to adore this' Carole Matthews

'As adorable as a Richard Curtis movie, as funny as that Welsh bloke in the baggy grey pants, this romantic comedy is the perfect way to pass a winter afternoon should Johnny Depp be unavailable' *Daily Record*

'An irresistible, feel-good story infused with infectious humour and sprinkled with Manhattan magic' Miranda Dickinson

When Darcy McCall loses her beloved Aunt Molly, she doesn't expect any sort of inheritance – let alone a small island! Located off the west coast of Ireland, Tara hasn't been lived on for years, but according to Molly's will, Darcy must stay there for twelve months in order to fully inherit. It's a big shock. And she's even more shocked to hear that she needs to persuade a village full of people to settle there, too.

Darcy has to leave behind her independent city life and swap stylish heels for muddy wellies. Between sorting everything from the plumbing to the pub, Darcy meets confident, charming Conor and sensible, stubborn Dermot – but who will make her feel really at home?

'A warm second novel - ****' *Daily Mirror*, Book of the Week

'Perfect easy reading'
Sun

'Charming story of adventure, discovery and affairs of the heart'
Candis

sphere

If you have enjoyed this book, you can find out more
about **Ali McNamara**'s books on her website

www.alimcnamara.co.uk

Or you can follow her on Twitter

@AliMcNamara

And keep up to date with

@LittleBrownUK
@LittleBookCafe

To buy any Ali McNamara books and to find out more
about all other Little, Brown titles go to our website

www.littlebrown.co.uk

To order any Sphere titles p & p free in the UK, please
contact our mail order supplier on: + 44 (0)1832 737525

Customers not based in the UK should contact the
same number for appropriate postage and packing costs.